The Simushir Island Incident

The Simushir Island Incident

A Josh Haman Novel

by

Marc Liebman

www.penmorepress.com

Simushir Island Incident by Marc Liebman
Copyright © 2020 Marc Liebman

This is a work of historical fiction. While based upon historical events, any similarity to any person, circumstance or event is purely coincidental and related to the efforts of the author to portray the characters in historically accurate representations.

ISBN-978-1-950586-67-7(Paperback)
ISBN 978-1-950586-66-0(e-book)
BISAC Subject Headings:
FIC014000FICTION / Historical
FIC032000FICTION / War & Military
FIC047000FICTION / Sea Stories

Editors: Chris Wozney, Robert Beeson

The Book Cover Whisperer:
ProfessionalBookCoverDesign.com

Address all correspondence to:

Penmore Press,
920 N Javelina Pl,
Tucson, AZ 85737
or visit our website at:
www.penmorepress.com

Other Books By Marc Liebman

TABLE OF CONTENTS

MAPS AND PHOTOS

THE ENIGMA THAT IS NORTH KOREA

Ever since 1905, Korea has been a challenge for U.S. foreign policy makers. In the Treaty of Portsmouth, President Theodore Roosevelt negotiated the end of the Russo-Japanese War. For doing so, he won the Nobel Peace Prize.

The treaty gave the Japanese full control of the Kuril Islands from the southern tip of the Russia's Kamchatka Peninsula all the way to its northernmost island, Hokkaido, in exchange for the southern half of Sakhalin Island. It also gave the Japanese control of the Korean Peninsula. Thus began a brutal occupation that lasted until the Japanese surrendered in 1945.

Fast forward to World War II and the Teheran Conference in November 1943, where President Franklin D. Roosevelt discussed with Josef Stalin the idea that Korea would be occupied by both countries for a short time and then become free and independent. At the Yalta conference in February 1945, Korea was again discussed, and the Soviet leader agreed to splitting Korea into two occupation zones and the Kuril Islands would be returned to the Soviet Union. Because the U.S. was bearing the brunt of the war in the Pacific, Roosevelt and then Truman wanted the Soviet Union to declare war on Japan.

Stalin waited until August 8th, 1945, after we dropped the first atomic bomb on Hiroshima, to declare war on Japan, and the Red

Army invaded northern Korea. His troops began moving into Korea and by August 24th had reached Pyongyang.

Meanwhile, Colonel Dean Rusk, the future Secretary of State, and Colonel Charles Bonesteel were tasked with drawing up the dividing line between what would become North and South Korea. Neither officer knew that the line they selected was nearly identical to the one proposed by the Tsar to the Japanese as a concession to end the Russo-Japanese war. To the U.S. government's surprise, Stalin readily agreed to the boundary we know today and committed to a short period of occupation and free and open elections in 1948.

Kim il-Sung and his Communist Party were not popular in either what would become North or South Korea and would lose any election. To ensure he would control the northern half of the peninsula, he declared a provisional government in 1946 along Soviet lines that later became the Democratic People's Republic of Korea (DPRK). The proposed elections under U.N. auspices were never held.

Neither Stalin nor Kim Il-Sung believed the U.S. would intervene when the DPRK invaded South Korea, now known as the Republic of Korea (ROK), in June 1950. Pushed by the U.S., the United Nations imposed sanctions and declared war.

The U.S. never did declare war, although it provided 90% of the foreign troops, aircraft and ships that fought under the United Nations banner. Eventually, 14 nations (in alphabetical order: Australia, Belgium, Canada, Columbia, Ethiopia, France, Greece, Luxembourg, the Netherlands, the Philippines, Thailand, Turkey, the United Kingdom and the United States) provided combat units to fight under the United Nation's flag. Six other countries—Denmark, Israel, Italy, Norway, Sweden and West Germany—provided medical units to support what is known as the United Nations Command.

The fighting stopped when the Korean Armistice Agreement was signed in July 1953. The agreement is not much more than a ceasefire, so the U.N. and the Republic of Korea are still at war with the Democratic People's Republic of Korea.

Since then, the DPRK has been a difficult foreign policy challenge. The country spends 23% of its GDP to maintain a large standing army, navy and air force. In contrast, the U.S. with its worldwide commitments spends less an 4% and the ROK spends 4.5%.

The DPRK continues to conduct terrorist acts and acts of war against the ROK. Since the armistice was signed, there have been over 120 incidents in which either a ROK or U.S. solider has been killed or injured. To be fair, the ROK has conducted raids into North Korea, usually in retaliation to an attack. In number, they are far fewer that those conducted by the DPRK.

The DPRK is not a nice place to live. Behind the public relationships facade lies a country where population and thought are tightly controlled by the government. Today, Kim Jong-Un maintains control through a security apparatus that would make Stalin smile in approval. Scattered throughout the country, the Ministry of State Security maintains internment camps housing between 150,000—200,000 people the government believes are politically unreliable. The same ministry also operates 15—20 re-education camps that house another 35,000—40,000 souls living in horrid conditions. The re-education camps are places one goes to die.

Economically, the country is a basket case. In 2017, the country's GDP per capita ranked 179th in the world at $1,300 per citizen per year, versus South Korea's 12th and $31,141.

North Korea is the only communist country in which the mantle of leadership has been passed down from father (Kim Jong-Il) to son (Kim Jong-Il) to grandson (Kim Jong-Un) without a major civil war. The consistent foreign policy tenet has been and will always be ensuring that the Kim dynasty maintains power.

The basis of its nuclear weapons program is to make any aggressor think twice about attacking the DPRK. The Kims have made it clear that if attacked they will respond with nuclear, chemical and biological weapons.

Other than iron ore, the country has few natural resources. Its harsh climate is similar to the U.S. Midwest and most of the arable land is on the western side of the country. Its collectivized farm industry, based on Stalin's model, cannot provide enough food to feed the country.

Citizens of the DPRK have suffered major famines—the last of which occurred between 1994 through 1998—in which, depending on the reporting news source, between 240,000 and 3.5 million of its 22 million citizens died from starvation.

So how does the DPRK government generate cash? Eighty-seven percent of what is manufactured inside North Korea is sold in the People's Republic of China. India takes 2.5%, the Philippines 1.9% and Pakistan absorbs 1%. Its products are shoddy and wouldn't be competitive in a western economy.

Hidden away in a building on the third floor of the Workers' Party Headquarters building are three organizations known as Office 35, 38 and 39. Officially, they are Central Committee Bureaus 35, 38 and 39 of the Workers' Party of Korea. They were created by Kim Il-Sung in 1970.

Office 35 is focused on intelligence gathering on foreign businesses and stealing business intellectual property. Like its neighbor across the Yalu River, North Korea doesn't honor patents or copyrights which govern the rest of the world's business community.

Office 38 handles the legal work for financial transactions created by the largest of the three, Office 39. Through a network of shell corporations that sell illegal products, such as counterfeit medicines and illegal drugs, Office 39 generates about $1 billion a year in cash for the regime's leadership. Most of the money generated by Office 39 goes into a slush fund to pay for perks for the ruling elite.

The above just touches the surface about North Korea and its illegal activities which are the background for the plot of this novel. All the events and conversations, however, are the product of the author's imagination.

Enjoy the read.

Marc Liebman
September 2020

Simushir Island is about halfway down the volcanic Kuril Island chain, which runs from the southern tip of the Kamchatka Peninsula to the northern-most Japanese home island of Hokkaido. In the winter, windswept Simushir is covered in snow. In summer, its mountainous terrain is a mix of brown and green. Three features dominate the geography of the 37-mile-long and 8-mile-wide island:

- Broutana Bay, on the northern end of the island, is a four-mile-long, kidney-shaped, deep-sheltered harbor, which is protected by a 1,200-foot-high ridge starting on the north side and ending at the 2,881-foot Mount Uratman to the southeast.
- Zavaritzk Caldera, in the middle of the island, is a large lake in a volcano crater.

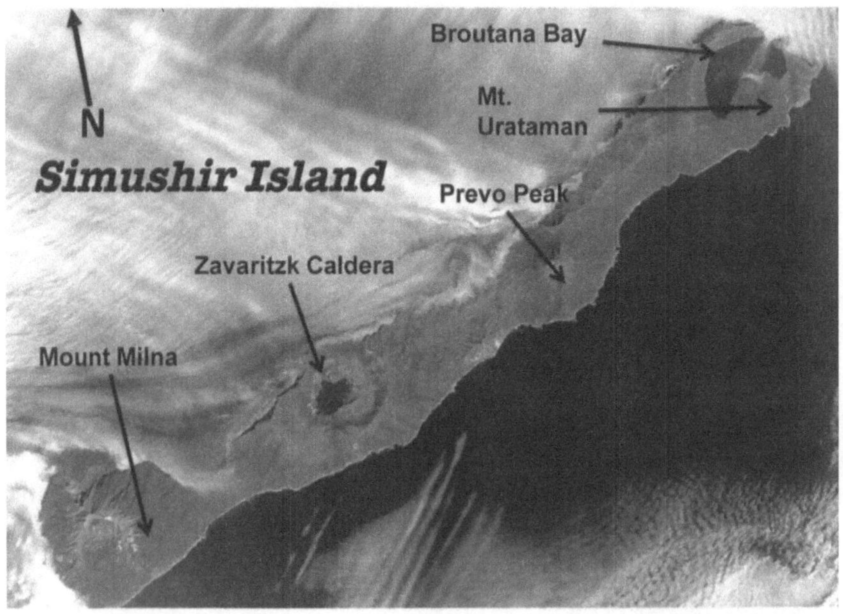

- Mount Milna is a pimple-like 5,050-foot mountain on the island's southern tip.

East of the Kuril Islands are the rich fishing grounds in the cold and stormy waters of the Northwest Pacific. The relatively shallow Sea of Okhotsk washes up on the island's west side. Much of it is ice-covered in winter and just plain cold in the summer.

In 1945, the Soviet Union re-occupied the Kurils, reducing Japan to its five main home islands—Hokkaido, Honshu, Kyushu, Okinawa and Shikoku, plus about 6,000 smaller islands, of which only 630 are inhabited.

Ownership of what Japan calls the Northern Territories—Iturup, Kunishir, Shikotan and the Habomai Island group in the Southern Kurils—is an international dispute. The Japanese want the five southernmost islands back, and the Russian Federation wants to keep the largely uninhabited islands. Despite several attempts to negotiate a solution, Russian ownership of the islands continues to be a source of friction between the two countries.

Chapter 1: RENDEZVOUS

Monday, November 14th, 1994,
1945 local time, Newport Beach, CA

The parking lot of the office building on the corner of MacArthur Boulevard and Birch Street was still half full of luxury cars and SUVs. Acuras, Audis, Corvettes, BMWs, Lexus, Mercedes and Porsches were common models, and most were less than three years old. Their owners either hadn't left for the day or had come back after dinner for a few more hours of work.

An arriving 5 Series BMW fit right in. The driver, an Asian man, pulled into a spot and shut off the lights, windshield wipers and ignition and got out of the car. He looked like any one of the hundreds of professionals who went in and out of the building throughout the day.

By hanging around the building at different times, the man, born and raised in North Korea, had learned that the lot began filling up around 6 a.m. It partially emptied around 11:30 for lunch but was full for most of the afternoon. There was a mini-rush hour around 5:30, when many workers left; beginning around 7 p.m., cars started returning.

The noise from a jet taking off from Orange County's John Wayne Airport caused the man to glance up as he walked briskly towards the brightly lit entrance, a few yards behind a returning professional. Rain dripped off, but didn't soak through, his black Gortex jacket. The security guard watched him walk toward the bank of elevators, then went back to his copy of *Sports Illustrated,* thinking, *Another yuppie back to pile up more billable hours.*

The office suites housed software and technology companies, accounting and legal firms, regional offices for Fortune 1000 corporations and consulting partnerships. The North Korean didn't glance at the directory on the wall. He knew where he was going. He carried a black eel-skin attaché case and wore thin, expensive-looking black deerskin gloves. In the elevator, he pressed the button that sent the elevator rising to the eighth floor. Exiting and turning left, he strode down the hall until he found the plaque for Suite 822, occupied by Jimenez, Gomez, Rodriquez and Associates, LLP, CPAs.

He swiped the security card that had been included in the package mailed to him. The door unlatched with a soft click. Inside, the thick pile of the expensive dark-gray carpet let him walk silently through the suite. No one was at the reception desk to stop or announce him. He headed for a corner office and opened the unlocked door.

An annoyed Enrique Gomez looked up from his desk. "Who are you, and what are you doing here?" He never heard an answer. His head jerked back involuntarily as a 7.62-millimeter 85-grain jacketed hollow-point bullet sent fragments throughout his brain. Blood flowed from the hole just above his nose, dripping onto his cream-colored shirt and the gold cuff links made from genuine US ten-dollar gold pieces.

At the other end of the hall, Julio Rodriguez was sorting papers on a table when he saw a man's reflection in his office window.

Surprised, he turned, clearly annoyed that an unknown person was in his firm's inner sanctum. "Who the fuck are you?"

The stranger said nothing. He aimed the North-Korean-made Type 68 pistol with a long suppressor screwed on the barrel and squeezed the trigger. The bullet entered the accountant's left eye and pulped his brain.

Jesús Jimenez had just come back from the bathroom and was headed to his plush, high-backed chair when the assassin stepped from behind his office door, gun in hand. Jimenez started to dive toward the protection of his large desk. Before he could get his own gun from the holster he kept under the table, one shot shattered his breastbone and destroyed a lung. A second went into his head.

The North Korean picked up the spent cartridges in each office, just as he had been trained to do at the Special Operations Officers School in the Democratic People's Republic of Korea, and put them into his pocket. He put the Tokarev back into his elongated shoulder holster, designed to hold the pistol with the silencer attached. In Rodriquez's office, he spotted a safe mounted in the credenza. He turned the handle and was surprised when it opened.

Inside, he counted 10 bundles of cash, stacked in two rows of five, under a journal and an address book. The cash went into his briefcase; he left the papers and spun the safe's handle to lock it. Next, he looked behind pictures and in the credenza of the other offices for more safes. Finding none, he walked out of the office. Barely five minutes had elapsed since he'd entered.

At a 7-Eleven near the junction of California Highway 55 and Interstate 405, he stopped to buy a bottle of Coca-Cola and two packages of Hostess Devil Crèmes, for which he had developed a fondness since arriving in the U.S. six months earlier. Both were impossible to get in his home country.

His desire for the cylindrical chocolate-crème-filled pastries satisfied, he made a local call from the pay phone and stayed on the line long enough to say in English, "Done," before being told another package was in the mail. This was his sixth mission since he had walked off the flight from Hong Kong at Los Angeles International Airport.

Tuesday, November 15th, 1994, 1456 local time, San Diego

Josh Haman stared at the black rotary phone. A petty officer in the Commander, Naval Air Forces, Pacific's administration department had just called to let him know his ticket had arrived. The process leading to his pending flight to Japan had started back in September, when the detailer responsible for assigning captains to new billets had told him that the Commander, Seventh Fleet had asked for him—by name—to be his Chief of Staff for Operations and Plans in Yokosuka, Japan. Normally an eighteen-month assignment for officers with dependents, it could be reduced to a year if he went alone.

He'd asked the detailer about a ship CO billet, which was what he really wanted, only to be told that none were available for helicopter pilots. Carriers were the exclusive province of fighter and attack aviators. Josh had pressed his point about becoming the CO of one of the larger amphibious ships, which were essentially helicopter carriers. He was told that surface warfare officers were getting those commands. Once again, Josh felt that Naval Aviators who flew helicopters throughout their careers were getting screwed. Without a ship command, it was hard to be competitive before the flag officer selection board.

Several times the detailer had made the point that being asked by a three star to be on his staff would be good for his career, but Josh was skeptical. As a naval officer, he wanted command of a ship.

Josh then had a difficult decision to make: accept the orders or retire? After coming back from Moscow in September 1991, he'd requested and received a shore duty billet in San Diego, which had been good for his family. Assigned to the tactical training group he'd helped create, Haman ran exercises for carrier and amphibious battle groups preparing to deploy. Fifteen months ago, Josh had become Commander, Helicopter Anti-Submarine Warfare Squadrons Pacific. The helicopter squadrons assigned to the Pacific fleet flew a mix of older SH-2s and SH-3s, along with new SH-60Bs, and getting the squadrons ready to deploy was a training and logistical challenge.

He'd been a captain for almost five years; next year his record would be briefed to the flag selection board for the first time. History said that a captain had one, maybe two "shots" at being selected for Admiral.

In the Navy, there was a saying, "You can only say no to a set of orders once." At this stage of his career, saying "no" to the orders to Seventh Fleet would have meant he'd decided to retire and his dream of commanding a ship was over. He was not ready to call it quits. Being selected for Admiral would be nice—but more than that, he wanted a ship command.

Josh first broached the subject of an unaccompanied tour in Japan to Rebekah, his wife of 25 years, while they were sitting on the deck of their house enjoying a sunset and a glass of wine. Rebekah was sitting sideways on the couch, facing Josh. She reached out and touched the hair on the side of Josh's head. "You're getting grayer by the day. Do you really want to take this assignment?"

"I do."

"I'm a veteran at being a single mom with a husband someplace over the horizon, so I guess we can do it again. Are you sure it is only for a year?"

"Unaccompanied, it is a year from the day I report. That's what the detailers tell me."

"And you believe them?"

"I do. Will it be exactly three hundred and sixty-five days? No. My guess it will be closer to thirteen months, allowing for prep and travel."

"Unless something dramatic happens. And it seems like it always does."

Josh didn't say anything as he sipped his wine. Predicting what would happen at the pointy edge of the sword was impossible.

Rebecca poked him playfully in the stomach. It was softer than it had been when she'd married him. Back then he'd had a firm six-pack. Now, despite his diligent work-outs, he had a small paunch. "Just promise me that you will remember you are no longer twenty-five and don't try to do something you are not physically capable of."

"So, you don't mind me taking this Seventh Fleet assignment?"

"Mind? Yes. I don't like being left behind, but moving Sean for 18 months is a non-starter. He won't want to leave his friends, and you promised him you wouldn't move him once he started high school. At least Sasha and Sara are off in their own world at college. Will I stand in the way? Because you believe it is good for your career, *no*. This time I'll have the advantage of having my mom nearby. We'll just figure it out… as we always have."

"Sara and Sasha can come with you to Japan during the summer. I'll figure out how to take some leave, so instead of coming back to the States, you can bring everyone over."

"That's exactly what I was thinking. Hmm, I may drag them to Hong Kong and Seoul. Maybe even Australia. I've never been there!"

The Simushir Island Incident

Josh knew where this was going. Rebekah was planning a lengthy vacation to places she'd never been, with or without him. "Sydney is a long ten-hour flight from Tokyo."

Rebekah leaned over and kissed her husband. "You'll be working long ten-hour days at sea on the *Blue Ridge*. If you can endure it, so can we."

Thursday, January 12th, 1995, 1046 local time, Washington, DC

After meeting with the minority leader of the House of Representatives, Steven Higgins returned to his office, smiling. His staff noted that his demeanor, normally very serious, had lightened. As a third-term representative from Wisconsin, he was still junior in terms of seniority, so he'd been surprised when the minority leader assigned him to the Armed Services Sub-Committee on Readiness. For an Annapolis graduate and a former Naval Aviator, it was a dream come true.

Friday, January 13th, 1995, 1425 local time, Glendale, CA

It was a typical LA winter day—not hot, but sunny enough to require sunglasses to counter the glare. Cho Rhee stopped her black BMW M5 in front of a heavy steel gate. Her mirror Ray Bans served another function: with them on, the guards could not see her scanning the premises. The window motor whirred softly after she pushed the button to run the driver-side window down.

A swarthy Hispanic guard, who looked as though he ate far too many tacos, waddled over. Cho could see a second man behind him, cradling an M-16 and trying, but not succeeding, to stay out of sight behind one of the pillars that flanked the gate.

"My name is Cho Rhee. I'm here to see Luis Padilla. He is expecting me."

The man grunted and had a discussion in rapid Spanish into a handheld radio. "Boss, it's not a he, it's a *she*." At the end of the conversation, he pointed up the driveway. "House is up there."

Cho raised the window and released the clutch. She took her time driving the quarter mile to the top of the hill where another armed guard pointed to a spot, and Cho parked the BMW. As she got out, Cho admired the view of the San Gabriel Mountains and studied the security arrangements, knowing the guards could not see the movement of her eyes behind her darkly tinted glasses.

This guard was short, stocky and had thick hair that glistened. She wondered if the slickness came from pomade and sniffed delicately. Yes, it did. He put his arms out, indicating that he intended to search her. Cho opened her black blazer wide to show a harness with a pair of magazine pouches and a shoulder holster filled with a Walther PPK/S. As the guard took in her weaponry and her breasts, she spotted two more armed men in the shade of the portico. The guard spread a small towel on the hood of her BMW and pointed to her Walther PPK/S. Cho dropped the magazine out of the pistol and racked the slide to eject the round from the firing chamber. The German-made semi-automatic pistol, the recently ejected magazine and single round, along with the two spare magazines in the shoulder holster, she placed in a neat row on the towel. Smiling, Cho put two more seven round magazines taken from the pocket of her blue blazer next to the others. She hoped they would stay untouched until she returned. Without a word, the guard—reeking of garlic—patted her down. He squeezed her breasts, then he slid his hand down and fondled her vagina. Behind her Ray Bans, Cho's eyes glinted like steel.

Next, the guard pointed to her black eel-skin briefcase. This she also placed gently on the hood. Cho popped the latches and stepped away so the guard could see its contents: a single three-by five-inch card and a brick-shaped object wrapped in black plastic.

"She's clean," the man yelled in Spanish and gestured her toward the door.

Cho pressed the latches shut on her briefcase. Her first step was toward the guard who'd searched her. In rapid Spanish, she whispered in his ear, "Feel me up like that again and I'll kill you so fast you'll be dead before you hit the ground."

As Cho strode to the house, the man muttered, "Asian bitch" under his breath. He admired her small, tight ass, well defined by her black pantsuit, and wondered what she would be like in bed.

What the guard didn't see was Cho's smile. Like most men who searched her, he'd found the pistol and been more interested in feeling her up than thoroughly searching her. What he hadn't found was the eighteen-inch *wakizashi* in a scabbard attached to the back of her bra. The hilt of the traditional Japanese short sword nestled between her shoulder blades, just below the base of her neck. Its scabbard provided another benefit; it forced her to sit up straight. The short sword was ideal for hand-to-hand combat. It was longer than a knife, and a skilled user like Cho could filet a man's chest in two strokes.

Cho stepped onto the veranda, with its redwood beams and two large ceiling fans. Slate gray flagstones were set into the concrete, and she saw that extra care had been taken to smooth the cement so that it was flush with the edges of the stone: the work of a skilled craftsman. As she approached, Luis Padilla stood up. Padilla was a slightly built man, five-foot-eight, with piercing black eyes that presented an almost Asian slant.

"I was not expecting a woman, let alone such a beautiful one."

Cho wasn't sure if he meant he didn't like dealing with women or was just trying to be gallant. "My first name loosely translates as 'beautiful' in Korean, but most Americans don't know one Korean name from another."

Padilla nodded a "thank-you-for-not-embarrassing-me" acknowledgement and pointed to the only other chair at the glass-topped table. A servant came out of the house, and Cho paused to allow him to pull out the chair. She brushed long strands of black hair off her face as she sat down.

"Drink?"

"Water with lemon or lime. Thank you."

"Would you like something stronger, like a glass of wine?"

Cho shook her head. "Thank you, but no. I am driving." *If this doesn't go as planned, I don't want my brain affected by alcohol. I don't believe you'll try to drug me, but you never know. Also, I have a legal concealed carry permit. If I were stopped for a routine traffic stop and the police smelled alcohol on my breath, good-bye permit!*

"Yes, it is a long way back to…?"

"Los Angeles." Cho wasn't about to tell him she lived in Laguna Beach.

"Ah yes, LA." Padilla didn't pursue the question; if she had wanted him to know what suburb, she would have told him. He'd thought about having whoever arrived for the meeting followed home, but had decided against it. Now he realized it was probably the right decision. His gut instinct that had kept him alive for a quarter century in a dangerous business said, *Do not mess with this woman.*

The servant withdrew, after putting a small tray holding a glass of water and wedges of lime and lemon next to Cho.

"You are a long way from the barrio, no?" Cho's accent gave a lilt to her voice that men found sexy. In Hong Kong, the Queen's English was taught starting in what Americans call kindergarten. At the University of Southern California, Cho had learned American slang and Spanish to go with the Cantonese, Mandarin, Korean, and English she spoke with ease.

Padilla wasn't sure what Cho meant, but assumed she was suggesting that his house in the mountains kept him a long way from the DEA and the LAPD. "Yes, it allows me to stay away from trouble."

Cho Rhee leaned forward. "Let's get down to business. We are the only ones who make Asian Pure and can deliver a metric ton every month. The question is, can your organization handle it?"

A metric ton of heroin consists of one thousand one-kilogram bricks, or about twenty-two hundred pounds. Padilla leaned back and waved his hand dismissively. "No one can deliver that much every month."

Cho brushed more hair from her face as the breeze picked up. "We can. In fact, if you can sell it, we can deliver a ton every two weeks. We control the process from the opium fields in Southeast Asia until we deliver the finished product to you. Asian Pure is the best there is and is already sought after on the streets. Your distributors should know; their customers are asking for it."

"And I am sure you brought me a sample."

"I have a kilo with me, which—if we agree to do business— you can keep as a gesture of good will." She put the briefcase on the table, opened it, and rotated it so Luis could see the contents.

Cho, if we can't make a deal, and if you piss me off, I can call the cops, who will arrest you with a kilo of heroin.

Luis snapped his fingers. A chemist, who was waiting just inside the French doors leading into the house, stepped forward and took a sample from the brick and left. "Assuming you can deliver, what are the commercial arrangements?"

"You agree to buy at least five hundred kilos each month to start. When you place each order, we give you the delivery date and you deposit half the price in an offshore account. When you take possession of the drugs, you deposit the other half. This way, we have half in case you fail to make the second payment. If we fail to deliver, you have paid only half. This way we share the risk equally."

"Why are you talking to *me?*"

"The other organizations in southern California can't handle the volume and don't—" Rhee hesitated. "—like our terms. Whereas your associates in Mexico agreed that they were acceptable." Rhee had evaluated each cartel's local drug organization before determining that the Sinaloa Cartel had the best distribution and smuggling network. Other organizations would have trouble distributing a half a ton a month.

For his part, Padilla knew that the Los Zetas and the Gulf Cartel didn't like dealing with Koreans. Now, he'd recently learned, many of their top people in LA were dead, and their distribution networks were disrupted. Even the cartel's sources in the LAPD didn't know who had done the killing.

"And you are sure *we* can?"

Rhee nodded. "That is what I have been told."

"What does your organization get out of this?"

"A steady customer who takes all the volume we can produce. It makes security simpler. In a year, we discuss changing the buy to a thousand kilos. You will have an exclusive deal—except for the Chinese and Korean gangs, of course. We will continue to supply them directly."

"Miss Rhee, what do you get out of it?"

"Money. Just like you." Cho Rhee's tone was matter of fact.

"Tell me about the logistics?"

"We bring it to North America by freighter. The ship slows to three to five knots off the Mexican coast—outside the twelve-mile limit—between one and three a.m., and the heroin is transferred to your boat. We know our delivery method works. We own the freighters and pay the crews extra to keep quiet."

"And you are the only source of Asian Pure?"

"Yes."

"Okay. How much per kilo?"

Cho waited to answer. The chemist had just finished with his test and returned. He spoke in soft Spanish to Luis, who nodded, clasped his hands and rested them on the table. "My chemist says this is the purest heroin he has ever seen. It is almost 99.5% pure. Like the old Ivory soap advertisements."

Cho smiled at his reference to the soap maker's old claim—*99 and 44/100ths percent pure!* "One hundred and fifty thousand dollars a kilo," she finally answered.

"That is ridiculous."

"Not when you consider you can cut it as many times as you want and it will still be better than anything you currently sell on the street."

"Seventy thousand."

"One forty." Cho took a sip of the water. She believed negotiating with men was very predictable when they wanted something badly. It was like dating a man who wanted to get her into bed. She would win this game. Cho had told her uncle that Padilla would settle at over $100,000 per kilo, or about 50 million dollars per 500-kilo shipment.

"One hundred thousand, Padilla countered."

"One hundred and twenty-five thousand dollars," Cho countered back.

"One-oh-five."

"One-fifteen. We're giving you a quantity discount at this price."

Padilla took a sip of his iced tea and smiled. "One-ten and no more."

"Done." Her agreement with Half Moon let Cho keep anything over ninety thousand as her commission. Now, each five hundred kilo shipment would add ten million dollars to her personal offshore bank accounts.

"When will the first shipment arrive?"

"Now that we have a deal and your order, I'll let you know the exact date as soon as I get it."

She took the three-by-five-inch card from her briefcase and slid it across the table. On it she had written the rendezvous latitude and longitude, along with her firm's offshore bank name and account number, a phone number in Macao, and a code word to identify Padilla's organization. "This will be the location of the first drop of five hundred kilos. If you are late or have a security problem, the ship will not wait around to let that become our problem too. The heroin is dumped over the side. We lose the heroin and you are out your deposit of twenty-seven point five million. Call the phone number to place each additional order."

Padilla nodded. *These people must have tons of Asian Pure if they'd rather dump it than deliver it late. Any captain of ours who doesn't make the rendezvous on time won't get a chance to miss a second one.* "I gather I should have someone call from outside the U.S?"

"Perfect." Rhee sounded like a Valley Girl when she spoke the word as if it started with "Purrrrr."

Padilla snapped his fingers on the corner of the card, thinking the street value of the first shipment would be well in excess of a hundred million dollars. Even with losses and expenses, that would put a cool forty-five million or more in his and the cartel's pockets. It was a good afternoon.

Monday, January 16th, 1995, 1315 local time, Pyongyang,
Democratic People's Republic of Korea (DPRK)

Captain Chin Hae Kim of the North Korean People's Army shivered as he waited in the headquarters of the Ministry of State

The Simushir Island Incident

Security. In Pyongyang, it is always damp and cold in January, and there was no hot air coming out of the vents. Yet it was the gnawing fear in Kim's gut that made him feel cold, not the room's 17 degree Celsius (63 Fahrenheit) temperature.

The country's founder—the late Kim il-Sung—and now his son, Kim Jong-Il, told his fellow citizens that winters had to be endured. Surviving in the cold with limited heat and food toughened them and better prepared them to fight the country's imperialist enemies.

The 28-year-old captain looked around at the dull-gray concrete walls. Then he looked at the polished marble floor. He had no idea the stone had been imported at great expense. But experience living in the field had taught the captain that stone held the cold unless it was heated, and the thought made him feel even colder.

A single row of plain wooden chairs with thin red cushions were pushed up against one barren concrete wall. Two-meter tall pictures of Kim Jong-Il—the "Dear Leader"—and his late father, Kim il-Sung—the "Great Leader"—hung on a wall opposite the country's national flag. They and the cushions were the only decorations giving the room any color. A small vase with burning incense gave the room a pleasant smell of cinnamon and sandalwood, two aromas from his childhood he hadn't enjoyed in years.

When he'd entered, the two thick teak doors had closed behind him with a soft thud. Kim thought it odd that the doors he'd come through had handles, yet the steel doors on the opposite wall had none. They were painted gray, like so many buildings in North Korea.

To straighten any real or imagined wrinkles, the captain tugged at the bottom of his uniform blouse, which bore the insignia of the DPRK's elite special forces. He had been ordered to appear in his dark brown dress uniform rather than the more comfortable—and warmer—camouflaged utilities he wore on a daily basis.

After his last mission, no matter how hard he tried, he could not get out of his mind the image of the coarse cloth of his camouflage fatigues spattered with blood, brain matter and bone fragments. Captain Kim wondered why he continued to follow his orders. That last special arrest, like the previous nine, had been murder in the name of the state. It was getting harder and harder to justify his actions.

Captain Kim made sure his empty holster and magazine pouches were snapped shut. Knowing he was unarmed made him even more uncomfortable. As the commander of a special arrest unit, Kim was one of the few men in the country allowed to carry his sidearm wherever he went. Burt when he'd entered this building, he'd been required to put his pistol and his four spare eight-round magazines in a basket. Based on the Soviet TT-33 semi-automatic pistol, and firing the same 7.62 x 25mm Tokarev round, the Type 68 pistol was made in North Korea.

The threads on the Tokarev's slightly longer-than-standard barrel had intrigued the guard. After examining it closely, he'd dropped the magazine out and pulled the slide back to eject the round in the firing chamber. Watching the soldier inspect the well-used weapon, the young captain could see the soldier's mind working as he ran his fingers over the worn grooves on the slide. *Yes soldier, it is well used.*

The wait in the conference room gave Captain Kim time to think about the events of the previous Friday. He had been told that Major General Gam would be in his apartment waiting for his staff car to arrive. A delay was arranged by an officer in the Ministry of State Security, timed so that Gam's wife would be at work and his children in school.

At any sign of resistance during the arrest, Kim was authorized to use deadly force. The general was accused of black-marketing, a crime punishable in North Korea by death. In school, Kim had been taught that the Constitution of the Democratic People's Republic of Korea gave every citizen the right to face his accuser during a trial. According to his late father, however, individual rights in the People's Republic were a fiction.

As he'd rapped on the door with his left hand while holding his pistol behind him in his right, Captain Kim had wondered what the general would do. He had three other men waiting to rush in and apprehend the general. Major General Gam unlocked the door, and Captain Kim shoved the Tokarev into the General's face.

"General Gam, you are under arrest for black-marketeering."

With a gun in his face, Major General Gam did the natural thing. He backed up. "Bullshit, Captain. I did nothing of the sort."

When he got enough separation from Captain Kim, Gam went to a small desk and pulled out a folder. He turned to a page in a centimeter-thick report. "Here are the names of the black-marketeers. They are the ones stealing diesel fuel and food from the Army and the people and then selling it. Go arrest them."

Captain Kim looked at Major General Gam. "My orders are to arrest you. That document is evidence; and if true, it can be used to clear your name."

Gam glared at Kim and the soldiers. "I am not going anywhere. Our Dear Leader personally ordered me to investigate the theft and write this report." He pulled open a drawer in a small desk. Captain Kim saw a black object and, thinking it was a pistol, fired one shot into the side of the general's head. The small black phone book in Gam's hand went flying.

That was the first "arrest" of the day. After lunch, they stopped Lieutenant General Rang near his corps headquarters, 40 kilometers north of the Demilitarized Zone, in the town of

Kumchon. Rang thought he was going to a conference at North Korean People's Army headquarters in Pyongyang. When Captain Kim approached Lieutenant General Rang's staff car, the driver remained at the wheel. Rang waited for Captain Kim to approach, assuming it was a routine security stop.

Kim held his suppressed Type 68 hidden behind his back while he opened the rear door on the driver's side. The general was sitting on the passenger's side. "Lieutenant General Rang, please get out of the car." He was commanding, but civil and respectful of a senior officer. He had to be—this time he had a witness, the driver.

"Why? What for? Who are you? I am Lieutenant General Rang. You have no right to order me out of the car."

"I am Captain Kim, and I have a warrant for your arrest from the State Security Department of the Ministry of State Security. So please, General, get out of the car. You need to come with me."

"Captain Kim, this will end badly for you. This is a mistake."

Kim nodded to the soldier standing on the other side of the car, who opened the rear passenger door. "Lieutenant General Rang. There is no mistake. Get out of the car, and I will show you the warrant."

"No. I am going to an important meeting at Army headquarters." Rang faced forward and spoke in his command voice. "Sergeant Baek, take me to Pyongyang."

Kim heard the soft pop of a suppressed Tokarev at the same time he felt warm blood and bits of skull hit his face. The soldier on the far side of the car had shot the general in the side of his head.

The time between the first and second arrest and the drive back to Pyongyang gave Captain Kim time to read the documents taken from Major General Gam's apartment. Assuming they were true, he concluded that Gam had done his duty. Kim suspected General

Gam's real crime was exposing a black-marketing ring run under the patronage of senior party members and likely the Dear Leader himself, or at least, some of his close confidants.

In the byzantine world of North Korean politics, Rang and Gam were a two-fold threat to senior members of the regime. They had found out about the theft of the diesel fuel, and if word got out, officials would be implicated and the Dear Leader would lose face. Therefore, someone high in the party and the government had decided both Gam and Rang had to be eliminated, without a trial, to save the country's leader from embarrassment.

A dull metallic sound interrupted Kim's replaying of the past Friday's events and drew his attention to the door without handles. It opened on well-oiled hinges, allowing four soldiers—wearing the insignia of the Dear Leader's personal guard and using the flat-footed goose step preferred by the Soviet Army and those it trained —to enter. The captain wondered if their shiny AKM assault rifles had ever been fired.

"Captain Kim. How are you?" A short, thin man entered the room. Kim recognized him as the head of the State Security Department (SSD), who reported to the Minister of State Security. The SSD were the secret police, and no one, unless they were Kim Jung-Il or someone close to him, questioned their actions. The guards took up positions in each corner and their boots thudded on the floor in unison as they came to attention.

Captain Chin Hae Kim came to attention and bowed slightly. At 175 centimeters (5' 9") and 65 kilos (143 lbs.), he was taller and more muscular than the man in front of him. "Deputy Minister Thaek. I am fine. Thank you for asking." His commanding officer had ordered him to keep his answers short and to the point.

"Good." Thaek reeked of stale cigar and cigarette smoke. As he came closer, Captain Kim smelled grilled *bulgogi* and wondered how much meat the man had eaten. His own lunch at the officer's mess had been a watery version of a spicy soup called *maeuntang,* made with hot chili paste, with three meager pieces of fish.

"Did you complete your mission?" Thaek looked into his eyes searchingly.

"Yes, sir. Both men resisted and are dead." Kim was sure Thaek already knew the answer to his own question.

"I see." The reed-thin Thaek relaxed for a second, then tensed again. "Did they say anything or confess to the charges?"

"No, sir." He didn't mention Gam's report. When he'd turned it over to his superior, Kim didn't say he'd read it. The corruption went to the highest levels of the army, and if it was true, he now understood why someone had wanted Gam and Rang out of the way with a suitable cover story. The day after their deaths, the Army had announced that "bandits and revisionist thugs" had murdered the generals and a manhunt was underway to bring the criminals to justice. The driver had been threatened that if he said anything about the death of General Rang, he and his family would be either executed or sent to a re-education camp.

Later this week, a state funeral for the generals would be held, attended by their grieving widows and children. Afterwards, the families would get into the limousines, not knowing the next stop was a slave labor camp they would never leave.

"Is there anything else you need to tell me?" The Deputy Minister of Safety and Security examined Kim as if he were studying an example of a new and unfamiliar brand of Cuban cigars. Captain Kim forced himself not to turn away from the unpleasant stench of smoke emanating from Thaek's clothes. The minister's tobacco breath made facing him difficult.

"No, sir."

"Captain Kim, what is in your formal report?"

"My report reads, 'When we attempted to arrest each general, he resisted and we used deadly force.'"

"Very good, Captain. You know your job well. Dismissed."

"Thank you, sir." With that, Captain Kim saluted, stepped back, did an about face and headed for the same door he had entered.

Now that he had completed a tenth operation of this type, Captain Kim suspected each one brought him—and perhaps his men—one step closer to being sent to a re-education camp or getting a bullet in the head so there would be no one to contest the official reports. *The longer I stay in this unit, the closer I am to being eliminated because I know too much. A request for transfer will raise suspicions. What can I do?*

Tuesday, January 17th, 1995, 0220 local time,
on board M.V. Crescent Star

Captain Sa'id Yamani ordered the freighter *Crescent Star* to slow to three knots so the ship's wake would not phosphoresce and make it easy to spot from the air. Its slow speed let the much smaller North Korean fishing boat chugging along at nine knots catch up and come alongside.

Based on the radar plot, the freighter was just inside the 12-mile limit measured from the tip of a small peninsula in North Korea, known as Changsan Got Point, that jutted out into the West Sea. The rest of the world might call the waters the Yellow Sea, but all Koreans—North and South—referred to the Sea of Japan as the East Sea and the body of water on the west side of the peninsula as the West Sea.

In a phone call with the ship's owners before leaving Hong Kong for Dalian in the People's Republic of China, Yamani had been warned that the South Koreans and the Americans photograph every ship entering North Korean waters. *Crescent Star* could not linger in this area for long.

On the bridge, the captain watched as the first of two pallets of black-plastic-wrapped heroin bricks was hoisted over the gunwales and into the hold of *Crescent Star.* On the return trip, the crane carried a pallet of food and consumer goods impossible to buy in North Korea, available only to those who ruled the country. Sanctions levied by the United Nations, the European Union and the United States against North Korea meant that goods like these had to be smuggled into the country. If one were caught buying or selling goods on the black market in North Korea, the penalty was death—unless one was a member of the ruling elite. Yamani wondered if the recipients enjoyed this rarified status or not. Was the production and selling of heroin unofficially/officially sanctioned, or were the heroin makers playing a very dangerous, if highly lucrative, game? He decided it was in his best interest to stop wondering. He was paid to deliver goods and be silent, not speculate.

In his stateroom safe, Yamani had the cash to pay his crew their bonus for their silence and the extra work; it amounted to twice their pay for an ordinary cruise. They got half when they reached Los Angeles and the rest when they returned to Hong Kong. The cash payments were made off the books and no record was kept either on board the ship or at Crescent Shipping, the company that owned *Crescent Star.* Yamani knew from experience that the members of his crew would hoard their cash until they returned to Hong Kong, where, depending on the man, it would go to their families or be spent on hookers.

A naval officer wearing the dark blue uniform of the North Korean People's Navy and gold shoulder boards came up the Jacob's ladder and headed toward the bridge. Yamani led the way to the radio room. The sailor on duty discretely exited, leaving the two officers alone. Without saying a word, the Navy captain handed Yamani a piece of rice paper with a 10-digit number beginning with 852, the country code for Hong Kong.

The Simushir Island Incident

It took seconds for the computers to make the connection from *M.V. Crescent Star* to an International Maritime Satellite to a ground station in Japan. Then it traveled by underwater cable to Hong Kong. There, another switch sent the signal to an office where a private switch dialed a number in Dandong in the People's Republic of China, just across the Yalu River from North Korea. The microprocessor in Dandong dialed a number in an apartment in Pyongyang.

When the phone started to ring, Yamani passed the handset to the North Korean, who spoke a few words. The men at both ends of the call kept it short to make it difficult to intercept or trace. Yamani did not speak Korean, but guessed the brief call told the person on the other end that the two-way transfer was complete.

Once the North Korean officer was back on the fishing boat, Yamani ordered *Crescent Star* to its most efficient cruising speed of 12 knots and onto a course into international waters. The heavy hatch covers were slid closed. Yamani's crew stowed the cranes, blocks, booms and cables.

Yamani made no mention of the transfer in the ship's log, which was a legal document and subject to examination by customs authorities in any country the ship visited. A note that *Crescent Star* transferred cargo to a fishing boat off North Korea would lead to questions for which there were no good answers. He made a mental note of the transfer time. Based on the times given to him, the entire transaction had been completed well within the gap in US satellite coverage. Once out of North Korean waters, Yamani used the loudspeaker system to congratulate his crew on completing the cargo transfer in less than 15 minutes.

Wednesday, January 18th, 1995, 0640 local time, Pearl Harbor, HI

There were three neat piles in the clear space in the middle of Uilani Ka'anapali's desk. It was an arrangement she used to keep up with message traffic and the daily review of photographs and electronic intelligence from her area of responsibility. In the center was the overnight message traffic she had to peruse and triage, then either keep for herself to draft a response, or distribute to her team members to handle.

The stack on the right was the second most important. It contained intercept transcripts and their summaries, marked with the location of the emitter as well as the source of the intelligence. Uilani's notes would be paper-clipped to the report for distribution to her 15 team members for action, further analysis, or filing.

The third pile had images from electronic and photographic intelligence aircraft and satellite passes during the past twenty-four hours, along with a map showing the route the reconnaissance platform took. Every day, Uilani's staff studied these. Any updates to previous analyses were passed on to her "customers" on the staff of the Commander in Chief, Pacific Command, traditionally known as CINCPAC, and subordinate commands authorized to receive the intelligence. Often, Uilani was copied in CINCPAC messages that requested more data to be gathered by the National Security Agency (NSA), the Central Intelligence Agency (CIA), the Defense Intelligence Agency (DIA), the National Reconnaissance Office (NRO), or a unit within the Pacific Command. Uilani took a lot of pride in knowing that her team's requests were rarely rejected.

Her area of responsibility was the Northwest Pacific and included the waters off eastern Russia, North Korea and the People's Republic of China. To make it easy to visualize the geography, Uilani had a map of the Western Pacific mounted behind a thin sheet of Plexiglas on the long wall facing her. It had grease pencil notes on current items of interest that either she or her staff updated as needed. The short wall, next to the clock, had a large map of the Korean peninsula. It too was covered with Plexiglas and had different-colored grease pencil notes in shorthand.

When Uilani had started as an intelligence analyst 14 years earlier, one of the first lessons she'd learned was never, *never* get behind on your message traffic. If you did, you'd be buried and there weren't enough hours in the day or week to catch up. If there was something that needed a response, get it done and move on. But before diving into the pile, there was the ritual of brewing a fresh pot of tea. Today's brew was Kilinoe Green Tea, grown only on her home island of Hawaii. As it brewed, Uilani could smell hints of dried cherries, caramel and citrus.

The clock on the wall showed 0702 when she finished surfing through the messages. All were routine, and none needed immediate action.

Every day around 0630, photos and data tapes of radio, radar and telephone transmissions recorded on daily flights by a U-2S high-altitude reconnaissance aircraft around North Korea were delivered to her office. The plane's U-shaped track paralleled the Chinese coast along the Yellow Sea over international waters before it turned south. Once it was 10 miles south of the demilitarized zone, the U-2 crossed the Korean peninsula before turning north over the Sea of Japan, staying 15 miles or more off the coast. It then continued up the Russian coast over international waters past Vladivostok before returning to Osan Air Base in South Korea.

Analysts working with the South Koreans were careful to ensure its analyses referred to the Yellow Sea as the West Sea and the Sea of Japan as the East Sea. Any intelligence products delivered to the Commander in Chief, United Nations Command, in Seoul needed to reflect that naming convention, or the South Koreans would reject the information without looking at it.

The photos and electronic intelligence collected by the U-2 were evaluated by Osan's photo interpreters and signal analysts shortly after the plane landed. A courier boarded a C-141, whose scheduled departure was timed to coincide with when the material was ready, and carried it to the Joint Intelligence Center, Pacific, known by its acronym JICPAC, pronounced 'jik-pack'.

Today, Uilani was very interested in the photos taken the night before. She wanted to scratch a mental itch that had started when she saw an intercept of an INMARSAT call made from a merchant ship well off the normal shipping lanes in the Yellow Sea and just inside North Korean waters. She wanted to know from what ship the call was made—and why the ship was there.

Chapter 2: THE DEAL

Thursday, January 19th, 1995, 1121 local time,
Wonsan, Democratic People's Republic of Korea

The icy-cold winds reflected their snowy origins in Eastern Siberia. They rattled windows, and their clatter told Vice Admiral Kim Sun Pak that spring was not coming any time soon. On his walk to the East Sea Fleet's headquarters, the raw dampness had penetrated the heavy woolen overcoat he'd bought years before, during submarine training in the Soviet Union. When Pak had been younger, his body had shrugged off the chill. At 54, he felt the damp cold in his bones and wished he lived in a warmer climate.

Suppressing a sigh, he returned his attention to the classified document he was reading. Pak was the commander of the North Korean Navy's submarine force. He was responsible for the training, support and operational deployment of its 22 submarines based at Mayang-do and Nanjin on the East Sea.

"Admiral…" Pak's aide said tentatively.

"Yes, Captain?" Pak was authorized to have a senior Naval officer as an aide. In other navies, an aide assignment was a captain's stepping-stone to a promotion. Pak suspected that was not the case here. More likely, Captain Chin had a collateral duty to report on his boss's activities to the secret police.

"Admiral, Lieutenant General Chun Lee Jang is here."

"Wonderful. Send him in and tell my driver I won't need him until later in the day. And, Captain, I won't need you until our next meeting at 1330."

"Yes, sir." Chin would use the time to catch up on paperwork while the Admiral had lunch with his friend. Major General Jang was commander of the country's elite airborne, reconnaissance and marine commando units, which totaled about a quarter of the 150,000 men considered by Western analysts as North Korean special forces.

"It is good to see you, General." At 195 centimeters (6 feet, 5 inches), Admiral Pak was tall even for a Westerner and towered over the stocky, tough-looking Army officer who entered, carrying his own heavy, dark-brown woolen uniform overcoat. The men clasped hands and the admiral gestured towards the large conference table.

"Where did you get this map?" Jang asked in a soft voice. The map on the table was of Simushir Island.

"A gift from our Russian friends. They have graciously offered exercise areas for our submarines and your commandos." Pak kept his voice at a normal tone as a signal to Jang to do the same. Both were paranoid about hidden microphones. Pak hoped that as long as they talked in businesslike tones around the *real* topic, they would be fine.

Jang took the hint. "It is good that our allies recognize our worth," he said in a normal tone of voice.

The admiral pointed to the northern end of Simushir and its harbor. "I think this is a perfect place for us. We can land and anchor our ships there. We will have to bring our own supplies, but that should not be a problem. Your commandos will find this an excellent training area, one where we can use almost all our weapons."

The general inhaled through his teeth with a hiss. "Very interesting."

"Yes, and I have permission to fly to Vladivostok and Khabarovsk to meet with our Russian friends to finalize arrangements. I will also stop in Beijing to chat with our friends and Chinese comrades about buying new submarines and much needed parts."

"Excellent." There was an enthusiastic nod of approval from the Army general.

The politics of Vice Admiral Pak's trip to Russia had life and death implications for both men. A ticket to leave the DPRK was a sign of trust by a government that treated airline schedules as a state secret. If you defected, your family left behind in the DPRK would suffer in the living hell of a re-education camp, worked to death while having to endure a constant barrage of propaganda, poor food, primitive sanitation and no medical care.

In Vladivostok, Pak would discuss transit and operating rights within Russia's territorial waters around Simushir. In Khabarovsk, he planned to arrange for use of a training area on the Russian coast on the west side of the Sea of Japan. That crucial discussion would take place in the offices of the Russian Far Eastern Military District at 15 Seryshev Street. The building was a kilometer from where the Amur River became the Russian/Chinese border. Khabarovsk was a thriving river port, the second largest city in Siberia. It was only about 400 kilometers, or 216 nautical miles, south of the Russian Pacific Fleet submarine shipyards in Komsomolsk, near the mouth of the Amur. The final agreements would be reviewed and signed by someone on the Dear Leader's staff, so if there was a problem, Pak would have someone else to blame.

"When will you leave?" General Jang asked.

"Next Monday. I go first to Beijing to give the Chinese a list of what we need." Admiral Pak let Jang study the map before saying, "Come, let us go eat. We'll walk."

The sky was steel gray with patches of blue. The cold wind from Siberia chilled the bare skin on their faces, but the four blocks would give them time to talk with little fear of being overheard. Admiral Pak spoke first.

"Our Dear Leader is excited about our plans for Simushir. The agreements give us a place to train our special forces and a factory far away from the prying eyes of the Americans. His approval gives me cover to meet with our relatives at Half Moon."

"Does he know the new factory on Simushir will more than quadruple our production capacity?"

"He knows he will get much more money each month, just not how much. I told him it would take a few months to ramp up to full production. We've given him a conservative estimate that we know we can comfortably meet. We can't set up this factory without him eventually finding out its true capacity, and getting his blessing is part of our cost to do business. Then, because he knows, he will discourage any other party from have us followed or investigated."

"Agreed." Jang said cautiously. "So, what is next?"

"Select a small team to send to explore Simushir. Later, we can base some of your special operations soldiers there to protect our workers. I was thinking a platoon or a company would be enough, at least in the beginning. The Russians had three thousand people based on the island before they abandoned it. Our factory will need thirty people, and running the port will need maybe thirty more. We can renovate what we need, starting with barracks, or build anew."

"That makes sense. I will select a team."

The Simushir Island Incident

Admiral Pak turned to his friend and spoke with utmost seriousness. "The team has to be led by a man you trust with the most sensitive missions. He will be alone and have limited communications."

"I understand." They walked almost a block before General Jang broke the silence. "I know just the man. He has been working for our Ministry of State Security on special missions. I need to get him back into the special forces before someone in the SSD decides he knows too much—and makes him disappear."

Tuesday, January 24th, 1995, 0945 local time, Pearl Harbor

Uilani studied the row of pictures. A box in the lower-right corner of each print showed the day, time, mission number, latitude and longitude of the location.

The U-2S's cameras produced large negatives on a special (and very expensive) fine-grain film so they could be enlarged many times. Before making the prints, a photo interpreter studied the negatives to select the ones best meeting her request.

One by one, Uilani looked at the photos showing a freighter with a fishing boat alongside it. The details of the two ships could be identified, and men could be seen on the decks.

Uilani sat back, swishing her shoulder-length, jet back hair. "Got you!"

Feeling triumphant, she bent over her desk and examined the print with a loupe. The lack of a wake—which would have been picked up by the infrared camera because of the temperature difference between colder water forced to the surface by the ship's screw and the warmer surface water—told her the vessel was barely making steerageway. The black square forward of the bridge on the freighter was an open hold. Unless the ship was there with the North Korean government's blessing, any vessel this close to the DPRK's 12-mile limit stood a good chance of being captured or sunk. *So, who are you and what are you doing? And why are there no North Korean naval vessels investigating you?*

Uilani picked up the handset and dialed an extension. "Jay, Uilani here. Can you bring me a list of freighters that left Chinese ports on the Yellow Sea during the past week so we can match some photos to the shipping registry?"

Jay Kirkland's office was less than 20 yards from Uilani's. He maintained a log of freighters going in and out of North Korean and Chinese ports.

It wasn't long before Jay entered, wearing the dark-blue wool shirt and black tie known in the Navy as "working blues." The "crow" on the left sleeve had three red chevrons beneath the insignia identifying him as a petty officer first class and an intelligence specialist. He was a trained photo interpreter who had made four deployments on carriers before getting assigned to shore duty at the Joint Intelligence Center, Pacific. Kirkland had spent most of his career studying ships or ground installations and matching them to other known data.

"Let's see what you have." He bent over and studied the photos on Uilani's desk. "I estimate this ship at about ten thousand tons and four hundred feet long. She looks like an old-fashioned break bulk freighter. There are thousands floating around. Most are based on the Mariner-class design we know as Liberty or Victory ships built during World War II. This one doesn't look like anything special."

"Okay." Uilani waited. Jay flipped through sheets on his clipboard.

"From the shipping notices, there are six possibilities. All left Dalian or Dandong in time to steam at around ten to twelve knots to be in this area. Let's see what they look like." Kirkland hefted a thick blue book onto the desk. Silver-white ink on the front announced it as *Jane's Merchant Ships 1987-88*. Jay flipped pages back and forth, looking for something that would identify the one in the infrared photo.

"This is the one. Ninety percent sure." Jay tapped a picture of *M.V. Crescent Star*. "Assuming about twelve to thirteen hours transit time, *Crescent Star* is probably our baby. Mitsubishi Heavy Industries built her in Japan in 1968. The shipping notice says it is carrying a cargo of clay pottery, solvents, and furniture to the U.S. It is due to reach Long Beach, California, in three weeks. Pottery was supposed to be loaded in Dalian. Ship is owned by Crescent Shipping. If Crescent is like most companies of its sort, most if not all of the company's ships have the word *Crescent* in their names."

"So why do you think she slowed up near the Korean coast?"

"Smuggling drugs or people out of North Korea would be my guess. I can't imagine anyone wanting to be smuggled *into* the DPRK. If it is people, they could be either escaping the regime or girls being sold into prostitution."

Uilani considered. "I'd bet on drugs. There's more money in drugs, and they are easier to smuggle. You don't have to feed them or provide some sort of sanitation."

"I agree that's the most probable scenario. Most of the people-smuggling comes out of the People's Republic of China." He picked up his clipboard and the heavy book. "I'll make you a copy of what's in *Jane's* and ask the Coast Guard and Customs to see what they have in their archives on the ship and Crescent."

Uilani's eyes narrowed. "Thank you, Jay. I'm going to give the guys at Seventh Fleet and CINCPAC a heads up so they can designate *M.V. Crescent Star* a target of interest and notify the Coast Guard."

Something about this ship is fishy, I just don't know what. At least not yet!

* * *

Three thousand and fifty nautical miles to the west of where Uilani was working, Marty Cabot stared at the ceiling of the Seventh Fleet command center and stretched the corded muscles of his arms. Hours in the gym and long runs and swims kept him physically fit and ready to go on an operation, but as a full commander in the SEAL community, going into the field with a team on an op had become a rarity.

Officially, he was the Navy Special Warfare Officer on the Seventh Fleet Staff. He had been strongly recommended to the fleet admiral as one of the most highly regarded operational planners in the small SEAL community. Marty had earned his stripes during two tours in Vietnam. In his second tour, he'd led a raid to take down a secret North Vietnamese missile base. And in 1982, he'd led the team that brought back six Americans POWs who had been held by a drug lord since the end of the Vietnam War. These and many other accomplishments made Marty Cabot a "wanted" man.

It was on long nights like this, when he had the watch and there was little to do other than sort messages, that his mind wandered.

He ran his hand through his sandy brown hair. It was cut short enough to meet Navy regulations, but long enough so that it wasn't a buzz cut. The streaks of gray were getting more prevalent. What was worse was he was seeing signs of baldness. Here he was in his 40s and already losing his hair. One reason he kept it so short was so he wouldn't see hair on the shower floor or in the teeth of his comb. This way, it looked like he had a full head of hair that was just cut short. How long he was going to keep up the fiction was anyone's guess. But, as both Marty and his friend, the helicopter pilot Josh Haman, were fond of saying, "That's my story and I'm sticking to it!"

Ruefully, he remembered a conversation he'd had with Josh about the gray strands in their hair. Both men had laughed when they discussed whether or not it was some of their harrowing missions or old age. Their conclusion: it *couldn't* be old age!

He'd been divorced now for almost 18 years and had not had a steady squeeze since his marriage had ended. Yes, he'd dated women, but the job of being a Navy SEAL always came first and interfered with building a long-term relationship. Before he'd taken the Seventh Fleet billet, he'd promised himself that when he retired he would find a woman who would take him for what he would then be: a retired warrior who wanted nothing more than to surf, have quiet dinners, and not worry about who was trying to kill whom.

In many ways, being a bachelor made life easy. He could come and go as he pleased. On the other hand, he was alone most of the time, with no one to engage in a meaningful conversation and no one with whom to share a hearty laugh.

In many ways, Marty envied Josh's long marriage. Somehow Rebekah and he made it work despite the long deployments, danger, and challenges that a Navy career brings. He wondered why *he* couldn't do it. What was wrong with him?

* * *

As Intelligence Specialist First Class Kirkland headed out the door, Uilani picked up the handset of the secure phone known by the acronym "Stew 3," which came from its designation STU-III or Secure Telephone Unit Model Three. The massive gray phone was about three times the size of a unit that did not have the computer and software to enable encrypted calls. Making sure she had her notes and the material from *Jane's* in front of her, she pushed the button labeled "C7F."

C7F was shorthand for Seventh Fleet and its flagship, *U.S.S. Blue Ridge*. If the ship was in port, it connected her to the staff's command center via normal telephone circuits and could dial the extension on the ship. If the flagship was at sea, a prompt appeared in the LED screen asking if she wanted to use the Navy's satellite phone network. If she selected "yes," the shipboard phone would ring at the duty officer's desk in the staff's command center, where a petty officer on watch could then switch the call to any office or stateroom occupied by a staff member.

"Good morning, Seventh Fleet Command Duty Officer. Commander Cabot."

"Good morning, Commander. This is Uilani Ka'anapali from JICPAC. I have some intel Seventh Fleet might find interesting. I'm going to send it out as a message and copy CINCPAC's N2 and N3. You may get a tasker out of it."

"Aloha, Uilani Ka'anapali. Let's go secure so you can tell me what has prompted this call. I'll initiate."

Uilani was taken aback. The voice on the other end had used the correct Hawaiian pronunciation of her first and last name, instead of stumbling over unfamiliar syllables. She made a mental note to ask Commander Cabot where he learned to speak Hawaiian. But not now, later; something told her this would not be the last conversation they'd be having about *M.V. Crescent Star*. It took about 10 seconds before the pale green letters Top Secret–C7F appeared on the display, telling her the phone was cleared for that level of intelligence.

"So, what is so important that JICPAC needs to call Seventh Fleet in the wee hours of the morning?"

It was 1030 Tuesday morning in Honolulu where Uilani was, but 0530 on Wednesday, the next day, where Marty was sorting messages on board *Blue Ridge*.

His pleasant tone was a surprise. She was used to sarcasm or the condescending tone often used by deployed operating forces when they talked to those closer to home. "Sorry to wake you, sir."

"Not a problem. Today I'm the command duty officer, so I'm up working." Cabot was enjoying the banter. It was a break from reading and sorting messages that had come in during the night. It also pushed his loneliness to the back of his mind, at least temporarily.

"Well, we got an intercept on a satellite telephone call made from a freighter inside North Korean territorial waters. It was off one of those islands just north of the DMZ and southwest of Nampo."

"I know that area well."

She took his statement to mean *I know of the place*. It was a heavily defended part of North Korea. But maybe Cabot, at some time in his career, had worked with South Korean Special Forces who went ashore there. Or, maybe *he* had gone ashore. "We got lucky, Commander. The U-2 took infrared photos of a break bulk freighter moving along at two to three knots with a fishing boat alongside and the front hold open."

"Even more interesting." Marty was wide awake now, and very focused.

"We're pretty sure the ship is *M.V. Crescent Star,* scheduled to dock in three weeks at Long Beach. I'm recommending the ship be classified as a target of interest and tracked until the Coast Guard boards her as soon as she enters U.S. waters."

"What do you think CINCPAC will want us to do?"

The question caught her a bit off guard. *He's asking for my recommendation!* "Maybe Seventh Fleet will be tasked to find and track the ship, and when it gets to the eastern Pacific, transfer the tracking to the Third Fleet patrol plane guys in Hawaii and San Diego."

"My thoughts exactly." Cabot made a note on his draft log. "I'll brief the admiral and my boss this morning." Another pause. "Uilani, what do you do for JICPAC?"

"I head the group that analyzes the intelligence we collect for the Northwest Pacific. We also get tasked with special projects, but there are just fifteen of us, so we stay pretty busy."

"Just for the record, I smell a rat. Most smart merchant ship captains wouldn't go within fifty miles of the North Korean coast without a gold-plated invitation and assurance they won't be sunk or shot. Sooooo, your message will result in some work for us."

"I don't know what to make of it. It could be nothing or something. But… my guess is drugs. Petty Officer First Class Kirkland, who works for me, says it could be emigrants fleeing North Korea—or worse, young girls sold into slavery."

Marty answered without hesitating. "I'd bet on drugs because you don't have to feed them or take care of them if they get sick. It is the one thing that has enough money in it for a captain to risk his ship, his life and his license."

Both had read intelligence briefs that stated that the North Koreans are one of the world's largest makers of counterfeit prescription drugs, uppers, and downers—and also heroin. The opium for heroin came from Myanmar, Laos, Cambodia, and Vietnam, and also from Afghanistan via Iran. The heroin was then smuggled into the U.S. and Western Europe. North Korean state-owned pharmaceutical companies also flooded the market with drugs made without any regard to international patent laws. Drug money flowing into North Korea helped keep the regime afloat. That was a two-edged sword. If Kim Jung-Il's government imploded, no one could accurately predict what would happen, despite many D.C. think tank studies. The DEA had confiscated North Korean-made drugs; but so far, no one had been able to catch them in the act of smuggling them into the U.S.

"Good work—*very* good work."

"Thank you."

The Simushir Island Incident

"How long have you been working for JICPAC?" Cabot asked. "I've been there several times and never met you."

"Almost fifteen years. After spending five years as a CPA, I wanted to do something more interesting than helping companies with their taxes. The Navy was looking for people with an analytic background, so I applied, and here I am. It's never boring!" Uilani wanted to keep the conversation going. "What's your billet at Seventh Fleet?"

"I'm the duty snake eater." Marty assumed she knew "snake eater" was slang for SEAL. "I work for the N6. He's a captain by the name of Josh Haman. Josh and I go way back. He was my personal helicopter pilot in Vietnam."

Cabot chuckled, thinking how Josh would react to that statement. On a numbered fleet staff, the N6 was the Chief of Staff for Operations and Plans and was a captain's billet. The N6's staff was responsible for long range operational and war planning. Qualifications for the billet were significant joint operational experience, a ship or squadron commanding officer tour, and either special or amphibious operations experience—preferably both.

"So, where'd you learn Hawaiian?"

"Let's go back to an unsecure line. The audio quality is much better. I'll switch." Cabot shifted into his chair and propped his feet up on the wastebasket next to the always present burn bag, stuffed with discarded messages, before continuing.

"Short answer is, my ex-wife came from a very traditional Hawaiian family who lived on the big island, and I learned from them. It also helped that I spent two years on the CINCPAC staff just down the street from your building."

"Oh..." Uilani wasn't expecting such a personal answer. Ex meant he was not married. She was pretty sure he would have said if he had remarried. They talked shop for another 20 minutes before he had to end the conversation and finish preparing for the admiral's morning message brief. Before he hung up, he said he would call her to let her know what Seventh Fleet planned to do.

Friday, February 3rd, 1995, 0230 local time, Mexico

The fishing boat *Mi Sueño* rendezvoused with *Crescent Star* 13 miles west of Colonet, Mexico, where the fishing boat's handheld Magellan GPS indicated the latitude and longitude given to the captain before he left port. Once alongside, a pallet was hoisted out of *Crescent Star's* hold and lowered to the deck of the smaller boat. A man with a pallet jack moved it forward, clearing space for the second pallet of 250 bricks. As *Mi Sueño* broke away from *Crescent Star,* a crew member was already slitting the clear plastic that held the one-kilo bricks of Asian Pure on the pallet, so the men could begin counting and neatly stacking them in the hold.

Mi Sueño anchored in 50 feet of water off a desolate beach, 20 miles south of Colonet, where five large Zodiacs were waiting. One hundred bricks were transferred to each Zodiac, which sped ashore to where the heroin was loaded into a waiting van.

From a distance, the *Mi Sueño* looked like a well-used fishing boat. Its black and white paint was fading in some places, but a closer inspection would reveal that it was very well maintained and had the latest in navigation and communication equipment. It also had a well-stocked armory with AK-47s, an M-60 machine gun and two RPG-7 launchers with six rockets. With the diesels pushing the *Mi Sueño* through the water at 10 knots and its mission complete, Captain Angel Torres dialed his satellite phone.

He didn't know that when he dialed the 213 number in Los Angeles, a switch automatically sent the call to another business in the 310 area before it was forwarded to a number in the new 909 area code for San Bernardino. The switching was by design and made it hard, if not impossible, to trace a call. What Angel Torres did know was that his bosses in the cartel would kill him if he deviated from "the scripts" or caused the shipment to be captured by the police.

The phone in San Bernardino rang only once before a voice answered. *"Hola."*

"Profesor, buenos dias. ¿te desperté?" [Professor, good morning, did I wake you?]

"No." Luis Padilla had been waiting for this call since 0400. It wasn't just because he had $55 million dollars on the line. If this deal fell through, his friends in Mexico would torture and kill him.

"Todos sus estudiantes están en el autobús." [All your students are on the bus.]

"Excelente. Gracias por llamar." [Thank you for calling.]

Padilla ended the call. Good. The Sinaloas had possession of the 500 kilos of Asian Pure. He now had to transfer the balance due from a bank in Lichtenstein to the account Rhee had given to him. If he didn't, he was sure that Rhee would send someone to collect, and the meeting would not be pleasant.

The next call would come in about five hours, after the vans drove the 220 miles up Mexico Highway 1 to a Sinaloa warehouse in Tijuana, Mexico.

Saturday, February 4th, 1995, 0846 local time, Newport Beach

After the third call to 911 informing the city that a large sailboat was floating loose in the bay, the police department dispatched one of its two 21-foot Boston Whalers to investigate. The callers were pretty specific about the boat's location and the danger it posed to other boats moored in the bay.

The police officers figured that last night someone had not tied up their sailboat properly. These calls were not unusual; owners were given a ticket, fined $250, and charged another $500 for towing their boats to their moorings or marina. The police officers would then watch as the chastised owner attached both mooring lines in the manner prescribed by the Coast Guard.

This drifting sailboat was a 60-footer, with a dark blue hull. After hailing it three times from 10 feet away and not getting an answer, the officers lashed their Boston Whaler to the side and Officer Harkness hopped aboard, expecting to find it empty.

He heard a door banging against the stop, so he yelled down the open hatch. When he didn't get a response, he peered into the cabin before stepping down the ladder. He drew his pistol when he saw a leg dangling limply over the edge of the bed in the V-berth, and yelled a warning. His partner called for backup before he jumped on board.

Harkness found a Hispanic man and a young woman of mixed black and Asian descent sprawled on the blood-soaked bed. Each corpse had a single bullet hole in the forehead. On the floor was a single brass cartridge, which he picked up with the tip of a pen and examined before putting it back where he found it. He'd never seen this type of necked-down casing.

Monday, February 6th, 1995, 0638 local time,
30 miles southwest of Long Beach, CA

Captain Sa'id Yamani sat in the captain's chair on the bridge of *Crescent Star*, sipping tea. The sun was now well up over the horizon. There was not a cloud in the sky and all was going according to plan. The drugs were unloaded on time and so now, if his ship was searched, there was nothing to worry about.

His hands were tented under his chin and his eyes followed a gray, four-engine patrol plane making a slow climbing turn to the east. During his career at sea, Yamani had seen many American patrol planes make low passes to identify ships and take pictures. This close to the American naval base in San Diego, the low pass was most likely part of a training mission. On the other hand, this was the fourth time since they'd left Dalian that they'd been "rigged."

To "rig" a ship, a patrol plane flies close down one side of the ship and then the other, taking pictures. Identifying a ship was the first step in determining if it was to be searched. Yamani smiled sardonically. Even if *Crescent Star* was stopped as soon as it entered U.S. territorial waters, they wouldn't find anything.

Twenty minutes later, the radio on the bridge came alive. "*M.V. Crescent Star, M.V. Crescent Star*, this is the U.S. Coast Guard cutter *Boutwell*. Please heave to and prepare to be boarded."

An orange HH-65A *Dolphin* helicopter was hovering less than 100 feet from the bridge, having flown up the ship's wake. Without any lookouts other than the watch officer, it was easy to sneak up on *Crescent Star*. Two armed men in orange flight suits were sitting on the floor of the helicopter cabin. The helicopter had to have come from *Boutwell*, but where was the ship?

The radio blared again. "*M.V. Crescent Star*, this is the U.S. Coast Guard cutter *Boutwell*. Please heave to and prepare to be boarded."

Yamani scanned the horizon with his binoculars. Off his bow, he could see the white V of a ship plowing through the ocean at high speed. If *Crescent Star* wasn't actually in U.S. territorial waters, it was damn close.

As he picked up the handset, Yamani drew his hand across his throat and commanded, "Dead-slow ahead." The helmsman, who had been watching him intently, nodded and moved the engine telegraph to "dead-slow ahead" twice before repeating the command as his acknowledgement that it has been executed.

"Coast Guard cutter *Boutwell,* this is the Motor Vessel *Crescent Star.* We will slow to two or three knots to maintain steerageway. Please board using the Jacob's ladder on the starboard side."

Yamani walked onto the starboard wing of the bridge and leaned over the railing. From his vantage point, he watched the approach of eight armed Americans in an orange Zodiac, all wearing the same kit: dark blue coveralls and orange life preservers, and carrying M-16s. He assumed they also carried pistols and were connected via short range radio.

A slim Coast Guard officer stepped onto the bridge and saluted Yamani. "Good morning, sir. I am Lieutenant Junior Grade Boyd Dickinson of the United States Coast Guard. Thank you for stopping. We have a warrant to search your vessel for illegal drugs. We would appreciate your cooperation."

Yamani casually returned the salute to the young officer. "We have nothing to hide. Where do you want to begin?"

"Please muster your crew on the bow. I'd like to have a look at the ship's papers, its log and the crew's identity documents. My team will start searching in the forward hold."

"No problem."

Yamani picked up the handset and spoke, first in English, then in Chinese. When he finished, he pointed to an open hatch that looked more like a door in a house. "Lieutenant Dickinson, my cabin is that way." Before he left the bridge, Yamani saw *Boutwell* 200 yards off the starboard side, pitching in the long swell on a parallel course.

In the cabin, Dickinson spoke politely. "Captain, unlock the safe and open it. Please do not reach into the safe until I give you permission."

After spinning the dial on the combination lock to the right and then left and back to the right, Yamani turned the wheel. The safe unlocked with a clunk and he pulled open the door.

Dickinson, a nine-millimeter SIG P228 in his right hand, leaned forward to look into the safe. "Hmmmmm…That's a lot of cash. What do you need it for?" Dickinson was thinking, *Bribes,* when Yamani responded.

"We pay the crew part of their wages in cash each time we arrive in port. In some ports, we have to pay for supplies or services in cash."

The 1989 graduate of the Coast Guard Academy nodded. He could see at least 10 bundles of $100 bills. There was probably a hundred bills in each stack. Since joining *Boutwell's* crew six months ago, he'd led several boarding parties and had never seen that much. He reminded himself that carrying that much cash, assuming the bills were not counterfeit, was not a crime.

"We'll start with the passports, shot records and identity documents for the crew; ship's manifest, log and insurance papers...."

Yamani nodded and handed him two folders and a bundle wrapped in rubber bands. The ship's log was the green ledger on his desk.

Dickinson gave the documents a once over. He didn't unwrap the passports. Checking them out would come later, when the ship reached the United States. "What port did you leave before heading for Long Beach?"

"Dalian."

"Where are you going after you leave Long Beach?"

"Magadan in Siberia. That could, of course, change."

"Did you take the most direct route to Long Beach?"

"Yes."

"Then why are you so far south of the shipping lanes?"

"Weather. We wanted to avoid a line of strong thunderstorms."

Dickinson eyed the captain. No bad weather had been reported. There was none on the satellite images the cutter downloaded on a daily basis. *Captain Yamani, that's your first lie. We'll escort you into Long Beach and then dip your tanks. We know how much this ship should burn on a daily basis and can figure out how much extra fuel you burned.*

"Did you rendezvous with any ships while you were en route?"

"No."

That's lie number 2. We photographed your ship alongside a fishing boat in North Korean territorial waters. Did you rendezvous again someplace else? Is that why you're so confident we'll find nothing?

In the forward hold, Petty Officer Second Class Haskell walked around the stacked pallets of cargo, examining each one for signs it had been recently moved. At the forward end of the hold, he came across a gap in the pallets where, instead of being six high, they were only five. While this was not unusual, it aroused Haskell's curiosity.

Haskell wedged his boot into the gap between 55-gallon drums and clambered up. *Crescent Star's* gentle rolling didn't bother him; he'd been in the Coast Guard for nine years and had grown up around boats. He stood on the corners of the pallet and shined his flashlight slowly across the tops of the drums.

Caught between the tops of two drums was a scrap of black plastic. On top of one of the drums, there was a small trail of white powder. Haskell reached into one of the pouch pockets on the left leg of his coveralls, pulled out a small camera and took six photos. Next, he pulled out an evidence bag from the corresponding pocket on the right side. He used tweezers to gently work out the piece of plastic and it went into bag. Then he scooped up as much of the white powder as he could with the blade of a pocketknife, and it went into another evidence bag. Experience told Haskell the black plastic came from a brick of either cocaine or heroin. Testing would tell which drug.

Once both were sealed, he took a marker from a sleeve pocket and wrote the date, time and location on each bag. Satisfied, he looked around for more indications of drugs. Finding none, he climbed down.

Dickinson's headset crackled. "Sir, this is Petty Officer Haskell. Please come down to the forward hold,"

"Be right there."

The young Coast Guard officer left two of his team on the bridge with Yamani, then worked his way down into the dimly lit hold. It had a pungent, chemical smell, suggesting it needed better ventilation.

As soon as the Lieutenant entered, Haskell held up a test tube with a dark reddish liquid. "Sir, I found a small amount of heroin." He held up the two evidence bags that were in his left hand. "There's a fine white powder coating, kinda like dust, on the drums. Either someone cut some horse here in the hold, or a brick leaked when it was lifted out. I'd like a day or two to go over this tub."

Dickinson put his hands on his hips and smiled. "I can make that happen."

Wednesday, February 8th, 1995, 1412 local time, Pyongyang

The narrow window on the second floor let the cold winter light into the small room. If there had been a sign in the front of the building, it would have indicated this was the administrative office of the Premier of the Democratic People's Republic of Korea. In the DPRK, addresses of government buildings were a state secret, as were maps.

Vice Admiral Pak was sitting alone in an office, with his hands tightly clasped. He had just concluded a call to a number in Hong Kong to schedule deliveries of opium and refined heroin. Using pre-arranged, coded phrases—Pak was sure that calls were recorded—the person at the other end had informed Pak that *Crescent Star* had been detained. The search for the informant was on. If he or she was inside the organization, Pak was confident the spy would be quickly found by the company's investigators.

At least they hadn't lost the heroin. They had to pay Kim Jong-Il a fee based on the number of kilos shipped to the U.S. If a shipment was seized or lost, it did not matter to their Dear Leader. They still had to deposit money in one of his Swiss bank accounts.

Friday, February 10th, 1995, 1600 local time, Pearl Harbor
Uilani waited until late in the afternoon before she dialed Marty Cabot's direct phone number. During the day, she'd forced herself to wait. There was something about Commander Cabot she liked, and she wanted to talk to him again. She'd found out that *Blue Ridge* was tied to a pier in Yokosuka; by time zones, Hawaii was 19 hours behind Yokosuka.

"Good morning, Commander."

"Good afternoon, Uilani. It is nice to hear from you," Cabot replied. "Should we go secure?"

"Yes. I'll initiate."

Cabot leaned back in his chair. All day he'd wondered when he would hear from Uilani again. The green LED screen flashed "Top Secret JICPAC," indicating the encryption algorithms were synchronized. The tone changed and the audio quality took on a tunnel-like sound.

"Commander, I have an update on *M.V. Crescent Star*."

"I was wondering what happened."

Uilani told him *Crescent Star* had been searched at sea, escorted to Long Beach and searched again. While they'd gotten a sniff of drugs, there wasn't enough to make an arrest, much less win in court. The heroin, however, matched what was being sold on the streets of LA as Asian Pure.

She shared the material that she had on *Crescent Star* and her three sister ships: *M.V. Crescent Moon, M.V. Crescent Sun* and *M.V.*

Crescent Galaxy, all of them chartered full time by Half Moon Trading from Crescent Shipping. Both *Crescent Star* and *Crescent Moon* were headed for Magadan in Russia, with a load of used heavy construction equipment bought from a local U.S. dealer. Uilani said she suspected that both Half Moon and Crescent had the same ownership because they shared the same suite of offices.

Out of curiosity, Marty asked if the equipment was on the approved list of material the U.S. could sell to the Russians. Uilani said yes. According to their intel, it would be used on Siberian oil and gas pipeline projects managed by Royal Dutch Shell. Her source was a Department of Commerce officer who'd contacted the Dutch-based company.

The U.S. military often helped U.S. law enforcement agencies outside the continental U.S. Illegal drugs meant that CINCPAC might task Seventh Fleet to track *Crescent Star,* once the freighter again entered their area of responsibility.

Chapter 3: THE PERILOUS ROAD TO RETIREMENT

Monday, February 13th, 1995, 1215 local time, Pyongyang

Vice Admiral Pak marveled at how fast the large white flakes accumulated on his woolen overcoat and made no attempt to brush them off. He enjoyed watching the snowflakes float down from the gray sky. It was negative 10 degrees Celsius (14º Fahrenheit), and there was barely a breeze. He was waiting for Major General Jang to emerge from the People's Army's headquarters. The building was another unmarked, flat gray structure, identical in style to all the others in the capital. When it had been rebuilt after the Korean War, Kim il-Sung had a chance to make it special. Instead, the architects had followed the Soviet style and the result created a boring sameness. But criticizing the blandness of the design of government buildings could result in an interview with the SSD.

The entrance was a quiet 50 meters from the street; there wasn't much traffic in Pyongyang. Remembering his childhood, Pak would have liked to throw snowballs against the building, but in the paranoid world of North Korea, throwing snowballs at a government building would be interpreted as a gesture against the regime and could lead to arrest, torture and residency in a re-education camp.

Jang exited the building. His thick-soled boots clomped on the concrete and left footprints in the snow; his purposeful stride suggested he was in a hurry. The general's dark brown Army winter uniform coat and red Korean People's Army insignia contrasted with Pak's dark Navy blue and gold.

Both their uniforms were custom made by tailors in Zhenxing, the city just across the Yalu River in the People's Republic of China. They fit and looked better than those issued by the North Korean government. Each officer had two sets of uniforms. One, purchased locally, was to wear around the men they led; the Zhenxing set was worn when they met with their peers, who also wore custom-fitted uniforms made by the same tailors.

Jang was cheerful. "I commend you, Kim Sun. Our Dear Leader can't wait to see the reports on the new commando training area. For thirty minutes, in our Army general staff meeting, he talked about how important the agreement with the Russians was, so you must have briefed him well."

"Thank you, my friend."

Jang asked the important question. "What did we end up paying the Russians?"

"The annual fee for the training area on the Russian coast along the Sea of Japan is two million rubles. The fee will be paid in small arms shipped to places of interest, so the Russians can deny they made them. Kim was happy we didn't have to pay cash and dip into our currency reserves. The lease for Simushir costs us only a half million U.S. dollars. It is a bargain, considering how much more heroin we can produce on the island. The two Russians with whom we negotiated the Simushir deal got one hundred thousand dollars each from Half Moon, and another hundred thousand to use as gifts. For the length of the ten-year agreement, Half Moon will deposit three thousand U.S. dollars a month into each of their accounts in the Japanese Sumitomo Mitsui Bank, which has a branch in Vladivostok."

"Excellent." General Jang nodded his head, then pointed off to the right, toward an army officers' mess where they planned to eat in a room set aside for senior officers. "When did you meet with our Dear Leader?"

"Yesterday. Our Dear Leader smiled when I told him we could ship the raw opium and chemicals into Broutana Bay without having any police officers to bribe." Pak quickened his step. He was hungry, and while the snowfall was beautiful, the chill had penetrated his coat. "We talked about the island's history. He was interested in how the Japanese used the Kuril Islands during the Russo-Japanese War and World War II."

Jang's internal alarms went off. "I hope he is not thinking of using Simushir as a military base."

Vice Admiral Pak laughed. "The agreement we signed with the Russian Maritime Ministry gives us the right to a small security force on Simushir, without defining its composition or size. It gives our country a base on Russian territory. I told our Dear Leader we could use your Special Forces units for security."

"You didn't answer my question." Jang turned to face his friend and they stopped walking.

"No one knows what's on the mind of our Dear Leader. I didn't spend much time on the potential military aspects of the island, other than to remind him that the Russians had a base on the island from 1987 to 1994 and then abandoned it because it was too hard to support. Our main discussion was about how much more money he would get from the heroin trade. I have to meet with the men in Room 39. They will tell me where the additional money will be deposited, in which offshore account, under what business name.

Our Dear Leader is more of a capitalist than a socialist when it comes to money."

Jang put his hand on Pak's arm and spoke in grave tones. "My friend, we are playing a very dangerous game. Our drug business exists because we have made our Dear Leader and a dozen members of his inner circle very wealthy. But he could kill us and our families without thinking twice or feeling any remorse."

Pak met his friend's gaze. "It would be difficult for him to replace us. No only are we his largest supplier of illegal drugs, we have reliable supplies of opium and a distribution network that takes everything we produce. Through us, he makes several times more than all the other suppliers combined. He knows it, and we know it. He has gotten addicted to our money machine. I keep telling our Dear Leader we are part of his grand plan to destroy America by making it dependent on his drugs."

Major General Jang nodded thoughtfully.

Pak continued. "We have contacts that no one in his inner circle has. He doesn't like it, but he is a realist. We put steps in place so if he kills us, he and his friends are frozen out of our network. Without us, our Dear Leader would have to start over. He won't admit it, but he knows that if he removes us, it would take years to get back to where we are today. Getting rid of us would cost him a fortune, and he's a greedy bastard. And right now he is very pleased with us. The Russian agreements give us a place to build a factory as big as we want, and gives our Dear Leader one thing he's never had—training areas outside our country, away from the prying eyes of the Americans and their allies in Seoul. My friend, I am just as concerned as you are, but as long as we are careful and cater to our Dear Leader's whims and greed, we should be safe."

"Still, we must try to anticipate, so we can so we can retire when we want to."

The Admiral bobbed his head vigorously. "On that, we are in agreement. The sad part is we cannot enjoy our wealth here."

Jang changed the subject. "Come my friend; we have a lunch to eat and a captain to interview."

Tuesday, February 14th, 1995, 0912 local time,
on board U.S.S. Blue Ridge

No matter how hard Josh Haman tried, his desk remained cluttered. He, like every member on the staff, was inundated with reports and messages, all of which had to be read, digested, and in some cases, responded to. Keeping up with the message traffic was one aspect of the job he hated. One day as he was dividing the overnight message traffic into piles, he vowed that if he ever became CNO, he would find a way to get rid of 90 percent of the message traffic and stick to the essentials.

Josh would have preferred command of a ship to a department head billet on a numbered fleet staff. He was sure Marty Cabot was behind the admiral's request; he was not sure if it was just a case of misery loves company, or if Cabot thought this post was good for Josh's career. Over the years, they'd both annoyed more than their fair share of desk jockey officers who concentrated on administrative tasks and "looking good" to their superiors. The derogatory term for such officers was "shoe clerks", and shoe clerks usually hated warriors. Here at Seventh Fleet, it was good, for a change, to be sought after by an admiral who understood warriors.

Jeff Gainesville, a friend from his first tour in Vietnam, who had just been selected for his third star, had called before Josh left San Diego and told him to keep the faith—this assignment would help him make flag. What Gainesville couldn't tell Josh at the time was that he—Gainesville—was about to become the Chief of Naval Personnel. In that billet, he either selected or approved the selection of all the officers assigned to promotion boards and reviewed all ship, squadron, air wing and battle group commanding officer assignments. In that billet, he could make sure that his friend would get a well-deserved ship command.

Josh was engrossed in editing a message when the black, "normal" phone on his desk rang. He was amazed that the Navy persisted in installing black analog, rotary-dial phones designed in the 1950s. As he reached for the phone, he was careful not to spill the mug of hot chocolate that he suspected was now at room temperature. "Captain Haman."

"Good morning, Captain Haman. This is Captain Nagumo."

"Good morning, Captain Nagumo." Josh recognized the precise English of the Japanese Maritime Self-Defense Force officer assigned as liaison officer to Seventh Fleet. Nagumo had a delicate job, because he had to keep his chain of command informed about what he learned about Seventh Fleet's operations so that they could compare this to what the Commander, U.S. Forces Japan, passed on. Often, the information did not match. To solve the problem and not cause any Japanese officer to lose face, the two captains coordinated what would be passed on. They'd met in Yokosuka in December, and Josh had been a guest for dinner at the Nagumo's house just three days before. The man's English was accented, but impeccable, polished from the two years he'd spent at the Naval War College. "Your family is well, I hope."

"They are." The pleasantries were in keeping with Japanese formality. "There is an article in Friday's *Asahi Shimbun* about Simushir." Anything about the Kuril Islands was newsworthy in Japan. "The article says a new, Macao-based firm called the Kuril Island Development Company has announced it is refurbishing the abandoned Soviet submarine base at Broutana Bay."

The words Broutana Bay and Simushir got Josh's immediate attention. They wouldn't make the news in the states, but they would in Japan, and anything happening in the Kurils was news for the Seventh Fleet staff.

Nagumo continued. "The article and news release says they are going to provide a refuge for fishing vessels operating off the Kurils. Once the facility is open, the company is going to issue a Notice to Mariners detailing what services will be offered."

Josh asked, "What are the Russians saying about this?"

"An official in Russia's Pacific Maritime Agency said they welcomed the investment and support this new commercial venture. It will be open to commercial vessels flying any flag."

"Who is providing the money?" Anything in the Kurils would take a ton of money. Reconnaissance photos showed the abandoned Russian base facilities were in disrepair.

"We don't know. The reporter was kind enough to share what he learned from the Russians and gave us the Macao address and phone number for a law firm that is the Kuril Island Development Company's registered agent. But neither the company nor the agent would grant an interview."

"That's odd. You'd think anyone who is going to invest in this kind of venture would want all the publicity they could get. Do you know when it will be operational?"

"The article says by the end of this coming summer, and that work will start as soon as weather permits."

"What is the Japanese government going to do?"

"Nothing, because this is a commercial venture. I suspect some of our fishing vessels with an intelligence officer as a member of the crew will stop there when it opens. Japan gave up its claim to Simushir in 1945, along with the rest of the Kurils. We are only trying to get the Northern Territories back."

"The Russians don't need the base anymore." Josh was thinking out loud. "It was built to give their diesel submarines more time on station in the Pacific, but now those subs don't leave the Sea of Japan or the Sea of Okhotsk. If their nuclear boats have a problem, they go to Petropavlovsk or Vladivostok for repairs. I think this development is worth watching."

"In my fax of both the release and the article, I will include the journalist's phone number."

"Thanks. I'll let you know what we decide to do, if anything." In other words, if it turned out there was more going on at Simushir than a way station for commercial shipping, Josh would share non-classified intel. That was how Josh answered the question that Nagumo couldn't ask. Like so many of their conversations, what *wasn't* said or asked was just as important as what was spoken.

The call ended with a click, and Josh went back to his message; but his mind was reeling. What the hell was going on? He'd need more info before briefing the admiral, and he'd better get it fast, before the admiral received a query from CINCPAC.

The fax machine started to whir, and he read the release as it was printed. Time to go see the admiral.

1026 local time, Broutana Bay

From the bridge of the 465-ton *M.V. Island Sun,* Chan Ho Lee looked out at the gray sky. The wind-blown snow mixed with rain had finally stopped hitting him horizontally.

Island Sun had been chartered by the Kuril Island Development Corporation to support a survey crew at Broutana Bay, because it was small enough to easily fit through the narrow inlet that led to the bay and anchor close to shore.

The small coastal freighter was one of 318 built to the same basic design by 25 American shipyards during and right after World War II. This vessel had been commissioned in 1944 as the FS-316 by the U.S. Army, then transferred to the U.S. Navy in 1947 and re-named *U.S.S. Metomkin* (AG-136). She had been decommissioned and struck from the Navy list in 1952. Since then, she'd had an unremarkable history as a coastal freighter. Crescent Shipping had acquired and overhauled her in the late 1960s. *Island Sun* was one of 16 of these small cargo ships the company had acquired after the U.S. government abandoned them rather than spend the money to sail them home. All now flew some flag of convenience and spent their days going from port to port between the east coast of India and the Philippines.

Three days ago, before it began to snow, Lee had spent a full day ashore. His training as a civil engineer made him ideal for the job of determining what could be repaired and what needed to be replaced. Cost, he was told, was not an issue. That was good, because most of the buildings either weren't worth repairing or would be expensive to make habitable.

He sighed. Born and raised in Hong Kong, the raw, damp cold wind rattled his bones. Just the thought of being back outside made him shiver. Well, if cost was no object, he would be sure that any repaired or new building would be well heated—and insulated.

1140 local time, on board U.S.S. Blue Ridge

When Josh told the Commander, Seventh Fleet about the new activity on Simushir, the admiral laughed and said it was just one more thing the staff would have to monitor, and since Josh had taken the call, he would have it as an action item. Josh promptly tasked his friend and former copilot, Jack D'Onofrio, a Naval Reservist on active duty for three weeks with the Seventh Fleet staff, to come up with a surveillance plan.

Two years junior to Josh, Jack was still a commander. He had left the Navy in 1976 and gone into the real estate business— initially buying, renovating and renting homes, and now doing the same with small apartment complexes. Until the business had become self-sustaining and generated a healthy profit, he'd supported his family by flying in a reserve helicopter squadron and doing as much active duty as possible. Now, with an income Josh could only imagine, D'Onofrio could afford to spend as much time as a naval officer as he liked, serving his country in the service he loved on his own terms. In any given year, between drill weekends and active duty, he averaged playing Navy 150 days a year.

From the staff's files, Jack gathered all the information it had on Simushir. Spread out on one of the command center's glass-topped tables was a Tactical Pilotage Chart F-11A for the central Kuril Islands that gave both officers terrain details for Simushir. Next to it was the most recent satellite imagery for the island, taken on a clear day late in November 1994, just before the first snow. The photos confirmed the Russians were gone.

Simushir as shown on Tactical Pilotage Chart F-11A
(US Defense Mapping Agency Aerospace Center, compiled 1969, revised 1993)

Josh looked over the map and tapped the fax of the release. "Okay, Jack—you're a businessman.

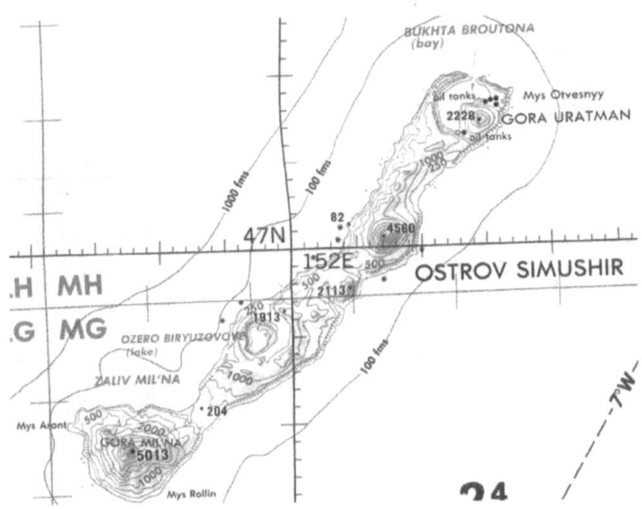

Why would someone invest millions in an operation on a desolate and unpopulated island in the middle of nowhere? Even the Russians, who are paranoid about their borders, no longer use it."

"I think we have to start from the other side. Let's look at this as a real estate play. When you buy real estate, it is all about location. So why Simushir? What about its location is so attractive? Think like a businessman. How much revenue will they generate from services? They'll sell fuel and charge for services. Will the profit be enough to make it viable?"

"That makes no sense. There just aren't that many fishing boats operating east of the Kurils who would need a refuge. Most are big fish factories that act as mother ships to a small fleet and have the supplies to stay on station for months at a time. They are big enough to ride out storms. So it has to be something else."

Josh tapped a lined yellow pad with his forefinger that was on top of the map. On it he'd written the questions that had occurred to him since his conversation with Nagumo. "Here—start with these questions and add your own. Then put them in a message to JICPAC asking for the most recent overhead images of Simushir."

"Josh, trust me. It is all about money. So the question is, what will generate enough profit to justify the expense?"

"Okay, Jack, go find the money."

Josh was dog tired when he left his office, still studying the map, but today was his turn as the Command Duty Officer. As such, he was supposed to work out of the staff's command center until he was relieved at 0730 tomorrow morning.

He was sipping a Coke between making notes on the margins of a message, hoping the caffeine would help keep him awake, when he heard one of the secure phones ring.

"Captain Haman," the petty officer of the watch held up the handset, "one of CINCPAC's watch officers wants to talk you on the STU-III."

"Switch him to the battle watch commander's phone. Thank you, Petty Officer Jamison."

Josh could hear the phones synchronizing as he put the headset and mike assembly on. "Seventh Fleet Command Duty Officer, Captain Haman speaking."

"Good morning, Captain. This is Captain Billingham. I'm the sub operations officer on the CINCPAC staff."

"Captain Billingham, what can I do for you?"

"We just got a flash message from *U.S.S. Olympia* operating off Mayang-do."

North Korea's largest submarine base was on the island of Mayang-do, off the North Korean coast in the Sea of Japan. It was complete with underground sub pens and maintenance facilities. For a sub conducting surveillance to break radio silence to send a contact report was very unusual.

Josh glanced at the status board. *Olympia was* a nuclear-powered *Los Angeles*-class submarine. To get more information on the sub's mission, he'd have to talk to the Seventh Fleet sub ops officer, because the details of *Olympia's* patrol area were known only to him and his subordinate.

"*Olympia* has a first convergence zone contact at about thirty-five nautical miles on a North Korean *Romeo* southeast of Vladivostok. Sub is moving north-northeast in deep water, paralleling the coast. When *Olympia* sent the message, the North Korean sub was snorkeling."

"Can you give me the reported position for the North Korean sub?" As Josh repeated the numbers Billingham gave him, Operations Specialist First Class Jeremy Jamison marked the location on a chart of the Sea of Japan.

Josh guessed *Olympia*'s towed array had picked up the noise from the sub's diesel engines as it charged its batteries. A convergence zone or CZ contact came after the noise from the source bounced off the bottom as it radiated out and headed back toward the surface in rings several miles wide. The first bounce was the first CZ, and the weaker second reflected signal was known as a second CZ contact, and so on. While the width and distance between the CZ rings varied based on the temperature and salinity profile of the water and the type of bottom, anti-submarine warfare experts' rule of thumb was that CZ rings are about thirty-five miles apart.

Josh looked at where Jamison put an upside-down chevron with a dot in the center on the map of the Sea of Japan. "Captain Billingham, he's about one hundred nautical miles east-southeast of Vladivostok and way out of the North Korean's normal sub operating areas in the Sea of Japan. The course and speed have him paralleling the Russian coast. Tell your boss that Seventh Fleet will send out an 'op immediate' message on the submarine broadcast, instructing *Olympia* to continue trailing the *Romeo*, to gather all possible intelligence, and report when feasible."

"Concur, and will inform my boss." Billingham would now be able to tell his boss, the four-star admiral who commanded all the U.S. forces in the Pacific, that Seventh Fleet's intentions agreed with their own. Josh had learned that when flag officers' heads nodded vertically, it was a good thing. When they shook laterally, staff action officers faced long hours of additional work.

There were times Josh missed flying missions. On the other hand, he knew that when he did his administrative work well, pilots had a better chance of accomplishing their missions and coming home.

The Simushir Island Incident

Wednesday, February 15th, 1995,
1522 local time, 100 feet beneath San Ysidro, CA

For the second time in less than an hour, the underground trolley had fallen off the track. Despite ventilation fans at both ends of the tunnel, Miguel Martinez was sweating as he walked along the rails within the six-foot-wide, six-foot-high shaft used to move drugs and people from Mexico to the U.S.

To enter the tunnel from a house on O'Keefe Street in San Diego, Miguel had rolled up the rug on the living room hardwood floor and lifted a concealed hatch. Before backing down the ladder, he'd flipped on the light and fan switches. The fan at the U.S. end of the tunnel sucked air through a two-foot diameter pipe hidden in a modified wall that went up through the house to pull fresh air in from a vent on the roof. Another fan, at the southern end, sucked stale air out and released into the warehouse in Tijuana, Mexico.

The floor of the concrete-reinforced tunnel was 100 feet below the house and passed under the Tijuana River and the U.S./Mexican border. It had taken a year to dig and equip, but now a dolly on a set of tracks, connected to winches, easily moved cargo north and cash south. Except when something went wrong.

Miguel had repeatedly warned the people on the Mexican side to only load 20 bricks at a time, but they kept overloading it. The first time this cargo had fallen over, the trolley had been only a few hundred feet from the Mexican side of the border. This time, it was closer to the U.S. The drill was always the same—unload, lift the trolley back on to the tracks, make sure the wheels were in the grooves, reload.

At the U.S. end, there was a wide area to stack bundles of marijuana or bricks of heroin, and a small hoist with a 100-pound capacity. The basket size was a limiting factor; only 10 bricks could be pulled up at a time.

The house overhead was in Miguel's name. On his mortgage application, he was listed as an electrical contractor who cleared $500,000 a year, with one assistant on the payroll. Miguel's real business was delivering product to Sinaloa factories in Southern California's counties where the pure heroin and cocaine were cut and put in baggies for the big customers, and marijuana was bagged for the small time buyers, all to be passed on to distributors and pushers. The farthest north he'd gone on a delivery was Bakersfield, about 240 miles.

Even without delays, it took the two of them almost four hours to get all 500 kilos across the border, up into the house and into his panel van in his garage.

Once his assistant left for the day, Miguel dialed a number and waited for a familiar voice to say "Hola."

"Acabamos de recibir toda la orden." ["We just got the full order."]

"Que tardó tanto?" [What took so long?]

"The idiots keep overloading the trolley."

"Any damage?"—*as in any bricks torn and heroin spilled.*

"No."

"When are you going to make deliveries?"

"Tomorrow."

Padilla was smiling as he hung up. Tomorrow the Asian Pure would be cut, distribution would begin, and the money would start rolling in.

Wednesday, February 15th, 1995, 1336 local time, Long Beach, CA

The marine layer—the cold, damp fog that hovers over the Southern California coast—made everything look grey. Special Agent Gavin Dawson emerged from the swirling mist and approached the headquarters of Gainey Heavy Equipment. This was the firm's office building, with only a small lot and maintenance facility in back. According to Dawson's research, a much larger 200-acre site in Ontario, CA was where most of the company's inventory was kept, as well as the maintenance and overhaul facility. Gainey's annual revenue of over $1 billion made them one of the largest Caterpillar dealers on the West Coast. It was not a place where an FBI agent can just casually drop in and ask to speak with the president. That morning, it had taken Dawson several patient and firmly polite minutes to convince the individual answering the corporate number to connect him to the president's office. Then he'd spent another five minutes convincing the president's administrative assistant that (a) he was really from the FBI and (b) it was a matter of national security that he talk to the president, Bill Whitman.

Inside the lobby, Dawson gave his name and showed his badge to the woman who'd thought he was pulling a prank when he made his initial call. She profusely apologized for her initial suspicion, explained that part of her training was to deal with prank callers, and then called the president's office.

Whitman's office surprised Dawson. He'd expected large, which it was. What he was not expecting was what was on the "I Love Me" wall. Instead of pictures of Whitman with the rich and famous, there was his diploma from Pepperdine, off to one side, and framed citations and certificates for Silver and Bronze Stars. There were several photos of Whitman as a young Marine officer in Vietnam, as well as several plaques thanking Whitman for his contributions to organizations that help disabled veterans.

Whitman was average size, with close-cropped hair. It was clear from the way his arms filled out the sleeves of his golf shirt with the Gainey logo that he still worked out. His handshake was firm.

"Special Agent, what can either Gainey or I do for the FBI?"

"Thank you for taking time from your busy schedule." Dawson waited for a nod from Whitman before continuing. "The FBI has been asked to collect some information on two of Gainey's international customers."

"Which ones and why?"

"Half Moon Trading and the Kuril Island Development Corporation. I can't tell you why, other than it is a matter of national security."

Whitman pursed his lips and nodded. His large wedding ring tapped noticeably on the table in cadence with his words. "Don't bullshit me, Special Agent Dawson. I spent 10 years as a Marine Recon officer. You've got to be more specific than 'a matter of national security.' "

"Sir, I wish I could. I have been asked to visit with several companies who have sold material and equipment to either Half Moon or a new company, Kuril Island Development Company. More, I don't know."

"What kind of information do you want?"

"Financial data. Apparently, the equipment you sold them is being shipped to Simushir Island in the Kurils. We assume that before you offered them credit or accepted a letter of credit, you would have asked for financial statements. The FBI would like a copy of those statements and any other documents they may have provided about their business."

"Do you have a warrant?"

"I do." Dawson reached into his coat pocket and pulled out several sheets of paper that were folded into thirds, which he slid it across the table.

Whitman scanned the document. "Wait here." It was not a request. It was an order by a Marine officer. He dialed a number and spoke briefly. Less than minute later, an attractive, well-dressed woman walked through the door without knocking.

The Simushir Island Incident

"Special Agent Dawson, this is Margaret Huntsman, Gainey's general counsel. Please show her the warrant." Whitman didn't mention that the woman was also the granddaughter of the company's founder—and his wife.

Warrant in hand, Margaret sat at a small table on which rested a notebook, a calendar, and an address book. As she read, she traced each line in the warrant with her finger. When she got to the signature page, she nodded. Then she opened the address book. "Bill, may I use your phone?"

Margaret went over to Whitman's desk and tapped out a series of numbers. She smiled at both men as she waited for her call to be answered. Dawson noted that she had perfect teeth, probably the result of being born into a family that could afford orthodontia. "Abigail, hi, this is Maggie Huntsman. Is Judge Beckman there? I'd like to ask him about a warrant he signed yesterday."

Dawson sat quietly, watching Margaret Huntsman. She scrawled a few notes on a pad on Whitman's desk and turned to Bill after she hung up. "Tell the CFO to give this gentleman everything he asks for. This is a real deal. The warrant says that we are to provide information on any orders that either one of these two companies send us." She turned to Dawson. "So, Mr. Dawson, would you mind telling me what the hell is going on?"

Dawson opened his hands in a gesture of ignorance. "Mrs. Huntsman, you now know as much as I do. And thank you for your cooperation." He wished all his civilian contacts were this competent and cooperative.

Thursday, February 16th, 1995, 0822 local time,
on board submarine U.S.S. Olympia

Inside the control room, the only audible machinery noise was the muted hum of the fan pumping fresh air into the compartment. Roger Hornsby, the sub's commander, had ordered *Olympia* to rig for silent running as they crept closer to the North Korean sub they'd been following.

"Up scope." At five-foot-five, Hornsby had been just barely tall enough to get into the Naval Academy Class of 1980. He stood on his toes and extended his neck to loosen up while he waited for the eyepiece to appear in front of him. "Let's see what they're doing." *Olympia* was about 300 yards to the seaward side and up-sun of the *Romeo*-class sub. The captain hoped the glare of the morning sun and slow speed would make his periscope difficult to detect.

Hornsby spun the scope in a circle to make sure the sole object in his viewing horizon was the surfaced North Korean submarine. "Side number on the conning tower of a *Romeo* class submarine is sixteen, that is one-six. The sub is dead in the water."

"Captain, sonar… we're picking up a high-speed propeller. Sounds like a motorboat."

"Down scope. Let's creep a bit ahead of him and a little up sun and see what we can see." Hornsby waited patiently. At this speed, very little happens very fast.

"Captain, we should be about two hundred yards ahead of him now."

"Okay—that's damn close. Up scope." Hornsby tapped his fingers on the plotting table while he waited for the scope to rise. *Olympia*, like all the *Los Angeles*-class submarines, was one of the quietest nuclear subs in the world. Right now, it was submerged in about 200 feet of water, well inside Russian territorial waters.

Hornsby pushed the button on the camera to take pictures. "A small launch flying the Russian Navy flag is coming alongside the sub. Passengers on the deck of the sub are wearing People's Army uniforms. Down scope."

"Captain, we need to change cameras." *Olympia* had one of the older periscope systems and used a conventional, 35-millimeter camera body attached to the periscope. The petty officer maintaining the manual plot had the spare camera handy. As soon as the captain shot one roll, they swapped cameras and always had one with unexposed film ready to go.

"Captain, sonar. Launch is underway again. Bearing change suggests it is heading to shore."

"Okay, gents. Here's what we're going to do. We'll move seaward to give us some room under the boat but stay close enough so we can come back if we hear the launch return."

"Captain, sonar. It sounds like the sub's screws are beginning to turn. Am getting some flow noises, so she is moving on the surface."

"Let's ease off five degrees to give him some room. I want to stay at periscope depth in case we need to take a look."

Commander Hornsby had taken command of *Olympia* six months before, and this was not the first time he'd been on a sub deep into Soviet—now Russian—territorial waters. "XO, this may take a while, so let's condense the watch teams into port and starboard and maintain the silent routine. We have no idea what kind of sensors the Russians have out here. If we trip one, we'll get lots of company in a hurry." XO, spoken as letters, meant Executive Officer, the boat's second in command.

"Yes, sir."

"Captain, sonar. Am picking up faint aircraft noises from a four-engine plane down low—a Russian IL-38 May, not one of our P-3s. I can tell the difference."

The captain took off his glasses and rubbed his eyes. "Our orders are to follow this North Korean puppy and gather intelligence." He looked at the depth gauge. "Ops, get started on a message to Seventh Fleet and CINCPAC reporting what we just saw."

"Captain, sonar. The noise signature of the May is getting louder. Believe he is much lower. Will let you know if he starts dropping stuff."

Everyone in the cramped control room understood "stuff" could be anything from sonobuoys and small explosive charges, known as noisemakers, to depth charges or acoustic homing torpedoes.

"Captain, sonar. The May just passed over the *Romeo*. *Romeo* is shutting down its diesels and opening vents. Sounds like he is pulling the plug."

"Oh, shit. We may be right in the middle of an ASW exercise."

"Captain, sonar. We're getting a bearing shift. The sub is turning toward deeper water. It looks like he is going to parallel our course. Estimate contact Sierra Eight is four thousand yards off our port beam." The contact designation indicated this was the eighth sonar contact the sub had picked up since the start of the patrol.

"Turn starboard to zero five zero. Ease the boat down to maintain about a hundred feet off the bottom until we get down to two hundred and fifty feet. Hold at three hundred feet. Where's the layer again?"

He was referring to the depth known as the layer—which can vary from about 100 to 300 feet. The layer begins at the depth where the temperature starts to decline rapidly. At this depth, which varies by season and location, the rapid change in temperature causes the acoustic properties of the water to change significantly. Sound waves from a surface transmitter are split, with some of the energy refracted back to the surface and some bent downward to the bottom. This area of "sonar shadow" can be used to hide a submarine from a sensor above the layer.

The salinity of the water affects sound propagation, but not as much as temperature. Accurate measurements of the temperature/

salinity profile of the water enable submarines to use the layer to hide from surface ship active and passive sensors.

"Sir, the layer was at one hundred and eighty-four feet depth. We're passing one hundred and fifty feet."

"Okay, here's the plan. We'll ease our way out of the immediate area and let the two of them play. We'll record everything we can. If new players enter the game, we'll re-assess. Let's all hope we don't get caught in the May's sonobuoy barrier."

Fifteen minutes later, the captain was studying the charts when someone handed him a cup of coffee with a "you need this" look. He took a few sips.

"Captain, sonar. Am hearing splashes like those made by sonobuoys. Will have location of the line in a few minutes, but it looks like it is behind us. Doppler shift indicates that Sierra Eight is turning in our direction."

"How far behind us is Sierra eight?"

"Sierra Eight is one-fifty relative and heading about zero six eight, range twenty-two hundred yards. Estimate he will cross about one thousand yards behind us."

"Depth?"

"One hundred and fifty feet."

Hornsby was worried the *Romeo* might damage his towed array, which trailed several hundred feet behind *Olympia*. Besides being embarrassing, it would be career ending. "All stop."

"All stop, Aye."

Now the captain risked catching the array on the rocky bottom or a sunken ship. If they had to guillotine a snagged array, it, was another career-ending move. "Let me know when Sierra Eight has crossed our stern."

"Captain, sonar. Estimate Sierra Eight will pass astern in about five minutes. His depth is still about a hundred and fifty feet."

"Thank you." The captain wondered if the North Koreans' calculation for the layer was same as what his crew used.

"Captain, sonar. More sonobuoy splashes—eight, about four seconds apart. Bearing two four zero relative, about six thousand yards. That gives the May two lines at right angles to us."

Hornsby went over to the plotting table where a petty officer was drawing the lines and using a calculator to estimate the spacing between the passive hydrophones. He had a publication open to the page with the airspeed and altitudes at which the anti-submarine version of the four-turboprop engine IL-38 transport dropped sonobuoys. It also had tables showing the estimated detection ranges of the Russian acoustic buoys.

"Captain, Sierra Eight has passed our stern."

"Captain, aye. Make turns for five knots." As the distance between the subs widened, the nervousness in the control room lessened; and when the separation between the two subs was just over 10 miles, *Olympia* slowed to three knots and raised its electronic signal gathering mast to record radio and radar signatures. The crew of the May might spot the scope; but at this distance, it was unlikely and worth the risk.

Hornsby looked at his watch and wondered how long the May could stay on station. It had now been four hours since the Russian/North Korean anti-submarine warfare exercise began. *Olympia* was finishing its fifth lap around the racetrack pattern Hornsby had ordered to keep close to the exercise.

"Captain, Sonar. Sierra Eight is blowing its tanks and making sounds suggesting it is surfacing."

"Sonar, make sure there are no other surprises out there."

"Sonar, aye."

A sudden growl from Hornsby's stomach turned heads, and reminded him he hadn't eaten since being called to the control room at 0700. Someone handed him a ham and cheese sandwich, and he took a bite gratefully. Around a mouthful he said, "XO, make sure that the galley hands out some chow."

"Already done, Skipper. The tray is sitting outside the control room. We were waiting for you to okay bringing food in here."

Sheepishly, Hornsby smiled. "So, handing me the sandwich was a hint that all of you are really hungry."

The executive officer was laughing when he replied. "Sir, your stomach spoke for all of us!"

The Captain looked at his number two, who grinned as he waved to one of the operations specialists. Books and charts were rearranged on one of the plotting tables to make room for one tray, piled high with sandwiches and cookies, and a second with a selection of soft drinks.

"Captain, sonar. Sub is starting its diesels. Clanging noises indicate it folded its dive planes."

"Captain, aye." The words were muffled by another mouthful. He looked at the current plot relative to Sierra Eight. "Turn thirty degrees to starboard." Another bite. "As soon as we steady up on course two two five, we'll go 'all stop' and coast in."

"New course two two five and 'all stop' when steady, aye."

"Sonar, distance to Sierra Eight?"

"Distance to Sierra Eight is thirty-one hundred yards, and we're closing very slowly. She appears to be dead in the water."

"The sub is waiting for someone. Let me know when we approach two thousand yards."

"Sonar, aye."

A little later, "Captain, Sonar. Am picking up the same type of screws we heard this morning. Doppler shift shows they are coming our way."

"I want a short sprint just to get ahead of him. Slowly add turns for ten knots and then go to all stop."

The crew felt the gentle surge forward; the captain hoped no one heard the knuckle made by the sub's propeller blade as power was added. He was also concerned about the extra flow noise as the sub accelerated.

"Captain, all stop."

"Distance to Sierra Eight?"

"We're inside three hundred yards."

"Is the camera ready?"

"It is loaded and cocked."

"How far is the launch?"

"About a thousand yards from Sierra Eight."

"Sonar, let me know when you think the launch is alongside, then we'll raise the scope, get a few pix and, as he starts moving, we'll slide into a trail position to the east in deeper water. If they spot us, we'll sprint away to the east and then slow down. Everybody got it?"

There was a soft chorus of "Aye, aye"s.

"Captain, sonar. High speed screws are slowing. I'll let you know when he cuts his motor, which will give you time to get the scope up."

"Perfect." The captain drained his can of soda.

"Captain, sonar. Screw noises stopped."

Hornsby counted *one one-thousand, two one-thousand*, and when he reached five, said, "Up scope." He turned it to where he guessed the North Korean sub was.

"Gotcha." The clicking sound of the camera's motor drive was the loudest noise in the control room. "Down scope. Hope these pictures turn out. Saw six guys in army uniforms get back on board. Make turns for five knots. I don't think they saw us; no one on the sub is reacting. Let's move away and out to sea where we can follow him to his next stop."

The Simushir Island Incident

Monday, February 20th, 1995, 1518 local time, U.S.S. Blue Ridge

Except during mealtime, Seventh Fleet staff officers used the wardroom for meetings, or just to find a quiet place to spread out working material. That was fine if one didn't mind the occasional visitor interrupting, or asking the stewards for donuts, cinnamon rolls, cookies or other between-meal snacks.

On the white tablecloth, Jack D'Onofrio had spread out the contents of the package from JICPAC. The material was neatly collated, noted and gathered. Photos of the *Crescent* class of ships were paper-clipped to the listings in *Jane's*, along with their ownership history and other records dug up by JICPAC. Jack sorted shipping records for the four ships based on U.S. Customs and Immigration records of arrival dates and cargo.

In his second pile, Jack had financial reports for Half Moon. Where and how the intelligence community acquired them, he could only guess. In the third stack were press releases and an article in the *South China Morning Post* on both Crescent Shipping and Half Moon Trading, focused on the companies' history, growth, number of employees and global customers.

Jack was used to reading his own profit and loss statements, and these financial reports, incomplete as they were, drew his attention. Both the incorporation filings and the tax returns listed the same Hong Kong law firm as Half Moon's and Crescent's agent. JICPAC had thoughtfully provided two documents summarizing how the Hong Kong profits tax was calculated and what was taxable and what was not. He thought it odd that profits generated by overseas subsidiaries were not taxable. *No wonder companies want to do business in Hong Kong.*

Jack looked at the filings of Half Moon first. It reported revenues of close to 900 million Hong Kong dollars. At a nominal exchange rate of six Hong Kong dollars to one U.S. dollar, their revenue converted to about $150 million. And, he mused, Half

Moon didn't have to report any income from sales from overseas offices in Bangkok, London, Los Angeles, Seoul, Singapore and Sydney. JICPAC would have to get tax filings from each country to calculate its total income.

JICPAC had also provided a document listing the 32 countries offering flags of convenience. When a shipowner registers in another country and the ship flies the flag of the country of registration, it is a flag of convenience. It is often done to circumvent taxes and reduce operating costs—as well as to avoid union contracts. Crescent had registered shipping agents, all law firms, in 10 of the countries on the list: Athens, Dubai, Genoa, Ho Chi Minh City, Hamburg, London, Los Angles, Manila, Singapore and Sydney. Nothing odd about their office locations; all were major port cities.

But the more he looked at the shipping company's tax statement, the more Jack suspected something was missing. *Where, and what, was all that profit coming from?* He went back to the Hong Kong profits tax guide, and then the 1992 and 1993 tax returns. It took a few minutes to figure it out. The Inland Revenue Department of Hong Kong requires an audited profit and loss statement, as well as a balance sheet. On Crescent's balance sheet, there was a number under assets for "ships owned" but no corresponding entry for debt under liabilities.

How can you own ships without debt? If you own them, you get to depreciate them on the Profit & Loss statement, unless they were already fully depreciated. And lease expenses should be on the on the P&L as an operational expense, with the total value of the leases as a liability on the balance sheet. The only explanation is if Crescent leases ships through wholly owned subsidiaries in tax havens outside of Hong Kong where Crescent doesn't have to report its ownership on its return.

The Simushir Island Incident

The next ripple was when ownership history of the four ships showed they were purchased, not leased. Cash on hand at the end of the year was 12.6 million Hong Kong dollars. *How do they generate the cash to purchase ships without a loan?*

Sensing the stewards wanted to begin setting up for dinner. Jack gathered up his material and headed back to the Operations and Plans Office.

To get into the compartment, one entered a six-digit sequence on the nine-button cipher lock. Inside were two separate offices, one for Josh and one for the Marine amphibious warfare officer, off the main workspace, a.k.a. the "bullpen," where six officers and eight enlisted men worked at desks. The space, about 12 feet by 20 feet, was made smaller by rows of safes: unusually sturdy, four-drawer filing cabinets with combination locks, bolted to the floor and bulkheads—the traditional nautical term for what served as walls on a ship.

Next to each desk was a brown paper burn bag with distinctive red stripes. By noon on most days, these were full and sealed. The enlisted men rotated the task of taking bags to the compartment where the papers were shredded before being incinerated.

Jack entered Josh's 10- by 12-foot private office. Seeing the look in his friend's eyes, Josh didn't waste any time; he called in Marty Cabot.

"You up for a fire drill?" Jack D'Onofrio plunked the documents onto Josh's desk. "I just spent a couple hours going through the material we got from JICPAC."

"What did you learn?"

Jack arranged the material the same way he had it in the wardroom. "I'm going to start with the punch line, which is: How does a company with $150 million in annual revenue, or two companies with a combined revenue of less than $300 million, have enough money to purchase ships for cash?" Jack looked at his two friends. "Let me make this simple. Ships are like houses. Most people put 20 percent down and finance the rest. Crescent Shipping doesn't have any debt, but they own ships. The only logical explanation is, they buy the ships with cash, or they have subsidiaries buy them. I think the cash—and it has to be a *lot* of cash, because if you think houses are expensive, try paying for freighters—comes from someplace else. Again, I'm not a bean counter, but that is what I'm seeing."

Marty put down the tax return he was holding. "Uilani *is* a CPA. Let's call her and see what she can tell us."

"You've been talking to her a lot during the past few weeks, haven't you?" Josh said.

"She's fun to talk to, and besides, she knows her shit."

"Is there a dinner date in the future? Even our esteemed reservist and former career bachelor here, Commander D'Onofrio, is now a happily married man. It took a while, but finally he succumbed and managed to become a father of two. You should try it!"

"I have sworn off women for, oh," Marty made a show of looking at his watch, "at least twenty-four hours, and have considered but rejected celibacy at least three times in the same time period. But Uilani has a team that knows how to dig up good information and separate bullshit from reality." Marty said levelly. *There is no way I am going to tell them a relationship between Uilani and me is brewing. I don't want to deal with their good-natured ribbing. And I am afraid that it will end like many before, in failure. Josh and Jack don't mention those. They helped me get through the painful disasters. They know me well enough to know when to kid me and when not too. I just don't want to give them any ammunition—at least not yet.*

"So call her." Josh's tone was more teasing than commanding. "I'll even close the door so my speaker phone on the STU-III doesn't bother our shipmates. Far be it for me to distract them from doing their duty." A balled-up piece of paper came flying through the door of the office before Josh managed to close it all the way.

"Uilani, this is Marty."

"Good afternoon, Commander Cabot."

"Miss Ka'anapali, I've got you on the speaker phone because Captain Haman and Commander D'Onofrio are with me. We have some questions. Do you have a few minutes?"

"Sure, and good morning, Captain Haman and Commander D'Onofrio."

"Good morning to you, Miss Ka'anapali. This is Captain Haman. Commander Cabot says good things about you and your team."

"Thank him for his kind words." Uilani sounded pleased.

Marty jumped in. "Uilani, we've got some sensitive data, so let's go secure."

The change in the sound quality told them Uilani had initiated the cryptographic capabilities of the STU-III.

"I see you are in the office of the N6 Plans Officer."

Marty answered. "Yup, we give him a private office to keep him out of our way so the rest of us can be productive."

From this, Uilani could tell that Josh, Jack and Marty were very close friends. Her chuckle was audible even through the encryption. "Fire away."

Jack D'Onofrio spoke up. "Uilani, this is Commander D'Onofrio. I provide the adult supervision for Marty and Josh." This time she laughed merrily. "Did you do any analysis on either Crescent's or Half Moon's ability to carry debt?"

"Yes—we looked at them all, and on the surface, they appear to be healthy and profitable."

"How do you explain their ownership of a fleet of ships?"

"That's a great question. We have a forensic accountant trying to follow the money trail."

"Uilani, this is Josh. Could you fill in the blanks on both companies? What are we looking at?"

"Sure. Let's start with the Half Moon Trading Company. Here's what we know." Uilani looked at the notes she'd written during on a conversation with a DIA asset in Hong Kong, who'd visited Half Moon's and Crescent's well-furnished offices, which happened to share the same plush reception area in the same building. Over the next several minutes, the four on the call discussed the consequences of the following points on Uilani's yellow pad:

- Factories in Shenzhen and Dalian make pottery & fireworks that are shipped all over the world.
- Ownership is hidden in maze of corporations with law firms as agents with attorney-client privilege in force.
- Crescent Shipping operates as both owner & broker, and either charters its own ships or charters others. Found two dozen ships owned by Crescent, suspect more.
- Brits confirmed founders came from Korea during the Korean War. Info pulled from immigration officers' interview notes when they arrived in Hong Kong.

Josh jumped in. "So, there is a long-standing Korean connection?"

"Looks like it."

Jack jumped in. "Uilani, I think if we figure out where they got the money to buy the ships, it will tell us a lot about Half Moon, Crescent Shipping and Broutana Bay."

"I agree. To my suspicious Hawaiian female mind, only illegal drugs can spit out the kind of cash needed to fund Broutana Bay, or buy ships, even old ones, without having to take out a loan."

"Bingo!!!" exclaimed Josh. "North Korea is known for counterfeit prescription drugs, not to mention meth and heroin production. What else do you have?

"That's it." Her tone had an air of finality to it.

"Uilani, thanks a lot. This has been helpful. I'll call you later." Marty hung up, smiling.

Josh laughed. "Just friends, huh?"

Friday, February 24th, 1995,
1020 local time, Broutana Bay, Simushir Island

Newly promoted Major Chin Hae Kim, wearing a down jacket, stamped his feet as he waited for the next lighter to come ashore with his team and their equipment. Movement kept him warm. Each time he stood still he shivered, and he wondered if the involuntary movement was caused by the cold or by fear of the unknown.

Front loaders had cleared the area around the old pier, the piles of snow made gray-black by volcanic soil. A muddy road went up from the piers to the entrance of a three-story building and several smaller structures, all of which needed extensive repairs.

The trip to Simushir had taken 12 days for Major Kim and his team of 11 North Korean Special Forces soldiers, who were outside their country for the first time. They had boarded a train outside their base in Haeju, North Korea that had chugged along to the Chinese/North Korean border. A second train had carried them to the Chinese port city of Dalian, where they'd boarded the *Crescent Sun.* Only when the freighter was out of sight of land had Major Kim told his men where they were headed. It had taken 10 days to sail the 4,680 kilometers (2,527 nautical miles) to Simushir, going south through the West Sea and between the Japanese islands of Yakushima and Toshima and into the Pacific before turning north toward the Kurils.

Kim and his men had been startled by the amount and quality of the food served. Each meal offered a bewildering array of choices and consisted of more food than a North Korean family normally ate in a week.

Major Kim had also marveled at how well the machinery on the ship worked. There were no frantic attempts to get something poorly made to function properly. He'd concluded his country had a lot to learn from the rest of the world when it came to designing and building machines.

Now, as he looked around, Major Kim compared the data from the Russian maps he'd studied to what he saw. None of the photos adequately portrayed the stark natural beauty of the sea-filled caldera. He admired the stark, white wilderness surrounding him, and the harbor's calm, slate-gray water.

He pulled his East-German-made binoculars from their case and studied the boat pulling away from the ship. Seeing his men and equipment were on the lighter, Kim turned to study the terrain around the bay.

To the south, the looming,1,500-meter Prevo Peak dominated the central part of the island. But it was Mount Uratman, on the northern end of Simushir, that called to mind his orders. *"Reconnoiter the northern third of the island first. If you encounter someone, determine why they are there and bring them back to Broutana Bay by any available means. If necessary, eliminate them."*

Kim estimated it would take five, maybe six days to scout the designated terrain with his team. Later, when the weather got warmer, he would lead them to Prevo Peak—he wanted to look down into the crater at the top, explore the Zavaritzk Caldera, and climb Mt. Milna, the tallest mountain on the island, 45 kilometers to the south.

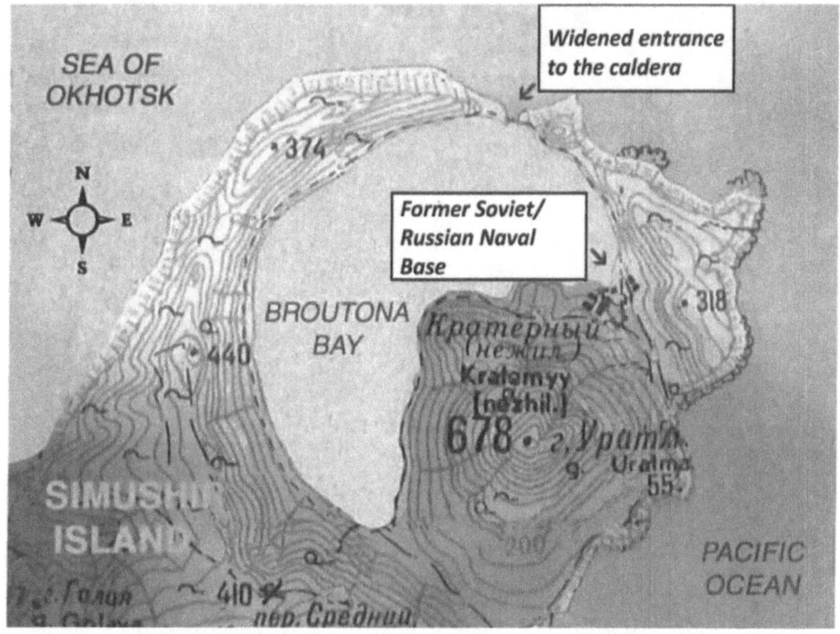

Soviet Map of Broutana Bay Given to Major Kim

Each man's pack had rations for six days, tarpaulins for shelter, and a light weapons load—an AK-74 with six 30-round magazines, and two fragmentation grenades, plus three liters of fuel for the two stoves they carried. Melted snow would provide water. To his own load, Major Kim would add his familiar Tokarev pistol, three spare magazines, his binoculars, maps, a compass (with another for his senior sergeant), a camera with a half a dozen rolls of film, and some pens and a notebook for a diary.

Kim wondered how the island would look in summertime. Transformed, no doubt, and not just by the change in seasons. He had been told that there would be many ships coming and going in the coming months.

Chapter 4: POLITICS OR POLICY

Saturday, February 25th, 1995, 0826 local time, on board U.S.S. Blue Ridge *100 nautical miles east of Honshu*

Whether at sea or in port, during the work week Josh Haman and his peers had a quick breakfast in the flag mess and worked until six or seven in the evening. At sea, the only difference in the routine was that, for those who lived ashore, the commute to the *Blue Maru,* as it was often called, was reduced to a short walk from their state rooms to the flag mess and their offices. Living on board let them sleep at least half an hour longer. Josh, as a "geographic bachelor," i.e., a married service member on an unaccompanied tour, lived on *Blue Ridge.*

The ship had been commissioned in 1970 as an amphibious command ship. But when the World War II era light cruiser *U.S.S. Oklahoma City* (CG-5) was decommissioned in 1979, *Blue Ridge* became the Seventh Fleet flag ship. Except for nine-and-a-half-month deployments during Operations Desert Shield and Storm, *Blue Ridge* rarely went on cruises longer than a month.

Officially, Saturday was a day off, but Josh quickly found out this claim was a cruel joke. The admiral's message and intelligence brief was at 0800 instead of 0630. Most of the staff stayed on the ship until lunch, and department heads considered themselves lucky to be off duty by three.

The flag mess served three meals a day. In one of the cabinets above the desk in his stateroom, Josh kept a stash of snacks, mostly dried fruit and crackers, which he bought in the commissary, or which Rebekah sent in a care package. Next to the sink, he had a small refrigerator for orange juice, cheeses and other items that needed refrigeration. And in the small safe that was supposed to be for classified material, he kept bottles of his favorite scotch and tawny port for an occasional and unofficial glass in the evening. Officially, American navy ships had been 'dry' since teetotaler Secretary of the Navy Josephus Daniels issued General Order #99 in 1914, which closed the bar in the wardroom.

The head, a.k.a. the bathroom to landlubbers, was down the hall. It smelled like any other on a Navy ship—a mix of seawater, urine and chlorine. Trips to the head to shower now required a bathrobe because, in the modern Navy, female sailors could be in the passageway. In the old days, a towel wrapped around one's waist was enough. But old habits die hard. A week after he'd arrived on *Blue Ridge,* Josh had been on his way toward the head wearing flip-flops and carrying a soap dish and shampoo with a towel wrapped around his waist. Around the first corner, he'd come face to face with a young female ensign. She'd smiled, assumed he was a senior officer, put her back against the bulkhead and stood at attention.

As he'd passed, Josh had mumbled a weak, "Good morning, as you were," and continued on his way, trying not to blush.

Josh's biggest inconvenience as a geographic bachelor living aboard ship was a car—or the lack of one. He didn't want to buy one for just a year, so he walked everywhere on the naval base. He'd taken the train into Tokyo several times on a Sunday. It was an easy 20-minute walk to the train station, and 30 minutes later, he was in the downtown area of the country's—and the world's—largest city. If he decided to take a few days off, he could take a high-speed train from Tokyo to almost any city on Honshu, Japan's largest island.

Surprise, surprise: Exercise Foal Eagle '95 was cancelled by the President; he had done the same thing in 1993 and 1994 as a way to appease the North Koreans. For the staff of N1 (Administration), N2 (Intelligence), N3 (Current Operations) and N6 (Operations and Plans), the cancellation meant sending out a blizzard of messages, ranging from cancelling active duty orders for several hundred reservists to redoing ship schedules. Thankfully, his predecessor had saved the messages sent in the wake of the previous cancellations. In many cases, it was merely a matter of changing names and dates and resending. In this case, Josh thought, plagiarism was a productivity enhancer.

Josh was about to initial the revised schedule when the phone rang. It was the flag lieutenant, a.k.a. "the rope," asking him to come to the admiral's office.

Josh scribbled his initials and dropped the approved schedule on the action officer's desk on his way to the admiral's office. When he arrived, the N3, by trade a fighter pilot who was hoping to get command of an air wing or a carrier as his next assignment, handed him a message. "Read this, and tell me if a first-class goat fuck isn't headed our way."

Josh enjoyed his fellow captain's sardonic and often sarcastic sense of humor. He laughed and started reading. The subject line indicated a congressional visit (which the press would refer to as a junket) to the Pacific, starting with a visit to CINCPAC (PACCOM) in Hawaii. Next stop was Commander, Seventh Fleet and Commander, U.S. Forces Japan. From there, the delegation planned to go to Korea and the Philippines and make a stop in

Guam before returning to Washington. Their first briefing in Hawaii was scheduled for March 16th. The message gave desired times for the briefs, which were to be confirmed by respective staffs. *Well, at least we won't be running a major exercise and war game with congressmen underfoot.*

After the itinerary, the message listed the members of the delegation. Josh stopped reading when he saw a name he'd thought he'd never see again.

Steven Higgins.

"Aw, fuck!" Bad memories of a botched rescue, a pilot disposition board, and civil lawsuits rose like a red tide in his mind.

The N3 is right—but for the wrong reason.

Josh was still staring at the list when Admiral Maize folded himself into a chair at the head of the table, which had a blue cover and three white stars. He nodded approval when he saw Haman already had the papers in hand. "Now that you two know the what, you can get to work. A briefing book on each member of the delegation should arrive tomorrow on the helo that brings our mail. The delegation's focus is supposedly on training and readiness, and there's a request for a threat brief. My part will cover how we'll fight wars in our op area. Our intel guys will focus on the threats from Russia, the People's Republic of China, and the rest of our area of responsibility. Ops, you'll lead the effort and cover current operations. Josh, you're going to talk about future exercises and war plan updates."

It all meant more busywork. Josh waited until the operations officer left, then said, "Boss, do you have a minute?"

"For *you*, I've got *five*, what's up?"

"Steven Higgins, sir. He's a big problem—for the Navy and for me."

Vice Admiral Maize, about to pick up a folder, stopped. "He's a Naval Academy graduate."

"Sir, it's a long story."

"I'll make time. Out with it. Please close the door."

Josh summarized the salient points. Higgins, who had been his first aircraft commander in Vietnam, had refused to make a rescue because the helicopter was being shot at. As a result, they'd left a man behind to be captured and tortured by the enemy. Nine years after the war ended, Josh flew the helicopter that rescued the aviator and five other men. They'd been held by a man who converted opium into raw heroin as he masqueraded as a North Vietnamese Army lieutenant colonel.

A few weeks later, Josh had wanted to take off and attempt to pick up a downed pilot, but Higgins had refused to go. Josh had gone ahead and rescued a pilot under fire off the coast of North Vietnam, even though he hadn't been a qualified aircraft commander.

Higgins then accused Josh of mutiny. The ensuing pilot disposition board had exonerated Josh, and the subsequent investigation into Higgins' behavior had led to him being offered a choice—resign from the Navy under less-than-honorable conditions, or be charged with cowardice in the face of the enemy and falsification of government records.

Higgins had then filed unsuccessful but resource-consuming civil lawsuits against Josh and the Navy. Josh finished with, "Sir, I can put you in contact with Gary Nash, the Navy JAG officer who supervised the investigation. He is still a reservist and can answer any questions you may have."

"What do you want me to do?" the admiral asked.

"Sir, I think it best that I'm not around when Higgins is here. I don't want to risk a scene that will be hard to explain and might embarrass you."

"Or, you can stay here, and if Representative Higgins says or does something stupid, you have witnesses."

"Sir, it's your call."

"Josh, how well do you know Vice Admiral Gainesville?"

"Sir, we're good friends. When he worked for General Feltzer, the Chief of Staff for Operations on the Joint Staff in the Pentagon, he had a hand in my posting to Moscow. He was a lieutenant on the *Sterett* with Higgins and me. Why do you ask?"

"I've got a message from Admiral Gainesville asking me to call. In the meantime, do what you have to do to prepare for this delegation."

February 25th to 28th, 1995, Simushir Island

Every day, Major Kim urged his men to keep forcing their way through knee-deep snow, thickly encrusted with ice. The effort wore them down. Each step meant the point man had to break through the jagged ice that pulled at clothing and flesh, sometimes ripping and cutting both. The next few men in line made the break wider, so that by the time the fifth or sixth man came stomping along, there was a passable track. Every hundred meters, Major Kim had the point man step aside and let the man behind him become the "trail breaker." The shift gave the former point a brief respite as the rest of the team trudged past so he could take his place at the end of the line.

The footing under the snow was slimy and slippery from rotting vegetation. A fall often meant a nasty cut from the sharp volcanic rocks, which would need cleaning with melted snow so the coarse volcanic granules wouldn't create an infection. It was, he told his men, a battle of will—man versus the elements—and they were going to win.

When it wasn't raining or snowing, the sun was painfully bright. Special Russian-made dark snow goggles protected their eyes from the blinding glare reflecting off the ice crystals.

As they trudged through the sparse patches of trees marked as "forests" on his map, Kim decided most of the trees weren't worthy of the name. They were more like tall bushes with roots deep enough to keep them from being blown off the island.

One day, they waited out a heavy fall of wet snow mixed with rain, grateful they could stay under makeshift tarpaulin shelters.

Each night, Major Kim took the midnight-to-0200 watch, which gave his men a chance to get six to eight hours of sleep. He enjoyed the solitude, and the time to think. At first, his thoughts were about practical matters concerning the mission: *I have to find a better way to get around on this island. How did the Russians do it? Did they have skis or snowshoes?* But as the silence deepened around him and the moonlight illuminated the branches of the "trees" overhead, his mind wandered.

My parents were department heads at Hamhung University of Education. Why were they demoted to instructors? They died when I was 18. I could tell they were sick, but the doctor claimed there was nothing he could do. They never would tell me why they were denounced and demoted, and now they are gone. The small, three room house felt empty without them. He was amazed that the government had allowed him to keep it.

Why did my parents insist I learn English?

He remembered a morning, years ago, when his booted foot had kicked an almost entirely submerged steel stake in the little garden where he still grew the herbs and annuals his mother had planted: lettuce, coriander, gochu chili peppers, and crown daisies. He'd knelt down and started digging. He'd unearthed a buried wooden box of books in English, written by Kipling, Twain,

The Simushir Island Incident

Thoreau, Bronte, Hemingway and others. All the books had been wrapped neatly in several layers of wax paper.

Why was I promoted to major two years before my peers? Why did General Jang pull me out of the Action Unit of the Special Security Department?

The musings made it hard for him to sleep.

Wednesday, March 1st, 1995, 0712 local time, U.S.S. Blue Ridge

In the large conference room, Vice Admiral Maize stood up and faced his staff. "Gentlemen, we've been tasked by CINCPAC to watch the commercial development on Simushir Island, since it is in our backyard. Captain Haman has volunteered to take it on as an action item." Several of the officers in the room chuckled at the word "volunteered". "Voluntold" was more like it.

Admiral Maize didn't have to hide behind his rank to be impressive. The six-foot, seven-inch admiral had played basketball at Annapolis and had been selected to the all-conference and all-academic team three years in a row. In his junior year, he made the All-America team. At the end of that season, three different sports agents had assured him that the NBA could get the Navy to reduce his commitment or even get permission for him to leave the academy early. But he'd sent a certified letter to the league, saying he planned to honor his full six-year commitment and would not allow himself to be drafted. As he said to anyone who asked, he'd rather serve his country than sit on an NBA team's bench.

Maize's height had left him with just one military option—surface warfare. His performance as an officer, not his ability to dunk a basketball, had earned him command of a frigate as a commander and then a cruiser as a captain. A Pentagon tour as an executive assistant to an Army three star on the Joint Staff in the Pentagon helped his chances of being selected by the flag officer promotion board. After being selected for rear admiral, he'd spent

18 months as an amphibious group commander. While managing an acquisition program in the Pentagon, Maize was promoted to vice admiral before being assigned as the Commander, Seventh Fleet.

While the admiral didn't exactly hand pick his staff, Maize had worked with many of the officers in previous assignments. As a courtesy, the detailers who assigned officers to his staff's department head billets called him before they issued orders. He was also allowed to request specific officers for key billets and to veto those he didn't want.

Vice Admiral Maize moved to podium and rested his left elbow on it. "Captain Nagumo, our Japanese Self-Defense Force liaison, tipped us off to the initial news release. Even though some of the material in Captain Haman's briefing comes from open sources, much did not. Our analyses make what you are about to hear Top Secret/Sensitive Compartmented Information. Captain Haman— and in his absence, Commander Cabot—will be the only two officers authorized to communicate with other commands about what we know. Simushir is now an *update* item on CINCPAC's intelligence brief, so if either Captain Haman or Commander Cabot —or their reservist side kick, Commander D'Onofrio—ask you for assistance, assume the request is coming from both me and our four-star boss."

The admiral nodded to the two officers standing off to the side. "Captain Haman and Commander Cabot." As the admiral sat down, Marty went to the projector with a pile of acetate slides, designed to re-acquaint members of the staff with the island and its history. Josh moved toward the screen, pointer in hand, and gave a commentary on what the photographs showed. Marty plopped the last slide in place, the most recent image of the island.

"I saved the best for last. In the last few days, several people have taken a hike through the snow," Josh said. "You can see their trail and where they made camp." He tapped the screen in several places. "It looks like they are exploring the island. Ops, we're going to ask you to task one of the P-3s equipped with long range cameras to take pictures when we have clear weather and to return on an unpredictable basis so as to catch them when they think we are not looking. We're assuming they know when our satellites will be overhead."

Friday, March 3rd, 1995, 1417 local time, Pyongyang

When one was summoned to the presence of the country's Dear Leader, the only acceptable answer to anything he asked you to do was "yes." Any other reply could be, at best, career shortening and, at worst, life threatening.

Before his aide, Captain Chin, could get out of the car to open the door, Admiral Pak put a hand on his shoulder. "Don't wait for me. Go back to headquarters, and when I am done, I will call you. If you don't hear from me by 1700, go home and enjoy the rest of the weekend. Trust me, nothing bad is going to happen. This is not the first time I have been summoned without notice to meet our Dear Leader, and it won't be the last. It comes with the job."

Admiral Pak got out of the staff car, knowing that, despite his reassuring words to his aide, he could be walking up the steps for the last time as a free man.

The guards at the door saluted, then waved him through to the next level of security, where he was searched. The guard flipped through the envelope in his breast pocket to make sure it contained paper, not an explosive device.

On the other side of security, one of the Dear Leader's many aides stood at attention waiting to guide Admiral Pak to the conference room. Once there, Pak prepared to wait. It was important to be "on time" for a meeting with the Dear Leader. This meant that one was in the room 15 minutes before the meeting was scheduled to begin. One's arrival time was reported to the Dear Leader, and being on time was viewed as respect for the Dear Leader's time, even though he was almost always late. In the DPRK, everyone waited for our Dear Leader. It was one of the ways he demonstrated his power.

The aide, an Army major, bowed respectfully. "Welcome to our Dear Leader's offices."

"I am always glad to meet with our Dear Leader so I can learn from his wisdom." Admiral Pak hoped he didn't sound insincere or sarcastic; a recording would be reviewed by senior officers in the Defense Ministry. Any negative report would not be good for his career.

The aide smiled and bowed so low his back was almost at a 45-degree angle to the floor. Then he rapped on the polished wood door. When it opened, it revealed another aide, who motioned Pak into a cavernous room dominated at one end by paintings of Kim Jong-Il and his father, Kim Il-Sung.

At the other end of the room, a large national flag hung from where the wall joined the ceiling. Between the two ends, there was a polished teak table that Pak estimated to be four meters wide and 15 meters long. Pak noted the neatly aligned chairs were exactly the same distance apart from each other and from the table. Someone had used a ruler or a template to make their positioning so precise.

The second aide wore no insignia on his drab gray suit. "Admiral, our Dear Leader will be with you in a few minutes. May I get you some tea or mineral water?"

"Thank you. Tea, please."

"As you wish." Tea was placed in front of him with some cookies, and he was left alone.

To pass the time, Pak made notes on one of the blank sheets of paper he'd brought with him, scribbling reminders of things he needed to do. When he finished, Pak glanced at his watch. It was 1428.

The turning of a latch broke the silence and Vice Admiral Pak stood.

Both French doors opposite him were opened simultaneously by two guards to allow two other guards to enter the room with their weapons leveled. There was a slight pause before a third person, a severe-looking older woman, came in and announced, "Our Dear Leader."

"I see you have been well taken care of." Kim Jong-Il waved toward the teapot and empty plate. "I am glad you could take time from your busy schedule to meet me. I assume our submarine fleet is performing well."

"Yes, sir. Our crews are ready to defend our country." *I know better than to tell the Dear Leader his submarines need replacing or, at the very least, a major upgrade. Even worse would be telling him the real truth—deploying them on wartime missions against the Japanese, American and South Korean navies would be sending their crews to certain death.*

"Excellent." Kim Jong-Il pulled out the chair at the head of the table—the largest chair in the room—and sat down. That was Vice Admiral Pak's signal to do likewise. He left an empty chair between them. A small chair was brought in for the woman, who was not important enough to sit at the table, and she sat down, notepad in hand, just behind and to the right of Kim. The Dear Leader then leaned back in his chair. It was a practiced gesture to give him an air of casual superiority.

"I understand we already have access to the new exercise area on the Russian coast of the East Sea."

"Yes, we have. Our submarines are taking small commando teams there once a month. Our agreement specifies that each time one of our submarines takes a team there, we participate in an anti-submarine exercise with Russian ships and airplanes. It is very good training."

"Excellent. You must be very proud of them."

"Yes, sir, I am."

"Are you sure our submarines can meet General Jang's needs?"

"Yes, they can. We practice putting men ashore and picking them up, even in the winter. It is a regular part of our training."

Kim smiled at Pak's intimation that the Soviets were softer than their North Korean allies. "What about taking our submarines to Simushir?"

"Dear Leader, our submarines have the range to make the round trip to Broutana Bay." *But long deployments will lead to breakdowns. What happens when we have to tow a sub back? The government will lose face if we have to hire a sea-going tug to bring it back. As punishment, I would be sent to a re-education camp in disgrace, even though the decisions that created the limited capabilities were not made by me. Then there are the Americans and Japanese. They will want to know why our subs are operating so far from home.*

"I hear food could be a problem on longer voyages."

"We can carry enough as long as the mission doesn't take more than 30 days."

The Dear Leader leaned forward in his chair. "You should ask our Chinese and Russian comrades for larger, longer range submarines when you meet with them."

"Yes, sir, they have a 641-class, which the American Imperialists call *Foxtrots*. They are much bigger and have a much longer range than our *Romeos*. That is an excellent idea, and I will inquire at once about purchasing some. I am sure either country will be happy to sell us enough to meet our needs." *They're obsolete and are being phased out of their inventory.*

The Simushir Island Incident

"Tell our Chinese and Russian comrades money will not be a problem. We will find it." The man with the high voice and round face sat back, pleased with his command. "How does the construction go on Simushir?"

"We enlarged the width of the harbor entrance channel to just over 35 meters. Channel depth is now 30 meters, so we can get larger freighters into the harbor."

Kim Jong-Il's head bobbed in acknowledgement.

Admiral Pak didn't mention that they'd nearly run out of explosives because their engineers had underestimated the difficulty of the job. Their experience was in tunneling into mountains, not widening the entrance into an ocean-filled caldera.

"Dear Leader, rebuilding the main piers needs less work than we thought. But the large barracks will need much more work to be repaired, so additional permanent housing is en route. When it arrives, it will be unloaded and the workers will move ashore. Soon, we will be able to start on the factory. So far, we are maintaining our schedule." *We're ahead of our plan and the first phase of pier repairs may be done by the end of next week. I am not telling you that, because if I do, you will ask for something outlandish to be completed on a ridiculous schedule.*

"The island is uninhabited, yes?"

"Our reconnaissance team found no one. As soon as the snow melts, we will finish exploring the island."

"Good. Keep me informed of your progress. Let us talk again soon."

Kim Jong-Il got up and left the room, followed by the two guards. Once he was gone, the older woman nodded and left without saying a word to Admiral Pak, who was left standing alone.

Marc Liebman

Sunday, March 12th, 1995, 1236 local time, Honolulu

This was going to be the first time Higgins had been on a Navy base since he had driven away from Norfolk on Saturday, February 13th, 1971. He'd gotten what he wanted—out of the Navy—but not on the terms he'd wanted.

He'd driven to New York in his 1968 Camaro SS, the manila folder containing his discharge papers unopened in his briefcase. The "other than honorable" discharge meant he would not receive VA benefits of any kind. Nor would he be eligible for benefits under the GI Bill.

In New York, he'd joined the Vietnam Veterans Against the War and participated in protests. To the organization, he was perfect—decorated, an officer and a Naval Academy graduate. He didn't tell the organization that he'd been run out of the Navy on the proverbial rail. It wasn't any of their business.

Money had not been a problem. When he'd graduated from Annapolis, his father had given him 75,000 dollars. Steven had invested the funds, and along with the money he'd added from his officer's income, by the time he left the Navy his portfolio was worth over $175,000.

In early May 1971, he had been accepted by the University of Wisconsin's Law School. He'd started taking classes in June, determined to graduate as fast as he could and finished in the top five of his class. While he was in law school, Higgins' relationship with his father got worse instead of better. The older man had served in World War II and still carried shrapnel in his body from wounds received at Anzio. He'd been awarded Silver and Bronze Stars for his actions in the war. When Steven had finally admitted the type of discharge he'd received, he'd seen surprise, then pain, then disgust in his father's eyes. Nonetheless, at his mother's insistence, he lived at home in a tense atmosphere until he finished law school. As soon as he graduated from law school and got a job, Steven moved out.

Though he was respected, even admired, for the quality of his work as a public defender, no law firms tried to recruit him. Nor did the district attorney's office ever ask if he wanted to become a prosecutor. After three years of practicing law, Higgins hoped his record of accomplishment would make him an attractive employee. He was wrong, and blamed his discharge for the rejections from in-state and out-of-state firms.

Higgins appealed to the VA to see if his discharge could be changed to a General Discharge for Administrative Reasons. The VA rejected his filing. Higgins immediately filed a lawsuit against the Navy, saying the discharge was prejudicial and he had never been charged with any offense that warranted a general discharge under other than honorable conditions. As soon as he learned a JAG lawyer from the Navy would offer into evidence the case the Navy had prepared to bring against him in a court martial, he withdrew the lawsuit.

He was good looking, trim and fit, and knew how to use a smile. While he might be awkward socially, once he walked past the bar in a courtroom, Higgins transformed into a confident, self-assured—some might say arrogant—public defender. His ordinary shyness was a character trait some young women found attractive at first, perhaps because they thought they could shape him to their own liking. But no woman he dated allowed a long-term relationship to develop. The excuses varied. He told himself they stopped dating him because he was never going to get rich as a career public defender.

When a fellow public defender asked Higgins to work as a volunteer for the Democratic Party in Wisconsin, he leapt at the chance. He excelled at the grunt work, and it got him noticed by the local party leaders. When the party's district congressional nominee dropped out of the race after nearly dying from a heart attack, Higgins volunteered to run. He was perfect—ultra-liberal, a public defender, a veteran and an anti-war activist.

During the weeks leading up to the election, his discharge—which he'd listed as a General Discharge on the forms he was required to fill out—never came up. Maybe, Higgins thought, no one cared or would notice. He hoped it was finally behind him.

Higgins easily carried Wisconsin's heavily Democratic and very liberal Second District. As a member of the U. S. House of Representatives, Steve Higgins had perks he'd never realized existed. From living on a Wisconsin civil servant's pay, he now had more money than he could spend.

As a junior member of the House of Representatives, Higgins was careful to ask to sit on committees that did not require a security clearance or work with the Department of Defense. He was afraid of what would happen if the Office of House Security did a background check on him.

When Higgins boarded the flight to Honolulu, he'd been in the House of Representatives for four years, and the leaders of the Democratic Party was confident he would run for re-election and win handily.

Higgins was met at the Honolulu airport terminal by a member of CINCPAC's staff and taken to the Hilton Hawaiian Village in Waikiki where a suite was reserved. The military congressional liaison officers accompanying the politicians were given rooms at the Hale Koa Hotel—a DOD-run facility and a very short walk from the Hilton. In Hawaiian, *hale koa* means house of the warrior.

Higgins was restless. It was lunchtime in Honolulu, but his body clock told him it was time for dinner. In the hotel's Hau Tee bar, Higgins took a stool where he could see the beach.

As women walked by, he amused himself by trying to guess if they were single, and if they were, could he get them into bed?

The Simushir Island Incident

Four years as a bachelor congressman had done much for his confidence with women, even if he still did not have a steady girlfriend. The bartender put his cheeseburger and French fries on the counter, along with a second glass of beer. He was studying a woman who was walking past when a man sat at the bar two chairs down from him. Higgins instantly tagged him as being in the military, which, given the number of military bases on Oahu, wasn't unusual. The woman moved on and he went back to his cheeseburger.

"Excuse me, but are you Representative Steven Higgins?"

He looked over at the stranger with a cold stare.

"Sorry, I didn't introduce myself. I'm Rear Admiral Jeremiah Jeffers—Chief of Staff for Operations on CINCPAC's staff—and I recognized you from your picture. Tomorrow, I'll be briefing you on Pacific Command's current and future operations. I'm waiting for my wife to finish shopping, so I came here for a beer."

"Oh." The man's name matched one he'd read on the prep documents. "Yes, I'm Congressmen Steven Higgins from Wisconsin's Second District." Higgins held out his hand.

Jeffers shook Higgins hand vigorously, thinking that getting to know a congressman would be good for his career. "Welcome to Hawaii."

"Thanks."

Higgins tried to decide whether or not to take advantage of a social opportunity. Polite conversation was not his strong suit, but this might be a chance to glean background information about the people he would meet in the next few days. He asked a question about who else would be attending.

Jeffers gave him a quick précis of the officers and their backgrounds. Although Higgins hadn't paid attention to the Navy in many years, his time at the Naval Academy and on active duty helped him understand the lingo. "Thanks. That's very helpful."

That was true. Some of what Jeffers had said was not in the briefing book he'd studied before the trip. "Tell me about Seventh Fleet."

Jeffers pursed his lips, and Higgins was sure he saw a flash in his eyes. He was not sure what it meant, but he sensed here was someone who wanted to say something but was reluctant to say it.

"Vice Admiral Edward Maize is well respected. He had two ship commands and an amphibious group before getting Seventh Fleet. There are some who think he is being groomed as a future CINCPAC or CINCLANT and then as a possible CNO. He's an academy graduate."

"I sense there is something more you are not telling me."

"All I'll say is, he requested several officers to join his staff as department heads whom I would never allow to work for me."

"Interesting." The public defender wanted to continue to question the witness, but now was not the time or place.

Jeffers changed the subject. "So, Congressman Higgins, are you still leaving for Japan on Tuesday morning?"

"Yes. Our itinerary says we're being picked up at 0800. Why?"

"If you have nothing on your schedule for Monday night, why don't you join my wife and me for a home cooked dinner? We can talk off the record about key members of the Seventh Fleet staff and the challenges the command faces. Every one of the stops on your tour is in their area of responsibility, which is the largest of any Navy numbered fleet."

"Sounds interesting. On Monday we have a wrap-up meeting at five, but that should be over at six. I am free afterwards."

"Excellent. I'll take you to our quarters and bring you back to the hotel. We can chat more then." *And I can tell you my thoughts on Josh Haman, Marty Cabot and Seventh Fleet's commander.* The smile on Jeffers' face was self-satisfied, and malignant.

The Simushir Island Incident

Monday, March 13th, 1995, 0715 local time, Pearl Harbor

"Welcome to Pearl, Commander Cabot. Rear Admiral Jeffers wants you to call as soon as you've checked in." The petty officer of the watch wore the insignia of an aerographer (Navy's rating for weathermen and women) on her sleeve. She stamped his orders, noting his time of arrival at CINCPAC's headquarters, then handed Marty a yellow government phone message form with a number to call written in black ink. She pointed at the standard black, Navy-issue rotary dial phone. "Sir, you can use this phone."

Marty dialed. Rear Admiral Jeffers' aide told him that Admiral Jeffers could squeeze him in for a 1300 meeting.

Marty arrived five minutes early. The aide ushered him into the admiral's office, where Marty came to a relaxed position of parade rest three feet from the front of the large wooden desk. Behind the admiral, there was a blue flag with two embroidered white stars on the left, and a U.S. flag on the right. The credenza had half a dozen framed black-and-white photos representing highlights of the admiral's career.

"Sir, Commander Cabot reporting as requested."

Jeffers did not offer the courtesy of responding. No greeting, no thank you for coming, no "At ease." A warning prickle went up Marty's spine and began to semaphore messages to his hind brain.

This will be interesting. Using his peripheral vision, Marty noted the admiral had lots of "I was there" ribbons and several representing "excellence in performing administrative duties." None denoted he was a combat veteran in an era when many surface warfare officers of his generation had served in Vietnam.

The word on Jeffers was that he was a shoe clerk who'd risen through the ranks due to political skills. Friends on the CINCPAC staff had told Marty that in one of Jeffers' first staff meetings, he'd informed his subordinates that they were there to help get him his third star. Leadership 101 suggests this is the exact opposite of what a leader should say. That was bad enough. Worse, Marty knew first hand that in times of war, shoe clerks got warriors killed.

The admiral stayed seated at his desk, focused on a single piece of paper on the center of the green blotter on the desk used by many famous flag officers before him. There were two neat piles of folders on either side.

Jeffers picked up the piece of paper and then let it go, as if it were contaminated. "The CINC has been watching what is happening on Simushir…" He left the island's name hanging, and pronounced the acronym CINC as "sink" with added emphasis on the k. "*I* have been following the events in the Seventh Fleet area of responsibility with great interest…"

So has my boss, Commander Seventh Fleet, who has three stars and talks almost on a daily basis with your boss, who has four. And before Maize talks to CINCPAC, he asks Josh or me for the latest info on Simushir. So what are you implying? Marty's facial expression must have given his inner thoughts away.

"Commander Cabot, the unusual cruises by the North Korean submarines have implications well above your pay grade or expertise. The commercial facility on Simushir Island is a matter for the State Department to deal with, not commanders and captains. Or even admirals of numbered fleets."

Jeffers raised his voice noticeably. He wasn't shouting, but his tone was harsher and decibels higher, as if Marty were a Naval Academy midshipman.

"The reason you are standing in my office *AT ATTENTION,* Commander Cabot, is so I can give you some flag guidance you should take to heart. I want to make sure you understand CINCPAC will not allow—no, let me restate, *will NOT tolerate nor permit* the type of freelancing you and your friend, Commander Haman, are prone to do. If either of you go off half-cocked, it could cause a great deal of embarrassment to our country or even start a war, to say nothing of costing you what remains of your career."

"Thank you, sir. I will take your guidance on board. I am sure the admiral knows that Commander Haman is now *Captain* Haman, and the admiral may also know we were both requested— no, let me restate that, *asked*—no, let me use a more accurate word, *required* to volunteer to serve on the Seventh Fleet staff." Marty mimicked the phraseology used by Admiral Jeffers, but not his tone.

"Don't be a wise ass, Commander. I was on the selection board and Haman was promoted despite my best efforts. And on the next O-6 board, I assure you, there will not be a friend in court for you unless you stop being a cowboy."

Marty flipped his mental recording switch on. *You, asshole admiral—just broke three sacred promotion board rules.* First: never discuss the deliberations about an officer whose record appeared before a selection board. Second: never threaten to blackball an officer before a future selection board. Third, the selection of officers who make up a promotion board is classified, and no one is supposed to serve on the same board two years in a row. *You expect to get Vice Admiral Gainesville to break the selection board rules? You just fucked up, Admiral!*

"Commander, let me make this clear. If either Haman or you go off the reservation, I will make it my personal mission to ensure you are court-martialed and run out of the Navy. Haman is on my permanent shit list for what happened in the Philippines, and I just hope you do something stupid so I can have the pleasure of getting you shit-canned, too. Believe me, the Navy will be a lot better off without you."

Marty stared at the wall, determined not to respond.

"I didn't hear an acknowledgement from you, Commander." Jeffers was now standing and leaning forward, his hands flat on the desk.

Marty was not going imply he'd accepted this "guidance" unless the admiral made it an order. He didn't think even this black shoe admiral was that dumb. "Admiral, is that all?"

Jeffers flushed. "Commander, I expected an 'Aye aye, sir' to acknowledge the direction given to you by a senior officer and the words, 'I will do my best to ensure it will happen.'" His lips pursed. "But that would be too much to expect from you, isn't it? Dismissed!"

Marty put his right big toe behind his left heel and performed an about face that would make a Marine drill instructor proud. As soon as he found a vacant desk away from Jeffers' office, he wrote Jeffers' comments verbatim, along with the time and place, knowing his meeting should be in Jeffers' official log. *Lord only knows what the aide will enter as the meeting topic!*

After his last meeting of the day, Marty stopped off at the officers' club. To use his best friend's words, his "beer-low-level light" was on.

Marty took a seat at a small table in the corner and waited for the waitress to bring him his drink, along with a small plate of beer nuts. He planned to go over his notes from the conversation with RADM Jeffers, but his mind stalled on the question, *Why do Josh and I keep running afoul of assholes like Jeffers?*

Before his brain could get into gear, the waitress had put an iced glass on the table and poured the Tecate.

He took a long sip, savoring the flavor and the zing of the lime juice the waitress had squeezed into the glass before she poured the beer. As the beer reached his stomach, his mind started answering the question.

The Simushir Island Incident

Some men and women are warriors; others are not. Beyond that, the answer became more complicated, because it lay in the difference between those who are at the pointy edge of the sword and those who are in rear headquarters. It was a matter of perspective.

The farther one worked from the front lines, the more ship and plane movements were just arrows on a map or symbols on a screen. Those in the command centers often didn't know those who were doing the fighting and dying. The human element of war is overrun by statistics and strategic theories. Combat is an intensely personal business and one needs to start with *Plan A* knowing that once the bullets start flying, you're going to have to shift to *Plan B* or *C*—or worse, create a new plan.

The German Admiral Karl Doenitz had supposedly said in his debriefing at the end of World War II, "The reason the American Navy does so well in wartime is that war is chaos, and the American Navy practices it on a daily basis."

That, Marty thought, *is why officers like Jeffers hate men like Josh and me—because we tend to be unorthodox and we can see through the chaos and make decisions that enable us to succeed. Sometimes the actions we take are considered pretty, sometimes they're ugly, but the result is the same—mission accomplished with minimum damage to the good guys. But Jeffers and others of his ilk are more interested in following instructions and orders to the letter, without thinking of the consequences. They can't deal with the chaos and unpredictability of a firefight and they see us as a threat because what we do could affect their ranking and chances for promotion. Operational risk is seen as promotion risk, and to their orderly minds, reaching the next rank is more important than mission accomplishment—or lives.*

He knew it was a rationalization, but Marty was pretty sure it was also the truth.

Thursday, March 16th, 1995, 0901 local time,
on board U.S.S. Blue Ridge, *Yokosuka*

The boatswain's whistle, piped over the ship's main communication system from the quarterdeck, let everyone know that dignitaries were coming aboard. After the whistle, the ship's bell rang three times, followed by an announcement. Josh forced himself not to wince when he heard, "The Honorable Congressman Steven Higgins, Second Congressional District of Wisconsin, arriving."

It was only a matter of minutes before Higgins and the other congressmen would be ushered into the flag mess, where the stewards had laid out cinnamon rolls and sticky buns on china plates with the navy gold and blue ring and the Seventh Fleet logo. Coffee and juices were sitting at either end of the table.

Vice Admiral Maize stood by the door at the head of a receiving line to greet their guests. Next to Admiral Maize was his chief of staff and, as a courtesy, *Blue Ridge's* captain. The department heads came next and were lined up by number so that Josh, as the N6, was at the end.

When Higgins entered the room, his head swiveled, searching for Josh. The two of them locked eyes. The admiral's aide touched Higgins' arm and guided him to the receiving line.

Each "N head" introduced himself by rank and his title. When Higgins got to Josh, he held onto his hand and with a smile, hissed, "Hello, asshole—still the do-gooder in uniform fucking up lives, I see." The N5, who was the staff's communications officer, forced himself not to turn around when he heard the remark.

During a break, Vice Admiral Maize reminded Josh to write down everything Higgins said to him, and to provide a formal memo once the visit was over, with the names of any possible witnesses.

The Simushir Island Incident

1839 local time, Yokosuka Naval Base

Rather than have the formal reception on board *Blue Ridge,* the staff reserved a large room at the officers' club. All the Seventh Fleet staff officers and chief petty officers were invited. The cocktail party was the last event on the congressmen's Seventh Fleet agenda. Tomorrow, they were scheduled to tour the Yokosuka Naval Base before going on to Yokota Air Base for briefings provided by the Commander, U.S. Air Forces Japan.

Josh was near the end of the table with the hors d'oeuvres when he was shoved in the back. He managed to juggle his plate and prevent it from spilling or crashing to the floor. As he turned around, he saw Higgins with a malicious grin on his face.

He tried to retreat toward a table, but Higgins got between Josh and his destination and forced Josh toward a corner where no one was nearby. He smiled and spoke softly in an icy tone. "Haman, I am now in a position to fuck up your life, just like you did mine. If you come before the flag board next year, I will make sure you are blackballed. If you are selected, I will do everything in my power to hold up all the Navy's promotions until you are removed from the list. Remember, Congress has to approve *all* promotions, particularly new flag officers. So get your retirement papers ready, Haman, because I now have friends in high places in the Navy who want your ass on a silver platter as much as I do."

"Higgins, don't threaten me. You were damn lucky that the Navy didn't court martial you in 1970. If it had, you'd still be pounding big rocks into little rocks at Leavenworth. Remember, once I retire, I can encourage several members of the Washington press corps who would love to write a juicy story about a member of Congress who was given a choice—resign his commission or be tried for cowardice in the face of the enemy. So my advice to you, Higgins, is leave sleeping dogs lie. If not, they may bite you in the ass! Now, excuse me while I go speak to officers and enlisted men who do their duty." Josh picked up his plate and started to walk toward where others on the Seventh Fleet Staff were standing.

"Haman, I'm not done with you!"

Rather than turn around and give Higgins the satisfaction of a response, Josh kept walking. *If Higgins tries to interfere with my career or my life, he is playing with a fire that will turn him into a crispy critter. I'll bet money that Higgins doesn't know Gary Nash is a senior captain in the Navy's JAG corps and Jeff Gainesville is the head of the Bureau of Naval Personnel. Both men know the truth and, given the chance, both are ready to fry his ass for leaving pilots to be taken prisoner by the Vietnamese. One of whom is a friend and just retired as a rear admiral.*

Friday, March 17th, 1995, 0021 local time, Hong Kong

Three men swathed in light-devouring black waited, while a fourth worked to pick the high-security lock on the door next to the Man Yee Building's loading dock. Finally, the dead bolt gave up its security and the four men slipped inside.

The four men, all specialists in breaking and entering from the 65th Reconnaissance Brigade of the North Korean Special Forces, went past the freight elevator and avoided the double doors to the lobby and the eyes of the attentive men who manned the elegant, manually operated elevators—the last in Hong Kong. The Man Yee Building's owners took pride in knowing that most of their elevator men had been employed there since the building opened for business in 1957. But the Man Yee was scheduled to be demolished in 1999, to be replaced by a new 35–story office building. Those on the current building's staff who had 30 or more years of service would get pensions. Younger employees would be retained and retrained on the new building's elevators and security systems.

The Simushir Island Incident

Every hour, one of the night staff checked the locked doors. Tonight, about 12 minutes after the burglary began, an elevator man making his rounds discovered the unlocked door. He alerted the concierge, who called the police.

Ten policemen from Hong Kong's Special Duties Unit showed up eight minutes after the call. They were backed up by a dozen more police officers, who took up positions on the loading dock, the stairwell entrances and the elevator doors in the main lobby.

On the fifth floor, when the door of the elevator clanked open, the point man of the Special Duties Unit peeked out and was greeted by a bullet from a suppressed Tokarev. He dropped to the floor with a hole in his forehead.

The team leader, trained by the British SAS, pulled back into the elevator and held up his balled fist and then one finger. He nodded and counted down from three to one. On the word go, the team leader ran out of the elevator in a low crouch while the second man in the stack aimed his Heckler & Koch MP-5SD down the hall.

No one was in the hall. The elevator operator had pulled the body of the policeman back into the elevator. Five more men arrived on the floor in another elevator, and all nine men—four on the side from which the shooter had fired and five on the far side—began to slowly work their way toward the doorway.

They were halfway to the office suite when a man peered out the door. The team leader had his MP-5 pulled back against his shoulder and squeezed the trigger. His MP-5 was set for a three-round burst, and the target collapsed on the terrazzo floor.

At the door to the office suite, once his men were in position with five on the left side of the double doors and four on the right, the team leader shouted. "This is the Hong Kong Police, you have 10 seconds to come out with your hands up!"

He waited 10 seconds and shouted again—still no answer. He pulled a flash bang grenade from his vest. The man on the other side of the door mirrored his action. They pulled the pins and tossed the grenades into the office suite.

Both grenades went off with a deafening bang. The nine policemen, wearing night vision goggles, charged through the door. Inside, the robbers had turned desks on their sides to create cover and concealment. Blinded and stunned by the flash-bang grenade, they fired wildly at the Special Duties Unit policemen. Bullets smacked into the police officers' bulletproof vests. Three times, the police MP-5s spat out bullets. Three times, the targets died.

With their goggles off and the lights on, the Special Duties unit and the police inspectors quickly found the burglars' objective—a large safe in the file room. Its hinges had been wired with det cord that had not yet been ignited. Other file cabinets had been jimmied open and rifled through.

The building's manager had arrived on the scene just before the firefight began. With a police inspector standing next to him, he dialed the senior partner of the law firm—King, Nae, Ru and Partners—which leased almost the entire fifth floor. The senior partner agreed to come to the offices immediately with other partners to help the police determine what, if anything, had been taken. The manager thanked him deferentially.

Saturday, March 18th, 1995, 1826 local time, Makakilo City, Oahu
Marty pulled into the driveway of the address Uilani had given him. As he walked to the door, the pleasant scent of jasmine filled the spring air.

Blind dates weren't Marty's thing, and Uilani agreed, so they'd exchanged official pictures by mail. She called it a "fuzzy glasses date." She'd also told him that she was 5-foot-2, and she'd let her hair grow and no longer wore the pixie cut in the outdated, official photo.

Even after all the conversations, he still wasn't sure what to expect. But from working with Uilani, Marty she was smart and very good at her job. *What's not to like?* He smiled as he approached the door.

"Hi!" Uilani swung open the door, ready to meet him. She knew already that Marty, a San Diego native, was a former collegiate swimmer at USC and an avid surfer. He'd been candid when he told her his wife had left him because she didn't like what he did for a living. The picture hadn't done him justice. She liked what she saw. *Where have you been all my life?*

"Uilani, you look lovely. These are for you." Marty's eyes drank in the petite woman in front of him, and he handed her a dozen pink roses mixed with fragrant small white flowers.

"Oh wow. These are beautiful." Uilani held them up and sniffed them. "Mmmmm," she exhaled. "If you'll come in, I'll put them in a vase, and then we can go." The pink roses—unlike, for instance, white ones—said that this was a real date, at least as far as Marty was concerned. It was 1995, so sex, if not yet on the table, was at least on the menu. He had no way of knowing that what Uilani was thinking was, *I want this hunk of a man to sweep me off my feet and carry me into the bedroom to make mad passionate love to me.*

Marty followed her into the kitchen and was fascinated by the shape of her body—wide, muscular shoulders and a back that tapered to a narrow waist. It was a surfer's body, and surfing was something they could enjoy together.

At the restaurant, after they'd finished eating, Marty enjoyed the texture of her hands as he held both of them. *I am going to play this carefully. There may be more here than a one-night stand!* "So, here's what's next. Based on an extensive reconnaissance of the local terrain, there's a great place for us to take a romantic stroll. I see the moon, what there is of it, is out." He looked in her eyes, which were smiling.

"You're on—let's go."

They walked to the overlook where they could hear the surf pounding the rocks a hundred feet below. Marty wrapped his arms around her waist as he stood behind her, and Uilani placed her hands on top of his. She leaned back and nestled her head just below his collarbone.

Her jet-black hair, blown by the soft sea breeze, tickled Marty's face as they stood enjoying the view. The smell of the sea, mixed with the delicate scents of hibiscus and jasmine, filled their nostrils. Marty put pressure on one side to twist her around to face him. She released his hands and held up a finger to make the gesture that said, "Wait a second." Then she put her hands on the back of his head, and pulled him in for a kiss.

Monday, March 20th, 1995, 1130 local time, U.S.S. Blue Ridge

When Marty arrived at his stateroom, he found a note taped to his door, asking him to stop by the boss's office. There was only one boss on *Blue Ridge,* and he wore three stars on his collar. Marty tossed his bag onto the rack in his stateroom and headed out, carrying his book with all his notes and a half-used pad.

The admiral waved Marty to one of the blue covered chairs in front of the steel desk. It was like many of the other offices in Seventh Fleet's spaces on *Blue Ridge*—blue tiled floors, with safes and tables bolted to the deck and bulkheads. Instead of four or six desks, the Admiral's office had one large steel desk, and a separate table covered with a green cloth.

"How'd it go?"

"It was a great conference. We had the special warfare guys from every command there, along with the Aussies and Brits. Our

SEAL teams and Marine Recon units are going to use the Brit's jungle training complex in Borneo and the Aussie's desert facility out near Darwin later this year."

"Glad to hear it. Nothing like training in terrain where we may have to operate."

"Admiral, sir, here's the big winner. The Thais, Filipinos and Singaporeans want to participate in a Special Forces-only exercise in Borneo. The wrap-up report, a preliminary exercise plan, and next-step recommendations should be in your in-box."

"I saw it. Thank you. Make it happen. Is there anything else I need to know?"

"Yes, sir. Rear Admiral Jeffers required I meet him in his office."

"Required?" The word got Maize's attention. His facial expression and tone said, "Tell me more."

"Sir, there was a message for me when I checked in asking me to call Jeffers' aide, who told me that Jeffers wanted to see me. I thought it was going to be about the conference. Instead, I got a very explicit guidance that was almost, but not quite, an order about not going off the reservation, which I was also directed to pass on to Captain Haman."

"That was out of line. You don't work for him."

"Yes, sir. I know that, and you know that, but I am not sure that he recognizes that nuance."

"That son of a bitch." The admiral winced, knowing he'd just violated one of the Navy flag officers' commandments: "Thou shalt not criticize a fellow flag officer in public."

"Sir, there's more and it gets worse." As Marty recounted the conversation, he tore off the sheets from the pad on which he had his written recounting of Jeffers' words. "Sir, this is not a transcript, but it is as close as I could make it. I wrote it as soon as

I could after the meeting. When we talked, the door was closed and there were no witnesses."

"Typical Jeffers. He's still an asshole." That was two criticisms in less than two minutes.

Admiral Maize pressed his intercom button. "Would you please ask Captain Haman to join us? Tell him it's important!"

Josh came in with a quizzical look on his face and holding a pad, assuming he needed to take notes.

"Have a seat." The admiral waited until Josh sat down. "Commander, I'm going to assume you told Captain Haman about the flag guidance you got from Rear Admiral Jeffers."

"Yes, sir, I did, but I did not share the second part of the conversation."

Josh glanced at Marty, giving him a 'What's going on?' look.

"I understand that Rear Admiral Jeffers is not one of your fans." The admiral held up his hand. "That is a statement, not a question, because it is unfair and inappropriate to ask you to comment on a flag officer. Tell me about what happened at Surigao City so I can have an intelligent conversation with someone."

Memories of 10 days of intense flying came back to Josh. In 1987, he had been the commanding officer of the helicopter squadron on *Midway* during an exercise in the Philippine Sea, southwest of Guam, using both ASW and special operations versions of the H-60 helicopter.

"Sir, a number of small islands just off the northern tip of Mindanao were hit hard by a typhoon. The battle group hurried over, with the intent of providing assistance. About a hundred miles out, I launched in one of the HH-60s to take a look at Dinagat Island, and another helo headed for the smaller islands around it. They were all a mess."

The excitement of the effort returned as Josh spoke. "I landed on Dinagat where Filipino Army troops were setting up large tents for shelter just outside the town of San Jose. Their commander informed me that the island had no power except for a few generators. The port captain said that the water was 60 feet deep by the piers. Back in the air, I flew around San Jose's harbor, scouting for sunken ships in the channel. On my way back to *Midway,* I reported our findings. The commanders of the frigates *Sides* and *Crommelin* came up on the radio and said they would dock at the pier in San Jose."

Maize said, "That's pretty standard, assuming they can get their ships safely into the port."

"Yes, sir. However, at the time, they worked for Jeffers, who was the escort force commander. He came on the air and said the harbor was too shallow and might be blocked by sunken fishing boats. He ordered the frigate captains not to go into the harbor, so both skippers launched their helos to pick up the harbor pilots and conduct a reconnaissance of the harbor. When *Midway* was about 30 miles off the coast, the skippers radioed they could have their two ships dockside in a little over an hour. Jeffers, back on the destroyer *Hewitt,* again ordered his two frigate skippers not to go into San Jose. One skipper replied that our allies needed humanitarian aid and it was his duty to provide it. The frigate skipper implied that if it cost him his career, so be it."

Admiral Maize held up his hand. "Do you know if any of this is in writing?"

"Yes, sir, it is all documented in the after-action reports, including the radio transmissions."

"Do you have a copy?"

"Yes, sir, I have both my squadron's and Carrier Group Five's as well."

"As soon as you can, please make me a copy of each."

"Yes, sir, I will. Admiral, you might want to chat with Admiral Grindl, who was the battle group commander at the time. He could give you his perspective."

"I know Admiral Grindl well. He's retired, but I can track him down. Continue."

"Yes, sir." Josh looked at Marty, who was nodding confirmation. "The H-46 helicopters from our supply ship flew the Marine detachment and several of our plane captains to clean up the pier and keep people out of the LZ for safety purposes. As the frigates approached the harbor, their helicopters scouted for sunken ships."

He described how, over the next 10 days, seven of his squadron's eight helos, plus the two from the frigates and the two H-46s from the supply ship, flew almost 20 hours a day. Navy hospital corpsmen were flown to villages all over the island, where they triaged the injured. The most badly hurt were flown out to *Midway.* Those who needed intermediate-level care were flown to the pier and treated in the ERs set up in the frigates' helicopter hangars.

Helicopters on their way back to the island brought volunteers from the battle group to help get the Filipino hospitals operating again, along with medical supplies, food, and Jerry cans of fuel for their generators. The American helicopters also carried Filipino government officials, who organized the relief effort throughout the province. Josh didn't describe the dangers of flying in and out of very small clearings in helicopters that were either at, or over maximum takeoff weights. Despite the difficult conditions and helo crews averaging 14 to 16 hours a day in the cockpit, there were no accidents.

Admiral Maize interrupted, "It was good work and made us a lot of friends. What about Jeffers?"

The Simushir Island Incident

Josh grinned inadvertently. Jeffers' crew had dubbed him "Captain Chicken of the Sea." Jeffers loved Chicken of the Sea tuna fish and had cases of the canned fish in his cabin. But the nick-name had another meaning. Jeffers shied away from any ship maneuver that might entail risk. He only allowed flight operations when the seas were calm, and he never allowed the ship to heel more than five degrees during maneuvering drills. Between his risk-averse command style, and his tendency to mete out punishment for minor infractions that his sailors thought were chicken shit, "Captain Chicken of the Sea" was not a term of endearment.

None of this he told Admiral Maize. "Sir, late on the first full day, Jeffers came up on the air with his call sign Bentley Zero Zero Actual and asked for situation reports every four hours."

"Are you shitting me?"

"No, sir. Jeffers insisted on a detailed situation report from me as the helo squadron commander, so I gave him one while I was flying. He radioed back, saying I didn't give him enough data to determine what to do next, which was odd because he wasn't directing anything! The guys in *Midway's* combat information center provided the operational control, based on directions from Admiral Grindl. My biggest concern, besides helping the relief effort, was aircraft availability and safety. Hell, I didn't know how many people we treated; or how many sorties or hours we'd flown; or how many of our people were on the beach until I saw the tallies a couple of days later. Jeffers again ordered me to get him all the data within two hours. That's when Admiral Grindl came on the air and told me to ignore Bentley Double Zero's instructions."

Admiral Maize chuckled. He could imagine Admiral Grindl in the flag command center hearing Jeffers on the air, then grabbing the mike and countermanding the order. "That was it?"

"No, sir. Jeffers kept his ship's helos grounded. The helo det O-in-C on the *Hewitt* managed to get airborne on the fourth day on a make-believe maintenance test flight. When he landed on the *Midway,* supposedly to get parts, he told us that Jeffers had ordered him not to fly, and to keep his two SH-60s in reserve. Both helicopters were fully operational. We just shook our heads, because we could have really used those two birds."

The admiral looked disgusted.

"All the ships except Jeffers' got Meritorious Unit Citations. The captains from the *Sides* and *Crommelin* got meritorious Bronze Stars, along with the corpsmen and doctors. Pilots and air crewmen received Air Medals, and some were awarded Distinguished Flying Crosses. All of which were well deserved, sir. But Admiral Grindl specifically ordered his staff to make sure no medals went to anyone on the *Hewitt,* which was Jeffers' ship."

Admiral Maize's eyes narrowed. "Are you sure about that last bit?"

"Yes, sir. There is an addendum to the battle group's final after-action report listing all the awards."

"I'm looking forward to reading it." Maize took off his glasses and cleaned them. "What I am about to say cannot leave this room. Understood?"

The "Aye, aye, sirs" were almost simultaneous.

"Commander Cabot has told me Jeffers made inappropriate comments about the promotion board on which he was a member and that selected you for captain. By doing so, he broke the sanctity of promotion board discussions."

Admiral Maize was tapping the table in front of him with his forefinger. Each tap made a noticeable thunk. He was clearly trying to control his growing anger. He knew that Jeffers' sugar daddy and former Naval Academy roommate had been the Chief of Naval Personnel and had pressured CINCPAC to take Jeffers. Maize also knew people who worked with Jeffers who said he was an incompetent asshole. Unfortunately, his sugar daddy and fellow Academy classmates managed to ensure he was promoted. Jeffers' comments about the selection board, bad though they were, wouldn't be enough to shit-can him unless CINCPAC had enough other ammunition to force Jeffers out of the Navy. "For the life of me, I can't figure out how he got to be a flag officer," Maize muttered under his breath, then looked at both officers. "As far as the events off Surigao go, I am not sure if CINCPAC knows the whole story, but he is good friends with Admiral Grindl, so he will know shortly. If there are any additional inappropriate conversations with Jeffers, I want to be apprised right away. Now get out of here—you two should have work to do!"

Both men smiled at Maize's mock annoyance. "Yes, sir." Again, the words were almost synchronized.

2123 local time, on board U.S.S. Blue Ridge

The new khaki shirt was spread out on the bed. On the desk behind him, Josh had, in a loose pile, his name tag, rank insignia, wings and ribbons waiting to be pinned on the shirt so it was ready to put on in the morning. It was the first uniform shirt he'd bought that he didn't need to have taken in at the waist. It was, he told Rebekah in a tape he would mail tomorrow, recognition that his body was changing as he aged. The tight stomach and six pack of his twenties and thirties was gone, despite his vigorous workouts. Josh ruefully smiled. He was still growing. Instead of upward, it was outward!

Chapter 5: RETURN VISIT

Tuesday, March 21ˢᵗ, 1995, 0900 local time, Nampo, DPRK

It was the first day of spring, and the temperature was 10 degrees Celsius, so Major Kim walked from the train station to the naval base. The comparative warmth was a nice contrast to the damp, freezing cold of windy Simushir.

For the train ride, he'd taken Hemingway's *For Whom the Bell Tolls* from the box in his parents' garden and wrapped it with a new cover made from a two day old copy of *Joson Inmingung,* the official newspaper of the Korean People's Army. If anyone asked why he was reading the novel, he would say he was practicing his English. If a police officer examined the book, Kim would be able to point out that it had the required stamp and serial number allowing a few trusted citizens of the Democratic People's Republic of Korea to own and read such a book. Without these, he could be imprisoned for possessing and reading Hemingway's Pulitzer-Prize-winning novel.

But for most of the ride, rather than reading, Kim watched at the countryside rolling by.

The Simushir Island Incident

Seeing a farmer digging a hole at the edge of a field brought back a flood of memories. *Now I see! My parents buried these books before they died. They were probably denounced and demoted for daring to suggest that there are great authors besides those on Kim Jong-Il's very limited list. And after that harsh interrogation that cleared me, I was sent to work for Thaek as a way, I think, for me to prove my loyalty. And, when the government decides I am no longer valuable, then they'll either kill me or send me to a re-education camp. My parents never told me about the books, and that protected me. Now I understand why the interrogators asked so many questions about what I read. But I am sure my parents wanted me to find the box. It was buried near the perilla, and my parents knew I loved to sniff the minty leaves.*

Kim closed his eyes as he thanked his parents for their courage in hiding these books. They must have realized that the Ministry of Education stamps, authorizing them to have the novels, would not be enough to save them. Now that they were his, he was legally supposed to go through the re-authorization process. If he didn't, possession of the books could lead to a death sentence.

He entered a well-furnished office, which was much nicer than anything he'd ever seen before. Major Kim was surprised to see both Admiral Pak and General Jang waiting. Admiral Pak waved him towards a chair in front of a table piled with food, mineral water and tea.

"Thank you, sir." *In a country where many have very little food, the people in power have a lot,* Kim reflected.

"Did you enjoy your stay in Hong Kong?"

"Yes, sir. I don't know whom to thank for the money. It was more than enough."

"You're welcome. We thought you and your men deserved a treat. What did you do in Hong Kong?"

"I bought some clothes, a pair of Nikon binoculars and a camera." *These men are my sponsors, but they have their own agenda. How much should I say? How far can I trust them? Hong Kong was a great place to practice my English and Chinese, and it is so different than North Korea. It is free!* The clothes he'd bought were much better than what he could get in Pyongyang. He kept them in a footlocker in his closet.

When Kim had led his men down the gangway into Hong Kong, a representative from the Kuril Island Development Corporation, rather than a member of the North Korean consulate, had met them. All they had with them were their packs—their weapons and ammunition were left locked in the old torpedo magazine on Simushir so as not to violate Hong Kong laws. Their packs went into the back of the two vans, and on the way to their hotel, they were told that each man would find four sets of civilian clothes in the right sizes waiting for him in his hotel room.

At the hotel, the representative, who never introduced himself, had given Major Kim an envelope for each man containing money to pay for meals, along with their North Korean passports with the appropriate Hong Kong entry stamps and visas. The rooms were prepaid. Major Kim was warned to make sure his men didn't create any incidents; if they did, the perpetrators would be dealt with harshly when they returned home.

Kim had mustered his men each day at 0800, 1400 and 2200, and he'd ordered each man to choose a "travel buddy." He reminded them that if a man defected, both families would suffer.

Kim had been astonished by what he saw on his forays into the city. The bright, electrified nighttime streetscapes were unlike anything in North Korean cities. Hong Kong enjoyed a robust free press and a thriving movie industry as part of the British stewardship Hong Kong would continue to enjoy until 1997, when governorship reverted to China, in accordance with the Nanking treaty of 1842. He'd seen newspapers from dozens of countries and found stores that sold books in many languages, including Korean —books not available in North Korea. Kim had discovered he liked martial arts movies, and had taken all his men to see Jet Li in *Fist of Legend.*

After three days and nights, a message had arrived, directing them all to the airport for a flight to Dalian. Then they'd traveled by train to the border town of Zhenxing, and by bus across the Yalu into North Korea. Their international passports had been taken from them and their North Korean internal passports returned. Then they were brought to an isolated barracks, told to keep honing their hand-to-hand combat skills, and excused from their normal duties. They were not allowed to mingle with any other soldiers or personnel.

Admiral Pak inclined his head. "Tell us about Simushir."

There was not much Kim could add to his official report. Snow, cold—more snow, more cold, and wind.

The trek had taken a miserable eight days instead of the planned six. At the end of each day, the men had been exhausted from the effort of breaking trail in the ice-encrusted snow, their bodies bruised and battered. Stretching out their food supply contributed to their exhaustion, and Kim had wondered if they were going to make it back to Broutana Bay. The 11-day ride on the freighter to Hong Kong had given their bodies much needed time to recover.

"We want you to go back to Simushir."

I figured as much. They may not like my demands.

"Not right away, toward the end of April, when the weather is warmer and much of the snow has melted. Our Dear Leader wants to know more about the island."

"Is this going to be a covert reconnaissance or an exploration?"

"Good question. Why?"

"If we are going back to Simushir to explore, then we can use vehicles, which will let us complete the task much faster."

"What kind of trucks would you need?"

"Trucks won't work on the island. The only roads are around Broutana Bay. Here's what we'll need." Kim pulled brochures and a spec sheet, along with a price list, from his briefcase. "These are called MULEs, Multi-Use Light Equipment." He pronounced the name of the small two-seat vehicle in English, then switched back to Korean. "They are perfect for moving around rough terrain."

He waited while Admiral Pak and General Jang flipped through the brochures and studied the large glossy photos. "They're made by the Japanese firm of Kawasaki. We need the four-wheel drive versions with the most powerful engines and the optional big tires. The platform on the back can hold equipment for two men, fuel, and spare parts for two weeks of operations. We will need training on how to maintain them so we can service them in the field."

Admiral Pak tossed the brochure on the table. "Where did you get these booklets?"

"I saw a red MULE in a Kawasaki motorcycle dealership and examined this amazing machine in detail. The brochure says they come in dark green or brown, good for seasonal camouflage."

"Anything else?"

"Yes, sir, a question. Why do I need to go back? It is a Russian island, and surely they have explored it. They should be able to tell us everything we need to know."

General Jang steepled his fingers and looked steadily at Kim as he answered. "A company owned by our government has a lease from the Russians to build a fishing support facility on the island. It is a commercial venture, but through the wisdom of our Dear Leader, we received permission to have the People's Army be there to provide security for the business as well as to train. We need you to explore the island so we can learn more about its potential to serve our needs."

What Jang said was not completely accurate. In reality, the lease gave them permission to "protect their assets from intruders and criminals."

Using the People's Army's Special Operations Forces to provide protection for a methamphetamine factory and heroin refining facility was stretching the intent of the clause in the lease. Their Dear Leader really wanted the soldiers to protect an operation putting millions into his Swiss bank accounts.

"When you go back, two civil engineers and two geologists will accompany you."

"Are they fit?"

"Yes. They are all in the Army."

Kim thought that over. It made sense that the Army would need geologists and engineers to help build the tunnels the People's Army uses to house submarines, airplanes, tanks and artillery. The country was, in many places, one immense cave.

"What are we looking for?"

"Places enemy Marines and special forces could land that will need to be defended." Jang's training drove his answers. "Hiding places on the island. Locate any cave entrances which we may explore later, and evaluate how we can use terrain to train special forces soldiers."

"In that case we'll also need radios. We need to be able to communicate with Broutana Bay."

"No radios." Jang was definite.

Ah, they're afraid of American eavesdropping aircraft and satellites. "How will we communicate with the facility?"

Pak looked at his friend Jang before he spoke. "We can provide short range radios that will be monitored by the facility manager.

And the manager can communicate with us via secure satellite phone."

Kim nodded. This was progress. "General, can you provide the MULEs?"

"We'll have them on the same ship taking you to Simushir. We will arrange for a technician who can train your men on how to maintain the MULES. He will stay at the base to make repairs and will be well supplied with spare parts."

"I want the same team, plus the rest of the platoon, so I'll have thirty-six men." Major Kim was enjoying making demands and hearing "yes" instead of "no."

"Agreed. How long do you think it will take you to complete a survey?"

"It depends on the weather and how long we stop at any one place. I estimate three weeks, more or less. With the MULEs, we can carry more supplies, and if we run out, we can drive back to Broutana Bay to get more. If we have radios, we can call Broutana Bay for a small resupply convoy. The island is not that big. On the reconnaissance, I will take eleven men plus the two engineers and two geologists. At two men per MULE, that's eight vehicles. I suggest you buy at least twelve MULES, or better, sixteen. The spares will be left at the base to support the remaining twenty-four men. We will need a building for a shop to maintain the vehicles and store our equipment and supplies. If we are to prepare defensive positions, we'll need more ammunition, mortars, and rocket propelled grenades."

"Done. I will arrange with the facility's manager to have a building to house only your team and to have workers repair one of the old buildings for you to use as a storage facility and workshop. I understand you left your weapons in the torpedo magazine. Is this acceptable?"

"Yes."

The Simushir Island Incident

On the train back to Haeju, Major Kim's mind raced. *Do they not realize that more of my men will see the West and be exposed to the lies of the regime? It will be impossible for the Dear Leader's secret police to keep them all quiet unless they are killed. How can I prevent them from being murdered by our own leaders?*

Friday, March 24th, 1995, 0415 local time, U.S.S. Blue Ridge

Jack D'Onofrio arrived on *Blue Ridge* well before sunrise, with a briefcase chained to his wrist. After having his orders stamped and the date and time of his arrival recorded, he dropped his bags off in a corner of the flag mess; he'd have to wait for the chief steward to arrive to be assigned a stateroom. Jack's next stop was the Operations and Plans office. He hoped they hadn't changed the code as he used the tip of his index finger to push in the six numbers. The cipher lock released and Jack turned the knob. Thankfully, no one had locked the handle. Inside, Jack flipped on the lights and cleared a space on the four desks grouped together and used as a table. Then he detached and unlocked the briefcase, and withdrew a package that consisted of several sealed courier envelopes.

His orders had been amended so he could pick up classified material in Hawaii and hand-carry it to *Blue Ridge*. Those same orders had designated him as a courier with the highest priority, and he'd been given a seat on the first plane out. It would have been better if he'd taken the second, for when a fire warning light came on, the C-141 had diverted to Wake Island. The problem proved to be a broken wire, and the crew had decided to fly to Japan where it could be fixed rather than waiting for several days on Wake for parts and a technician. Instead of arriving early in the evening, the C-141 had landed at 0207. Then the duty officer had to wake up the base transportation officer and find a driver. On the plus side, the 40-mile drive from Yokota to Yokosuka that during the day could take as long as two to three hours, at 0300 in the morning took only fifty-five minutes.

With scissors he found lying on one of the desks, Jack cut the packing tape binding the envelopes together. Two were addressed to the N6, the third was for the staff's intelligence officer. It was set aside.

He opened both envelopes addressed to N6, and dumped out 8 x 10 photos taken of Simushir Island, along with an inventory for someone from the N6 shop to use as a checklist to verify that all the classified material had arrived. Jack slid the inventory back in the envelope and began to sort the pictures.

Images of the whole island went into one pile. Enlargements of ships in the harbor went into another. A third had blowups of the buildings around Broutana Bay. The fourth pile had photos taken through a periscope of a Russian *Petya II*-class corvette and a North Korean submarine.

Sorting done, Jack went back to the flag mess and made a cup of coffee for himself. The stewards were just taking a batch of cinnamon rolls out of the oven, and he was offered two. Back in the N6 spaces, Jack studied the pictures and didn't pay any attention to the clock.

As he entered numbers on the cipher lock, Josh saw light shining from under the door. It wasn't usual for one or two of the enlisted men to be in early—or for the last person leaving to simply forget to turn out the lights. What did surprise him was the person studying the photos spread out on the desks.

"Jack, when did you get here?"

D'Onofrio answered without looking up. "About three this morning. My body is still on California time."

"How'd you get active duty orders so fast?"

"I have my ways."

The Simushir Island Incident

"Uh huh, and how long are you going to grace us with your presence this time?"

"Two weeks. I can get it extended, if needed. Josh, I just couldn't stay away. This Simushir thing is a puzzle that needs solving."

"It is. And it's good to have you on board."

Jack held up a picture. "I'm just trying to figure out which photos are the best ones for the morning briefing."

Marty showed up, and after a quick hello all three loomed over the photos spread on the desk. "This one," Marty said. "This one shows work on the pier and two ships in the harbor." Josh tapped a another. "In this one, it looks like they've reopened a road to a structure they've begun to rebuild."

Jack unfolded a small map showing the route that North Korean subs had taken between Mayang-do and the Russian coast, and placed beside it a photo taken from a submarine's periscope. "So far, there have been at least four trips by *Romeos* to the Russian coast on the west side of the Sea of Japan. Same routine each time: transport commandos, put them ashore for three or four days, then recover them. While the sub is waiting, a Russian plane and a *Petya II*-class corvette or an *Udaloy*-class destroyer come out to play for three to four hours each day. We are getting great intel on their noise signatures and Russian anti-submarine warfare tactics."

Josh's cobalt-blue eyes were focused on the row of photos. "It doesn't take commandos to establish a resupply base for merchant ships. I think the admiral is right; we just keep watching and monitoring, and sooner rather than later, something will pop."

"Yeah, but—" A ringing phone interrupted the conversation, and Marty picked it up. "Commander Cabot.... Yes." Marty's sudden, clumsy movement to sit in a chair while he was listening to the phone raised alarm bells in Josh's mind. "I'll be there as soon as I can and will call when I land."

Josh could see tears welling up in his friend's eyes. "What happened?"

"My dad just had a heart attack. It doesn't look good. I need to go back to the States." Marty stood up, looking dazed. Josh hugged the man who was one of his two best friends. Jack D'Onofrio was the other.

"God, I'm so sorry. Marty, go pack. I'll get the admin officer to issue emergency leave orders and get you a seat on a non-stop flight back to LA."

"Okay…thanks." It was a weak answer from a warrior.

Tuesday, March 28th, 1995, 1953 local time, Los Angeles

From where he sat on a wooden bench, Jaime Gomez watched his pushers work the park. Each took up his nightly position on a bench or a low concrete wall. Customers would amble up, and at some point in their elaborate, pantomime hand greeting, cash and a baggie of heroin would be exchanged. Elsewhere in the park, Gomez had two more distributors, who sold syringes for two dollars a syringe. Gomez paid five dollars for a stolen box of 24 new hypodermic needles; it was his personal attempt to minimize the spread of AIDs by providing low-cost, sterile syringes so his customers didn't have to reuse old ones. Dead addicts made poor customers.

His pushers only carried a dozen baggies at a time for two reasons. One, it minimized the potential sentence if the pusher was tried and convicted. Two, it reduced his potential losses if they were arrested and the drugs confiscated as evidence. He never had syringes or drugs in his own car or on his person. Instead, he had a mule on call, who could be on the scene to resupply a pusher in just a few minutes.

The Simushir Island Incident

It was a good night at this location, one of the four that Gomez "owned." They were, in fact, "franchises" issued to him by the 18th Street gang, whose leaders could, if they so desired, give any or all of them to someone else at any time.

By nine p.m. the six pushers in the park had been resupplied three times. At five dollars a bag, he figured his take here was going to be, along with needle sales, north of $1,200.

A normal night brought in a grand in cash. For estimating purposes, a week was worth $7,000. The math was simple—this location, like the other three, generated $28,000 a month, $336,000 per year per location, roughly $1,344,000 per year. After costs, he netted over a half million in cash.

Gomez was also "paid", via an additional discount on the drugs, to run one of the two cutting-and-bagging facilities for the 18th Street Gang. Satisfied all was going well at this park, he drove to the building to check on the second shift.

Men and women worked in their underwear. All wore the same cheap, foam shower shoes and painter's masks to prevent them from inhaling and becoming addicted to the powder in the air. At the end of the shift, the workers were allowed to take a shower if they chose. Before they exited the building, each employee was patted down. On random occasions, Gomez conducted cavity searches to send a message—he would not tolerate stealing.

One time, after he pulled three baggies out of a woman's vagina, he tied the offender to a chair in the storeroom. After two hard slaps she confessed that her brother was an addict and she was helping support his habit. Rather than fire her, he told her that every day she would be issued whatever her brother needed and the cost would be taken out of her pay. What she didn't know was that her bags were mixed with crushed aspirin to increase the chances that the young man would die. One morning, the woman told him that she no longer needed the baggies because her brother was dead When he heard the news, Gomez just nodded, caring only that the message "do not steal my drugs" was clear.

The package Dae Ho Muk received at his UPS store P.O. box included a map, the address and instructions to kill the rival operation's guards and the manager, but let the workers go. He was also supposed to destroy the lab. A box containing Semtex, a plastic explosive with which he was very familiar, and detonators arrived separately. To keep the telltale almond-like smell of the explosive from seeping out, each brick was packed in three layers of Zip-Loc bags before it went into the box.

He did not know where his orders came from, only that he was here in the U.S. to carry out direct action missions. He was to leave no witnesses. If he was arrested, he was on his own. While he was in the U.S., his family in North Korea received extra food rations and double his salary. Should he defect, his family would be arrested and taken to a re-education camp. If he was killed, they would get a stipend and told their son was a hero to the DPRK.

Muk parked his car about a hundred yards from the entrance to the factory and walked up to the guard. He stuck his Tokarev in the man's face before the man could react and told him to open the door. As soon as the guard complied, Muk put a bullet in his head, then shot a second guard stationed just inside the door. He paused to pull down his ski mask, which was folded up on his ski hat.

One of the two guards patrolling the tables spotted the black-clad intruder, shouted a warning and started to raise his AK-47. The second guard also started to unsling his AK-47. Before either could pull the trigger, double taps from Muk's Tokarev into each man's chest put both guards down.

When the shooting started, some of the workers screamed, and all of them dropped to the floor. A fifth guard came out of Gomez's office, firing five high-and-wide rounds from the AK-47 at his hip before two red splotches appeared on his wife-beater T-shirt. He, too, fell to the floor, dying. To make sure the guards were no longer a threat, Muk fired a round into each one's head. Then, at gunpoint, he commanded the five male workers to drag the bodies into the storeroom, where bricks of uncut heroin were stacked three-deep from floor to ceiling on one side. On the opposite wall, barrels of alcohol and cardboard boxes of small plastic bags, painter's masks and shower shoes were neatly arranged. Once all the workers put their clothes on, he locked them in the storeroom with the corpses and the heroin, and made sure it wouldn't open by kicking several wedges in place.

Alone, Muk used det cord to burn off the hinges of the floor safe in the office and removed stacks of bills wrapped with the standard American Banking Association currency bands. Red bands denoted there were 100 five-dollar bills in each bundle.

On one of the tables, Muk arranged 15 stacks, each consisting of four packages of five-dollar bills. The packages with the mustard-colored bands, denoting they held 100 one-hundred-dollar bills, and those with the brown bands, signifying 100 fifties, went into his own pack.

As Gomez walked up to his building, he saw the security guards were gone and there were blood smears on the ground. It looked like someone was muscling in on his turf.

The only drawback to running an illegal operation was that he was on his own. He couldn't call the cops, and if he asked for help from the organization, they'd decide he was too weak to keep his territory. He drew his pistol, a full size .45 caliber Model 1911A1 and cautiously pushed the door open. No one was in the production area.

Dae Ho Muk heard the door open and crouched below a table that gave him a good view of the door. If Gomez heard the pop of a suppressed Tokarev, his brain didn't have time to process the sound before it was pulped by a hollow point bullet.

With the intruder down, Muk scanned the street for more attackers before closing the door. He took three sand colored one-kilo bricks from his backpack that any explosives expert would have instantly recognized as the Czech-invented plastic explosive, Semtex.

Muk kicked the wedges out from the storeroom door and let out the workers. In Spanish, he told them there was one stack of money for each of them on the table. He warned them not to call the police or he would hunt them down. Any of them who were in the country illegally and wouldn't dare call 911.

Alone once more, Muk pulled off his ski mask and levered out one of the bricks in the middle of the stack of heroin, replacing it with a kilo of Semtex. Next, he pushed in a blasting cap for which he'd cut a three-meter det cord "tail." He set three bricks and attached all the det cord tails to a detonator, then set its timer for seven minutes. Just before he exited the storeroom, he used a pocketknife to slit open several bottles of alcohol.

He was a block away when the Semtex went off. Neighboring buildings were rocked by the concussion. The size of the fireball assured him that the building and its drugs were incinerated.

In his home country, killing people was Muk's job. He enjoyed the challenge of arriving unannounced and delivering a death blow to his targets. It occurred to him, however, that in the U.S. he could become rich as a hired killer. The Dear Leader's propaganda was wrong—capitalism did have its benefits.

Friday, April 7th, 1995, 1156 local time, Honolulu
Marty's sunglasses fogged from the heat and humidity as he stepped off the plane from LA. By the time he walked into the

baggage area, the glasses had cleared, and he saw Uilani running toward him.

She hugged him tightly before they kissed, passionately. Uilani put her head on his chest. "Marty, I'm so sorry to hear about your dad."

"The good news is I got to say good-bye before he died."

The couple held hands until they got to her car. Marty tossed his bag on the back seat. "Where are we going?"

"My house." Uilani didn't say out loud, *Because I am going to fuck your brains out! I'm pretty sure you need it, and I know I do.*

Afterwards, Uilani encouraged Marty to talk. At first he focused on his father, whom he'd deeply admired for his dedication to his job. Ed Cabot could have found jobs that paid him more, but he liked teaching. It was his passion and he never wavered from it.

Late in the afternoon, Uilani loaded two surfboards on the rack of her minivan, and the couple headed toward Sandy Beach. There, between rides, Marty continued to unwind and talk about his past relationships. They'd sit on the boards, waiting for a wave, and Marty would unload, starting with his ex-wife.

Uilani listened, and realized that Marty loved what he did and wasn't going to give it up. She sensed he felt guilty; he thought he was being selfish about his career. Now she knew the avenue to his heart. Her mission: reassure this wonderful man that she was as proud as he was, if not prouder, of his dedication and accomplishments. And she would take what came, no matter what.

Monday, April 10th, 1995, 0615 local time, U.S.S. Blue Ridge

Josh was already at his desk, having come in early enough to take a quick glance through the messages before breakfast and the morning intelligence brief. He heard the greetings as Marty came into the N6 compartment, so he came out of his private office. "Welcome back to the salt mines."

"Thanks."

"I am very sorry to hear about your dad. Are you sure your sister can handle everything?"

"I'm sure. We sorted things out after the funeral. All my dad had was his two-bedroom condominium, a Mercedes 300D, stocks, and some personal stuff. After we probate the will, we'll split the mortgage payment on the condominium until we decide whether to sell or lease it. She doesn't want the Mercedes because she's got four kids and needs a van, so when I get back to the states, I'll get it!"

"And, the rest of the trip…how did it go?"

"I stopped in Hawaii and did a little surfing. Uilani says hello."

Josh noted that his friend seemed less wound up than usual. He suspected he knew the reason—Marty was in love. He hoped this time it would have a happy ending. In the past, he'd spent hours talking with Marty after a breakup. Each time, it tore at Josh's heart. "Is this getting serious, or is she just another babe in a port?" Josh's sparkling eyes told his friend he was teasing.

"I am going to invite Uilani to come here or to meet me in LA for a week or so the next time I can take leave. Does that answer your question?"

"Yes."

For the next few weeks, work was going to be Marty's refuge as he dealt with his grief. Even when separated by thousands of miles, he and his father had been close. "What's the latest on Simushir?" he asked.

"Come to the briefing, and you shall find out!"

* * *

The Simushir Island Incident

Josh began his portion of the brief with the usual reminder that the information was Top Secret/SCI and should not to be shared with anyone unless authorized by the admiral, Marty or himself.

On the screen was a satellite photo taken the day before. As Jack D'Onofrio adjusted the focus, a question came from the staff.

"Captain, what's a caldera?" Josh recognized the voice of a new supply officer who'd been on the staff less than a month.

"A caldera is formed when a volcano's magma chamber collapses deep underground as the magma and gas vent out. It leaves a deep crater—really, a sinkhole—that, over time, fills with water. Simushir has two, the landlocked Zavaritzk Caldera and Broutana Bay."

Jack put up a photo of the harbor on the projector, and Josh tapped the northern end of the island with his pointer. "The Kuril Island Development Company has made the entrance channel deeper and wider, so it is now approximately 115 feet wide and, based on the ships that come into the harbor, at least 60 feet deep. We estimate that there are between 75 and 100 men working on the island, and they've been busy. They have just brought in ..."— Jack changed slides—"...large generators." The image showed two diesel generators, one in the air as it was being slung over the side of a ship, and one on the pier. "These are mounted on giant sleds with temporary wheels, which suggests they may also want to move them around."

Jack plopped another slide onto the projector. "These new portable buildings were just brought ashore and are similar to those used by oil companies in the Arctic. Until now, everyone has been living on a small freighter anchored off to the east of the piers. That ship is now gone. Our spooks in McLean are working on getting us details on the buildings. We know that everything is being bought through firms in Hong Kong. And according to the Brits, all the workers boarded ships in Hong Kong." Josh nodded for Jack to change slides. "If you look at the northwestern side of the bay well away from the old base, you will notice a new, rebuilt structure where there used to be an abandoned whale-oil processing facility. We can also tell it has a newly refurbished pier by comparing it to photos taken two years ago. A road along the shoreline connects it to the old Soviet base.

"Photos taken by P-3s have helped us identify each vessel that has stopped at Broutana Bay, and to be honest, right now everything seems to be on the up-and-up. Nonetheless, Simushir will continue to be a location of interest."

After the meeting, Josh was summoned to the admiral's office, where he found Marty Cabot already there. Admiral Edward Maize had a very serious look on his face when he said, "Marty, tell Josh what you just told me."

"When Uilani and I were having lunch at the O Club, Rear Admiral Jeffers came by. He told Uilani and me that we needed to 'stick to our knitting'. He said, and I quote, 'Some half-assed renegade captain who doesn't have the brains to be an ensign shouldn't be involved in a State Department matter.' He added that if I wanted to make Captain, I should not associate with or participate in any operations that encroach on the State Department's areas of responsibility." Marty took a deep breath. "And then he said that if we were not careful, we could ruin the career of a very promising three star."

"It is so nice that Admiral Jeffers is worried about my career." The admiral made a face to emphasize the sarcasm in his voice. "And will Uilani testify under oath to what Jeffers said?"

"Yes, sir—she will do so with pleasure." Marty was adamant. "She hates Jeffers' guts because he treats people like dirt, and he ridiculed her team's analyses in front of CINCPAC, even though events proved they were spot on. Most people just shut up when

Jeffers goes after you because they are afraid of what he'll do to their careers."

"Thank you, gentlemen. I'll handle this with CINCPAC. Now I want to move on to a different subject. CINCPAC is going to be here on Monday, along with Jake Garza, the DEA liaison agent assigned to his staff. He's a West Pointer who did two tours in Vietnam as a platoon and company commander with the 101st Airborne. They want a private briefing. Apparently, the DEA can trace some of the opium shipments from Southeast Asia to North Korea, but then they lose track of it until the junk shows up in the U.S. They've got some ideas they want to bounce off the two of you."

Thursday, April 13th, 1995, 1012 local time, Washington, D.C.

Representative Steven Higgins walked towards the podium. The left wing of the Democratic Party had been looking to bring legislation with specific content forward for several years now, and were gambling that Higgins, a graduate of the United States Naval Academy, was the perfect person to cosponsor and introduce it.

Higgins was now making more than three times his old public defender salary, and wealthy constituents and donors quietly opened doors to other lucrative sources of income. Every time he looked at his portfolio, it reassured him that he was on his way to becoming a rich man.

He'd bought the tailored charcoal grey suit, pale blue shirt with French cuffs, and the red and blue striped tie at Brooks Brothers just for this speech. The cameras were going to record what he—Steven Higgins—had to say.

At the podium, Higgins turned to the Speaker of the House of Representatives, a Republican, who nodded and rapped the gavel sharply two times. "The Honorable Steven Higgins from the Second District of Wisconsin has the floor."

Higgins took a deep breath. This was his chance to put his name on a piece of legislation that could change America's defense posture and significantly reduce its defense budget. The courtroom had taught him how to speak persuasively to a jury of 12 men and women whose decisions would affect the life of his client. In court, his tone had to be measured, with the right amount of passion for the innocence of his clients. This was no different. His clients were the citizens of the United States and the tax burden they had to bear. The jury were his fellow representatives. Higgins was speaking on the second-largest stage in the U.S.—only the president had a bigger "bully pulpit"—and he was confident his words would be heard around the world.

"My fellow representatives, today it is my honor and pleasure to introduce H.R. Bill 1269. It is cosponsored by five of my fellow representatives and is called the Foreign Entanglements Reduction Act. At great cost in blood and treasure, America has won the Cold War; the conflict President Kennedy called the 'long, twilight struggle.' The Soviet Union is no more. It dissolved four years ago on December 26th, 1991, and it is a shadow of its former self. The Russian Federation is no longer a superpower. Surely, it is time that our national strategy and our national priorities reflected that fact. It is time that the American people began to enjoy the fruits of that victory. Tax monies once spent, year after year, 'to provide for the common defense,' can now be spent—*should* now be spent —'to promote the general welfare,' or to pay down the national debt, a matter about which my esteemed Republican colleagues often speak yet rarely act."

This last sentence produced a small ripple of laughter from the floor and a lone but clearly-heard whistle from the gallery. "H.R. 1269 is a landmark bill because it offers the United States the means to disentangle itself from the alliances that could drag our country into an unwanted and unnecessary war similar to the one in which I fought. It will bring home tens of thousands of men and women in our armed forces now serving abroad. HR 1269 reduces the risk they will become targets and killed or maimed unnecessarily in an incident that may cause us to act—or worse, overreact—inappropriately, as we have done so many times before. This bill will save hundreds of billions of dollars over the next decade."

Higgins looked around the chamber. It was only three quarters full, but those present on the floor and the people in the packed gallery were paying attention. "If passed, with the exception of NATO, H.R. 1269 ends all participation by the U.S. Armed Forces in military exercises outside the United States. The bill lists by name the exercises that will no longer be funded. It requires the Pentagon to develop a plan to bring the men and women serving outside NATO home within three years. The bill also requires DOD's plan be approved by the House Armed Services Committee by the end of *this* calendar year. If it is not, in the next defense appropriations bill, *all* funds for overseas military exercises will be eliminated. And last, HR 1269 requires the State Department and the Pentagon to review all of our treaties whose terms require the United States to come to the defense of other nations. Any secret protocols will be made public so the American people will finally understand the commitments this country has made to foreign governments. This review will be conducted with the oversight of the House Foreign Relations Committee, and it too must be completed by the end of this calendar year."

When he finished, those in the gallery erupted in applause. They'd been invited because they were members of left-wing groups critical of U.S. foreign policy or because they were Libertarians who opposed U.S. foreign aid and entanglements. Some members of the House of Representatives figured the Speaker was allowing Higgins and the left wing of the Democratic

Party to do a little grandstanding and present a bill that would never make it out of committee, or if it did, had zero chance of passage. Some thought his apparent generosity reflected the mostly unwritten congressional rules of polite conduct, allowing representatives who disagreed fundamentally on policy issues to nonetheless work together toward the common good. Others thought the Speaker was cynically allowing the opposition party all the rope it wanted to hang itself before the next election cycle. Some thought that Higgins' bill was a joke. But Higgins was, as they say in Texas, serious as a heart attack.

Tuesday, April 18th, 1995, 1203 local time, Simushir

When the incline became too steep, Major Kim slowly angled his MULE up the mountainside. They'd already rolled one of the MULEs; they had all been surprised that when they got it upright, it had started up as if nothing had happened. They'd reloaded the backpacks, crates of food and fuel cans back onto the bed and continued.

At last, they reached the Zavaritzk Caldera's southern rim. Despite the bright sun and warming temperatures, the glacial lake still had sections of ice. All around, the gray-black volcanic landscape was beginning to change to green. Four MULEs could be seen headed south along the western side of the island, toward its narrowest section. Kim and the geologists would catch up with them by nightfall.

After taking a long look around, Major Kim approached Dr. Ryu, the senior geologist, who was writing in his notebook. The older man looked up and volunteered, "This island is very interesting."

Kim agreed. "Yes, it is a fascinating place."

"Major, I don't think we can expand any of the caves we found around the caldera. It is just too dangerous. If we punctured a sealed vent, it would fill the cave with water, toxic gas and lava. Worse, it could trigger an eruption. So far, the only caves we can safely expand are around Broutana Bay or on the west side of the island, where the water keeps the rock cool. I am not saying it would be easy—the dense volcanic rock here will chew up our boring tools—but it would be safer." The geologist closed his notebook and scanned the island, stopping when he faced Mount Milna to the south He actually grinned. "While studying for my doctorate, I read textbooks about volcanoes. Now I am exploring them."

"I am glad you are finding this useful," replied Kim, "and I hope our motherland will benefit from your work."

1213 local time, on board Aphrodite Zero Three

The long canoe-shaped fairings on the top and bottom of the fuselage, the disk-shaped bulge under the nose, and the 30 blade antennas of different shapes and sizes reduced the maximum cruising speed and range of the specially-modified P-3. On board was a flight crew of five, plus 18 "passengers" in the back—a mix of linguists, sensor operators and intelligence specialists. It flew over eastern Hokkaido and paralleled the Kuril Islands, heading northeast. After passing the Russian naval base at Petropavlovsk, the EP-3E made a wide 180-degree turn to the east and headed back down the Kurils.

The weather had changed. The cloud deck that had covered the island had moved off to the east. Passing the egg-shaped island called Ostrov Rasshua, about 44 nautical miles northeast of Simushir, the pilot eased the nose down to descend to 10,000 feet, the optimum altitude to take pictures in the cold, clear Arctic air.

In the cabin, the crew started the large telephoto cameras as soon as Simushir came into view. When the sensor operator spotted men on the top of the Zavaritzk Caldera, he zoomed the camera to get a close-up image. Their weapons and the camouflage pattern on their fatigues were easy to identify.

Wednesday, April 19th, 1995, 0732 local time,
Atsugi Naval Air Facility, Japan

For Josh, flying was a relief from the day-to-day pressures of a desk job. Occasional "stick time" on nearby station aircraft was one of the benefits of being on the admiral's staff.

"Navy Eight Alpha Two Four, you are cleared to take off. Wind zero two five at ten knots. Contact departure on one two two point five when airborne. Squawk 3615." Squawk was the transponder code assigned to the flight.

After his copilot "rogered" the radio call and told the tower they were "switching and rolling," Josh released the brakes and eased the throttles forward. The C-12 started to move from the taxiway onto the runway. Using his feet and differential power, he lined up the plane's nose with the runway's centerline, then Josh rolled the yoke from stop to stop and pulled and pushed it to make sure the elevators and ailerons were free.

He turned to his copilot, Gary Curtain. "Ready?"

"Yes, sir. Let's go. I'll back you up on the throttles."

Josh pushed the throttles forward and kept the plane stationary with the brakes as the twin PT-6 turboprops spooled up. As the torque gauges and prop rpm began to increase, Josh dropped his heels to the cockpit floor, releasing the brakes. The C-12 surged forward.

Once the plane started rolling, Josh pushed the throttles to full power and eased in a little right rudder to keep the plane centered on the runway. At about 20 knots indicated airspeed, Josh gently pushed the rudder pedals to the right and then to the left, noting how the airplane's nose changed direction, and called out, "I have rudder control."

The Simushir Island Incident

As the C-12 rushed forward, gathering speed, Josh kept his eyes focused on the runway centerline, his left hand on the yoke and his right hand on the two throttles. The airspeed indicator showed the King Air was passing 70 knots. With only two passengers and a full load of fuel, they would have a takeoff weight of around 11,500 pounds.

Scanning the instruments, Curtain reported, "Eighty knots—gauges look good."

Everything looked and felt normal. Passing 90 knots, Josh eased back on the yoke and the C-12's nose rose to the takeoff attitude.

BANG! Josh felt the nose of the airplane start to slew to the right, so he fed in enough left rudder and aileron to keep the nose straight down the runway.

THUMP. There were no warning lights, but the noise was loud. As the King Air lifted smoothly off the runway, Josh keyed the intercom, "Don't raise the gear. That felt like a blown tire. If we get it up, we may not be able to get it down."

Gary Curtain nodded and flipped from the normal takeoff-and-climb NATOPS checklist to the one for emergency procedures, bordered with blue and black hash marks.

Josh saw the right engine torque gauge flicker and slowly unwind, telling him the engine was no longer producing full power. It was accompanied by a slow yaw to the right. He keyed the intercom. "Gary, I think the right engine is failing. Confirm we have secondary indications."

Out of the corner of his eye, Josh saw the altimeter pass 200 feet and the vertical speed indicator show the plane's rate of climb as just 200 feet per minute. Airspeed was at 105 knots, so they were now above the minimum airspeed for flying on one engine. By lowering the nose by a degree or two, Josh allowed the C-12 to accelerate.

Curtain ran his finger down the right column of engine gauges. The top gauge for inter-stage turbine temperature was dropping. The propeller rpm was also dropping, and the engine torque was approaching zero. "Sir, the right engine is dying."

The windmilling prop on the right engine was creating enough drag to slow the airplane. Despite full power on the left engine, the C-12 had stopped accelerating and climbing. They were in "no man's land" at just over 300 feet, and unless they shut down the right engine and feathered the propeller, they might not make it back to Atsugi.

"Gary, shut the right engine down and feather the prop right now!" Josh reached down and pulled the rudder boost switch up out of the detent and forward to give him more rudder authority.

"Sir, we've still got some engine rpm and torque. I'd recommend trying an air start."

Josh pointed to the fuel flow gauge. "Fuel flow is at zero, and the fuel low-pressure warning light is on. With no fuel flow or pressure, we'll never get it running. I'd rather fly it single engine and get rid of the drag from the right engine than dick around with trying to restart a windmilling engine at low altitude."

"But, sir—"

Josh was in no mood for a debate. "Shut it down NOW! We don't have the time or altitude to monkey around with a restart."

"Roger that, sir."

Curtain, a member of the Naval Academy class of 1990, had finished flight training a year after Desert Storm. During the drawdown, he'd been sent to Atsugi as a station pilot while he awaited assignment to a fleet squadron, a.k.a. a "fleet seat." While he had over 300 hours in the C-12, far more than Josh, he was junior to the captain flying the airplane. If they crashed, the Navy accident board would hold Josh, as the senior pilot on board, responsible.

The Simushir Island Incident

Josh made damn sure his hand was on the *right* throttle and pulled it back to the detent normally used to shut down the engine. Then he moved the prop control for the *right* engine to the side and farther back to the feather position. Assuming the propeller governor worked as advertised, the three propeller blades would soon align themselves with the C-12's flight path.

Almost immediately, Josh felt the plane surge forward. The airspeed, which had been hovering around 110 knots, just 14 knots above the minimum single engine control speed for their takeoff weight, began to increase.

"Gary, raise the flaps. I want to minimize the drag on the airplane.

"Are you sure, sir? Takeoff flaps give us additional lift."

Josh was trying not to be curt. He was concentrating on flying. Way back in the training command, his instructors had hammered into his brain that during an emergency, you *aviate* first to keep the airplane in the air and under control. Then, once you have the airplane controllable, *navigate* and figure out where you are going. The last item was *communicate*—tell whomever you need to tell what had happened and what you intend to do. Right now, he was still aviating. "Yes."

Once the C-12 passed 600 feet, Curtain switched the radios back to the tower and declared an emergency—they were flying on one engine and returning to Atsugi.

At 800 feet, Josh called for Curtain to recheck to make sure they'd completed all the items on the single-engine checklist. At 1,000 feet, Josh began a gentle right turn to the south.

"Gary, ask the tower if any helos are airborne. If so, I'd like to have them look at the right landing gear." A short exchange told them that an SH-60 from Helicopter Anti-Submarine Warfare Squadron Two was airborne on a maintenance test hop and would call when they got a visual on the C-12.

Two minutes later, the radio crackled. "Navy Eight Alpha Two Four, this is Golden Falcon Eight Zero One, have you in sight. Am closing on the starboard side. Looks like you've lost one wheel entirely from the right main mount and the other tire is pretty shredded. We can see hydraulic fluid all over the wheel well, and fuel is coming from both the wheel well and holes in the wing."

After Gary Curtain rogered the call, Josh turned to him and asked, "What are our options?"

"Sir, I'm not sure."

"Gary, is this your first real emergency?"

The young officer nodded.

"Well, Lieutenant, consider this a teaching moment. We have to tell the tower how we're going to get this plane on the ground. They heard the report, so now what do you think we should do?"

Curtain's blank look told Josh he didn't have a clue. This was not in the NATOPS manual, and when he'd gone through training, single-engine landings with fuel leaking and one main mount all fucked up probably wasn't an emergency they covered.

"I think we have two realistic choices. One, land and hope the strut doesn't collapse or rip off, causing us to ground loop. Two, see if we can get the gear up and then land it wheels up. If the back-up hydraulic system doesn't raise both main mounts and the nose gear, we'll have a different and unknown configuration. We can't bail out because we don't have parachutes. Ditching isn't a good option with the wheels down. Anyway, this time of year, the water's really cold." As he banked the airplane to begin a wide downwind leg to enter Atsugi's landing pattern, Josh could see Curtain contemplating their choices. He didn't look happy.

"Okay—I'll make it easy. I vote for landing the way it is and asking Atsugi to foam the runway. We'll put the right main mount down in the foam, and if it comes off or collapses, so be it. Once we have the runway made, I'll shut down the left engine to minimize the chance of a fire."

"Sir, what if we have to go around?"

"That, Lieutenant, is not an option. We get it right the first time. Next question, flaps or no flaps?"

"Sir, I'd use flaps because it will allow us to fly slower."

"And if the flaps on the right side don't come down or get jammed, then what?"

"I see your point. So, this is going to be a no-flap approach?"

"You got it. I'll keep it above the minimum single-engine speed, but once we drop below 500 feet, we're landing one way or another."

Josh saw Curtain's eyes widen as he shifted in his seat and looked at the feathered right prop. He turned back to Josh and said, "Okay."

"First things first—we tell the tower, who may want us to fly around while they foam the runway, and then we'll brief our two passengers. While I'm doing that, you shut down every piece of electrical equipment on this plane, except for the radio, to make sure there are no sparks. It goes off when we get on short final. Pull the circuit breakers to make sure they're all off."

"Yes, sir."

The tower informed them that it would take 10 minutes to foam the first 1,000 feet of the runway just past the numbers. Fire trucks would be waiting beside the runway.

Josh flew a wide circle, maintaining 115 knots. At a mile out, he started easing off the left throttle. The King Air crossed the runway threshold at 25 feet and Josh closed the left engine throttle and pulled it back into the detent to shut it down.

To compensate for the loss of power, Josh eased back on the yoke and the C-12 glided toward the runway at 90 knots. As they descended, Josh rolled the airplane slightly to the left and raised the nose a bit more to flare. Once the left wheel was on the ground Josh kept easing back on the yoke to slow the airplane and feeding in left aileron to keep the right main mount off the ground for as long as possible.

At about 50 knots, the right wing slowly came down and Josh ran out of control authority. The rim of the right wheel screeched when it touched the concrete, leaving a long trail of sparks that died in the foam.

The right wheel came off with a crack and the strut dug into the concrete. The C-12, now down to 40 knots, slewed to the right and was heading toward the edge of the runway when the sound of tearing aluminum, followed by the scraping of metal on concrete, told them the entire right main mount had come off the airplane.

The C-12 lurched, and the right wingtip hit the ground as the plane slowly pivoted to a stop. Once it was motionless, Josh yelled, "Out, out—everyone out!"

Marty didn't need any encouragement to open the passenger door. He and the intelligence specialist ran through ankle-deep foam. Men in silver suits were running toward the plane, while others were already dowsing the right wing with foam.

Josh walked through the foam, which smelled like someone had just taken a dump in the toilet, to look at the damage. He then boarded a van waiting to take them to base operations for the inevitable debrief and paper drill. Marty leaned forward from the back seat, grinning from ear to ear. "Guess we're not going to get to Misawa today!"

Chapter 6: SHELTER NEWS

Friday, April 20th, 1995, 0803 local time, San Diego

Gary Nash glanced out the window of his office. He could see the sailboats in San Diego Bay. On the far side of the bay, two carriers, *Kitty Hawk* and *Nimitz,* were tied up at the carrier pier at NAS North Island. He returned his attention to his desk and glared at his business calendar. Everything on his schedule for the next two months and beyond would have to be rescheduled. Meetings and court appearances would be delayed.

The cause of the chaos was a call from the office of the Judge Advocate General of the United States Navy, who was also a Vice Admiral, requesting Captain Gary Nash, JAG Corps, United States Naval Reserve, to report for at least two weeks of active duty at the JAG Corps headquarters in D.C., preferably no later than May 1st. Apparently, Steven Higgins was making trouble, again! And Nash was the Navy's resident expert on former Lieutenant Steven Higgins.

After leaving active duty in 1977, Gary Nash had formed the law firm Nash & Partners, LLC, which developed a stellar reputation in southern California as a litigator in civil court. Nash

& Partners grew from just Gary Nash to a small, thriving law firm with six lawyers: two other partners and three associates, supported by a staff of ten paralegals and secretaries. *Well, they'll have to hold the fort without me for a while.*

The admiral had recommended bringing a couple of suits appropriate for a courtroom appearance. Nash deduced from this that it was shaping up to be round four in the matter of *Higgins v. the Navy.*

Saturday, April 21st, 1995, 1814 local time, Simushir

The engineers spent a full day exploring the relatively flat area south of the Zavaritzk Caldera and the base of Mount Milna. In the afternoon, Kim found a rocky beach that gently sloped down to the water. It was large enough to support a small invasion force, so it would have to be watched, even mined, if the North Koreans wanted to fortify the island. Landing on this beach would mean invaders would have to make their way north over easily defendable terrain. Small clandestine teams, however—special operators or reconnaissance troops—could land almost anywhere on the island, hide amongst the volcanic rocks and crevasses and conduct raids all over the island.

Kim was looking up at Mount Milna, wondering how difficult it was going to be to get to the top, when Dr. Soon came to his side and suggested they walk to a small cliff on the south end of the beach. There, the trees would conceal them from view, and the sound from the waves beating against the rocks would frustrate anyone's ability to record or overhear their words. This meant, Kim realized, that Soon wanted to have a private conversation.

Soon towered over the Special Forces soldier and literally looked down on most of his fellow countrymen. The state had wanted to turn Soon into a world-class basketball player; but, as he explained it, they had been unable to find the athlete in his centimeter-tall (6' 10") body. Instead, Hak-kun Soon had earned a doctorate in civil engineering from Kim-Il Sung University, specializing in designing roads and runways.

"I understand Dr. Ryu has shared with you some of his findings." The tall engineer looked out over the surf as he spoke.

"Yes, he has."

Senior Geologist Nam-il Ryu had completed his doctorate in civil engineering and seismology at Peking University, where he'd learned more than political slogans. Ryu became one of his country's top seismic experts after he showed his superiors how the South Koreans regularly found North Korean tunnels under the DMZ—they were making too much noise building them and were detected by acoustic sensors. Ryu used his knowledge of the uneven sound propagation characteristics of rock formations to help North Korea mask some, but not all, of their tunneling activities from South Korean seismic sensors.

Major Kim waited for the real reason for the walk.

"Major, do you know the true purpose of our trip here?"

Major Kim looked up at him, appreciating that the engineer trusted him enough to ask the question. *So how far do I trust Soon?* "My mission is to escort you and the geologists, determine whether or not the island is inhabited, and look for areas which could be used for military training."

"I see. Well, I am here to find where we can build an airfield. In the area we explored today, we can build a 3,000-meter runway, but only after much blasting and grading. Senior Geologist Ryu thinks the island is stable enough that we don't have to worry about erupting volcanoes, but the area has frequent earthquakes." Senior Engineer Soon faced inland, surveying the terrain with a practiced eye. "There is no place on this island that is already flat, and we can't put anything underground. There is too much risk of breaking into pockets of lava or deadly vapors. Or having the cave collapse in an earthquake. Just building a road to get the equipment here will take years, and the cost will be enormous. I can't understand why we want to build a 3,000-meter runway. I don't know if we have airliners or military transports than can fly here from our country."

Major Kim was cautious. He wasn't sure if Dr. Soon was baiting him to reveal his inner thoughts that could be reported to State Security, or if his concern was genuine. But he, too, was curious. "Who told you to look for a possible location for an airfield?"

"An Air Force colonel on our Dear Leader's staff, who showed me a map of the island. I didn't dare say anything discouraging, so I just listened and said, 'We will find out.'"

"Do you remember his name?"

"Yes, Hwang Soo Pong. It is a very common name, but I also have the phone number he gave me. He said to call as soon as I was back."

"Good, give that to me. I will tell Vice Admiral Pak and General Jang when we get back."

Monday, April 27th, 1995, 0828 local time, U.S.S. Honolulu

The keel of the *Los Angeles* class fast attack submarine ('fast' being a one-syllable way of saying 'nuclear powered rather than diesel powered') was 250 feet below the surface of the Sea of Japan. Its depth put it beneath the layer and 2,000 feet above the bottom.

Air-conditioning kept most workspaces at a comfortable 72 degrees. To minimize noise that might be detected by sonar, everyone on board wore soft-soled shoes. All the machinery was mounted so that mechanical vibrations were isolated from the submarine's hull.

"Bridge, sonar. Contact Sierra Eleven has changed course and looks like it is heading zero four two. Speed is still about five knots."

The officer of the deck, a young lieutenant on his second cruise on a fast attack submarine, used a drafting pencil to plot the new course for one of the two *Romeo* submarines they'd been tracking since the North Korean boats had left Mayang-do.

Contact Sierra Ten followed the route now referred to in submarine logs and official messages as "the Kimchi Highway," which ran from the North Korean submarine base at Mayang-do to the area south of the town of Olga, on the Russian coast on the Sea of Japan.

Sierra Eleven had departed a few hours after Sierra Ten and then gone ultra-quiet. The computers on *Honolulu* had detected the man-made machinery and the steady beat of two different sets of screws amongst the ocean noises. When each sub snorkeled to charge its batteries, *Honolulu's* crew added data to that sub's sound profile.

Extending Sierra Eleven's north-northeast course took it to the La Pérouse Strait, a narrow strip of water between Russian-held Sakhalin Island and the Japanese home island of Hokkaido. No North Korean submarine had ever ventured this far from Mayang-do.

The lieutenant rubbed his chin as he contemplated the situation. *Honolulu*'s skipper would have to make a choice. They could trail and track Sierra Ten or Eleven, but not both. It was decision time. "Call the captain to the bridge."

* * *

On board the *Blue Ridge*, Special Agent Jake Garza finished his presentation on sources of drug being smuggled through the Seventh Fleet area of responsibility. Besides Garza, in the admiral's office were CINCPAC, Vice Admiral Maize, Josh and Marty—who was just about to ask a question—when Admiral Maize's "rope," a.k.a. flag lieutenant, interrupted the meeting to deliver an Operational Immediate Flash message. Maize looked at Garza. "Jake, will you excuse us for a few minutes. I don't believe you are cleared for submarine operations."

Garza nodded, picked up his mug of coffee and left. Admiral Maize summarized the contents for those in the room.

Honolulu was trailing two North Korean *Romeos.* One was headed up the Kimchi Highway, and the other seemed headed for the La Pérouse Strait. CINCPAC asked his host to dial a number at his headquarters. As soon as it started ringing, CINCPAC pushed the secure button and selected the speaker function. Captain Roger Billingham answered and CINCPAC identified himself as well as the other three officers in the room. "Captain Billingham, where is the second *Romeo* now?"

"Sir, according to what *Honolulu* sent, its last reported position was 46 degrees, 30 minutes north; 141 degrees west—heading roughly southeast. Speed is five knots."

"Southeast?"

"Yes, sir, according to the message, the sub made a loop around a small island on the west side of Sakhalin called Ostrov Monoron. The water there is only 100 fathoms deep and noisy, so unless it was a navigation exercise, the only reason to go there would be to make it difficult for one of our subs to follow. Up until the sub made the dogleg, she was headed straight for the La Pérouse."

"Standby, Captain—we're getting a chart."

Admiral Maize pulled a rolled chart of the Sea of Japan out from a stack in a tub in the corner of his office and spread out the nautical chart on the conference table. Two coffee mugs, a stapler and a tape dispenser were plunked down on the corners to keep it from rolling back up.

The Simushir Island Incident

The two admirals found the location on the chart. "Is there anything else in the report?"

"*Honolulu* intends to stay in trail of this submarine unless otherwise directed, which means she'll be out of her patrol area. We'll lose coverage of the other submarine on the Kimchi Highway."

"Understood. Assign another sub to the Kimchi Highway as soon as you can."

"Aye, aye sir."

"Thank you, Captain." The four-star admiral ended the call and turned to the other admiral in the room.

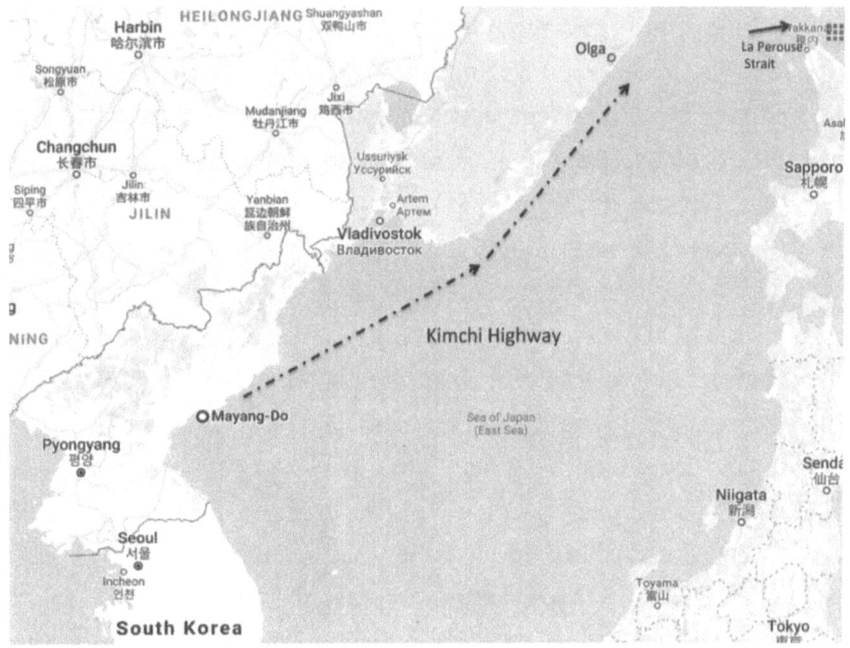

The Kimchi Highway

"If the North Koreans set up a military base on Simushir, it's a game changer. It will outflank the Japanese and make life difficult for us—it'd be harder to re- supply Japan or help them defend their islands. Vice Admiral Maize, if you need anything to ascertain what the North Koreans are doing on Simushir, and you don't have it, let me know. I'll get it if I have to rip it out of the chairman's hands myself!"

Marty looked down to hide his smile. The chairman was CINCPAC's boss, the Chairman of the Joint Chiefs of Staff. Decisions made and direction given.

1426 local time, Los Angeles

No one in the group of young Hispanic men paid any attention to a short, stocky man leaning against the fender of a battered Chevy parked at the end of the street. He wore dark sunglasses and a light blue windbreaker that hung loosely over his jeans.

Dae Ho Muk, First Lieutenant in the Special Forces of the People's Army of the Democratic Republic of Korea, seconded to a succession of shell companies in Macao and Hong Kong, in the U.S. for "special tasking" marveled at the accuracy of the intel he'd received. The group of men, including his primary target, were right where he'd been informed they would be. By now, he'd figured out that whoever was paying for his services was slowly eliminating the leadership of rival organizations that sold drugs. He didn't care; he enjoyed the killing.

Ignacio Hernandes—"That's with an S, not a Z, and don't you forget it!"—was holding court with his *colegas,* his "colleagues". All were in their mid-to late twenties and had already spent at least two years in jail. Ignacio leaned against the dark, metallic-green Malibu lowrider that was his pride and joy. Around him were four of his West Side La Mirada lieutenants and two bodyguards—Jesús Ortiz and Hector Ordonez. They were cousins, his *primos hermanos,* and their sole purpose in life now was protecting him. Blood was thicker than water, and keeping him alive and their drug and prostitution operations profitable was good for the whole family.

They were laughing and making jokes. The afternoon gathering was a daily ritual. It was one part staff meeting and one part "man party" where testosterone flowed. Ignacio would share words of wisdom and guidance before they headed out to check on the pimps and drug pushers they controlled, as well as to make sure no other gang encroached on their territory. Each man had a roll of cash in his pockets, and much more was stashed in their apartments. Life was good.

A close look at any one of them would reveal the butt of a pistol sticking out of a waistband under a shirt not tucked in. They were in the heart of their turf; this was their area, and they controlled it.

When the man with the dark Ray-Bans finished his soda and put the bottle into an overflowing trash can, no one around Ignacio noticed or cared. Nor did they notice when he crossed the street and headed toward them. They were still laughing at Hector's last joke. Then Ignacio spotted the approaching man and nodded to Jesús, who touched Hector's arm. Seriousness replaced laughter as both men sauntered toward the stranger in their best "I'm a cool Chicano dude who's a big man in La Mirada" manner. They walked in the rolling gait Tom Wolfe referred to in *Bonfire of the Vanities* as the "pimp roll."

Jesús moved to flank the stranger while Hector headed for him. Locals knew not to approach this gathering without prior approval.

When they were about 15 feet away, Muk pulled two Tokarevs with suppressors from shoulder holsters under his unzipped jacket. Before either Hector or Jesús could react, they were falling—dead —with bullets in their brains. The other gang members reached for their weapons, but the stranger moved too quickly. Each time he fired, a bullet went into a gang member's head. Only one of

Hernandes' lieutenants got a shot off with his .357 Magnum. The bullet went wide and flew 500 feet past Muk and popped a basketball before it stopped in the brain of a 10-year-old boy.

Ignacio pulled out a pump shotgun from the back of his car. By the time he was turning to point the gun at the attacker, the stranger was squeezing the Tokarev's trigger from just five feet away. Ignacio saw the flash of flame, and then he, too, was dead.

Wednesday, April 26th, 1995, 0915 local time, Los Angeles

The office of Captain James Randall, the head of the Special Investigations Unit of the Los Angeles Police Department, was tucked away in the back of the second floor of the police headquarters building. The location gave them easy access to the department's leadership on the top floor, as well as to its crime labs.

Randall tossed his reading glasses onto the desk and scrutinized the six plastic bags he held in his left hand, each containing brass cartridges from shootings at different locations Three others with similar casings sat on his desk. Across from him sat Lieutenant Proudfoot, the detective assigned to find the mystery assassin who was killing members of drug gangs. He was a full-blooded Apache who'd grown up in New Mexico and spoke fluent Spanish.

"So, the ballistics folks at both the FBI and ATF say that these special, subsonic hollow point rounds are used only by the North Korean Special Forces."

"Yes, sir. The Russians don't make them, nor do the Czechs or the Bulgarians."

"And did each shell come from the same weapon?"

"No. Looks like we're dealing with four pistols, which means we could have four shooters, or one shooter who used four different pistols, or something in between. No fingerprints on any of the shells. This last incident, all the shots were head shots—one shot, one kill, and fast. Only one of the La Mirada gang members got a shot off. Unfortunately, all it did was kill a young kid—collateral damage. Witnesses say the shooter had black hair, wore dark sunglasses, jeans and a light-blue windbreaker."

"You're saying the gangbangers were not murdered. They were executed."

"Yes, sir. The right word is executed. This was a professional hit. Someone gave this dude a mission and he fulfilled it."

"What about the 18th Streeters' warehouse that was blown up?"

"Same MO. It was professional."

"How are the gangs reacting?"

"The Westside La Miradas and 18th Streeters are vowing revenge—but against whom? They don't know, and our gang unit has warned them not to start a war."

"Are there any connections among the victims of any of these hits?"

"That's a very goooooood question." Proudfoot elongated the o's in the word for emphasis. "Some were CPAs and attorneys who we thought were clean, until they were killed. Now we know they worked almost exclusively for suspected cartel or gang members. The targets on the yacht had set up legitimate businesses so gangs and cartels could launder money. All that the firms will tell us is that their safes were emptied of cash. The owners are claiming privilege and won't tell us what else was stolen. They've tried to pass off the killings as murders of opportunity, with the safes and the cash as the objectives, but there's no doubt in my Apache mind that these were professional hits."

Captain Randall had worked with Proudfoot long enough to know that when he invoked his Indian heritage, he was convinced he was right. "So, Lieutenant, have you a theory?"

"We have two. One is the hits are part of a power play, and someone has hired North Korean hit men, which means they have connections inside North Korea. Theory two is that someone already in place wants to start a gang war and then pick up the pieces. That would certainly explain the hit on the La Mirada gang and the 18th Streeters. If this is the case, Machiavelli would approve of the move!"

Proudfoot hesitated, then continued. "Then there is the vigilante theory. It could be a Charles Bronson wannabe doing an LA version of the movie *Death Wish*. But none of us buy that theory because it would take years—and a hell of a lot of resources—to get the intel needed for these hits."

One side of Randall's mouth twisted in a non-smile and he asked, "What does your gut tell you?"

Proudfoot took a deep breath before answering. "There's a new-source heroin on the street called Asian Pure. I think the hits and distribution rights to Asian Pure are connected."

"Ronnie, do you want help?"

"You mean DEA, FBI or ATF help?"

The captain nodded.

"Beyond ballistics … not yet. Narcotics is putting heat on its informants to see if they can identify someone connected to the shooter or shooters." Proudfoot paused to let his brain catch up to his mouth. "On one hand, whoever's behind these executions is saving our taxpayers the cost of investigating and prosecuting pushers and white-collar crooks. On the other, we can't let this go on. Call it what you like, it is still murder, which unless I am mistaken, is against the law in Los Angeles."

The captain tossed the bags back to the lieutenant, one at a time. "You've got two weeks. If you don't have enough evidence to make an arrest, we're asking for help from the feds, starting with the DEA."

The Simushir Island Incident

Wednesday, April 26th, 1995, 0910 local time, U.S.S. Blue Ridge

The visiting Commander, Pacific Command, a.k.a. CINCPAC, had sent for Captain Haman and Commanders Cabot and D'Onofrio, and he addressed them now. "Vice Admiral Maize tells me you are the best, most innovative operational planners around. He said your suggested revisions to Operations Plan 5088, including what you called the Kuril Wedge Sanctuary off Hokkaido, were validated in war games by the Naval War College. I loved the idea of a battleship attack, using 16-inch guns to take out the airfield and fuel depot on Burevestnik. I also think the idea of using avalanches to shut down the flow of supplies to Petropavlovsk is brilliant. My compliments to all three of you. Well done."

The admiral nodded, then continued. "The Commander, United Nations Forces, Korea, is as curious as we are as to what the North Korean subs are doing. He thinks the Russians are involved up to their still-deeply-Red eyeballs. Admiral Maize is his naval component commander, so both of us have been briefing him by phone on a 'for-his-ears-only' basis. This brings us to what I want to talk about." The four-star admiral eyed the men around the table keenly. "What do you think is happening on Simushir?"

Josh looked over at Marty, who was the guy with the most operational experience—and possibly the most recent intel from Uilani. But Marty gave him the returning look, which translated to, '*You're the senior guy, answer the admiral's question.*' Josh was confident that Marty would bring him back to reality if he got too far ahead of the data.

"Sir, we—that's Commanders Cabot and D'Onofrio, Uilani Ka'anapali and I—believe this is all drug related." He summarized the evidence Uilani had found, indicating that Half Moon Trading and Crescent Shipping were behind the Kuril Island Development Corporation.

The admiral's eyes widened in appreciation. "I've been briefed by Uilani many times, she's very good."

Josh continued. "Sir, I recommend we initiate a full-court press to find out more about Half Moon Trading and the Kuril Island Development Corporation and what connections they have with the Russian Maritime Ministry."

"I'll get CIA, DIA and NSA help, and set it up so Seventh Fleet doesn't lose control, but you'll need to keep pushing. When, not if, you get the idiot treatment or unacceptable delays or poor-quality info, let me know through Vice Admiral Maize, and I'll turn up the heat. Meanwhile, I'll try to keep the State and Commerce Departments out of this. They've begun to make noise that the fishing facility is a State and Commerce Department 'issue', not a DOD one. It may turn out that way; but right now, North Korean soldiers on the island make it a military problem. Both State and Commerce refuse to consider any military implications of a North Korean base in the middle of the Kuril Islands. The Secretary of State is convinced his department can deal with our former Cold War adversaries in Moscow. They think Russia is in a death spiral and anything not involving the Western half of the country is a sideshow. My takeaway is this is a turf war in D.C. But that's my problem, not yours. What else?"

"Sir, we—that's Jack, Marty, Uilani and me—think a sneak and peak on Simushir is needed."

"Can it be done?"

Josh opened his hand to his friend as if to say, "*Your turn.*"

"Yes, sir." Marty took up the thread. "There are many places we can come ashore safely if we go before the end of October. Once on the island, however, there are few places to hide, so it is going to be at most a four-day op. Day one to land and get to where we want to be, two and three to watch, and four to get back to our egress point and get out. Josh thinks an anti-submarine warfare exercise in the area can be used as a cover, and to provide close air support or helos to extract the team if we run into problems."

"Why ASW?" The four star used the letters because all those in the compartment understood that ASW stood for anti-submarine warfare.

"Sir," Josh replied, "It is the most logical. We can do it with the amphibious ready group assigned to Seventh Fleet, augmented with a couple of cruisers and destroyers from the carrier battle group. We can involve the Japanese because ASW is their area of expertise, and it will demonstrate our mutual and continued interest in their getting the Northern Territories back."

"I need a plan ASAP from you that will pass muster with the snake eaters on my staff," CINCPAC said with a nod in Marty's direction. "Run it out of here. I don't want anything put in messages. I'll send you a list of who will have control of the need-to-know on my staff and who will be read in. Work through them. When you're ready, come to Hawaii for a face to face review. Understood?"

"Yes, sir."

"I'd like the recon sooner better than later. But to be clear, this is authorization to plan, not execute."

Marty shot Josh a look that said, *See, your reputation precedes you.* If they hadn't been in a formal meeting, Josh's rejoinder would have been in the form of a gesture involving a middle finger.

"Aye, aye, sir. We understand."

The four-star started grinning. "Excellent. Why are you sitting here?"

Thursday, April 27th, 1995, 0842 local time, Simushir

Managing Director and Project Manager Chan Ho Lee put down the phone and looked at his watch. His visitors were due to arrive in 30 minutes, which gave him time to put sensitive documents in his safe—such as the one with overhead times of U.S. and Russian reconnaissance satellites. No need for his Russian guests, and their supervisors, to know he had their satellite schedule.

Lee walked toward the pier and watched the *Ostrov,* a slate-gray, rust-streaked warship, enter the harbor at a gingerly three knots and drop anchor in the western part of the bay. The captain of the ship picked a spot that would let the corvette swing clear of a freighter unloading on the pier. The twin 57-millimeter guns on the stern turret were level with the deck. The surface-to-air missile launcher on the bow was empty.

By the time Managing Director Lee arrived, two men were climbing up the pier's ladder from *Ostrov*'s launch. One was wearing the uniform of a general in the KGB Border Guards. The other was wearing an unzipped ski parka and a heavy dark-gray wool turtleneck sweater.

"Good morning." Managing Director Lee spoke in English. He didn't speak Russian and suspected they didn't speak either Korean or Mandarin. Lee bowed slightly.

The Russians looked around, and then the civilian answered. Like many Russians, he left out the articles "a," "an" and "the", but his English, while hesitant, was precise. "I am Valeri Dimitriov, Deputy Minister Eastern Region of Russian Maritime Agency and responsible for Kuril Islands. This is Major General Boris Oborin, Federal Border Service of Russia. He is boss for Far Eastern Federal District and reports to Moscow. He has ships, planes and several divisions of border guards under his command. General

Oborin is responsible for who comes and goes in Kuril Islands. Out here, *he* rules."

"I am pleased to meet both of you. Welcome to Simushir." Managing Director Lee shook hands with the general. These were Very Important People. He'd seen their names in reports, but never expected to meet them face to face. That they were here on Simushir suggested that the Russians suspected there was more going on than a simple fishing boat support business. Or else they were being professionally paranoid, here to emphasize Russian ownership and control of the island. "What would you like to do?"

"We want, how you say, tour?" Dimitriov was used to demanding, not asking. The inflection of his voice was one of command.

"Just the two of you?"

"*Nyet*." Four other men had come over from the warship and were now standing by themselves on the pier. Two were in civilian clothes, and two were wearing the same uniform as General Oborin. Dimitriov pointed his thumb at them four men. "They come, yes?"

"Of course. I can show you the facility's plans, and then we can drive anywhere you want." Lee turned to lead the way.

"*Da*, good." Dimitriov pivoted on his heel. Oborin called out in Russian, and the four men jogged over.

In the conference room down the hall from his office, a pot of hot tea and disposable cups were ready for them. After his visitors helped themselves, he showed them the maps and drawings taped to the walls.

Dimitriov asked his next question. "Why were you picked as boss?"

Before he'd left for Simushir, Managing Director Lee had been told that the Russians had not been informed about the true purpose of the facility. He was to maintain the cover story at all times: this is a fishing boat service and support operation, nothing more. "Before the Kuril Island Development Corporation hired me, I managed construction projects." Some of the factories he'd built converted raw opium into heroin and precursor chemicals into what the Americans called uppers and downers, but that was none of the Russians' business. "They paid me well to take this assignment, which lacks the usual amenities."

Dimitriov grunted in acknowledgement. There was nothing about this location to recommend itself to a manager accustomed to the comforts of city living. "How long you here?"

"Until this facility is completed." Lee wanted to keep his answers short and simple.

"Then?"

"I turn this place over to someone else, and find out what my employer wants me to build next."

"Where is your family from?" Dimitriov demanded.

"My parents came to Hong Kong in 1952 from Korea." *That should be a safe answer that explains why I speak English. If the Russians researched the Kuril Island Development Corporation, they might find out that my parents came in the same group as the owners of Half Moon and Crescent Shipping.*

"You buy much Western equipment, no?" These were the first words that Oborin spoke, and Lee was glad of the change in subject.

"Yes. We buy used equipment to keep costs down. As I am sure you know, once we deliver equipment to Simushir, every month we provide a list to your government so it has an accurate inventory of what is here." In this way, Managing Director Lee explained why Kuril Island Development Corporation did not purchase the equipment offered by the Russian government, which was shit, expensive, and plagued by uncertain delivery.

The Simushir Island Incident

"Have you explored island?" General Oborin inquired. Despite his accent, his English was easy to understand.

"Yes, we had men drive around the island. It is important we know more about the island for Phase Two."

"Phase Two? What is that?"

This was potentially the most important and delicate part of the meeting. According to Lee's superiors in Hong Kong, senior Russian officials had been told about Phase 2 and paid the necessary bribe to expedite approval, but Lee did not know how far down the chain of command this awareness and approval extended. Apparently, not this far. Lee was convinced that the runway would raise eyebrows, but he was just the construction manager and would construct what his superiors told him to build. "We intend to build a runway between the Zavaritzk Caldera and Mount Milna." He pointed to the area on the large map of the island. "This would allow us to bring in supplies for emergency repairs quickly, even when sea navigation is difficult. Once we have a design, we plan to ask your government for approval to build it."

"And how big will this… airfield be?" Oborin inquired.

And this was the dangerous part. Lee didn't know how much detail had been shared with the Russian Maritime Ministry. "Our investors plan to build a 3,000-meter runway. We realize that pilots may have a hard time approaching and taking off, so the extra length is a safety feature to prevent expensive accidents."

"When will construction begin?" General Oborin was thinking hard and fast. His job was to secure the physical borders of Russia in his area. A few hundred foreigners from Hong Kong or Korea on this island, several hundred miles from the mainland, were not a risk to his homeland, even though they were on sacred Russian soil. But an airfield? With a 3,000-meter runway—long enough for heavy bombers? That was different! *Moscow must be told! What if the Americans start using Simushir as a place to refuel airplanes?*

On the other hand, a runway out here could prove useful to Russia, in more ways than one. A runway meant Russian customs agents would have to be stationed on the island to collect fuel taxes and entry/exit fees, fees which he could set—some of which he could pocket. He had the authority and legal right to do so. There and then, he realized it would be worth stationing people on this god-forsaken island out in the middle of nowhere, and not just as a punishment assignment.

"Could Russian Air Force use airport and buy fuel?"

Lee smiled. "Of course. We would provide the fuel at a discount to our host nation."

General Oborin nodded, thinking that the airfield would have to be big enough to handle several planes or it would not be worth much tactically. He studied the chart. The terrain was hellishly uneven; building a 3,000-meter runway here would be a logistical and engineering nightmare. Despite Lee's smooth words, Oberin did not for a moment buy the story of the Kuril Island Development Corporation's stated purpose that they could make a profit selling fuel and supplies to fishing vessels. Barracks and offices can be built cheap and fast, but runways must be constructed to endure hard usage, and quality construction does not come cheap. He tapped his fingers in cadence to the Russian equivalent of "cost overrun".

Meanwhile, Dimitriov had pulled a small 35mm film camera from his coat. "We take pictures."

"Please, take as many as you want. Would you prefer to walk? Or I can arrange for a driver."

"Drive. We must try machines." Dimitriov headed for the mud-splattered two-man MULEs.

Managing Director Lee stuck his head in the door of the building next to the office and barked instructions in Korean. *It will give some of Major Kim's men something to do.* Soon, six vehicles were quickly lined up, five with drivers.

"Minister Dimitriov, why don't you ride with me?"

"Excellent. We go there, yes?" Dimitriov pointed at the building on the northwest side of the bay.

"Certainly." *So much for the route I wanted to take.* Lee had hoped his explanation that the building was a storage facility for parts would make it sound too boring to visit. In fact, it was to be a heroin and meth lab, and no one was allowed inside other than a few chosen workers. Lee drove slowly toward the almost-finished building. Thankfully, it was not yet in operation.

1806 local time, Los Angeles

Cho Rhee kept one eye on the TV as she chopped vegetables for a stir fry. She was waiting for a highly touted interview with the head of the LAPD's gang unit, scheduled to begin at 1830. The teasers for the half-hour special segment said the police captain would answer questions about the recent murders of LA residents alleged to have ties to several local gangs.

When the show was over, Cho smiled a feral smile. *They still haven't figured it out.*

Two years ago, while working in her native Hong Kong, Cho had approached her uncle after overhearing a conversation about smuggling drugs into the United States. At the time, Cho was working for Half Moon, having spent six years in the United States earning a bachelor's degree in bio-medical engineering from the University of Southern California and a master's degree in business administration from its Marshall School of Business. When she'd returned to Hong Kong, Cho had started at the bottom, living and working on the production line at Half Moon's fireworks factory in Shenzhen before she was given a shift to run. That led to a year in Dalian, where again, she'd had to start at entry level, making and painting pottery before becoming a shift supervisor. Her father, one of the founders of Half Moon, had insisted that an apprenticeship was required if she wanted to work in the family business.

The youngest of four children, Cho was one of two working at Half Moon. The number two son had opted out of the family business to become a doctor, and the number three was what her father called "lost at sea." The last time anyone had heard from him, he was meandering around Europe, searching for himself.

Family history was important to the Rhees. Cho's father couldn't convince his oldest brother to leave Korea, but her uncle was good friends with the Democratic People's Republic of Korea's founder, Kim il-Sung. The two brothers had fought the Japanese during WWII as members of the communist Northeast Anti-Japanese Army. After the war, both brothers started running chemical and pharmaceutical factories, but Cho's father didn't trust the Soviets. When the UN forces moved north in late 1950, Yoon Pak, then in his late thirties, had seen his chance to escape and come to Hong Kong. Once there, they all—her mother, three brothers and Cho—changed their family names from Pak to Rhee in honor of the leader of South Korea.

On November 18th, 1994, Cho Rhee had been appointed as the new Financial Director of Half Moon, U.S. Inc. and moved back to Los Angeles. As a student, Cho had worked in the Half Moon LA office part time as a clerk in the shipping and logistics department, and later in sales. Now she was back, as head of finance and administration. Cho was the only one in the U.S. who had any knowledge of what her father called, the "dirty side" of the family business: drug smuggling.

When the president of Half Moon, U.S., was interviewed by the DEA and Customs, he was not lying when he said that he had no knowledge of drugs being carried by *Crescent Star.* He explained that while Half Moon chartered the ship for its cargos, it had little or no control over what the captains did as long as their designated cargos were safely delivered.

Cho worked with a Hong Kong law firm to set up the subsidiaries of the chain of corporate entities chartered in Macao, Mauritius, the Cayman Islands and the Seychelles to move the money to pay the assassins' stipends and arrange for their cars and houses. Tasking came through the dummy corporation in Macao. Once in country, each North Korean paid his own bills from his own checking account. Knowing how to do that was part of their training in the Democratic People's Republic of Korea. Through her uncle Admiral Pak's connections and another Half Moon founding family, the Jangs, Cho's father negotiated the fee paid to the communist nation for the "services" provided by the young men.

The assassin list had been developed during the time she was in Macao, with input from a man named David Seul, who was a cousin of General Jang. Seul had flown to the Portuguese colony from Hawaii and given her a who's who of the illegal drug business in Southern California. Together, they'd identified key players who had to be eliminated for Half Moon to quickly increase its market share and approach the Sinaloas.

Cho turned off the TV with a satisfied smile and the press of a button. *Only eight more to go, and the cops still don't have a clue. We'll be done before they know where to look, and they'll be scratching their heads with the same hand they use to wipe their asses.*

Chapter 7: EXTORTION

Monday, May 8ᵗʰ, 1995, 0814 local time, U.S.S. Blue Ridge

Monday in Japan was Sunday in the U.S., therefore, Mondays were light on messages. Josh was in his office finalizing the draft of the last reply he had to send when the STU-III on his desk rang. "Captain Haman."

"Hi, Josh, it's Roger Billingham."

"How are you doing? It is Sunday in Honolulu. Shouldn't you be on the golf course?"

"I wish. Let's go secure. I'll initiate."

Josh hated the secure phone because it always sounded as if you were speaking in a tunnel with your voice distorted by high winds.

"I called to give you the latest from *Honolulu,*" Billingham said. The *Romeo* had moved through La Pérouse and up into the Kurils, staying close to the islands for the most part, well inside the hundred-fathom curve as it picked its way north. "It's now headed southwest in the Sea of Okhotsk after surfacing for four hours a mile off the entrance to Broutana Bay. A Zodiac style boat came out from the harbor and took some people ashore."

The Simushir Island Incident

"Just how tough is it to maneuver a sub in close to the Kuril Islands?"

"Not hard. There's a lot of current going back and forth between the Pacific and the Sea of O. You just have to know where you are in relation to the bottom. The west side of the Kurils is pretty calm. The islands are the tops of volcanoes, so the water deepens pretty fast. You can get very close."

"Spoken like a man who's been there."

"No comment."

"Thank you. The info is very helpful."

"Captain, why are you asking?" Billingham's sudden formality was meant to remind Josh that, even though they were both captains, he was senior. The former sub commander was using a tone a superior officer uses when talking to a subordinate officially.

"The *Romeo* is way out of its sandbox, so I am curious. The North Koreans are big on using their subs to insert Special Forces."

"So are we. Does your question have anything to do with *La Jolla* and its SEAL dry dock shelter heading your way?"

"Sir, I can't tell you. Thanks for the info. Please keep me informed." Josh ended the call before Billingham could ask another question.

Tuesday, May 9th, 1995, 1456 local time, Glendale, CA

When Detective Proudfoot arrived, uniformed policemen were setting up barricades on the street to keep the gathering crowd at bay. The forensic team and two individuals from the medical examiner's office were waiting outside the house. He asked them to not move the body until he had a chance to look over the crime scene.

Doug Proudfoot pulled on a pair of latex gloves, hoping he could get in and get out before the media arrived. He crossed the threshold, closely followed by William Grayson, senior forensic investigator, into a spacious kitchen, and stopped. He'd viewed many murder scenes, and all of them were grisly. Violent human death is never pretty; but in his 18 years as a police officer, eight walking a beat and 10 as a detective, this one was a first.

The body was slumped in the corner, wedged between two cabinets. Muscle and tendon on the man's right arm were hanging loose, almost sliced completely off. His breastbone was exposed. The last wound, and probably the one that actually killed the man, was the slash that had nearly decapitated the victim. Blood was splattered everywhere. Large quantities had soaked the man's clothing,

Proudfoot wondered how long the fight—if you could call it that, it looked is if it had been damned one-sided—had lasted. The attacker must have been an expert with a sword, so it had probably been brutal and over in seconds. But what kind of assassin in this day and age uses a sword? Images from what he referred to as "chop-sake" movies, with ninjas and martial arts experts, ran though his mind.

After they studied the blood-splattered kitchen, Proudfoot walked through the rest of house. In a small bedroom, a large TV monitor sat on a desk next to a video recorder and a small pile of VHS videotapes.

Proudfoot tapped the space bar, and the monitor came on, showing images for four different cameras. "Bill, do you mind if I play this back?"

William Grayson, like Proudfoot, always seemed to draw the challenging cases. "I don't mind; but if you fuck up the video tape, there will be hell to pay, and it will come out of your hide!"

"Can you send me copies?"

"As soon as we can make them. Probably this afternoon."

"Any sign of forced entry?"

"The lock to the back door was picked, as was the one on the back fence. Looks like the killer surprised the victim in the kitchen —not much sign of struggle, just lots of dying. Driver's license says Hector Garza. Vice thinks he's high up in La Miradas. Here, let me show you the safe."

Grayson opened the door to the closet in the bedroom. In it was a safe, bolted to the floor, empty except for some bands used for bundling currency. "We'll check it for ink residue. It won't tell us how *much* was here, but it *will* tell us if there was cash.

"I want to look at the camera locations."

"Sure, knock yourself out. Can I have the ME guys remove the body now?"

"Yeah, I've seen enough blood and guts for the day."

Out back, Proudfoot vaulted over the fence so as not to interfere with forensic's assessment of the fence and stood in the alley, gazing at the camouflaged camera that should have recorded the attacker's movements. Did the security system have alerts to tell Garza someone was at his back door?

Four hours later, just as Proudfoot was about to call it a day, Bill Grayson walked into his office and plunked two VHS cassettes on the table, along with a fuzzy image of a young, Asian male. "One is cued up and shows an Asian in the alley, clearly studying Garza's house. The second, three days later, shows the same man kneeling by the fence. A few seconds later, the man enters the back yard and starts to pick the lock on the back door.

"Thanks. I'll study them and see what I can come up with."

"Doug, this man is the killer. Go detect and find the bastard."

Proudfoot nodded. "That's my job."

After Grayson left, Proudfoot sat staring at the picture. "Who the fuck are you? Who trained you? And who hires you?

If he'd had the capabilities to compare the image he held with passport photos, he would have learned that he was looking at the face of Jintao Yi. What the passport wouldn't have told him was that Yi was a first lieutenant in the Korean People's Army and an expert in using a *wakizashi* or short sword.

Tuesday, May 19th, 1995, 0930 local time, Pyongyang

The building that contained the offices of the general secretary of the Communist Party in the Democratic People's Republic of Korea was designed to be imposing, not a thing of beauty, and succeeded in its goal. It was also boring to look at, a stack of gray concrete rectangles.

General Jang, looking worried, met Vice Admiral Pak, outside the building and demanded "What is going on?"

"Our Dear Leader called me in to talk about Simushir. Maybe he wants to tell me he has struck a deal to buy more decrepit submarines, or maybe he actually ordered the newer ones we want."

"Don't make light of this, Chun Lee." General Jang was very serious. "He can have us killed and won't think twice about it."

"You worry too much. He needs us, and he knows it."

"I will eat lunch at the ministry of defense's cafeteria and stay there as long as I can. Look for me there first. If not, we will find a way to talk." Jang didn't wait for an answer and headed back toward the Army headquarters building down the street. If they met too often or too long, it would make some paranoid people in the State Security Department suspect that they were plotting a coup.

Vice Admiral Pak looked up, enjoying the spring sunshine, and then he looked at his watch. It was, unlike the counterfeit ones made in China and worn by many of his counterparts, a real Rolex Submariner. It was, he saw, time to enter the dull, drab building.

As usual, he suffered through the rigmarole one endured before one might be graced with the presence of the country's Dear Leader. It amused Pak that the guards tested the sheets of paper he brought to meetings to make sure that they weren't laced with some kind of explosive. This time, he had summaries of submarine operations, as well as a separate one on the "side" business.

"Vice Admiral Pak, it is so good of you to come." The Dear Leader held his hands wide, then grabbed Pak's outstretched hand in both of his. The guards took their customary stances in the corners of the room. The same severe-looking woman took up a place behind and to the left of the Dear Leader. Pak assumed anything spoken in this room was recorded by hidden equipment, so the secretary's presence was at once a facade and a visible reminder that whatever one uttered would be written down, scrutinized, and manipulated.

Two other men followed dressed in civilian clothes and bearing scrolls of paper.

One man introduced himself as Senior Engineer Soon. He unrolled the drawings he carried onto the table, and used four polished steel disks to hold down the corners. Dr. Soon then pointed out where they could build an airfield on Simushir. There was no discussion of the cost or time needed. If the Dear Leader wanted an airfield, an airfield he would have. When he was finished, he resumed his place against the wall and came to attention. Now it was the Geologist Ryu's turn.

Ryu described how North Korean engineers could expand caves on the island so that large vehicles could be parked and hidden from spy planes and satellites. He did mention the risk of the construction team encountering a vent, but this he glossed over. He said nothing about the deaths that would result, and no one else asked. Nor did he mention the danger of earthquakes and what they might do to the caves. Like Soon, Ryu spoke mechanically, providing responses carefully composed to validate the Dear Leader's idea. Pak was impressed. These men understood how to survive in the Democratic People's Republic of Korea. When

Senior Geologist Ryu finished, the two scientists were excused and marched out of the room.

The Dear Leader leaned forward in his chair. "Admiral Pak, Simushir is a perfect place for us to establish a base outside our country. It is an opportunity to show our Russian comrades and the rest of the world the skills of our engineers and our ability to complete complex projects. Our foreign minister has already spoken to the Russian Foreign Ministry. He has approved the airfield, and when it gets built both countries get to use it!"

Vice Admiral Pak forced himself to smile because he could see the Dear Leader was very excited. *The airfield, Dear Leader was your idea, not mine or General Jang's. We do not want Russians on Simushir to observe our drug operation, and neither should you! It's bad enough their border guards are making regular visits. An extensive Russian presence will mean that they will want a cut of the income from drug sales. We picked Simushir expressly to avoid the need for bribes!*

Whenever bureaucrats and senior military officials were assigned special projects by their Dear Leader, they always made sure they had a scapegoat in place before they began the task. He wondered whom Ryu and Soon had chosen—or were they potential scapegoats themselves? It was, Pak thought, a most Darwinian situation.

The Dear Leader's high-pitched voice was continuing. "So, you see, your island has lots of possibilities for our country. I understand from your reports there will soon be accommodations for six hundred men. Is this true?"

"Yes, sir, it is. When we finish renovating the barracks, it will house three hundred. New buildings will give us accommodations for two hundred more, and the one hundred employees of the Kuril Island Development Corporation have their own quarters."

"Excellent. How many are on the island now?"

The Simushir Island Incident

"The number changes as installation teams come and go, but on average there are one hundred workers, plus thirty-six of our special forces soldiers."

"We are going to increase the number of soldiers. Our Russian friends had three thousand people on the island, so I want to have at least that many. I am sending another, larger survey team under Senior Geologist Ryu to examine in detail the caves he found. They will develop a plan to expand them. Senior Engineer Soon will oversee building the runway. I am sure you can arrange the transport of both the survey teams and a battalion of our special forces soldiers to Simushir, along with any vehicles they may need."

Pak nodded stoically. *This is wrong, wrong, wrong!!!*

The Dear Leader smiled, savoring that the admiral didn't have any idea of what he was about to shove down his throat next.

"We are going to store chemical and nuclear warheads in the caves, along with the missiles to carry them. We're going to build launch sites on the shores of the Zavaritzk Caldera. We'll assemble the missiles in the caves, and when we need them, we can use them against our enemies."

Admiral Pak swallowed. *You're fucking nuts!!! The Russians will never let you store chemical and nuclear weapons on their land, much less the rockets to deliver them! How the fuck are you going to get the missiles there? They won't fit in my submarines. Once the Americans and the Japanese find out they are on commercial ships, they will stop or sink them. When I was training in the Soviet Union, the instructors openly talked about Khrushchev's failed attempt to base missiles in Cuba. The Americans forced him to remove them—and we're not the Soviet Union.*

"Once they are there, our Tae Dong I rockets launched from Simushir will be able to reach all of Northern Japan, and our Tae

Dong IIs and IIIs can hit Washington and New York. I have issued orders to have special crates designed to carry the missile parts and to put them in ships leaving from Dalian or Dandong. The warheads are small enough so they can be shipped in our submarines."

The Dear Leader was smiling, sure his strategic thinking had surprised the admiral. He believed that neither Pak nor General Jang had ever thought about putting ballistic missiles on Simushir. Their thinking was too small, too narrow, just like the rest of the flag officers on the general staff, and *that* was why *he* was North Korea's thought leader and ruler. "I will be assigning a member of my staff, Kwang-sik Thaek, to work with you on this. He is waiting for you to call so you can meet this afternoon. Assume he is speaking for me in terms of what I want done. He will also advise you of any new security measures to implement. You will show him how to work through the Kuril Island Development Corporation to purchase equipment from commercial contractors. The missile base and runway on Simushir have the highest priority, and I want work to begin as soon as possible."

"Yes, sir." Vice Admiral Pak knew any reluctance would mean the end of his career, and his life. The Dear Leader was like a spoiled child with a new toy, so excited by the prospect of nuclear missiles that he didn't even see how he was jeopardizing the plans for the extremely lucrative heroin production and distribution out of Simushir.

"And one more thing." The Dear Leader smiled again. He was about to ram the most important issue up Pak's ass. "I want to increase our drug exports to the U.S. What better way is there to weaken the Americans? I want you to make sure we find more, what do you call them, 'pushers' in America. If you need help from our intelligence services, let Thaek know. He will want to know more about your drug distribution operation."

The Simushir Island Incident

Vice Admiral Pak said nothing. The message was clear: *You are not indispensable.* The more Thaek learned about their operations, the more "dispensable" Pak became. *General Jang is right to be worried.*

"To help pay for this operation, I am adding a two-percent tax on the drugs you sell, beginning the first of next month, so the state will now get twelve percent. The new factory on Simushir increases your output and will make us both more money."

His declaration complete, Kim Jong-Il stood up. "Vice Admiral Pak, thank you for coming. I am assuming you will assist Deputy Minister Kwang-sik Thaek to the best of your ability, just as you have served my father and now serve me."

Vice Admiral Pak stood up and came to attention. After his commander-in-chief left the room, he didn't leave right away. The thought that kept running through his head was, *He's going put our whole drug operation at risk, and he wants to start a war we cannot win.*

The time to retire was fast approaching. The question was, how? He and Jang were wealthy men living in a country where any show of money could lead to denouncement, accusations of being capitalists, and death by firing squad or worse—by starvation or disease in a re-education camp.

Pak fumed quietly as he exited the building. These new plans were insane. The Americans were taking pictures of Simushir, and the facility needed to look just like what was said in the news release. *We can tell the press we are starting to build a road to the southern end of the island for a new airport, and that road will require tunneling. But what about the missiles? How do we get them to the island? In international waters, ships can be stopped. What if the launchers are discovered? How are we going to explain missiles and chemical weapons to the Russians, or anyone else?*

And Thaek was going to be a problem. *Jang warned me about him. He's the stinky bastard who uses Special Forces officers for "special arrests. The man doesn't even speak English or Chinese, nor has he ever left North Korea, so how is he going to communicate with anyone in Hong Kong?* Admiral Pak paused in mid-stride, struck by an idea. *I can use his lack of knowledge of languages to our advantage, even as he thinks he is making decisions. Give him choices that will minimize any risk to us. It will be difficult, but I will find a way.*

The sooner he met with General Jang, the better. They had a lot to discuss.

Wednesday, May 10th, 1995, 1340 local time, Pyongyang

Deputy Minister Thaek's stomach churned as he stood before the Dear Leader. He needed a cigarette and the calming effect of nicotine flowing through his system, but smoking in the presence of the Dear Leader was forbidden. He didn't like unscheduled meetings with the Dear Leader because they didn't leave him time to check his sources to see which way the wind was blowing.

"Tell me what you know about Admiral Pak."

"We monitor all his conversations and carefully study those he has with Half Moon Trading in Hong Kong to see if there are any hidden codes or meaning. So far, he has never said anything that could be construed as disloyal. We have operatives in Hong Kong and Macao watching their relatives. We know Half Moon has three heroin processing factories there, plus the two they have in Nampo where they also make counterfeit drugs. We don't know how many kilos of heroin they produce in Hong Kong because they are well guarded. We've tried getting someone inside or bribing a senior manager, but so far, we have not been successful. Shipments are concealed in other products." Thaek flipped through his binder and looked at his notes. "They never talk specifics when they are on the phone."

"Where do they keep their money? How much do they really have?"

"Dear Leader, we have agents looking. We suspect they have Swiss bank accounts, but we do not have proof nor any estimates of their fortunes, because they work through law firms in Hong Kong and in Lichtenstein." Thaek looked at his Dear Leader for signs of disinterest or boredom. Seeing none, he kept speaking. "His relatives in Hong Kong are wealthy; however, they keep their wealth well-guarded. A few months ago our men tried to break into the law firm they retain, but they were killed during the robbery, so we learned nothing."

Thaek decided to share another tidbit he didn't think his Dear Leader knew. "Pak's daughter has another full year at an advanced medical school in Beijing. You personally approved her visa. His wife has been approved to go there to visit when Vice Admiral Pak meets with the Chinese Navy."

"What is she studying?"

"When she returns to our republic, she will be one of our best trained cardiovascular surgeons."

"And his son?"

"His son Seong is a marine engineer at the number five shipyard in Haeju. He has severe asthma and is not fit for military service. The last doctor who treated him said he will not live long."

"And what about Major General Jang?"

"His wife works at Kim Il-Sung University as a senior administrator. They had one son, who died young." Their only son had followed his father into the special forces and had been killed in a plane crash during a training exercise. The pilot of that plane had received his wings not because he was skillful, but because his father was a friend of Kim il-Sung, and no one had dared wash him out of the pilot-training program. He had been assigned to fly AN-2s, a World War II-era biplane that was easy to fly. What was not so easy was flying up and down mountain valleys under cover of darkness, trying to avoid being detected by radar. One night, the pilot crashed headlong into a mountain, killing himself, his copilot, and the twelve soldiers in the cabin, Jang's son among them.

Kim Jong-Il stared at Thaek. "And this Major Kim who went to Simushir?"

"I know him. He was handpicked for special arrests and completed ten for me with satisfactory results. Each arrest was handled well. My men who were on his arrest teams say he is an effective leader, and very loyal. Major General Jang reviewed several officers before recommending him for the Simushir assignment."

"Is there a family connection between Major Kim and General Jang or Vice Admiral Pak?"

"No." Thaek desperately needed a cigarette.

"How reliable are Kim, Pak and Jang?"

Is that a hint to create a fictitious conspiracy the Dear Leader could use to arrest these three officers? The Dear Leader had just implied he didn't trust the admiral and the general, who had wealth outside the country that Kim Jong-Il didn't control. Kim Jong-Il controlled their daily lives, but not their wealth. Money made these men independent, and to the Dear Leader that was intolerable. They were allowed to live only because they were making the Dear Leader wealthier. Thaek suspected it was only a matter of time before one of two events happened. Either their value to the Dear Leader diminished, or he figured out how to seize their money. Then they would be eliminated. Thaek just had to make sure the Dear Leader's finger never pointed at *him*.

He hesitated before speaking. "I can vouch for Major Kim. I have studied Jang's and Pak's files and can say they all have served their country well. We have nothing to suggest they are not true patriots who will do their duty when asked."

Kim Jung-Il wrinkled his nose at the stench emanating from Thaek. He had little sympathy for men addicted to tobacco. "Watch them very carefully. I want to know about their money, where it is and how much they have. I want you to find out how their business works and develop a plan to take it over. When you do, I will make sure you benefit. You will report in person only to me on this every week."

"Yes, Dear Leader."

"And two more tasks. Have your agents tell the police in Hong Kong and Macao about the drug factories. I want them raided and put out of business to put pressure on Pak and Jang."

"At once, Dear Leader. That is a brilliant move."

Kim il-Sung nodded at the compliment, as if to say, *Of course, it is brilliant—it came from me.* "Second, the Russians are telling us the Americans have become very interested in our little operation on Simushir, and that makes the Russians curious. Do what you can to discourage the Americans, which will lessen the Russian interest."

Friday, May 12th, 1995, 1830 local time, Oahu

Bill Hamilton, wearing a Hawaiian shirt, Bermuda shorts and a pair of running shoes, tried to look inconspicuous in the crowded lobby of the Hilton Hawaiian Village Hotel. It felt odd not to be wearing the dress shirt and slacks he habitually wore at JICPAC, where he was a signals analyst working for Uilani Ka'anapali. The mounting tension he now felt was mental and physical. He was afraid, very afraid, and sweating because it was getting harder to control his fear. Bill slowly turned his head from one side to the other, searching. Despite his attempt at surveillance, he was surprised by a jab in the ribs and a voice from behind.

"Come along, Bill. We're going for a short ride. Don't worry, you're worth more alive than dead. Act as if we're your buddies." Hamilton felt a firm grasp on his triceps.

As they walked along, Bill could smell Old Spice cologne, but he didn't turn his head to see who was guiding him toward Kealakekua Avenue, on the other side of the park of the Fort DeRussy military reservation. The old coastal defense battery that once guarded the entrance to Pearl Harbor was now a museum. Despite his escort's assurance, fear gnawed at Hamilton's stomach.

The rear door to a maroon Ford Crown Victoria opened in front of Hamilton. Hands moved up and down his sides and legs, checking for weapons or a surveillance wire. Then he was ordered, "Get in."

The man in the front passenger seat turned around. It was his bookie. "Good evening, Bill. We're going to go meet an acquaintance of mine."

"Why?" Bill Hamilton found his voice. For some reason, his brain began reviewing the highlights of the 45 years he'd spent on this earth. There weren't many.

The car pulled out into traffic, and his bookie continued. "Why? because of the forty-two thousand, six hundred and twenty-five dollars you owe me, you little shit. With the vig on the money, I don't think you can ever pay it back."

Hamilton didn't answer, because what his bookie said was true.

"So, I was thinking. How do I collect? I can break a few of your bones, but that won't get me paid. You live in an apartment, so you don't have a house to give me. And killing you as an example isn't always good for business. So I came up with a different idea."

The Crown Victoria pulled over to the curb.

"See that man over there on the bench? He likes to be called Mr. Seul. Go talk to him. He's going to offer you a deal you can't refuse. If you cooperate, he will pay your debt in full and make both of us happy so we can go our separate ways. Now get out."

Hamilton was too scared not to do as he was told. Two well-muscled men stood on either side of the bench scanning the park, one small sector at a time. As Hamilton approached, the nearest one held out his hand, palm raised, indicating he wanted Bill to stop. "I… I am here to see Mr. Seul," he explained. *I thought I was expected.*

The man took a picture from his shirt pocket, looked at it, then looked again at Hamilton. The picture and face evidently matched, for he pointed Bill to the bench. Hamilton wasn't patted down, but then, they must have known he'd been searched already and didn't want to make a scene in a public place.

Hamilton sat on end of the bench, which looked out over the ocean. "Mr. Seul?" He noticed the man was reading a book in Hangul and had a Chinese language newspaper on his lap.

"Yes." He made a small ceremony of placing a bookmark between the pages before closing it. As Mr. Seul turned to face Hamilton, he put his arm on the back of the bench. Well-manicured fingers draped loosely over the top slat of green painted wood. "I understand you have a debt you cannot pay. Is that correct?"

Hamilton nodded. Seul's voice had a light, almost feminine lilt to it. For a moment, he wondered if Seul was a fag.

"And you would like the debt to go away."

Another nod, this one more vigorous.

"Then we can transact business."

"What do you want me to do?"

"Provide information."

"Such as?"

"I am associated with several companies that are being studied by your co-workers. I want to know what is known by them."

"So… you want classified information."

"Yes."

"And the companies are?"

"Not so fast. Do we have an agreement?"

"So, I provide you the information you request, and you pay my debt in full. If you mean that when that is done, I am a free man and there will be no more requests for information, then maybe we can work something out."

"Yes to the first, but I cannot guarantee the second part of your stipulation."

"Why not, once I get you the information you need?"

"I always need more. It is the price you pay for me taking care of your debt. Call it interest. It is a nice play on the word. Bookies don't like it when they are not paid. I am offering you an alternative with minimal risk. It is a choice only you can make."

Hamilton couldn't refute the man's logic. He looked at the tips of the well-manicured fingers resting on the top of the bench's backrest. If he didn't agree, he would never get out of the clutches of his bookie. "Will I get paid for the additional requests?"

"Are we negotiating fees?"

"Yes." Hamilton wanted to play along. His choices were to commit treason or turn the bastard in—and risk being killed. Before he did anything rash, he had to wipe out his debt, wait some time, and then decide what to do.

"I'll give you twenty thousand U.S. dollars for each additional request."

"Not enough. For this first one, we've already established the market at over forty-two thousand dollars."

"Very good. I am impressed. You *do* have some balls. Twenty-five thousand."

"Twenty-seven thousand, and you make three equal deposits in offshore banks in accounts I give you. That keeps the payments under the feds' radar. First payment is deposited when the request is made, the second when the delivery is scheduled, and the third within twenty-four hours after I deliver the material."

"Done."

"Then we have a deal."

"Agreed."

"Mr. Seul, how long do I have to collect the first batch of information?"

"Let's plan on delivery on June 1st. It is a little over three weeks away."

"Agreed." *How hard can this be?*

Mr. Seul looked Bill in the face, taking his measure to determine if the man was desperate or scared enough to deliver. If not, he'd let the bookie deal with him and look for another source.

"What are the names of the companies?"

Mr. Seul handed him a folded hundred-dollar bill. Hamilton again noticed Seul's manicured fingers. "Use this for a cab back to where you parked. The companies' names are on the paper inside, along with a phone number to call to schedule delivery."

Hamilton found a small piece of paper folded inside the Benjamin. When he saw the names Half Moon Trading and Kuril Island Development Company, the air went out of his lungs. Breathing in, he put his head back and looked straight up at the sky thinking, *Oh shit!* By the time he turned back to the bench, Mr. Seul, his bodyguards, the bookie and the Crown Victoria were gone. He waited a few minutes so he could stop shaking before he walked to the street and hailed a cab.

Tuesday, May 16th, 1995, 1023 local time, Oahu
Captain Haman and Commander Cabot were sitting opposite CINCPAC's administrative secretary, waiting for the four-star to finish a conversation with the National Security Advisor, at the end

of which they expected the admiral to authorize them to execute Operation Glass Carat, the sneak-and-peek on Simushir Island.

While they waited, Admiral Jeffers' aide walked by and almost jackknifed when he saw the two officers. A few minutes later, he came back, ostensibly to check for an opening on CINCPAC's schedule for some mythical meeting with Jeffers.

When he left in an obvious hurry, Marty, Josh, and even Madeline, CINCPAC's admin, started laughing. With a twinkle in her eye, Madeline said, "We all have crosses to bear, and at PACOM headquarters, Rear Admiral Jeffers is ours."

The laughing stopped when CINCPAC opened the door. He didn't have to say anything. The look was enough to say, *What's so funny, Madeline?"*

"Sir, Rear Admiral Jeffers' aide almost fell over when he saw Captain Haman and Commander Cabot sitting here. Then he came by to check your schedule. It was a recon! I could see he was trying to eyeball your schedule to learn why these two officers were here."

CINCPAC harrumphed. "Before COB the one-sentence authorization message will be out. Admiral Jeffers is not on the list of those cleared for the op. I'll deal with him if need be."

The four-star wished them good luck and disappeared back into his office.

Standing on the veranda of the headquarters of the Commander in Chief, Pacific Command, Marty and Josh could see all of Pearl Harbor and the city of Honolulu. Again, they started laughing at the antics of Jeffers' aide.

Their enjoyment was overshadowed by the anticipated difficulty they would face in executing Operation Glass Carat. Besides being dangerous, the sneak and peek on Simushir could have ugly geopolitical and career-ending consequences if bungled.

The Simushir Island Incident

When they got to their rental car, Josh put his hand on the steel roof before he got inside. It was hot to the touch. "Are you going to stay the rest of the week?"

"Yup. There are some things I need to work out for an upcoming exercise."

"And spend time with the gorgeous Uilani? If she wants to come to Japan, let her. I'll move mountains to make sure you get some time away from the meat grinder to help the two of you out."

Marty took a deep breath. "It's scary letting another woman into my life. Especially a very smart one. But I think Uilani is the right one. I just wish I'd met her sooner. And… please don't push. I am trying not to rush it. I want Jack and you to help me enjoy the ride"

"Understood. Let me know what I *can* do to help. I'm sure Jack will say the same."

"No matter how this comes out, just be there for me. And don't let me do something stupid!"

Chapter 8: NO GOOD ANSWERS

Wednesday, May 17th, 1995, 0930 local time, Washington, D.C.

For Gary Nash, the past two weeks had been a whirlwind. His initial orders had been extended for two more weeks, and that was putting a strain on his law practice. Some matters could be shifted onto the shoulders of his partners or associates, but many could not, causing problems with impatient judges as well as disgruntled clients. All his scheduled court dates had to be postponed, and that was a major hardship for everyone involved.

He had spent long hours at the Judge Advocate General's office, reviewing material on Higgins, including the latest background information collected by both the FBI and the Navy Criminal Investigative Service. He'd briefed the Chief of Naval Operations, the Chairman of the Joint Chiefs of Staff, the Secretary of Defense, and the DOD's top civilian lawyer. All wanted to know why Higgins had been forced out of the Navy. Apparently, the name Steven Higgins was toxic, and Gary Nash was supposed to be the man with the antidote. Today's tasking was a meeting with the minority leader of the House, at the Rayburn House Office Building.

CNO had set up this meeting, and while the Minority Leader had not been told the exact topic, CNO had emphasized its sensitivity, its importance to the Navy and the Department of Defense, and had convinced the Minority Leader's aides that the meeting would be worth the Minority Leader's time. What surprised the Minority Leader of the House of Representatives was the length of the requested meeting—at least an hour. Usually, meetings were measured in minutes.

The Judge Advocate General, a two-star admiral, went with Nash to provide clout and context. Gary Nash's role was to present the material, starting with DOD's reasons why it could not issue Representative Steven Higgins a Top-Secret clearance.

Existing DOD policy prevented any federal agency from issuing a clearance to anyone given a discharge under other than honorable conditions. As a member of Congress, Higgins had been issued a Secret clearance as a matter of course when he was elected, and the DOD had looked the other way. On the committees to which he had initially been assigned, he was not expected to be granted access to classified material. However, assignment to the House Armed Services Sub-Committee for Readiness requires a Top-Secret clearance, and neither the DOD nor the Navy was prepared to issue such a clearance to Higgins.

All of this was carefully explained to the Minority Leader, a former Air Force intelligence officer. When the JAG admiral finished his explanation, the congressman sent his administrative assistant to bring him Representative Higgins' background file. When it arrived, he scanned the papers.

Concern registered on his face. "Representative Higgins stated he was issued a General Discharge. No other information. I need more information. Tell me why he received this discharge, which is unusual, to say the least, for an Annapolis graduate."

The JAG admiral asked Nash to walk the Minority Leader through the investigation and the subsequent charges. As he spoke, Nash handed the verifying documents to the Minority Leader so he could read them. He finished by describing the choice given to Higgins in February 1971—accept the General Discharge under Other Than Honorable Conditions or face a court martial for cowardice in time of war.

The representative shook his head. "This is not good news, but what do you want me to do? As far as the House's rules go, other than knowingly not listing his discharge correctly, which technically is a felony because it is falsifying a government document, he has done nothing to warrant impeachment. His constituents elected him not once, but three times."

Gary forced himself to control his anger. How many people were going to cover for this weasel? Didn't they understand? Higgins was a disgrace to the United States. He had left men behind to be killed or captured by an enemy known to torture their prisoners. Didn't anybody care? Sensing Gary might say something he shouldn't, the Judge Advocate General put his hand on Gary's arm as if to say, *"Let me speak."*

"The Navy wants all the briefing material Representative Higgins was given on his recent trip to the Far East, including his notes, as well as the return of any classified material in his possession. DOD is, as of May 29th, revoking his clearance."

Reluctantly, the Democratic Minority Leader nodded. Higgins was now a time bomb, and the fuse was lit. While neither Nash nor the admiral had said the information would be released officially, it could be leaked at any time and be a major embarrassment to a Democratic Party that had lost control of the House and the Senate. As he thanked the officers for coming and escorted them out of his office, the Minority Leader focused on the only viable option he had to prevent losing another seat.

The Simushir Island Incident

Thursday, May 18th, 1995, 1400 local time, Washington, D.C.

Steven Higgins was planning how to enjoy his Memorial holiday weekend recess when he was called to the House Minority Leader's office. When he entered, he was surprised to find the chairman of the Democratic National Committee sitting at one end of the couch.

The Minority Leader waved him to the empty end of the couch and Higgins settled into the armchair next to the chairman of the DNC. "Steve, have you formally announced your intention to run for re-election?"

Higgins smiled, resting one arm expansively over the back of the couch. *It looks like I'm being groomed for a leadership position. About time, after all I've accomplished for the party.* "No, sir, not yet. After all, I was re-elected to my current term only six months ago. I'm having a press conference on June 12th in Madison on my position on key issues. If asked that question, I will say yes. Why?"

The chairman of the Democratic National Committee was a former Army officer. He leaned forward. "The Party would prefer if you served out your term and did not run for re-election."

Taken aback, Higgins gave both men a puzzled look. Only two words came out. "Again, why?"

The Minority Leader answered, his voice quiet and deliberate. "Earlier in the week, the Judge Advocate General of the United States Navy and one of their lawyers paid me a visit. They walked me through the details of what was behind your discharge. You deliberately left off the words 'under other than honorable conditions,' and with your incomplete answer, you falsified a government record. Technically, it is an impeachable offense. Now that I know what was behind your discharge, neither the Party Chairman nor I will support your candidacy for re-election."

The public defender in Higgins took over. He sat up straight, tented his fingers and made eye contact. "Sir, I carried my district in three elections by margins of 12, 18 and 21 per cent. My constituents like my positions, and I have been open about my opposition to the Vietnam War, our involvement in the Persian Gulf during the 1980s, overt and covert support of the British to take back the Falkland Islands, and support of the South Africans against the Cubans in Angola. The list of our military entanglements is long, and I believe that no one in the House or the Senate knows the extent or the costs of all the commitments we have. There are hundreds of others in this country who have the same type of discharge, so why is this important now?"

"It *is* important. You are a member of the House of Representatives, not just anyone on the street. If this becomes public, it will be an embarrassment to the Democratic Party. We can't afford to lose any more ground. The DOD is pulling your clearance as of the 31st of May. Their long-standing policy is to deny a clearance to anybody with an Other-than-Honorable discharge. You need to deliver all of your classified material to my office by close of business next Thursday. The only graceful way out is for you either to resign immediately or to announce that you are not going to run for re-election."

The DNC's boss added, "And if you run, the DNC will not provide support of any kind and will find a candidate to run against you. What was behind your discharge is a ticking time bomb, and you should consider yourself lucky it hasn't already exploded."

Higgins felt his eyes narrow, his jaw clench. He felt himself flush with anger. *Those bastards Nash and Haman are behind this —I just know it! Those self-centered, self-righteous, self-serving fucks! They want to ruin my life. Why couldn't they just have left me alone?* He was oblivious to the irony of his complaint. He took a deep breath and stood up. "Are we done here?"

The Simushir Island Incident

At the door, Higgins turned to face the two men. His hand reddened as it gripped the steel doorknob as if he were trying to crush it and, through it, the throats of everyone who thwarted him. "Two things. One, I intend to run. And two, if this leaks out, my first two lawsuits will be against the DNC and you, Congressman. I know how both of you operate. Have a nice day."

Tuesday, May 23rd, 1995, 0754 local time, U.S.S. Blue Ridge

Josh sat in his office enjoying the smaller volume of the message traffic caused by the upcoming Memorial Day holiday. Usually he had to slog through messages until nine or ten in the morning; today, the clean center of his desk screamed, *YES, you ARE caught up!!!*

The only document on his desk demanding his review was the latest revision of Seventh Fleet's operational plan to support a war in Korea. He was about to dive into the three-inch thick document when he heard someone enter the outer office. Marty was looking haggard as he plunked a briefcase down on his desk.

"You look like shit," Josh observed.

"Plane left Honolulu late, so I stayed at a hotel in Narita and took the first train here. I got about three hours sleep."

"Glad you could make it back. How was the important part of the trip?"

"Great."

"Do anything special?"

"Yeah. On Saturday, we had dinner with her parents."

"How'd that go?"

"Fine. We talked about many things, including our favorite island. They're very nice people. But my Hawaiian is rusty!" Marty looked around the empty room. "Where is everybody?"

"Enlisted are off meeting with the admiral, and the officers are having a late breakfast. It is like a morgue around here."

"Oh." Marty pulled two sealed envelopes marked "Top Secret" out of his briefcase and plopped them on his desk. "Uilani's dad Ka'eo is a professor at the University of Hawaii, has a PhD in geology and is an expert on volcanoes. I picked his brain about dormant ones, and without any prompting, he used those in Hawaii and the Kurils as examples. He has a Top-Secret clearance for the seismic work he does for our government, most of which is in Korea."

"So, what did you learn?"

Marty crossed his arms and leaned against a wall. "Ka'eo said tunneling into volcanoes, even extinct ones, is dangerous work and not for amateurs. If a tunneler punctures a tube sealed by cooled lava, the tunnel will fill with hot, toxic gases and maybe even molten lava. The gas is mostly very hot water vapor, but contains enough hydrogen sulfide, carbon dioxide and sulfur dioxide to kill you, if you are not scalded to death first. If you are lucky, a leak happens slowly. Plugging a leak in a tunnel filling with volcanic gases and molten lava is very difficult, if not impossible. Best solution is to get out of the cave and let it repair itself, which could be days or weeks or never!"

Then Marty shared his newfound knowledge on how solidified lava eats up boring tools. Ka'eo was going to give Uilani a list of which companies made such tools so the CIA could track purchases of these very expensive, large, specialized, and custom-built machines, all of which were made in the U.S., Japan or Germany.

"That's good information. But I'm sure you did more than talk with Ka'eo. How else did you spend your time?"

"We hiked and surfed."

"So Uilani wore you out. That's the real reason you're so pooped. The snake eater can't handle a woman for more than one night?"

Marty made a face. "With all due respect, Captain—fuck you!"

"Sensitive, are we. I guess that's what happens when you're in love."

"Yeah." Marty didn't even try to deny it. He stretched and sighed. He couldn't help that his mind was still in Honolulu and on what a great time he'd had during the past four days. "So, what's going on?"

"Look at what got faxed to us yesterday. It must have been a slow news day in Hong Kong because all three English language papers picked up the same story." Josh slid a paper across the desk. "This one is from the *International Herald Tribune.*"

DEVELOPMENT PLANS EXPANDED
FOR KURIL ISLAND

HONG KONG—The Kuril Island Development Corporation (KIDC) announced plans for phase two of its project that significantly increases its investment in the facility being built on Simushir Island in the Central Kurils. Phase two includes building a 40-kilometers-long (24.4 statute miles) road from Broutana Bay on the northern end of the island to a relatively flat area south of the Zavaritzk Caldera, where the company intends to construct an airfield with a 3,000-meter-long runway. The airfield will have fuel for sale and ramp space and ultimately two hangars of 4,000 square meters each. The firm estimates it will take at least two years to finish the airport. Other than emergencies, flights to the island will have to be pre-approved by both the Russian Federation and the company.

Phase One, to renovate the Cold War-era submarine base and turn it into a facility designed to support fishing vessels operating in the Northwest Pacific and eastern parts of the Sea of Okhotsk, should be completed by the end of this year. When it opens, the facility will stock parts for commonly used engines, pumps, winches and other machinery found on ocean fishing vessels. The machine shop is already operating to support the renovation.

The Broutana Bay operation, which does not yet have an official name, will also have a small dispensary and frozen and canned food to resupply ships. Two of the three original piers left over from the Soviet submarine base have already been rebuilt. The company said it will have a year-round staff of approximately 75.

To house the construction crews and enable them to stay on the island year round, the company brought in housing of the type used by oil companies drilling in the Arctic. Redundant desalinization plants, diesel generators and waste processing equipment are already operational.

The release noted that the company was in negotiations with the owners of fleets of vessels that fish in the area to provide storage for their catch. This would allow the ships to stay on station longer and have other ships pick up the frozen catch and take it to their customers. If these negotiations are successful, the Kuril Island Development Corporation will construct a large refrigerated storage facility on the island.

The project has earned local Hong Kong businesses large commissions for the goods purchased and shipping contracts to move the equipment to the remote island. Local economists estimate that KIDC has purchased about US$30 million in equipment through local agents, and spent millions more in shipping fees and labor.

According to members of the crews of the ships who have been carrying equipment and their installment teams, the island's picturesque harbor usually has one or more ships either anchored or tied up to a pier. Sailors interviewed report construction crews are working 24 hours a day and are paid a premium for working on Simushir.

Fishing boats will have plenty of room in the sheltered, mile-wide Broutana Bay, located on the northern end of the island. The channel into the bay, previously widened by the Soviet Union, has been enlarged to at least 50 meters wide and 30 meters deep by KIDC.

The company said work has begun on the road south to the proposed airport location. Deputy Minister Valerie Dimitriov from the Russian Federation's Maritime Ministry, when reached by phone at his office in Vladivostok, said, "The Russian government has approved the construction of the airport. We think that this facility will help vessels operating in a very difficult environment. The airport will also facilitate emergency evacuation of injured sailors."

Mr. Dimitriov is the official responsible for the Far Eastern region, which manages activities in the Kuril Islands. He declined to answer any questions about KIDC other than to say, "The Russian Federation welcomes commercial enterprises who want to invest in operations and facilities within its borders."

Work on the airfield will not begin until the road, which will require some tunneling, is completed. Attempts to contact KIDC or its representatives to get more information or verify the facts in the press release were not successful.

Marty tossed the paper back on the desk. "Despite what this release implies, I still think the North Koreans are involved up to their Communist eyeballs. They're experts at tunneling and hiding stuff—tanks, missile launchers, airplanes, submarines, etc.—in caves. If they put missiles on the island, it puts the Japanese islands at risk from a different direction, and maybe even the West Coast of the U.S."

Josh nodded agreement. "My bet is the facility will be a cover for a military base. And yes, the Japanese won't like it."

"What I keep asking is, why would the Russians allow the North Koreans to put troops on the island? Or, do they not know they are there?"

"What do you mean?" As Josh leaned forward, Marty could see the fire in his friend's icy blue eyes.

"Look, Josh—assume the North Koreans *are* behind this. They get the Russians to give them rights to use the island. The Russians aren't dumb. They know the North Koreans better than we do. They allow this fishing support facility to be built as a cover for a base from which the North Koreans can launch Tae Dong IIs. They can always deny they knew about the military aspects of the facility. A North Korean base on the island is a strategic win for the Russians. So, is this another move in the chess game?"

"I don't know if I buy that." Josh rapped his pen on the desk. "It is awful ballsy, even for someone like Kim Jong-Il. Think of all the support equipment for the liquid-fueled rockets he would have to move there. I would like to think that is a line even someone as crazy as Kim Jong-Il wouldn't cross."

Josh tossed one of the surveillance photos on the desk. "Assume the Russians want to shut it down and the North Koreans say no. They would have a hard time invading Simushir against any kind of organized resistance."

"Exactly. That's my point, Josh. A blockade will take forever if the island is well stocked, and air strikes won't work if the North Korean defenders are in caves. An airborne landing would be a disaster because you'd lose most of the paratroopers to injury."

Marty tapped his heel. "Assuming the North Koreans are about to put a large force on the island is pure speculation. Right now, our guess is there is a platoon, maybe a company-sized force, on Simushir. So far, all the recon photos verify what is in the press release, and we don't have any facts to suggest anything else— *yet*." Marty paused. "This is why we're going to do the sneak-and-peak."

"Amen." They could debate the topic for hours, but not this time. "So, did you see Jeffers?"

"No, but I bumped into Roger Billingham at the Navy Exchange. He told me Jeffers is clueless as to what is going on. No one is telling him anything. He also told me that *La Jolla* will be in Yokosuka by ten June."

"Do you think he knows about Glass Carat?"

"He knows that *La Jolla's* deployment schedule was changed, so he knows we need a sub with a dry-deck shelter already installed. He's no dummy. He knows that a North Korean *Romeo* entered the Sea of O, went up to Simushir, steamed around awhile in the area and then returned home. I took his comment on Jeffers to mean that he didn't like his boss."

Wednesday, May 24th, 1995, 1822 local time, Oahu

Hamilton arrived 20 minutes early at the McDonald's on Ala Moana Boulevard in Waikiki. He was carrying a manila envelope stuffed with information and trying to look nonchalant. He wanted the package out of his possession as soon as possible.

Getting the reports out of JICPAC had been easy. The dozen photos had been much more difficult because they were marked Top Secret. He'd used an X-Acto knife to cut off the source, time and date information in the lower right corner from the recent satellite and air reconnaissance photos of Simushir.

One of the blowups showed a *Grisha III* anchored in the harbor and a boat bringing people ashore. He thought it would convince Mr. Seul that he was getting his money's worth. He wondered if the man's name was really Seul.

Hamilton had just sat down to eat his Big Mac and fries when Mr. Seul slid into the bench seat opposite him and said, "Good evening."

"Hello."

"Do you have the package?"

Hamilton nodded as he bit into his burger. As he chewed, he reached down and handed Mr. Seul the brown envelope.

Hamilton watched as Seul fanned through the contents under the table before sliding them back in the envelope. "Tell me what is in here."

"The top sheet is a table of contents."

"I see." He slid it out and went down the list. "This is most thorough. You have manifests, ship names, departure and arrival dates. And these photographs of the island are very good! I presume these were taken by U.S. satellites."

Hamilton was not going to answer his question. "On the back, I noted the time and date the photograph was taken."

"You cut out the block with the source details."

"That lowers my exposure if I get caught—or you do."

Mr. Seul pulled a photo out of the stack about a third of the way out and looked at it. "Excellent. I will pay your debt tonight."

"Thank you." Bill finished the last French fry.

When they shook hands, Hamilton thought that Seul's hand, while firm, was, well, *dainty* and again wondered if the man was gay.

"I will contact you in the future if I need something."

"You know how to reach me. If not, my bookie knows." He was sure he had been tailed several times during the week. If it was the FBI and this was a sting, he'd be arrested for espionage as he exited the restaurant or at home tonight. If this was real, he was out of debt, the bookie was out of his life, and he was uninjured. All in all, for a few pictures and reports, he rationalized, it was a fair trade. One he could live with.

Sunday, May 28th, 1995, 0716 local time, Yokosuka
One of the small joys of being a department head was that Josh had an office for privacy when he made phone calls. While it was Sunday morning in Yokosuka, it was 3:16 p.m. Saturday afternoon of the Memorial Day Weekend in San Diego. Yesterday, the staff had had a picnic in one of the base's parks, and while it was a pleasant break from routine, he'd have preferred to spend it with his family. He dialed the familiar number.

Rebekah picked up the phone on the second ring. "Hello."

"Hi, it's me." Because the call was covering about 24,000 miles, twice, he had to wait for Rebekah's response.

"Hi there. How's Japan?"

"Quiet. Its Sunday here and no one is working. And I wanted to talk."

"YOU wanting to talk. That's one for the ages."

Josh laughed because her teasing remark was a joke between them. The words *I want to talk* usually came out of her mouth. "Rebekah, be serious."

"I was. Do I need to sit down or call an attorney?"

"No, don't be silly. What's with the sarcasm? What did I do to piss you off?"

"Nothing, I'm sorry. I just had another fight with my step dad. He can be such an asshole at times, particularly when it comes to you. And I'm lonely, and I miss you."

"I miss you, too. Are the kids around?"

"Are you kidding? They leave in the morning, I get a phone call during the day and am lucky if I see one of their faces for dinner. I'm not sure I like empty nesting all by myself. What's on your mind?"

"Sometime late this summer, the dance for where the Navy wants to send me next will begin. Jeff Gainesville is pretty sure I'll get a ship, but one never knows. So, here's what I've decided. If I get a ship and it is based in San Diego, I stay in the Navy. If they offer me a shore billet that doesn't require moving, I stay in the Navy until the flag board meets. If I get selected, I stay. If not, I retire. It is binary."

There was a silence longer than the normal delay caused by the distance. "Rebekah, are you there?"

"Color me stunned. Are you sure?"

"Yeah. I like being at the pointy end of the sword. I'm not a bureaucrat. Out here, I'm a paper pusher who sometimes gets to do something productive. A ship will keep me doing what I love. A shore billet will be just a holding tank until I find out if I make flag."

"Do I tell the kids?"

"No. Let's wait a few months until we know. I thought I would tell you where my head is at as of today."

"Thanks. We'll talk about it some more. You can always be like a woman and change your mind. Sorry, that was nasty. I'm just in a bad mood. It just seems as if I am running a motel."

"It's O.K., I still love you. Anyway, I think this is the fork in the road. It took being buried in messages that ask dumb questions, written by people who have nothing better to do."

"I get it. I'm sorry if I was crabby."

"Rebekah, I love and miss you."

"I love and miss you, too." He heard the sigh and the smile in her voice, and it warmed him.

Monday, June 12th, 1995, 1300 local time, Madison, WI

The Madison Concourse Hotel was in the heart of the downtown area, close to the state government's offices. It was also just a few blocks from the local media offices. Its furnishings were a mix of traditional and modern versions of Colonial-style furniture. A press release had stated that Representative Steve Higgins would make a formal announcement on his home turf and take questions on his positions on issues coming up this fall. The start time was early enough for the political reporters from Madison TV stations to get their sound bites for their evening news broadcast.

Neither Higgins nor his chief of staff thought the press conference was going to be of interest to anyone other than Wisconsin newspapers and TV stations. So when Congressman Higgins walked into the room, he was surprised to find most of the

50 seats occupied. He'd expected half a dozen local reporters and three or four cameramen. Instead, national network reporters who covered Congress were in the seats and their camera crews lined the walls.

From the podium, Higgins looked for reporters he knew. They were outnumbered by those he didn't. "Good afternoon. Thank you all for coming. I want to make a brief statement, and then I will be happy to take questions." Higgins paused to let the photographers take pictures.

"As many of you know, I was not expected to win my first term. However, we campaigned on issues important to voters in Wisconsin's Second Congressional District, to the state of Wisconsin and the nation. We persevered, and much to the surprise of the pundits, we won. I ran for re-election twice, and each time I won by a larger margin than before—and I intend to run again. This time it will be different because I am running as an independent, free of any party affiliation and, therefore, free to express my views on any issue without the constraints of a party philosophy or platform. To that end, this morning I resigned from the Democratic Party and notified, by letter, both the Speaker and Minority Leader of the House that I will finish out my term as an independent."

Higgins allowed himself a big smile. Every columnist had predicted the district would go Republican when he ran the first time. They'd all been wrong, and he'd just rubbed their noses in it. After looking around the room to let his words sink in, Higgins nodded slightly. "I'll take a few questions, and you can contact my staff later to schedule in-depth interviews. Since there are many reporters here whom I do not know, would you please identify yourself when I recognize you." Higgins confidently pointed to a man in the front row.

"Representative Higgins, I'm Jim O'Day from *USA TODAY*. I have two questions. One of your colleagues has introduced a resolution in the House that is still in committee to change your discharge from a general discharge under other-than-honorable conditions to an honorable one. So my first question is, why? I'd also like to know why a Naval Academy graduate received this type of discharge. Depending on your answer, I have a follow-up."

Higgins forced himself to remain calm. "I believe the Navy made a mistake. The Navy, like most bureaucracies, has a hard time admitting it made a serious error, so I am pursuing a different avenue to get it corrected."

Smiling, Higgins pointed to another reporter so as not to give O'Day a chance for his follow-up question. "Bill Hanlon, *Washington Post*. Our sources say you were offered a choice between a court martial and a general discharge under other-than-honorable conditions. The list of charges includes cowardice in the face of the enemy, falsifying government records, conduct unbecoming an officer and others. Is any of this true?"

Higgins swallowed hard as he flushed and gripped both sides of the podium to help control his anger. "Mr. Hanlon, cowardice is in the eye of the beholder. In combat, someone who is cautious may be thought of as a coward when, in fact, he is not. One has to have been in combat to understand the difference."

Hands went up all over the room. Higgins pointed to another reporter, desperately wondering how fast he could end this press conference. Someone, possibly even the chairman of the DNC or the Minority Leader, had leaked information about his discharge. Now he was standing in front of a school of hungry media sharks who smelled blood in the water.

"Sir, I'm Geoffrey Sundstrom from the *Washington Times*. Can you tell us about the Field Naval Aviator Evaluation Board held in

November 1970? I would like to know why you were asked to appear and what were the recommendations of the board?"

"That was a long time ago, and it is not relevant to my candidacy to continue to represent Wisconsin's Second Congressional District or to my outstanding record in the House of Representatives. Are there any questions on my position on legislation coming to the floor of the House for a vote or on my voting record?" One hand shot up. Higgins pointed at the stranger.

"Jeffrey Donaldson, *Wall Street Journal.* Assuming my colleagues print stories about what they just revealed, do you think it will affect your ability to win re-election?"

"The polls show that the people of my district like the work I do in Washington, and I am confident they will value my tireless efforts to represent their interests over the unsubstantiated claims and prejudiced opinions of a review that happened twenty-five years ago. It is not only old news, it is not *news* at all. Are they any more questions about either my record or re-election campaign?" No one raised a hand. "Well, then, I need to get back to the people's business."

Higgins was about halfway between the door and the podium when Sundstrom, the *Washington Times* reporter, stepped in front of him. He was a former Marine officer who had earned a Purple Heart and a Silver Star at Khe Sanh. He held the microphone between their faces.

"Representative Higgins, do you want to give your side of the story? If not, we will be printing our analysis of the information we have on your Naval career and disclose the charges the Navy was planning to level at you as the basis of a court martial, as well as the recommendations of the board. In follow-up stories, we plan to interview one of the pilots who was left behind and became a prisoner of war because *you* personally failed to pick him up."

Higgins pushed his press secretary and chief of staff aside and pulled the *Washington Times* reporter's microphone close to his mouth. He spoke in a deliberate, icy tone.

"For the record, Mr. Sundstrom, I am a highly decorated naval aviator, who did my duty as I saw fit. If you print what you have, the *Washington Times* does so at its own risk. So, you better get your facts straight, or you will be out of a job."

* * *

That evening, Robert Higgins was sitting on the swing on the porch in the backyard. Its westward orientation allowed him to watch the sun set. Steve came out of the house and handed his father a beer.

"Dad, I just told mom… I decided not to run for re-election."

"Why, son? I thought you were very successful and popular." He'd not seen the local news or the clips from the news conference.

"Because the shit is going to hit the fan later this week. My past is going to be all over the papers. The *Washington Times, USA Today* and the *Washington Post* are running stories on what happened in the Navy. The backlash will be such that I'll never be able to raise enough money for a viable campaign. Potential donors are already refusing to take my calls."

"So, once again, what you did in Vietnam is coming back to haunt you." The World War II veteran finished his beer in one long swallow and then put it gently down on the redwood armrest. "I told you it would haunt you the rest of your life."

The older man got up and walked inside, leaving Steven Higgins to look at the sunset and contemplate his future, whatever was left of it. The perks he'd been enjoying for the past six years would come to an abrupt halt once his resignation took effect. *The law says I can keep what's left from my campaign contributions, and I have a portfolio worth well more than two million, but it's not enough for me to live on.*

Tuesday, June 13th, 1995, 1627 local time, Broutana Bay

Major Kim knocked on the door of the Kuril Island Development Corporation. Under the company name, in smaller type, were the words *Chan Ho Lee, Project Manager and Managing Director*. The new brass plaque was an indicator of how much had changed during his time back on the mainland.

Another change was the large pile of ashes off to the side of the pier farthest from the buildings—all that was left of the debris taken from the large building that would, in a few months, become the barracks for a battalion of North Korean soldiers. All workers were now housed in modular buildings.

His detachment was allotted two buildings, each with eight 4-man bunk rooms, plus lavatories and showers. For the North Korean soldiers who were used to quarters with 30 to 40 men in a room, four-man rooms were luxurious. In each of the buildings, there was a living room with a large TV on which they could watch shows from the STAR (Satellite Television for the Asian Region) network, broadcast from Hong Kong.

In the second building, his two officers shared a two-man room, and he had a room to himself. With the Kuril Island Development Corporation's help, they had removed a wall to create a meeting room and replaced the bunks in the other two rooms with desks and chairs.

On his way, Kim had passed dozens of pickup trucks and four-wheel drive Toyota Land Cruisers. He'd never seen so many in one location. His unit's MULE count was now 24. Three of them were in front of their building, covered with volcanic mud from the roads made from crushed lava rock. The MULE fleet was supposed to be 36 in number by the middle of summer.

Another building in the complex was a dining facility, open 18 hours a day. More than a military mess hall, it was a restaurant with a buffet and a limited à la carte menu. In another building, the Kuril Island Development Corporation had set up a recreation center filled with electronic games that the North Koreans were learning to play, as well as a game played on a green felt-covered table called "pool."

The old torpedo magazine was now their maintenance shop and armory. The reinforced steel doors, chain hoists and rails bolted to the ceiling had been cleaned of their rust and painted a matte black, or oiled where appropriate. Everything in the building worked.

Kim found Managing Director Lee in his office. Simushir's boss came out from behind his desk when he saw who had arrived and held out his hand in greeting. "Thank you for coming. I hope you are pleased with the changes on Simushir."

Major Kim was quite impressed, even as he worried that his soldiers were seeing way too much of the outside world. When they returned to North Korea, he was afraid they would not be allowed back into the general population and would be sent to a re-education camp or shot. But that was not a topic for this discussion. "The weather is much nicer this time of year."

"Yes, the flowers are in full bloom."

"Mr. Lee, more of my men arrived on *Crescent Trader*."

"I was told that, yes. Are more on their way?"

"We should expect another 60 or so."

"The plan is to give you buildings one through five until the barracks is ready."

"Thank you, that will be fine."

"Major, may I ask you a direct question?"

"I will do my best to answer it."

"Why are your men here? What is your actual mission?"

"We provide security for this facility."

The Simushir Island Incident

"To protect it from whom?" Managing Director Lee was on uncharted ground here. In his last conversation with his superiors at Half Moon, he had been told to expect as many as 500 North Korean soldiers by the end of the year. He was afraid that would compromise the facility's ability to make heroin and amphetamines without Russian interference.

"We are here to protect North Korean interests. We plan to use the island for training once the barracks is completed. What my role will be at that time is unknown." *Lee probably knows more about what my government is planning for Simushir than I do.*

"Very well, Major Kim. If those are your orders, please carry them out. If you need any help from the Kuril Island Development Corporation, my door is always open. You can use our satellite phone to call anywhere in the world, including North Korea."

"Thank you, Managing Director Lee, I will take you up on your generous offer in the future." He wanted to use the number given to him by Vice Admiral Pak, but he wanted to finalize his list of topics before he called.

Monday, June 19th, 1995, 0932 local time, Pyongyang

Deputy Minister Thaek sat in the conference room trying not to show his growing impatience. The Dear Leader enjoyed keeping people waiting to show his power. After three hours, Thaek tried pacing. All it did was make him more nervous. He desperately needed another cigarette. When Kim Jong-Il finally came in, Thaek had to keep his hands pressed against his legs so his Dear Leader wouldn't see the shaking.

"What have you learned?" The demand was abrupt. There was no greeting or warmth.

"Both Vice Admiral Pak and Major General Jang have been very cooperative and have been including me in every conversation and meeting about Simushir. From them, I have learned three interesting facts." Thaek watched his Dear Leader's face closely. He saw an eyebrow move up, indicating that he must prove that what he was about to say was indeed of interest.

"Three?"

"Yes, Dear Leader, three. First, Half Moon Trading now has a spy giving them excellent information on what the Americans know about Simushir. In Hong Kong, they have copies of aerial pictures taken by American planes and spy satellites."

"That *IS* very interesting."

"Second, Half Moon has an arrangement with the Sinaloa Mexican drug group, based in western Mexico, to smuggle drugs into America and distribute through their network. Pak mentioned a trusted cousin living in the U.S. He implied they are no longer worried about competition. I believe he means it has been eliminated."

"He has a cousin in America?" Kim Jong-Il leaned forward.

"We are not sure if it is a blood relative or he is using the word to describe an associate."

"Find out." The Dear Leader leaned back to his normal position. "What is the third thing?"

"Half Moon's vetting process is very thorough and will be hard to penetrate."

"Hmmmm. What do you know about the spy?"

Thaek made a mental note that the Dear Leader didn't seem to be interested in more information on how the drug dealers checked each other out. "The information is sent from Hawaii to Macao and then Hong Kong by a courier service. We don't know where the spy is located or who he is."

"Find out. Get me copies of the pictures."

Kim Jong-Il was angry that Vice Admiral Pak and his associates at Half Moon had a spy in the U.S. and were not sharing information with his country's intelligence services. He was unhappy that Pak had a relative in the U.S. that was not in his file. What else did they not know about the man? *I want the details before I have Thaek eliminate Pak!*

"Yes, Dear Leader, I will work as fast as I can. It may be difficult."

"I don't care. Get the information."

After his Dear Leader left, Thaek sat shaking and wondering why he felt exhausted. His vibrating fingers felt as if they were being moved by small electric motors.

As soon as he was outside, Thaek lit the first of the four-inch-long Cuban cigarillos in his briefcase, inhaled deeply and held the smoke in his lungs. Finally, the trembling in his fingers began to subside.

0833 local time, Honolulu

The Hawaiian DEA office was in a four-story building on Ala Moana Boulevard in downtown Honolulu. Jake Garza could see the street below and the harbor, a block away. It was a view that he liked to take in while talking on the phone. He flipped through his Rolodex, stopped at a number for a certain master chief machinist's mate and retired SEAL, and dialed.

A voice answered after two rings. "Jenkins."

"Hi, Master Chief, this is Special Agent Garza from the DEA. I need to buy you a cup of coffee and pick your brain. It will be a classified conversation."

"Okay, come over to CINCPAC at ten hundred, and I'll book a skiff." By "skiff," Jenkins was referring to a Sensitive Compartmented Information Facility. SCIFs were designed to protect conversations from eavesdropping.

"You're on."

* * *

They stopped for the obligatory cup of coffee, then Jenkins escorted Garza to a cipher-locked conference room.

"So, what brings you out to my humble office?"

Time was short, so Garza got right to the point. "Who uses suppressed Tokarev Type 68s and subsonic ammunition?"

Jenkins raised an eyebrow. "Far as I know, the North Koreans are the primary users. It is a favorite of the North Korean Special Forces. The round is a necked-down nine-millimeter, but still, it packs a pretty good punch."

"Master Chief, look at these." With that, Garza opened the sealed manila envelope he'd brought and spread out the investigator's reports and the lab analysis. He explained what was in the reports before concluding, "No one has seen the shooter either enter or leave any of the locations. He's a ghost. I'm thinking he was well trained by someone's special forces. Do North Koreans train guys like him and hire them out?"

Jenkins drummed his fingers on the desk and took a deep breath. "This is for your ears only—yes, they do. There are validated intelligence reports stating that the North Korean Ministry of Safety and Security sends officers to help tin-pot dictators in government-to-government contracts. They come in as trainers and sometimes do the dirty work. We suspect some have defected and now work as freelancers."

Jenkins took a sip from his mug of coffee, which on one side had the insignia of a Master Chief and on the other side the logo of SEAL Team One. "Despite what you see in the movies, good assassins who don't leave a mess are hard to find and expensive. So what is so valuable that someone would bring in an expensive outside hit man?"

The DEA officer discounted the idea that a cartel was cleaning house—operatives are just too hard to put in place and are too valuable. There were no signs of a war between any two cartels or gangs, so it had to be an outside organization trying to muscle its way in. "The reason is turf."

Jenkins nodded. "Next question: where is the assassin getting his info?"

"We don't have a clue." Garza shook his head. "We didn't even know some of the victims were players until they turned up dead and we started investigating."

"It is a very indirect strategy and, I hate to say it, very Asian." Chief Jenkins looked over the rim of his coffee mug. "Have you talked to Commander Cabot or Captain Haman during the last few days?"

"No, why? I met them when I went out to Seventh Fleet last month."

"Talk to them. They have ideas that may fill in some of the blanks."

"I hear they are loose cannons."

"You're listening to the wrong people."

Garza had seen Haman's and Cabot's decorations. From his own Vietnam combat experience, Garza believed that men who are awarded Navy Crosses and Silver Stars are among the best warriors around. When he'd heard the detractors speak, he'd wondered if there was professional envy at work or if the speakers were shoe clerks more concerned about paperwork than how to win a battle.

"Do you have time for a war story that will tell you a lot about these two officers?

"Sure."

"Before I tell it, you should know something. If either Haman or Cabot put the word out they need men for an op, candidates line up at their door, even fight to go. For either man, they'll charge the gates of hell. All they want to know is, do we use the doorknob or do we blow it down? Do you get my drift?"

Garza nodded somberly and Jenkins put his cup down. "Back in Vietnam, Haman was a full lieutenant and Cabot a j-g when I was on an eight-man team on a recon op in North Vietnam. An NVA battalion got on our trail, and they had dogs. Before we could disengage from our third encounter, the guy with the Stoner got hit in the leg and we had to carry him."

Remembering how close the fighting had gotten, Jenkins ran a beefy hand through his flattop. "We went to ground in a ravine. Cabot radioed for pickup while the other guys made a stretcher. The Claymores we'd placed to slow down the bad guys went off. So then, Cabot picks up the Stoner, along with a spare ammo belt, and says he's going to take out as many he can. He gives me the map and shows me two LZs. He tells me that if he doesn't make it back, I am to say *'Beach Boy* is gone.' Then Commander Cabot says, 'If you use the words *'Beach Boy* is down,' Haman will know I'm wounded. Tell him 'steep icy course' and he'll hurry. Use the code word Kneissl for our primary LZ and Kastle for our back-up extraction LZ."

Garza interrupted to ask, "Why the ski brand names?"

"Simple. Haman liked to use brand names of skis to designate landing zones. It was different and kept them secure because they weren't in any code books."

"Was that your normal operating procedure?"

"I'll get to that in a minute. We hear short bursts from the Stoner, and then the guy who'd gone with Commander Cabot sneaks back to our position and says, 'Follow me.' We walked about thirty meters, and there are dead NVA all over the place. Cabot is looking at a map he'd take from the body of an NVA major. *It had our primary insertion and extraction LZs marked!"*

"No shit?"

Jenkins's answering gaze was level. "Saw it with my own eyes. Their intel let them know just where to find us. Cabot sent me and my fire teammate to the LZ with the Stoner, and about an hour later Captain Haman landed the helicopter. I told Captain Haman that Commander Cabot and the others were about two hours behind us."

Jenkins tensed as the memories flooded back. "The helo didn't have much gas left. Captain Haman asked me, 'Do you know the route they're taking to get here?' I said yes. Haman said, 'Great— we'll take off and find the rest of your team.'"

Jenkins took a deep breath. "He followed the route we took. You couldn't see it from the air, so it was guesswork. To make a long story short, Haman held the helicopter in a hover, taking a lot of small arms fire, while his crew used a sling to bring up the rest of our team. Tracer fire all over the place, but he never wavered, and he got us all out of there. When we landed at the base on Nakhon Phanom, the helo had less than fifteen minutes of fuel left."

"That's… interesting."

"Captain Haman would always get us to the right LZ and would come back, no matter when or what it took and find a way to get us out."

"I want to hear more about that map and their intel."

"We concluded there was a leak somewhere in the system. Commander Cabot and our boss ran it up the chain of command, but never heard anything afterwards. But from then on, we never sent LZ locations or op details via message."

"Did you ever find any other evidence?"

"Yes, we did."

"When? How?"

"Sorry, I can't tell you what you're not cleared for. Get CINCPAC to clear you for an operation called *Sunlight Sam* and either Captain Haman, Commander Cabot or I will be happy to tell you about the proof, how we got it and what we learned. But without CINCPAC's blessing, no can tell."

"So, Chief, the net-net is I should call Cabot and Haman and listen to what they have to say."

"That would be my advice. You might learn something."

Tuesday, June 20th, 1995, 0333 local time, Broutana Bay
Major Kim was making his rounds of the four two-man fire team positions around the bay. He also had two-man patrols moving between the outposts. Halfway down the ridge, he paused. Something wasn't right about the security light reflections on the building on the north end of the bay. Two lights next to each other were out, and that made him suspicious. He'd often wondered what went on in the building that was off limits to everyone except a dozen Hong Kong workers who kept to themselves. Their leader spoke to just one person—Managing Director Lee.

Major Kim worked his way down the steep slope toward the darkened building. He decided that tonight was the night he would take a look at the building and pier on the northwest side of the bay. The trip down from the top of the ridge added, he figured, an hour to his nightly rounds.

He took care to test his footing on each step with one leg before he put his full weight down. The method took longer, but avoided a fall onto volcanic rock and a nasty gash or worse. When he got to the razor-wire-topped chain link fence around the building, he crept around the shadows, toward the pier.

Carefully testing the timbers on the pier's frame, Major Kim climbed up so he could peer over the top. He watched the security cameras until he was sure he couldn't be seen and then rolled onto the pier, suspecting that whoever had designed the camera layout either didn't care about the pier or assumed threats would not come from the water.

The Simushir Island Incident

The sliding garage doors were locked, but the side door was cracked open. Kim drew his pistol—a round already chambered.

Inside, dim internal security lights illuminated three pallets, each a little over a meter square. Each pallet was piled high with rectangular packages about the size of a large brick, held tightly in place with a thin plastic film. In the back of the loading area, an open door revealed what looked like a chemistry lab. Kim's first thought was that they were loading chemical bombs or shells, but there was none of the protective gear for handling chemical weapons. Nor were there any bomb or artillery shells stacked either inside or outside the building.

A loud snore froze him Kim. A second one, in a lower tone, came from a small office off to the side. He crouched behind the pallets and crawled toward the sounds of the sleepers.

After remaining motionless for a minute, he peered around the cellophane-wrapped bundles and saw a man on a chair, fast asleep. An AK-47, with two magazines taped together leaned against the wall. On the table next to the chair was a bandoleer with more of the distinctive crescent-shaped magazines.

On the other side of the doorway, another man was lying on the floor. The slow movement of his chest told Kim that he, too, was fast asleep.

Major Kim felt not a sense of danger, but an overwhelming feeling of unease. He backed out and debated for a few seconds before deciding to leave the area as he found it. Once back on the volcanic soil, he climbed halfway up the ridge before heading back to what Managing Director Lee liked to call "the settlement." As he walked, Kim debated whether or not he would tell Managing Director Lee about what he had seen. By the time he reached his quarters, he'd decided to mention the lights but not the sleeping guards—or the need to adjust or add more cameras.

Chapter 9: NEAT NEW TOYS

Thursday, June 22nd, 1995, 1845 local time, Waikiki

Bill Hamilton sat at a booth in the back of McDonalds, where he could be seen from the street, and unwrapped his Quarter Pounder with Cheese. It wasn't long before Mr. Seul slid into the bench seat opposite him. He looked even more effeminate than before. He wore a pastel blue golf shirt, and his fingernails were painted a pink so pale they were almost white.

This espionage thing, Bill reflected, was getting easier and easier. In a few months, the cash piled up in his offshore accounts from these weekly deliveries would give him enough to retire to someplace in the Caribbean. Hamilton slid a manila envelope across the table, and Mr. Seul hefted it—testing whether it was heavy enough to have what he wanted—before he opened the clasp and pulled out the table of contents.

Seeing notes on the DEA's interest on Simushir as a possible source of illegal drugs, Seul asked, "You have access to DEA files?"

Bill didn't want to let him know how often he met with DEA agents. "Only if it is related to what I am working on. If I request additional information, it is a crapshoot as to whether I get anything."

"Fair enough." Mr. Seul looked at him thoughtfully. "I will be in touch with another request. Good evening."

Saturday, June 24th, 1995, 0635 local time, Broutana Bay
Major Kim loved the dawn view from the top of Mount Uratman which, at this time of year, began around 0330. By 0430, the sun was already above the horizon. From their observation post in a shelf-like flat area below the peak and about 600 meters above the bay, sunrises and sunsets were spectacular. In the clear, pollution-free blue sky, he could see the peak on Ostrov Ketoy, the island across the Diana Strait to the north. The ship that had left the bay at six in the morning looked like a small a toy trailing a light blue wake that contrasted with the blue-gray waters of the Western Pacific.

Kim turned to study another ship through his prized Nikon 10 x 50 binoculars that were better than even the rare East German ones he'd left behind in North Korea. A few hours earlier, the small freighter had been barely visible. Now he could clearly see a Burmese flag fluttering from its fantail. On the bow of its rusty black hull, the ship's name, *Orange Flower,* was legible in a dirty white block script.

Major Kim watched it dock at the pier on the north side of the bay. One by one, six pallets of what looked like loaves of bread were hoisted out of the hold with the ship's own crane and sent swinging over the side and down onto the pier. There, workers transferred the sling from the incoming pallet to one waiting for pick-up. A wave, and the ship's crane operator lifted the outgoing pallet off the pier and lowered it into *Orange Flower's* hold. It was an efficient ballet, one which Kim enjoyed watching. More pallets were delivered than were loaded onto the ship. At last the empty crane hook swung away from the pier and the M.V. *Orange Flower* began to back away. Its diesel engine belched black smoke as the ship headed toward the caldera's entrance and out to sea.

Kim hadn't told anyone about his visit that night to the building that he now suspected was a drug lab. He had been taught in school that all opium usage had been eradicated from North Korea and only corrupt Chinese mainlanders and decadent Americans dealt in the stuff. Every day, Kim wrestled with what he should do. "Patience," his father had once told him, "be patient and good things will come."

As he watched another ship enter the harbor, Major Kim chatted with the four men manning the observation posts—one facing each direction—they'd built roughly 50 meters east of and below the mountain's peak. The position allowed them to see the southern tip of Ketoy on the northern side of the Diany Straight as well as providing a clear view of the Pacific. Camouflage netting covered the sandbags that rested on a sturdy wooden frame; a sheet of six-millimeter steel underlay the sandbags and further shielded the men from radiation from the radar antenna at the top of the mountain.

Like all the prepared North Korean positions around the ridge, it was connected to a small command center in a cave, manned 24 hours a day, and to the Half Moon office switchboard via redundant phone lines. The command center was now linked to Half Moon's satellite dish on the top of Mount Uratman that gave them a telephone link to anywhere in the world.

His men had found the cave entrance one day while walking along the edge of the bay, about a kilometer directly west of the settlement. Major Kim thought it was in an ideal location; if the island were ever attacked, the settlement would be the primary target.

The Simushir Island Incident

The top of Uratman was home to the British-made Racal Decca Marine Bridgemaster II radar purchased by the Kuril Island Development Corporation. Placing the antenna high up increased the radar's ship detection range to almost 40 kilometers. Two scopes, one in the headquarters building and one in Kim's command center, showed the same view that his soldier's had from observation post on Uratman.

The large freighter, the third ship he'd seen today, slowed as it glided toward the main pier. The field telephone rang.

"Sir, it is Managing Director Lee." A young soldier held out the phone.

"Good morning, Chin Hae. You might want to come down and watch what is about to be unloaded. Meet me at the pier." This was the first time Managing Director Lee had ever addressed Major Kim by his first name.

Major Kim drove his MULE down the rocky path to the settlement. By the time he got to the end of the pier, the *M.V. Crescent Sun* was tied up, and the hatches from her forward cargo hold were stacked on the bow.

Lee greeted him and, speaking in a low voice, as if he was afraid someone would overhear, said, "We have eighty-four minutes before the next American satellite pass, plenty of time to get one, maybe two of the vehicles off and parked under those large empty sheds."

Kim was stunned to see a Russian-made 9K33M3 missile system emerge from the hold. The technical term for the six-wheeled amphibious vehicle is the acronym TELAR—transporter, erector, launcher and radar. The 9K33M3 was a self-contained surface to air missile system and each vehicle carried six radio-guided, command line-of-sight surface-to-air missiles and its own fire control radars, so it could operate independently. The Russians called it the *Osa* which means wasp.

Both men watched the first *Osa* settle on its wheels, and then Managing Director Lee summarized what he read from the manual. "The H band radar can detect a target out to about thirty kilometers, depending on target altitude. The missile range is about thirty kilometers and can hit targets as high as twelve thousand meters. The operator directs the missile via a mono-pulse J-band radar, and a proximity fuse sets off the warhead. There is a smaller I-band radar that can control two missiles aimed at a single target. The *Osa* also has an optical tracking device. The reloads consist of 'three packs' because each contains three missiles. A trained crew should be able to replace both sides in fifteen minutes."

"Managing Director Lee, why they are here?" Lee started to speak, but the diesel engine on the *Osa* coughed and spat out a plume of black smoke as it started. He waited until the vehicle drove off before answering.

"Chin Hae, I was hoping *you* could tell *me* why. Sixteen *Osas*, plus thirty-six reloads and spare parts, are on their way here. I was told they are to be turned over to you. This shipment is the first: four of the latest export models. The remaining twelve will arrive later next month."

Major Kim said nothing. He stared at the second *Osa* as it emerged from the hold.

Managing Director Lee, a native and resident of Hong Kong, looked and sounded worried. "Your country will, I am told, send trained crews here."

Kim knew nothing about the *Osas*. "Ah, I have not yet received these orders," he stammered.

"Also in this ship's hold is a surplus Russian radar that NATO calls the Bar Lock. That I know about. My company bought it from the Syrians. The initial position will be on top of Uratman. Don't worry, we will install additional shielding so it doesn't affect your men or the Racal radar. Eventually, we will build a road up to the top of Prevo Peak and move it to a position where it does not affect the surface search radar. When we get it operating, it will tell us if anyone is flying around us out to about a hundred and sixty kilometers. Ultimately, it will be used in support of the airport."

"That makes sense," was all Major Kim could say. He didn't know whether he should be excited or horrified. Here was a missile system better than what his country had to defend the homeland, bought for this island. It did not make sense. Sixteen *Osas*!

Monday, June 26th, 1995, 2136 local time, Yokosuka
Neither man said much as they walked down the pier reserved for submarines at the naval base. Marty was lugging a sea bag slung over his left and carrying a briefcase in his right hand. Ahead was the *Los Angeles* class submarine *La Jolla*. A large cylinder mounted on the aft hull, the dry-deck shelter, dominated the back of the nuclear attack submarine. Shimmering and shining harsh yellow-orange light from the sodium-vapor lamps along the pier made the scene look right out of a science fiction movie.

Josh stopped short of the gangway and turned to his friend. "Good luck, Marty. Remember, the boss and CINCPAC said to break radio silence if something goes wrong. We're not at war."

"Yeah, I know." Marty took a last long look around the pier. "I didn't expect CINCPAC to send Uilani to hand deliver the latest imagery."

"It was an excuse to give you some time together. Call it a Navy good deal."

"It was most appreciated." Marty shifted the weight of his sea bag. His B-4 bag was already on board the sub. "Is the ASW exercise that will hopefully distract the Russians still laid on?"

"Yeah. I talked to Captain Nagumo on the *Belleau Wood* this afternoon. The Notice to Mariners went out two days ago, saying we're going to conduct an anti-submarine warfare exercise with the Japanese along the eastern edge of the Kuril Islands, seventy miles southeast of where you're going ashore. It starts the day before you arrive and goes on for six days. That should provide sufficient distraction."

"Good." Marty sounded reassured.

"In addition to Nagumo's four ships, the guided missile cruiser *U.S.S. Reeves* and two *Perry*-class frigates are part of the task force. The amphibious ship has a battalion of Marines, helos and Harriers, and a full load of live ordnance. The ships are going to make a practice amphibious assault on Okinawa after the ASW exercise. We're not leaving you out there alone." Josh was just reminding Marty—who, as the joint task force commander for Operation Glass Carat, was feeling the whole weight of his responsibility—of just how thorough their planning was. And, if needed, how powerful the 'covering show' was.

Marty shook Josh's hand. "See you in a few days. It's just a walk in the park or, in this case, on a volcanic island." He walked up the gangway, put his sea bag and briefcase down and saluted the officer of the deck. He took one last look at Josh, then disappeared through a hatch.

Chapter 10: KNIFE FIGHT IN A PHONE BOOTH WHILE BLINDFOLDED

Friday, June 30ᵗʰ, 1995, 0027 local time, Simushir,
on board submarine La Jolla

La Jolla approached the northeastern tip of Simushir from the southeast. None of its sensors detected any surface ships or submarines. On the surface, the northwest wind created whitecaps. Fifty-feet below, they had little effect as the SEALs slid the Mark VIII Mod 0 Swimmer Delivery Vehicle (SDV) out of the dry-deck shelter and clambered on board for the half-mile trip to the island. The sub's skipper, Commander Knowlton, would maintain the sub's position until the delivery vehicle returned.

Lieutenant Junior Grade Henry Adair and three other SEALs sat in the cramped passenger compartment, while two SEALs drove the submersible. When they got underway, the fathometer indicated the bottom was 600 feet below and the water temperature was 49 degrees Fahrenheit. A hundred yards from Simushir, it was less than 100 feet and shallowing fast. Finally, the SDV brought

Adair and his team to where the nose of the boat was just a few feet above the bottom and fifty feet from the surface. They each took one last gulp of air from the tanks on the SDV, then rose to the surface to swim the remaining 25 yards to the island.

Ashore, the four SEALs pulled off their fins and masks and stowed them in their packs. Using night vision goggles, Adair scanned the cliffs to orient himself. His handheld GPS receiver indicated they were 50 feet south of the ravine he wanted to use to hide their movement off the rocky beach. From there, they would work their way up and over the ridge. The SEALs planned to build a hide among the scrub trees and rocks that would give them a clear view of the bay.

From satellite images, they knew that all of the prepared defensive positions were located either between Mt. Uratman and the harbor, or along the narrow and relatively flat area connecting Broutana Bay with the island's western shore. There seemed to be nothing north of the old Russian base.

Adair motioned the other three men to follow. This was not his first time inside enemy territory. During Desert Shield, Adair had made four covert trips into occupied Kuwait. Once Desert Storm started, he'd gone deep into the Shat al Arab estuary to the Iraqi port of Um Qasir to place limpet mines on Iraqi Navy ships.

A little after two in the morning, they reached the top of the ridge and found a grove of alder trees. By 0445, when the sun came up, the shelter was up, they were hidden from sight, and ready to watch the harbor.

Adair made his second radio call since coming ashore. The first had been to let *La Jolla* know they were safely ashore and moving out. This one was to say that they were in position.

The Simushir Island Incident

0326 local time, on board submarine U.S.S. Honolulu

The screech of the fire alarm, followed by the words, "Fire, *fire,* **FIRE**—fire in the bow sonar equipment room. This is no drill!" sent Boyd Hensley tumbling from his rack. Hensley pulled his mask from its storage compartment and headed toward the control room. Fire on board a submarine was almost as dangerous as a hole in the hull. Flames consumed the available oxygen, and if the crew didn't put the fire out quickly, they would all suffocate or die from toxic fumes.

Lieutenant Junior Grade Jonathan Abrahamson, whose stateroom was above the forward torpedo compartment, leapt out of his top bunk, grabbed his steel-toed leather boots, and dashed to the forward damage-control station. Besides being the ship's assistant engineering officer, Abrahamson was the submarine's damage control officer. He pulled on his fireproof overalls and stuffed his feet into his boots. Next, he shrugged on the oxygen breathing apparatus and, along with four similarly-garbed enlisted men, went to the closed and dogged-shut waterproof hatch that led to the equipment compartment.

"Did you discharge the Halon?"

"Sir, we tried—it didn't work. We recycled the switches and the circuit breakers and tried again. Nothing happened."

"We have to go in with CO_2."

Abrahamson touched the door to see if it was hot. It was not, which was a good sign. Masks on, they un-dogged the hatch. Acrid smoke poured past Abrahamson as he led one other sailor into the confined space filled with electronic equipment that controlled the bow sonar. Each carried a 15-pound CO_2 fire extinguisher.

Toward the forward end of the compartment, he saw glowing wires through the heavy smoke. He struggled to get the long-flared nozzle into position. CO_2 whooshed out onto the glowing wires and burning insulation. But it wasn't enough.

The cramped space was too narrow for the enlisted man to pass, so they traded extinguishers. Abrahamson used half the bottle to smother the still smoldering insulation. Next, a jet of flame from a power supply at the bottom of the rack got a dose of CO_2. A third sailor squeezed his way into the compartment and took the empty bottles back while Abrahamson and his teammate searched for more sources of smoke. The third sailor came back with two five-pound bottles and shouted, "Sir, that's all we have left!"

Abrahamson used up one bottle dousing the last of the visible flames. As he stepped out of the sonar equipment compartment, the compartment phone rang. He pulled off his OBA mask to take the call. The tight-fitting mask left red lines on his face, and his clothes reeked of electrical fire smoke.

"This is the captain. What's the status of the fire?"

"Sir, I'm pretty sure the fire is out. We've resealed the hatch and we're going to wait a few minutes before we go back in. When we do, we'll pull out all the sonar cables to cut off power to the system. We've already pulled all the breakers to the sonar."

"Did you activate the fire suppression system?"

"Yes, sir. It didn't work despite showing it is fully charged. We tried using the backup controls to actuate it, and that failed as well. That's when we went in."

"What do you mean, didn't work?"

"Sir, the Halon never fired. We could hear the solenoids clicking, but nothing came out."

The sub's skipper, Commander Hensley, now had two major problems: a fire that might not be out, and a fire suppression system that was not working.

"Lieutenant, do we need to surface and vent the boat?"

"If the fire is out, the boat's scrubbers should get rid of the smoke and fumes. Fresh air would just do it faster. It's your call."

"Got it. Let me know when you are sure the fire is out. Captain out."

0811 local time, U.S.S. Blue Ridge, *pier-side in Yokosuka*

Josh made himself the "permanent" watch officer on the day the SEALs landed on Simushir. The admiral had designated the flag command center as a restricted space, so the watch team could monitor the operation and, if needed, communicate with *La Jolla* while Glass Carat was underway. Josh was reminding himself that no news was probably good news when a secured call from Roger Billingham came through.

Josh said, "Roger, how are you doing?"

"Things are great here, but just turned to shit in your neighborhood."

"What's the good news?" Josh tried to make light of whatever he was about to hear. Their friendship had developed over the course of many phone calls, and they'd agreed to have a beer the next time Josh was in Hawaii.

"*Honolulu* had a fire and is headed back to Yokosuka. You'll need to notify the task force off Simushir that *Honolulu* will be a no show. The *Bremerton* is off Petropavlovsk, so it will be a day or so before she can replace *Honolulu* on the ASW exercise. As soon as I can, I'll give you a guestimated time of arrival."

"Thanks for the heads up. I'll see if we can get the Japanese submarine already laid-on for later in the exercise to come earlier. We can adjust the exercise schedule once I know when *Bremerton* will show."

"Admiral Jeffers wanted to know what was so important about an ASW exercise off the Kurils that we needed to break off surveillance of Petro. I told him we didn't want to lose face with the Japanese."

"Good answer."

"Are you going to keep your promise to tell me what is going on?"

"I will, if and when I can."

"Fair enough. By the way—the Japanese diesel electrics will be very hard to find in the water around the Kurils. In close to the shore, they're invisible."

The phone went dead.

1013 local time, on board Aphrodite Two Two, north of Simushir

Simushir Island, 30 miles ahead, was visible from the cockpit of the four-engine EP-3E turboprop surveillance plane. Pilot Richard Harrison, a brand-new lieutenant commander, marveled at the contrast between the deep blue of the Pacific, the brown and green of the shoreline, and the snowy white cloud tops of the island's peaks. His attention refocused abruptly when the radar-warning receiver chirped. The intercom buzzed.

"Boss, we're being tracked by a Bar Lock air search radar that's a newcomer to this area. Nothing to worry about, unless we get painted by a fire-control radar."

The "Boss" was Bill Smith III, known in the squadron as "Bill Three". He was a Naval Intelligence officer, an expert on Russian radars, and the mission commander. He stood between the two pilots and peered out the windscreen as the plane neared the island. An air-search radar on the island was a major development.

Suddenly, the camera operator blurted out, "Holy shit, they've got SA-8s on Simushir!"

The mission commander calmly replied, "Say again?"

"Boss, I'm looking at four SA-8 *Geckos* with support vehicles and reloads. Two are in revetments, and I can see the front of two more in a shed. I'm getting video and stills."

Bill Three was alarmed. SA-8s were not listed in the North Korean order of battle. *This is supposedly a commercial venture. Are the Russians deploying SAMs to protect it?*

"I'm going to call Blackbeard and let them know about the Bar Lock and the SA-8s," said Bill Three. "Don't circle because it will alert them that we spotted something unusual. When we get back, the world is going to want copies of the photos and the data."

"The world" meant Commander, Seventh Fleet, and Commander, Pacific Command, the DIA and the CIA.

When Josh Haman got an alarming call from Bill Three, he wrote an "operational immediate" message to Marty. Then he called Admiral Maize.

1026 local time, on board the North Korean Submarine S-217
in the Sea of Okhotsk

Fifty meters below the surface, Lieutenant Commander Jae-sung Tae, captain of the North Korean Submarine S-217, ordered the crew to shut off all ventilation and electrical systems to minimize battery drain and noise as they tried to creep away from a Russian Navy *Udaloy*-class destroyer, 2,000 meters away.

At first light, right after they'd made their morning transmission on their high-frequency radio and finished charging their batteries, an alert lookout had spotted the *Udaloy's* KA-25 helicopter flying toward them. Tae had ordered a crash dive and taken the submarine down to 70 meters to get below the layer.

When they heard pings from the helicopter's dipping sonar, Tae ordered everything on the submarine not essential to maintaining depth to be shut down. Silently, he cursed the North Korean Navy's requirement to report every 12 hours via high-frequency radio. Although the political officer on board disagreed, Tae was sure the Russian ship had picked up his transmission or heard them charging their batteries and had sent its helicopter to investigate.

"Captain, sonar. It sounds like the *Udaloy*-class destroyer has sped up." Tae acknowledged and ordered a forty-degree heading change to try to take his sub out of the *Udaloy's* sonar detection envelope. He picked up the microphone to tell the crew his intentions. "This is the captain. We are being tracked by a Russian destroyer. It is our duty to evade. If we are attacked, we will respond. Captain out."

Tae took a deep breath and turned to the sailor standing at the torpedo status panel. "What is the status of the torpedo tubes?"

"Sir, bow tubes one through four are loaded. Both aft torpedo tubes are loaded. Do you want to load the remaining two bow tubes?"

"No." Loading torpedoes was a noisy evolution. Tae picked up the handset and ordered the crew to go to battle stations and close all watertight doors.

1026 local time, on board the Russian destroyer Admiral Yuri Rall

Captain (2nd Rank) Leonid Semenov gazed at the gray blue waters. This was Day 2 of a secret ASW exercise he was conducting with a Russian Pacific Fleet Victor III class submarine. His *Udaloy*-class destroyer was designed primarily to hunt submarines; the exercise was a test of tactics and sensor equipment. The area west of Simushir Island had been selected for its remoteness and water conditions. During the planning stage, the Russian Navy had predicted that no American or Japanese submarines would be in the area for the three days of the exercise.

But *Yuri Rall's* electronic surveillance system had picked up a high frequency transmission on the same bearing as machinery noises similar to those of a diesel submarine charging its batteries, detected by their Polinum variable depth sonar. Then the helicopter had observed a submarine crash diving. So he had an unknown submarine in the middle of his exercise.

The Simushir Island Incident

Semenov's orders were clear. If a foreign submarine was detected, he was to prosecute, i.e.: identify the type. For subs classified as diesel electric, he was to maintain contact until it was forced to surface when its batteries were exhausted. If the contact was a nuclear sub, he was to chase it away.

His rules of engagement were also clear that, for unidentified submarines, he was to drop five small charges in the water and then use the bow mounted sonar to send the letters I D K C A in Morse code. These letters, sent at the eight kilocycle frequency, are the international code used to signal a sub to surface and identify itself.

Semenov turned to his officer of the deck. "Send the men to battle stations. Get our sonar operators ready to send Morse code."

He went back to studying the waters where the unknown submarine might be. *Who are you? What are you doing in these waters? How much of our exercise have you observed?*

1032 local time, on board North Korean Romeo Submarine S-217

The bong of an active sonar pulse rattled throughout *S-217*. This was followed by a ping from the helicopter's sonar, then a second ping. Tae gave orders to turn and slowly descend to one hundred meters and stay at three knots. *They know where I am; I hope they do not guess where I go.*

Everyone inside the boat could hear the thrum of *Udaloy*'s screws. The challenge was to stay in the gap where some of the energy from the ship's sonar was reflected back to the surface by the layer and some went straight down.

The helicopter was more a problem. Every minute, the helicopter sent out a pulse. The helicopter's dipping sonar was probably below the layer, where it could hear the reflected sound waves from both submarines.

With only two decoys left, Tae was cornered. This was his, and any submariner's, worst nightmare—detected by two sensors that could triangulate his position and make it impossible to slip away. It meant the Russians had a firing solution and could plot every move of his sub. He wondered what was coming next. None of the tricks he'd learned during the free-play portions of exercises off Russia's coast were working. Tae made a mental note to include that in his cruise report.

"Planesman, ease up to thirty meters." Tae ignored the political officer who was, as usual, observing his every move. He did his best to be polite to the man who could, with one report, end his career and send him off to a re-education camp.

His planesman eased back on the wheel controlling the bow planes to create a gentle upward movement, careful to move them slowly so as to not to make any additional noise. Tae looked at the clock. The cat-and-mouse game had been going on for four and a half hours.

He had, at most, eight hours of battery life left before they had to surface or raise the snorkel to run the diesels and charge the batteries.

Submarine S-217 was in international waters and had every right to be there. Nevertheless, any public attention to its presence in these waters would be… awkward. Tae's mission had been to deliver four passengers to Simushir Island, which he had done, and then return home, which he was trying to do.

Tae debated his options. One would be to surface, show his colors and then submerge and continue home. But allowing the Russians to force him to surface would be an admission of defeat and a severe loss of face. It would not be good for his career, no matter what the circumstances. His political officer would insist on a court-martial when they returned to Mayang-do.

"Captain, the *Udaloy* is now headed right towards us and should be overhead in about two minutes."

"Captain, aye." Choice two was to continue to evade until his batteries were drained. Then he would surface, charge the batteries and head toward home. But every captain of a *Romeo* who'd tried to stay down too close to the end of a battery charge had run into problems because the batteries lost power quickly, which meant that the crews lost control. Tae decided he would stay submerged for six more hours to give himself a two-hour margin.

But then there was a new sound. It was a splash, followed rapidly by a second, third, fourth and then a fifth. After a delay of about ten seconds, five explosions detonated in rapid sequence.

The young sonar man yelled out. "Captain, we are being depth charged!"

"Negative, those are not depth charges. The explosions are way too small." *Is the destroyer using the explosions as a short-range sonar?*

"Captain, their sonar is making strange noises. It is a series of long and short pulses."

"Get the radio operator up to the conning tower on the double." The young man arrived, breathing hard. "Is that some kind of code?" The captain demanded.

"Sir, it sounds like Morse code."

"What is the ship sending?"

The young man listened to the series of pings. "Sir, they are sending the letters I D K C A in Morse code."

"Anyone know what that means?"

No one responded.

Tae turned to his political officer. In a stiff, formal voice, the officer said they were to defend themselves if attacked.

Bang, 10-second delay. Bang, another 10-second delay, followed by three more explosions. Another series of short and long pings, just like the first one.

Tae was confused and waited 10 minutes, keeping the sub on its current heading and depth. *What the hell is going on? Are we under attack?*

The Russian destroyer passed overhead and steamed away to a range of about 9,000 meters. The sonarman could tell when the *Udaloy* made a U-turn. "Captain, the destroyer is headed right for us and is accelerating."

Destroyers accelerate before they attack. "Range?"

"Eight thousand meters, bearing one seven zero relative. He is behind us."

"Ready aft torpedo tubes one and two. Open the doors. Prepare to fire on my command. Open the doors to bow tubes one and two in case we have to take any additional shots."

"Aye, aye, Captain. Aft torpedo tubes open, also bow tubes one and two."

"Sir, the anti-ship homing torpedoes are ready to fire. Anti-submarine torpedoes are also ready."

Tae deliberated. "Open the doors to tubes three and four. Ready the anti-sub torpedoes." The destroyer might have a Russian submarine playmate lurking out there, undetected. "Range? Speed of the destroyer?"

"Twenty-plus knots. Two thousand, nine hundred meters."

Tae could once again hear pinging from the helicopter's sonar. *Shit, they have us targeted. Are they attacking us or is this an exercise? Do I want to risk the lives of my crew to find out?*

"Captain, destroyer is at two thousand, five hundred meters."

Tae didn't say anything. His face was a grim mask. *The Russian destroyer already dropped explosives, so I have been attacked. So I have the right to defend my sub.*

"Captain, the destroyer is now at two thousand, two hundred meters and closing."

"Fire aft tube two."

Tae heard the pulse and felt the submarine lurch as it ejected a 1,300-kilogram Chinese-made Yu-3 acoustic homing torpedo. The high-pitched squeal of the torpedo's screws was audible. This was the first torpedo he'd ever fired.

"Turn left to one-nine-zero and take us down to one hundred meters."

S-217 was passing 70 meters when everyone on board heard a loud rumble from the torpedo's warhead. A shockwave rocked the sub a few seconds later.

"Captain, sonar. The Russian destroyer has stopped. Sir, I think we hit it!"

Tae had just committed an act of war. He had to get out of the area.

The sonar operator's voice changed to a higher pitch. "Captain, I am picking up two sets of high-speed screws that sound like torpedoes—relative bearing zero-three-zero. They're pinging, and I think they have us targeted!"

Tae didn't hesitate. "Fire tubes three and four at the source of the torpedoes. Guide them manually until they acquire a target."

Shit, shit, shit, there is *another submarine out there.* "Launch the last two decoys three seconds apart. All stop."

"Sir, our anti-sub torpedoes are pinging and locked on to a sub."

The high-speed screws of approaching torpedoes and their rapid, high-frequency pinging told Tae he only had moments to live. The sub's sonar man turned to his commander, eyes wide with fear. "Captain, a torpedo is going to hit us. *WHAT DO WE DO?*"

1040 local time, on board submarine K-264

Mikhail Dudnik had ordered his *Victor III*-class submarine to lurk as quietly as possible in the vicinity of the destroyer *Admiral Yuri Rall*. Their mission tasking for the day was to act as a "playmate" for the *Rall*. When the surface ship stumbled onto an unidentified diesel-electric submarine, the exercise had been abruptly abandoned.

The Russian sub captain suspected the contact was probably a Japanese Yushio class submarine that had stumbled onto the exercise. *K-264* would remain as quiet as possible until the other submarine was out of the area. Neither Dudnik nor Semenov wanted an unknown foreign power observing their tactics and recording their sensor performance.

The unidentified sub hadn't responded to the destroyer's Morse code signal. For practice, Dudnik's conning tower team had been maintaining a firing solution on the unidentified submarine for well over an hour. After all, if you cannot train one way, find another.

Passive sensors indicated when the unidentified submarine launched a torpedo. Hearing the high-speed screws of a torpedo in the water aimed at the destroyer, Dudnik ordered a torpedo fired at the unidentified submarine. When two were fired back at him, he ordered his *Victor III* submarine to flank speed and launched a string of decoys while he changed depth and the sub's course. But his best maneuvering only got *K-264* bow-on to the onrushing torpedo. Dudnik ordered the crew to blow all the ballast tanks and full up on the planes. The submarine was going almost 30 knots when the 300-kilogram warhead slammed into its sonar dome.

The 6,000-metric-ton submarine staggered from the explosion. Anyone not sitting down was thrown into a bulkhead or onto the floor. Bones broke on impact, and several sailors were impaled on fittings. Throughout the boat, lights went out. The explosion punctured the forward torpedo room and killed 21 sailors. Only the water flooding in prevented a catastrophic sympathetic explosion of the 18 torpedoes stored in the compartment.

Emergency lights came on in the conning tower. Dudnik pulled himself up and reached for the handset that connected the control room with the engine room. The submarine was still headed up, but the sonar transducer hung in pieces, dragging and slowing the damaged sub, and they had 30 more meters to go to the surface and safety.

"Emergency surface. Blow all ballast tanks. Engineer, how is the reactor?"

"Off line, sir. We don't know what the damage is. The good news is we are not leaking radiation."

"Shift to battery power. Give me all you have." Getting to the surface and stopping the flooding was the only way they were going to survive.

The depth gauge told Dudnik they were passing 25 meters, but he could feel the submarine slowing further. The sluggish response meant that that the boat was becoming nose heavy. "Forward berthing compartment, are you flooding?"

"Negative. So far, the bulkhead is holding."

Dudnik sent his executive officer forward to see what the damage was, and to make sure all the hatches are sealed.

Would they make it to the surface? Dudnik wondered if now was when they'd find out where the defects were in the ship's construction. Soviet, and now Russian, yards were notorious for skipping steps and performing shoddy work.

Dudnik took a deep breath. He had to tell the crew what they already knew. He flipped the switch so that all compartments would hear his voice. "This is the captain speaking..."

1046 local time, on board U.S.S. La Jolla

The fast attack submarine was in deep water, slowly completing a turn in the racetrack pattern it was maintaining north of Simushir. With the SEALs ashore, there was little to do other than keep the radio mast above the water and wait to make the pickup. Marty was handing a cup of coffee to his fellow UCLA Navy ROTC classmate and former gymnast, Commander Richard Knowlton, the sub's skipper. At five-foot-six, he was just above the minimum height for the Navy. Suddenly, the speaker bolted to the overhead of the wardroom blared, "Captain to the conning tower."

Knowlton made a face as he got up. "I'll bet it's about your op. The shit may have hit the fan. Let's go."

2235 local time, Broutana Bay

Now that it was almost dark, the SEALs packed up their hide and made their way cautiously toward the north side of the entrance to Broutana Bay. The plan had them spending two days on the north side and one on the south side of the harbor. Rather than hike around, Adair believed swimming the channel was the shortest, safest route to the other side of the bay.

One by one, the four SEALs slipped into the cold water. Overhead, a layer of clouds hid the moon and stars. While two SEALs measured and logged the depth of the channel, the other two towed all four packs to the north side. All four were relieved to climb onto the rocks.

Adair led the team around the northwest side of the island. After a brief rest, the SEALs headed up the ridge to where they would spend the night. At 0012, after waiting for a patrol of four North Korean soldiers to pass by, Adair called the *La Jolla* to let them know they were in position.

Marty didn't mention the two other subs and the destroyer. Instead, he asked Adair if the team could get a close look at the

Geckos. Adair said he would, but it would delay the rendezvous from just after dark to close to dawn, or even after sunrise.

0055 local time, Broutana Bay

Adair worked his way down the mountain toward the stand-alone building. The chain link, razor-wire-topped fence had a gate on the west side, where the road ended, and extended all the way to the edge of the dock.

At the water's edge, Adair and his fire-teammate paused briefly before entering the 48-degree-Fahrenheit water. Treading water at the base of the ladder, he shined an infrared flashlight up and down, looking for any signs of a security system. Seeing none, he pulled himself up and peeked over the edge. He saw no movement, no sign of guards. Staying in the shadows, Adair crept to the side door and tested the handle. It was not locked and opened with a barely audible click. Crouching down, he slowly pushed the door open and scanned the inside.

His night vision goggles turned the darkness into a green-black world. Arrayed in front of him were four loaded pallets. Peering around the closest one, he saw another partially loaded one in the back. He also heard two different sets of snores. Guards! Adair moved cautiously around the pallets, spotted the sleeping men, then edged his way into the back room—and stopped.

Adair had never seen a real drug lab, but had seen enough of them in movies and cop shows to realize he'd found one. Even in the darkness, he could discern that the bags of pills had different colors; from each pile, he took one bag. On the way out, he grabbed a black plastic-wrapped brick from one pallet and another loaf-shaped one from another pallet and stuffed them into his backpack before leaving the building the same way he came in.

Chapter 11: GRAND CENTRAL STATION

Saturday, July 1st, 1995, 1038 local time, U.S.S. Blue Ridge

Josh was working at the plotting table, making notes on messages he needed to answer, when the intercom buzzed and an urgent summons called him to the comm center, where an incoming message from *La Jolla* was being decoded. When he finished reading it, Josh had five takeaways:

- A North Korean *Romeo* had sunk a Soviet *Udaloy* destroyer;
- One of the *Romeo's* torpedoes hit a Russian *Victor III* class submarine and it was on the surface, dead in the water;
- The *Romeo* was itself sunk by a torpedo of as yet unknown origin;
- The *La Jolla* was not detected; and
- Marty wanted to continue the mission as planned and retain control of the op.

Message in hand, Josh headed toward the admiral's office. Over his shoulder, he said, "Call the rope and tell him I need to see

Admiral Maize now. Not in thirty minutes, not in ten minutes. Right NOW!"

Josh watched Admiral Maize's eyes widen as he read and reread the message. "Holy shit! The good news is, it doesn't involve us. This goes beyond FUBAR."

"Sir," Josh said, "we need to give *Belleau Wood* and its escorts a heads up, if they haven't already picked up radio traffic from the *Victor III*. Maybe they can help the Russian sub. And I suggest you call CINCPAC ASAP, so he can stay on top of this game."

CINCPAC's decision was to continue Glass Carat as planned. Then he had a suggestion. "Put Captain Haman's Russian to use. Tell him to call what's-his-face at Russian Pacific Fleet headquarters and offer our help."

"Yes, sir. I'll do that right away. We'll see how friendly he is without half a bottle of vodka in him."

Even though the encryption, they could hear the four-star admiral chuckle, then, "Madeline just handed me a note that the *Victor III* is sending encrypted messages but also talking in plain language via satellite to its base in Vlad. Transcripts are about thirty minutes behind the transmissions. I'll have them faxed to you. From what we can tell, the sub took the torpedo hit in the bow and is not in any immediate danger of sinking, but the reactor is all fucked up and they have a bunch of casualties."

Admiral Maize had an idea. "Sir, Captain Haman and Captain Nagumo, the Japanese flotilla commander, are good friends. Nagumo is our liaison officer and their deputy chief of staff for current ops, so he'll know if a Japanese sub was there. And he is on *Belleau Wood* as an exercise evaluator."

"Nagumo, as in the admiral who led the raid on Pearl Harbor?"

Admiral Maize nodded in Josh's direction. "Sir, that was his uncle. Captain Nagumo and I work out at the same dojo. Every session, his friends give me painful lessons in Kendo. I have dinner with Hitoshi and his wife Kimiko once a month."

"Let me know what you find out. I am going to read Captain Billingham into Glass Carat. It is time he knows what is going on. Then I'll task an Air Force Rivet Joint RC-135 to orbit in the area."

* * *

Admiral Maize issued a series of instructions to his aide before flipping through an address book and dialing a number. When the phone at the other end started to ring, he pushed the button to turn the speaker phone on. "All right, Haman, it's time to see how good your Russian really is."

At first, the Russian officer who answered the phone thought the caller was playing a joke. He refused to believe an American admiral was on the phone. It took Josh five minutes, speaking in both English and Russian, to convincing the captain-of-the-third-rank (equivalent to an American lieutenant commander) to turn the phone over to another officer, Captain of the First Rank Valentin Rostov.

"Yes, Admiral Maize, good afternoon. We met when *Blue Ridge* paid visit to Vladivostok." Captain Rostov spoke in English.

"Yes Captain, I remember you," Maize replied. "You were the commander of a *Sovremenny*-class guided missile destroyer called the *Stoykiy*."

"Admiral Maize, you have very good memory. Well, now we have established we really are who we say we are. Admiral Prokiev is in office and I will transfer you. Good day."

"Admiral Maize, why are you calling?" Admiral Prokiev, who had a nasty scar at the base of his neck, spoke in a high-pitched, raspy voice. Maize suspected damaged vocal cords.

"Admiral, we are listening to plain-language transmissions from a damaged Russian submarine calling for help in the Sea of

Okhotsk. The U.S. Navy and the Japanese Maritime Self-Defense Forces have ships participating in a routine exercise less than 300 kilometers away who can render assistance."

"We don't need help. Yes, nuclear submarine has problem but is not in danger of sinking." Prokiev, like most Russians speaking English, often dropped articles like "a," "an," and "the."

"Is it leaking radiation?"

"*Nyet.*"

"That is good to hear. But we understand there are seriously injured sailors on board who need medical attention. Plus, there are survivors from the *Admiral Yuri Rall,* which sent out an SOS when it was sinking. Our ship, the *Belleau Wood,* has a large, well-equipped hospital. We could fly doctors to the submarine and treat the most seriously injured in the ship's hospital. Then we can transfer them to your ships when they are in range."

"That is most generous offer, but we do not need American help."

Maize persisted. "Ships leaving Vladivostok are three or four days away, even at full speed. It is a long time to wait if you are injured. Waiting may increase the number of dead. Our ships could be there in less than twenty-four hours."

"Captain of sub says everything is under control."

"Please allow me to offer an alternative." Admiral Maize was trying to be both polite and helpful. "We can simply fly a medical team to the submarine to treat your injured. They will leave when your ships arrive."

"Again Admiral, I appreciate offer. We consider, and if we decide to accept, I call. I have number. Please instruct U.S. Navy ships to stay at least ten nautical miles away to prevent unfortunate incidents." Then there was a dial tone.

Admiral Maize blew out a breath. "Damn! Prokiev has my sympathy; he's between the rock and the proverbial hard place. But

I wish he didn't think the risk of us getting intelligence is worse than losing lives."

The admiral's aide stuck his head in the door. "Sir, *Belleau Wood* is on the line."

"Please transfer it here."

It took Josh a few minutes to bring both Captain Nagumo and the rear admiral who was the exercise commander up to speed. "Hitoshi, we know that none of our subs were in the area. Were any of yours?" Josh heard his friend sucking air through his teeth.

"Our submarines operate around the central Kurils all the time. If one of our submarine captains could not get away from an *Udaloy* or a *Victor*, he would be relieved."

Translation—it was not a Japanese sub that was involved. There's a Japanese sub in and around the Kurils someplace, but not near the incident.

"Thank you. We'll keep you informed." That was as much as Josh was going to get until Nagumo returned to Yokosuka and debriefed the Japanese sub skipper.

2347 local time, Simushir

For the past two days, Major Kim had been unable to shake the feeling that someone was watching the base. To allay his suspicion, he'd ordered increased patrols, each with four men. With only 40 men, he was limited as to what he could do—and if any group were ambushed, a tenth of his force would be gone.

Today, the feeling got more persistent. He was convinced intruders were on Simushir. *Maybe the Americans have finally sent a reconnaissance team.*

Kim was headed to the cafeteria when he saw a shape. Rather than stare directly at it, he looked out of the corner of his eye and forced himself to keep walking when he noticed two small green discs that he recognized as night-vision goggle lenses. The Americans, he knew, used them extensively.

Inside the cafeteria, Kim called his number two and ordered everyone not already deployed in a fighting position to meet him at the armory as fast as they could get there. He then tasked the command center to alert the fighting positions that intruders were on the island and this was not a drill. No one, he reiterated, was to fire unless fired upon or unless he gave the order.

* * *

Henry Adair pressed himself against the building. *Oh shit, I've been spotted.* Adair retreated into the darkness. Once out of the complex, he keyed the mike. "*Adman Two*, *Three* and *Four*, we're compromised. We need to bug out, now. *Three* and *Four*, what's your ETA to rendezvous?

"Be there in five mikes."

"Check your six to make sure you're not followed. *One* and *two* will be waiting."

Adair now had a problem. Looking at the *Geckos* had taken them across the island, away from the pickup point. And from where he was, there was no way or time to call in the cavalry.

2359 local time, Broutana Bay

While his men checked their gear and weapons, Major Kim ordered the remaining 16 to follow him.

Once out of the settlement, Major Kim ordered his men to spread out in a skirmish line. He, along with the two machine gunners and their assistants, walked five meters behind the center of the line. As they left the facility, they swept west to the shore.

Sunday, July 2nd, 1995, 0019 local time, Simushir

Each SEAL rested on one knee, part of an outward-looking triangle, pulling security while Adair, in the center, looked at the

255

map. Their plan was to move quickly and stay away from the North Koreans. Adair guessed they had a 20-minute head start. With a little luck, the four would be back aboard the *La Jolla* in three hours, unless Mr. Murphy showed up.

0230 local time, Simushir

Major Kim was about a hundred meters from the Sea of Okhotsk when word was passed to him that one of his men had come across four separate sets of foot prints. Examining them with a red-lens flashlight, Kim concluded that their quarry was not moving directly west, toward the sea. Instead, they were headed up the western peninsula, to the northwestern end of the island.

Major Kim took a deep breath and motioned for his men to move forward. He did not tell his men that the intruders had night-vision goggles that would let them see his men long before they saw the enemy. He inwardly cursed his failure to add night-vision goggles to the shopping list he had given General Jang and Admiral Pak.

0235 local time, on board U.S.S. La Jolla

Commander Knowlton found Marty in the small officer's wardroom and spoke bluntly. "Marty, we've got a problem. The SDV is tits up. The battery's completely discharged and the guys working on it think there's a dead short someplace. Even if we fix it, getting the batteries fully charged will take hours. There's no way we can get into position for the pickup without being detected. That's the bad news, now I need an honest answer to a question."

The churning in Marty's gut went into overdrive. It was bad enough a sub-versus-sub shootout had happened 70 miles from their covert ops—and now this. Mr. Murphy has just shown up. "What's the question?"

"How far can your guys swim in 48-degree water after being on the beach at the end of the op?"

"A couple hundred yards. Why?"

"That's enough. I've got a plan, and the next time your guys call in, we'll brief them."

0237 local time, Simushir

Adair's headset crackled.

"Hold up, boss." He recognized the voice of the man designated as "tail end Charlie". "We've got company. Looks like about a dozen bad guys, six hundred yards behind us, spread out in a skirmish line."

"Do you think they've spotted us?"

"Don't know, but they've probably picked up our trail."

"Okay. Let's move out and pick up the pace."

02420146 local time, Simushir

Major Kim and all his men knelt down, weapons ready, and listened. The one thing he didn't want to do was to lose half his men in the first few seconds of an ambush. SEALs were known for their accurate shooting.

Or am I simply afraid? Major Kim wasn't sure. He motioned his men to go forward.

0248 local time, Simushir

All four of the SEALs were in a semi-circle, 20 feet from the cold, black water. The waves slapping against the volcanic rocks were so loud, Adair was afraid it would conceal the sound of approaching North Koreans.

Adair rolled on his back, made sure the short-range radio was on and his earpiece plugged in before he keyed the mike. "Surfer One, this Adman Zero Zero, over."

"Adman Zero Zero, this is Surfer One, over."

"We're ready for pick-up."

"We've got a change in plans. The SDV is hard down. So, here's what we want you to do."

Adair listened, his mind racing. This was not going to be fun. They were all tired from hauling 50 pounds of equipment and lack of sleep. But hey, at least they had a viable option. He clicked off the radio and keyed the short-range radio the team used. "Guys, remember "Hell Week" and sitting in the surf? Well, we get to do it again, but this time, at least we get to swim to keep warm. We have to make a hundred and fifty yards in cold water. Two by two, let's get down to the surf and get our fins and masks on."

Before he low-crawled into the water as the last man off the island, Adair pulled a brass coin about an inch and three-quarters in diameter out of his pocket. He propped it up against a rock and made sure the cloisonné SEAL logo faced inland.

He heard a shout and then a short burst. AK-47 rounds ricocheted off the volcanic rocks behind him, sending green tracer-bits flying crazily above and around him. It was followed by another burst that stitched the water just to his left as he entered the surf. Another line of geysers of water erupted in front of him, short of the snorkels ahead of him in the water.

Each man was stroking steadily towards the submarine, and every third breath was coming up to take a look. The SEALs were a hundred yards into the Sea of Okhotsk when a black shape emerged. *La Jolla* surfaced so the deck was a foot out of the water.

A hatch opened and a red light beckoned the SEALs. Four sailors tossed a rope to the first SEAL, who wrapped it around one arm as he kicked with his legs. The sailors pulled each exhausted SEAL out of the cold water, one by one.

The Simushir Island Incident

0304 local time, Simushir

On the rocky shore, one of his soldiers handed Major Kim the brass coin. He gazed out over the dark waters, frowning. *SEALS. How long were they here? What did they learn?* But then his scowl transformed into a smile. *Did it matter?* This was Russian territory, leased to North Korea. *Whatever you know, there is nothing you can do.*

0721 local time, Pyongyang

Vice Admiral Pak alternated time at the sub base in Mayang-do, Wonsan, the East Sea Fleet headquarters, and Pyongyang, the nation's capital. By air, 200 kilometers separated Mayang-do and Pyongyang, and the People's Air Force made the forty-five-minute flight six times a day. If they went to war, Admiral Pak would stay in Mayang-do, but peacetime politics and a desire to stay alive kept him in Pyongyang four days a week.

So it was not long after receiving a call, summoning him to the command center, that Admiral Pak was speeding toward "downtown" Pyongyang and the Navy's headquarters, wondering what had everybody so excited it couldn't wait until Monday.

Admiral Pak waited to enter the command center until he heard Captain Chin call "Attention on deck!" Having subordinates stand when a superior officer enters a room was one of the few traditions Pak insisted the People's Navy borrow from the Americans and the British, as a sign of respect to senior officers. None of the other services did it. He felt it was a tradition they should maintain, even though his political officers frequently informed him the practice was very bourgeois and not appropriate for a classless society such as the Democratic People's Republic of Korea enjoyed. Each time Pak's senior political officer reminded him, Pak had a hard time holding back his laughter.

"What needs my immediate attention?" he asked the watch commander, Commander Kang, who wore the insignia of a surface warfare officer.

"Sir, there are three situations requiring your attention. One of our *Romeo* submarines—S-217—has failed to report for the second time. This requires us to notify the commander of the submarine fleet."

"In any of their earlier communications, did they say they were having electrical or radio problems?" North Korean submarines carried spare parts for the HF radio, but failures were common.

"No, sir."

"Where was S-217 when it last reported?"

"About seventy kilometers southwest of the northern tip of Simushir Island, in the Sea of Okhotsk. Its last message said it was heading home."

"When is S-217 due back at Mayang-do?"

"Sir, July 9th."

"And the second item is?"

"Sir, our listening stations are picking up radio transmissions from a damaged Russian submarine in the Sea of Okhotsk. They have many casualties, and a Russian destroyer sank. We made a transcript of the conversations."

A sailor behind Commander Kang thrust out several sheets of paper, then popped to the position of attention. Admiral Pak took the transcripts. "You said you had a third item."

Commander Kang looked down at his notes. "S-201, operating off Olga, reported a Russian *Victor III* and four Russian warships steaming at high speed toward the La Pérouse Strait, sir."

"So we have a submarine, S-217, that has not reported for two days, a damaged Russian nuclear sub, and an *Udaloy* type destroyer that has sunk—all in the Sea of Okhotsk. And now another Russian nuclear submarine and four warships appear to be headed from Vladivostok toward their damaged comrade at high speed."

"Yes, sir."

"Do you know the location of the damaged Russian sub and their sunk destroyer?"

"Yes, sir." The watch commander pointed to a small X on a chart.

Pak mentally computed the distance S-217 would have traveled at five knots. The result was alarmingly near the location of the Russian sub. He noticed that Kang had *not* plotted it on the chart, and he was not going to tell him to do so.

"Commander Kang, what do you propose we do?"

"Sir?" The look on Commander Kang's face told Pak the commander had never been asked by a superior officer for his recommendation.

"Commander, if you were in my shoes, what would you report to our Dear Leader?"

"Our procedures manual says if a submarine misses two reporting times, we need to notify the fleet commander. Our signals intelligence officers are recording the radio transmissions." Kang paused after repeating the textbook answer. Admiral Pak sensed his unease in giving his opinion.

"Very well. You have done that." Pak didn't want to deflate the man's zeal and desire to do his job, or cause him to lose face by pointing out to Kang that he had not answered the question. He decided to give the man something productive to do. "I need a full report with your analysis of what caused the damage to the Russian submarine and destroyer, and why you think S-217 is missing, as soon as possible. Start from the established facts, but use your imagination. Consider what other facts would be most illuminating or helpful, if they could be discovered, and give me ideas about how to do just that—discover them soon." Pak doubted the man had ever heard such an order in his life. "In the meantime, try to communicate with S-217 as per our procedures. For all we know, their problem is merely that their radio has failed."

"Yes, sir."

"When can you have your report finished?"

"In an hour."

"When you are done, deliver it to Captain Chin so I can use it to ask for guidance from our Dear Leader. Do not make any copies. If S-217 responds, have the watch commander let me know, immediately—day or night. We won't report it missing until it does not return to Mayang-do as scheduled on July 9th."

"Yes, sir."

Admiral Pak turned to leave, and Captain Chin called attention on deck.

On his way out the door, Pak guessed he had at most a week before the shit was going to hit the fan. *S-217 is lost. What if S-217 was involved in an incident with the Russians? Someone's head will be on the chopping block. I have to make sure it is not mine.*

Monday, July 3rd, 1995, 0917 local time, Yokosuka

Josh glanced at his watch as he turned the corner onto the pier, at the end of the which was the *Blue Maru.* He'd been running longer than he planned. His shirt was soaked front and back from sweat, but the long run was a stress-reliever as well as a way of burning calories. As he ran, he let his mind wander. Most often he wondered what his wife and children were doing. Today, as he headed toward the ship, he wondered if Operation Glass Carat had turned into a cluster fuck.

The officer on watch informed Josh that he was wanted in the command center as soon as he returned. So much for a shower! Josh made his way to the com center, sweat-damp and shivering in the draft from air conditioning, and was immediately directed to one of the radio handsets for an update on the situation. He was informed that life rafts were now lashed to the deck of the Russian sub. Three planes, an Air Force RC-135 Rivet Joint signals intelligence gathering aircraft, a Navy ASW P-3C, and a Russian Tu-95M, were all circling the disabled sub at different altitudes. And, passing by Simushir, an EP-3 had been tracked by two *Geckos* for about 10 seconds, as if the North Koreans were practicing target acquisition. That last item rang all sorts of warning bells in Josh's mind. It would definitely be part of the day's briefing.

The call over, Josh got up to head for that shower, but the phone rang again, and the screen indicated it was from CINCPAC Ops and Top Secret. He picked up the headset. "Haman."

"What the fuck kind of rogue spec ops mission are you running?"

"Sir?" Josh couldn't recognize the voice through the encryption. He pushed the record button connected to his phone.

"Don't play dumb with me, Haman. You know *EXACTLY* what I am talking about. Goddamn you!!! Seventh Fleet reported that a North Korean sub torpedoed a Russian submarine and sank a Russian destroyer. Where the fuck did you come up with that? Where's the intelligence to support that insane assessment?"

Josh still didn't know who was on the phone, but he had no choice but to listen and let the individual rant.

"*I* think something on the *Victor III* blew up by mistake. Now *you* have an amphibious task force steaming around some godforsaken island in the Central Kurils, and you have one of *my* submarines on some super-secret op for which I am not cleared! And the commander of the Pacific Air Force is telling the Joint Chiefs of Staff there are Russian surface-to-air missiles on Simushir! So, I ask you again, Captain—*WHAT the FUCK is going on in MY area of RESPONSIBILITY?"*

The voice was so loud Josh had to hold the phone away from his ear. The two petty officers present grinned as he grimaced. Now he knew the caller was Rear Admiral Jeffers, a.k.a. Admiral Chicken of the Sea. The not being cleared was the clue. "Admiral, you know as much as I do about the Russian submarine. We're getting the same messages. You should have seen the message traffic several days ago—or in briefings. And, for the record, sir, we're not sure the missiles are being operated by the Russians, only that they are Russian-made."

"Don't be cute with me, Captain. Simushir is sovereign Russian territory."

"Sir, we have not confirmed there are any Russian forces on the island. So far, we know there are people in North Korean Special Forces uniforms on Simushir."

"Whaaaaaat!!! That's bullshit and you're out of your fucking mind. Are you writing a fucking novel or a movie script? I can't wait to convene the board of inquiry that will fry your ass." Jeffers paused. "Then there's the *Bremerton*. Tasking *any* sub in the Pacific AOR goes through me. The submarine commander for the Pacific Fleet works for me. Roger Billingham works for me. Do you understand?"

"Yes, sir." *But if they are tasked as a Seventh Fleet asset, we can task them.*

"Now just what in hell are the SEALS doing?"

"Sir, I cannot answer your question." There was no way Josh could sugarcoat the answer. Jeffers wasn't cleared for Glass Carat. He could hear an explosion building in the silence.

"Captain Haman, are…you…*fucking*…telling…me…that… I…as…the… CINCPAC…N3…am…not…cleared…for…an… op…in…my…*fucking*…area…of…responsibility?" Jeffers enunciated each and every word. "Is that what you are telling me, Captain?"

"Yes, sir." Again, the less said, the better.

"That's more of your insubordinate bullshit, Haman. I am cleared for all—repeat, *ALL*—operations in PACOM's AOR. Running an off-the-books operation like this will end Admiral Maize's career. And with my help, CNO will have you and your slimy snake-eater friend Cabot hauled in front of a general court martial, and your careers in the Navy will be over. I repeat, OHHHHVERRRR!" There was a pause, then Jeffers spat out, "Cabot is on the *La Jolla*, isn't he?"

Josh grimaced as he spoke. "Sir, I can't answer the question."

"You goddamn well *will* answer the question, that's an order."

"Sir, with all due respect, I can't answer the question."

"I…am…giving…you…a…direct…order. Answer…the… *fucking*…question. Do you understand, *CAPTAIN HAMAN*? Answer, or I will have you charged with insubordination and relieved. Now, answer my question."

"Yes, sir, I understand the question. Sir, with all due respect, I cannot answer because you are not cleared for the operation."

"Let me repeat this for a moron like you, Haman, there is nothing—repeat, *NOT A FUCKING THING*—that goes on in this theater for which I am not cleared. That is a fucking bullshit answer, Haman. Are you going to answer the question?"

"No, sir. I cannot because you are not cleared. I suggest you ask CINCPAC to add you to the access list. Then I will be happy to answer any question you may have."

There was silence for a few seconds. Josh could tell Jeffers was fuming. "After I hang up, Haman, I am going to call CINCPAC's JAG officer and have you charged for disobeying a direct order. I hope you enjoy cold weather and making big rocks into little rocks, because you and your snake eater buddy are headed for Leavenworth."

"Admiral, are there any other questions you want to ask?" Josh ignored the threat. His question received the sound of a slamming hand set, then a dial tone in response.

"Did you tape that?" Vice Admiral Maize had entered the room at some point and was standing by the door. He looked at Josh, then at the enlisted men, all of whom were Operations Specialists.

"Yes, sir."

"We heard most of it, and as standard procedure, it was taped so we can put a transcript in the log," the senior petty officer on the watch team chimed in.

Admiral Maize held out his hand. "Good—I want the tapes now." The two sailors handed the cassettes from their recorders to the admiral. Both men were in their early twenties. One of the privileges of working in the command center was hearing things few enlisted men ever hear. Admiral Maize took a deep breath. "I will have the staff's legal beagle take statements from all of you attesting you heard the conversation, and ask you to sign off on the transcript once it is typed out. I am now giving a direct order: you are not to discuss anything about this conversation with anyone. Understood?"

"Yes, sir." All three answered.

"Good. Captain Haman, go take a shower, then report to my office ASAP."

"Yes, sir."

Tuesday, July 4th, 1995, on board U.S.S. Blue Ridge

Officially it was a holiday, but Josh didn't want to leave the command center until he had confirmation that Adair and his team were off Simushir. He'd set the alarm clock for 0600, thinking a message would arrive during the wee hours of the morning; now, twelve hours after their scheduled extraction time, he was still waiting. Naturally, just when he sat down to eat a breakfast of bacon and two poached eggs, the steward told him that a message from *La Jolla* had come through. Josh lunged away from the table and headed to the com center.

The office petty officer smiled as he handed over the message. "Another good op, sir." So he'd at least skimmed, if not read, the message. This type of operation was difficult to keep secret within the staff.

Sitting on the corner of the desk and ignoring the clanging tele-printers, Josh read the message. The report was succinct.

1. The team is back on the *La Jolla;*
2. Four Geckos and 36 missiles are on the island;
3. Building on north side of the bay refines opium paste into heroin and makes methamphetamines. Samples are being brought back;
4. Two Crescent Shipping—*Crescent Galaxy* and *Crescent Moon*—arrived, unloaded equipment and then each took two pallets from the drug factory;
5. Estimate of 50 North Korean special forces on the island; and
6. Island has desalination plants and generators along with extensive fuel suppliers.
7. *La Jolla's* acoustic sensors have recorded the incident between the Russian and North Korean ships in its entirety.

It was time to go see the admiral.

Wednesday, July 5th, 1995, 0954 local time, Broutana Bay
A rust-streaked fishing vessel chugged into the harbor of Simushir Island, smoke belching from the funnel. Fishing nets hung from its rigging. There was no name on the bow. Its captain cut the diesel and let the boat coast to the empty dock.

Forty-eight North Korean soldiers filed out of the hold and formed up along the pier. They put their weapons and packs in a neat row along the edge of the pier and formed a line to pass crates of ammunition—mortar shells, anti-tank and shoulder-fired anti-aircraft missiles—onto the pier where they were stacked neatly by munition type.

Major Kim responded swiftly, tasking his men to use six of the Kawasaki all-terrain vehicles to shuttle the weapons to the armory, where they could be safely stored.

The boat's diesel belched a cloud of black smoke as it clattered to life. Less than an hour after it tied up to the pier, it headed back out of the harbor. On the pier, a young captain approached Major Kim, came to attention and saluted.

"Major Kim, Captain Pyon Jung reporting, sir."

Kim returned the salute. "Welcome to Simushir, Captain."

"Thank you, Major. I have heard much about you, and it is my honor to serve you and our country."

"We both serve the people and our Dear Leader." Major Kim hated the trite statement, but it was required. "What unit are your men from?"

"The 154th Special Operations Company, based just south of Wonsan."

"Your company has conducted many raids in the south."

"Yes, that is true."

Major Kim always wondered why his country kept sending men south to conduct raids. Over 80 percent never returned. Most died when their submarines sank, or they were killed or captured by the South Koreans. "I see you have brought weapons to help us to better defend our little base."

"We look forward to completing our mission."

"Our mission is to defend the base if attacked. As soon as you are settled, I will introduce you to Managing Director Lee from the Kuril Island Development Corporation. He runs this place."

The captain looked surprised.

Major Kim read his mind. "Did you think this was a People's Republic facility?"

"I was told this will be a forward base of the Democratic People's Republic of Korea. When it is finished and all the weapons are here, we will have outflanked the capitalist Americans and their South Korean and Japanese lackeys."

"Who briefed you?"

"Deputy Minister Thaek. I have been working for him on a special assignment. He reports to our Dear Leader and no one else."

"I have met him." *Is this man here to arrest or kill me?* Major Kim struggled to maintain his composure amid his anxiety. *Probably not. If he were, he would have the sense to keep quiet about his "special assignment" work for Thaek.* "That may be the plan for the future. For now, we are guests of the Kuril Island Development Corporation, who have leased this island from the Russians. And for now, our mission is to defend this facility if it is attacked."

1840 local time, Las Vegas

First Lieutenant Jintao Yi stood in line for the cashiers' windows in one of the large slot machine rooms in the Sands Casino. Long lines, he decided, were good. The longer the line, the more pressure on the cashiers and the less diligent they would be. In his arms was a large paper bucket of chips he'd purchased several hours ago. This was the fifth casino he'd been to today, and in each, the process was the same.

Step 1—convert $9,000 cash into chips.

Step 2—play blackjack for an hour or so and lose less than $500. Casinos only had to report winnings to the IRS, not losses. Then take the remaining chips to a different cashier to convert them into a check. Each time, the clerk asked him for his driver's license, and each time he slid his California license through the slot.

Not once was Yi asked for his South Korean passport, with its long-stay student visa stamped on one of the back pages. On his visa application, he'd reported his home as Taegu, South Korea, when in reality he'd been born and raised in Wonsan—in the Democratic People's Republic of North Korea. Before he'd boarded the plane from Pyongyang to Beijing, he'd turned over his Korean People's Army identification card to an official, who had reminded him that his entire family was depending on him to complete his assignments and return to North Korea. Defecting meant they would be placed in a re-education camp.

From Beijing, he'd flown to Seoul and then on to LA, where a driver had met him and handed him the keys to a furnished house. There he found a low-mileage 1992 Chevy Malibu parked in the garage with the keys on the dash, a checkbook to an account where his salary would be deposited, his preferred weapons and ammunition, and a phone number to call once he'd arrived.

At first Jintao hadn't known what to do with the cash he took from the safes of his targets, so he'd kept the stacks of bills in boxes in an empty closet. Then he saw a bank advertisement, offering a free safe deposit box for a year with a new account. After the third hit, Jintao rented the largest safe deposit box the local branch of Bank of the West had to offer, and another one at a nearby Wells Fargo branch.

He divided and locked away the $1.6 million he'd collected. The bills, mostly 50s and 100s, were cash in hand, but the money was also in limbo; if he deposited a huge sum into a bank account, the transaction would be flagged and reported. Yi feared government agents might match it to unsolved thefts. Then it occurred to him he could use casinos to "launder" his wealth.

A few weeks back, a hit had got messy when his Tokarev misfired with a loud click. His mark had come at him fast, with a large Bowie knife. To defend himself, Jintao had drawn his *wakizashi.* The hit became the first real test of his skill with the eighteen-inch blade. A parry and side-step, and Jintao had slashed the man's forearm, nearly severing it above the wrist. An astonishing quantity of arterial blood had spurted out and the man had dropped his knife. Jintao had followed up, slashing open the man's chest, sending him into shock, and ended the fight by slashing his target's throat. He'd left the man's house splattered with blood—none of it his—taking the man's briefcase, which contained a quarter million in cash.

Yi had changed clothes in his car, a 1993 BMW 535i, then cleaned the seat and discarded the bloody clothes.

On Highway 99, he'd seen a sign for the Chukchansi Gold Resort, northeast of Fresno. Thinking it would be an ideal place far from LA to test his cash-to-chips-to-cashier's check scheme, he'd parked the Beemer and gone inside. And it had worked.

The first time he bought chips, the cashier had told him that all cash transactions of $10,000 or more had to be reported to the Federal government. So Jintao only bought $9,000 worth of chips.

The BMW he'd acquired by trading in the Chevy and paying the balance with a bank check. He'd wanted something more fun to drive than the mundane Chevy. Also, the change cut a tie to whomever had set up his cover. His next planned step to break the link was to move out of the house and rent an apartment. In North Korea, they were assigned by the government. In America, one could choose. Step by step, he planned to disappear.

The decision was painful because Yi and his parents understood the yin and yang of the decision. If he was killed, the North Korean government would treat him as a hero. If he disappeared or defected, there were dire consequences for his family. When Jintao had learned where he was going, he'd spoken with his mother and father. They'd approved of his decision to stay in America if possible. It was, his father had said, the family's Karma.

Later that evening, in his hotel room at the Mirage Casino, Jin-tao studied the brochures of attractions in Las Vegas. Yi had not slept with a woman since he'd left North Korea. There, officers in his unit were kept secluded from the rest of the People's Army. To fulfill their need for sex, the government sent companionship teams of women called *manjokcho* teams. They came from an unofficial organization known as *kippumjo,* which provided women between 18 and 25 years to the senior leadership of the country, and to selected others, such as the young men in his unit.

The flyer for a swingers club caught his eye, and he decided to call. After a short discussion with a with a representative of the club, he made a reservation. A $25 cover charge had to be paid in cash, and if he wanted something alcoholic, he had to bring his own.

At the Special Forces school, where they taught the customs of the countries to which they were headed, Jin-tao had developed a taste for Kentucky bourbons. He particularly liked Maker's Mark. In a nearby liquor store, he bought a bottle and went into the casino to play blackjack. The limo from Sappho's would pick him up at nine.

The limo dropped Yi off under a portico where a man in a dark suit and a woman wearing a mid-calf-length dress waited. The woman led him to a small room, where he handed over his bottle of Maker's Mark along with five 5-dollar bills. He was asked to sign a release. The female clerk, whose name tag read "Vicki", studied the well-built Asian in front of her. He filled out a golf shirt nicely. "Welcome. Follow the rules and have a good time. We expect a nice crowd tonight. I suspect there will be many who will be interested in you."

Inside, the house was larger than anything that Jin-tao Yi had ever seen in his life. The brochure said Sappho's owned a 10,000 square foot mansion that had 30 bedrooms on the upper three floors. The downstairs had two main rooms, one with chairs and couches where men and women were already making out. The other had the bar, tables with food, and a small band playing love songs.

The house rules said he could talk to any of the guests. If they shook their heads or said no, he was required to walk away. No meant no. Still nervous, he asked the bartender to pour him some of his bourbon. Drink in hand, he walked past the buffet and toward the living room. A very attractive blonde walked up to him. "Hi, my name is Kris, and you must be Jin-tao." The woman wore a black miniskirt and a loose fitting pink blouse.

"I am…. How'd you know my name?"

"My friend Vicki at the front desk said I should check you out."

Kris's smile, the way she looked at him, and the way she moved was like nothing he'd ever seen. Suddenly, he understood why. *She's here because she enjoys sex.* Shortly thereafter, in one of the rooms on the third floor, she was taking him places he'd never been before. Jin-tao thought he'd died and gone to heaven.

Chapter 12: MANNA FROM UNLIKELY PLACES

Thursday, July 6th, 1995, 1030 local time, Pyongyang

For three days, Thaek had dithered over where to hold this very important meeting. Finally, he'd decided that privacy and discretion were more important than impressing his guest with the imposing size of a large conference room, and opted for a small conference room down the hall from his new office. There were large photos of Kim Il-sung and Kim Jong-Il on the wall, along with one of Lenin. Considering who his guest was, Thaek had removed the photo of Stalin and replaced it with one of farmers in heroic poses.

Thaek didn't like to be kept waiting. Nor did he like to make others wait for him. He liked promptness. So as soon as his assistant informed him that their visitor had arrived and all was in readiness, he smashed out his cigarette and strode to the conference room, to meet with General Ryabkov.

"Welcome, General Ryabkov," Thaek said politely, scrutinizing the man. The general was stocky and built like a truck. His closely cropped hair was gray, speckled with black, rather than the other way around. "Thank you for seeing me on such short notice. It is always a pleasure to meet comrades in fraternal security organizations."

The Russian major general was the number three man in the Counterintelligence Department of the newly created FSB. His world was espionage, assassinations, recruiting spies, and supporting front organizations that helped Russia. Ryabkov's specialty was active or "wet measures," and the more notoriety they got the more he liked it, because they sent the message, "Don't mess with Russia."

"So, General, what brings you to the Democratic People's Republic of Korea?" Thaek hoped his meager Russian was understandable. If you wanted to advance in the Ministry of State Security, proficiency in Russian or Mandarin, or both, was a requirement, but languages did not come easily to him.

"I asked to see you because we have a common interest in the activities of two Americans."

Thaek blinked. "We take an interest in any Americans who support their South Korean puppets."

Ryabkov spoke slowly to make it easy for Thaek to understand. He didn't want an interpreter; the fewer who heard what he said, the better. "You will want to know more about two American naval officers who are taking a very active interest in the heroin facility on Simushir."

Thaek's face set in a stone mask. *How does he know about the factory? I am not going to react or confirm its existence.*

Ryabkov stared directly into Thaek's eyes. "Deputy Minister Thaek, I would not have brought these files all the way from Moscow if I didn't think they would be of use to you. Either talk with me now, or this meeting is over and I will not waste your time."

"I am sorry, General, but I am suspicious by nature. You must understand, people do not bring me gifts. I have to dig them out, usually by extreme means."

Ryabkov knew what extreme meant. The FSB, like its predecessor, the KGB, routinely got confessions through intimidation, imprisonment of family members, and torture. "I understand, Deputy Minister Thaek. And soon you will understand that this 'gift' is also a test of your ingenuity." He put his leather briefcase on the polished wooden table and popped open the latches. He lifted out two red folders, both almost six centimeters thick, and laid them on the table, side-by-side, before closing the case and putting it on the floor. He hoped the theatrical delay would increase the North Korean's curiosity.

"These are copies of what we have in our files." Ryabkov tapped each file in turn. "This man is a helicopter pilot by the name of Haman. This one is a SEAL whose name is Cabot. The two officers first came to our attention during the Vietnam War when they proved troublesome. In 1976, they engineered the defection of two of our scientists who developed our chemical and nuclear weapons. They were also responsible for shutting down a West German terrorist organization that was supported by our friends in the Stasi. In 1986, Cabot and Haman flushed out one of our agents in the CIA. In 1992, Haman was sent to Moscow and helped the civilian police arrest one of my comrades, Lieutenant General Volkov." Ryabkov didn't bother to mention that Haman had been part of a humanitarian rescue mission at the time, arranging famine relief for Russia's starving people. "I must warn you, they are very competent adversaries, so do not underestimate them."

It seemed to Thaek that these two American naval officers were Russia's problem, not his. *Are you trying to use my resources to do your work for you?* "How does this relate to the Kuril Island Development Corporation?" *And who told Ryabkov I was involved with the Kuril Island Development Corporation? The Dear Leader or one of his trusted minions will be getting a report on this meeting. I must do what is expected of me, or I will lose my position.* "And why are you bringing this excellent information to my attention?"

"Ahhhhh, the crux of the matter." Ryabkov leaned back in his chair. "Under our new leadership, my country has decided to desist from active measures against these two officers. Your country tends to be, professionally speaking, more realistic on these matters. And since both of these officers are stationed in close proximity to your facility on Simushir and have a long history of covert ops, I think you will realize that direct action on your part will directly benefit *all* your plans for Simushir."

Their meeting continued cordially. Ryabkov departed, hoping the North Koreans would succeed where the KGB had failed.

Friday, July 7th, 1995, 1126 local time, Pyongyang

Naval headquarters was another gray, concrete structure designed by an architect who was either disinterested in design or had been told to make it plain. The single ornamentation, the only indication that the building was the People's Navy headquarters, was a bronze statue of a sailor in a heroic pose.

A small, windowless office in the back had a phone from which one could dial international numbers without having to connect through an operator who would ask for a special authorization code and record the conversation. As he placed his call, Pak tried to relax.

"Hello, Cho Rhee."

Calls from North Korea had to be short and circumspect. As soon as she recognized her uncle's voice, Cho Rhee, who had been studying Half Moon U.S.'s June financial reports when the phone rang, got right to the point. "The package sent to Singapore arrived safe and sound."

"Thank you." Vice Admiral Pak hung up.

Cho had just confirmed that her aunt, So-yi, Pak's wife of 30 years, had arrived safely in Singapore. He had gotten her out of the country on a one-week visa to attend a medical conference in Beijing. Once there, she'd used a Singaporean passport kept at the Half Moon office in the People's Republic of China's capital to fly to Singapore. Now he had to get out with his daughter. Admiral Pak sighed. *I will save who I can.*

His son, Seong, would remain in North Korea. His job as a marine engineer precluded any type of travel permits. And there was the additional complication of Seong's health. There weren't any medicines readily available in North Korea to treat the severe asthma that had destroyed his lungs. Walking 25 meters left Seong wheezing. Cold, damp winters in poorly heated homes had aggravated his respiratory problems. In a pressurized airline cabin, he would slowly asphyxiate without supplemental oxygen. If Pak used his back channels in an attempt to acquire the kind of oxygen bottles a man with asthma would need to travel by plane, word of this would reach The Dear Leader—and it would not end well.

Seong was a realist. He did not believe he would live to age 30. He knew any attempt to smuggle him out of North Korea would probably kill him, and would jeopardize his family. This did not anger him, for he believed it was his karma to die in North Korea. If his parents and sister got out alive, he could die in peace.

After lunch, Admiral Pak met a representative of the Chinese Navy at their Pyongyang embassy to continue their discussion about buying more modern submarines. The Chinese were eager to sell the subs, but every deal required extensive negotiations that dragged out for months.

The Simushir Island Incident

Saturday, July 8th, 1995, 0530 local time, U.S.S. Blue Ridge

The message traffic never stopped. Waiting on Josh's desk Saturday morning had been a four-inch-high stack of messages to be sorted. All the department heads came in on Saturdays and Sundays for a few hours to make sure they kept up, otherwise they would be buried when they returned on Monday.

Josh had just about finished reviewing message traffic when the admiral's aide came in and handed him a blue folder with a single sheet of paper.

"YES!!!!"

His exclamation startled the young lieutenant and the two enlisted men at work in the flag command center. Grinning, Josh re-read the document for a third time.

```
FROM: CINCPAC
PERSONAL FOR:
COMMANDER, PACIFIC FLEET
COMMANDER, THIRD FLEET
COMMANDER, SEVENTH FLEET
COMMANDER, NAVAL FORCES KOREA
COMMANDER, NAVAL FORCES JAPAN
COMMANDER, NAVAL FORCES PHILIPPINES
COMMANDER, NAVAL FORCES MARIANAS
INFO:
CHIEF OF NAVAL OPERATIONS
CHIEF OF NAVAL PERSONNEL
CLASSIFICATION: SECRET NOFORN
SUBJ: RELIEF OF CINCPAC N3
1. (SECRET  NOFORN)—REAR  ADMIRAL  (UPPER
        HALF) JEFFERS HAS ELECTED TO RETIRE
        AT  THE  END  OF  THIS  FISCAL  YEAR.  HIS
        DEPARTURE IS EFFECTIVE JULY 7TH, 1995,
        JEFFERS  WILL  BE  ON  TERMINAL  LEAVE
        UNTIL THE END OF THE FISCAL YEAR.
```

2. (SECRET NOFORN)—UNTIL A NEW CINCPAC N3
       ARRIVES, CAPTAIN ROGER BILLINGHAM
       WILL BE MY CHIEF OF STAFF FOR
       CURRENT OPERATIONS (N3).

"You can go home now and get some rest."

A familiar drawl startled Josh. He turned to see Marty standing in the doorway.

They shook hands before they hugged. This was shaping up to be the best day Josh had had since this tour started. Admiral Jeffers was out and Marty was back!

"I thought it would be better to get the guys off the sub in the dark. They'll be back at eleven tomorrow for the debrief—after they check in their gear."

"Great."

"Go to your stateroom. You look like shit."

"I look that good?"

"No, Josh—you look that bad. Three people stopped me on the way in here and asked me to escort you there if you didn't go on your own accord. The admiral said he wouldn't give you an order you would probably disobey. He did say you're excused from all duties until you get some sleep. I'll stand down the watch team."

"Thanks. But you might want to read this first." Josh handed Marty the message. "It'll make your day. It is also proof that there is a God."

1020 local time, Pyongyang

Deputy Minister Thaek waited in a conference room that resembled a crypt, reviewing, for what felt like the hundredth time, the detailed notes he'd prepared for this meeting. He stood when he heard the door open.

"What do you have for me?" The Dear Leader took the seat at the head of the table.

"My people on Simushir confirm what you, our Dear Leader, suspected. Half Moon is processing much more opium than they report. They get the raw opium from suppliers in Myanmar and Laos and are shipping one metric ton of heroin every two weeks from the island. This is in addition to what they ship from Hong Kong, even after we tipped off the police and our republic to raid their production plants."

"Where is it going?"

"America. Ships chartered through Half Moon Trading unload it about one hundred miles south of the U.S./Mexican border. The Mexicans pay them and smuggle the heroin into the U.S, where it is sold. Vice Admiral Pak says their heroin is sold under the street name of Asian Pure."

"How do they get the money from the Mexicans?"

"The money is paid directly into banks outside America. I do not know the names of the banks. They have not told me yet."

"Find out."

"Yes, Dear Leader. I am already working it."

"Good. Do you know from whom they buy the raw opium?"

"No. Vice Admiral Pak has said he will share his contacts with me, but has not done so yet. We searched the homes and offices of both Pak and Jang, but found nothing, so they must keep the information in their heads. I suspect the ordering is done in Hong Kong."

"What about their spy?"

"We suspect he is in the Imperialist Americans' Pacific Command headquarters."

"Who controls him?"

"A relative of Major General Jang, who lives in Hawaii."

"How do you know that?"

"Research. During the War of National Liberation, some of our disloyal and cowardly countrymen deserted." Thaek was careful to use words acceptable to the Dear Leader. "About three hundred families went to Hong Kong, several hundred made it to Singapore, and another hundred or so went to what was then Burma. Thousands of others went to Australia, the U.S. and Canada. Most who went to the U.S. settled in Southern California while most of the ones who went to Canada now live in Vancouver or Toronto."

"Very interesting. Apparently, some of our investigators in our Ministry of State Security are not as thorough as you are. Do we know who these relatives are?"

Thaek realized that heads, maybe literally, were going to roll in the section of the ministry responsible for background investigations. But his would not be one of them. Poor bastards— there was no way they would have known or could have found out; but in the paranoid mind of the Dear Leader, that was no excuse. "Not yet, Dear Leader. Many of our records were destroyed during the war. My men went to Wonsan, where Major General Jang was born and raised, and to Chongjin where Vice Admiral Pak lived as a child to see what we could learn. They confirmed that Vice Admiral Pak has a brother and sister in Hong Kong, and we think Pak's brother is the President of Half Moon Trading."

Thaek stopped speaking in case his Dear Leader had any questions. Hearing none, he continued. "Vice Admiral Pak's wife is in Beijing at a medical conference. Her attendance was approved by the Ministry of State Security. Agents are monitoring those who attend."

"And Major General Jang?"

"The general had two brothers who left during the war. One works for Half Moon, and the other is a doctor in Singapore. There is another brother listed on the birth records, but we could not trace him. We did find a reference to an officer from Wonsan with the same birth date as the general's brother who was sent to Myanmar as an advisor in the early sixties. He never came back. Military records have no information on what happened to him, other than he was in our special forces."

"So, he could be a deserter and still alive? He could be the man in Hawaii?"

"Yes, Dear Leader."

"Interesting. What else?"

"We are monitoring every move Major General Jang, Vice Admiral Pak, and their families make."

"Excellent. Keep me informed."

"Yes, Dear Leader." Thaek hoped the meeting was over. His stomach was churning. He needed a cigarette and needed it badly.

"One more thing."

Thaek knew his Dear Leader loved making those below him squirm. He'd seen him do it to others. Now he was the target.

"How was your meeting with General Ryabkov?"

"It was very productive. He gave me files on two American naval officers that I am studying. I will come up with a plan for you to approve to eliminate them."

"Excellent. The Russians will pay us well if we do. You will profit from this success. We can't let the Americans interfere with our plans on Simushir. Getting a missile base there is a major strategic initiative of mine. You wouldn't want to be the reason we failed."

When he finally got outside, Thaek's hands were shaking so much he struggled to rip open a new package of Cuban cigarillos. It took him five strikes to get the match lit, and it wavered in his shaking hand as he brought it close. When the cigarillo was finally lit and his lungs were full of satisfying smoke, he looked furtively around to see if anyone had noticed his struggles.

Monday, July 10th, 1995, 0931 local time, U.S.S. Blue Ridge

The air conditioning was set to 65 degrees Fahrenheit, which struck Josh as overcompensating for the summer heat, but the setting was out of his control. To keep from being chilled to the bone, he used silver duct tape to block the vent above his desk. It kept the frigid air from cascading down on his shoulders and neck. The room was still cold, but at least he wasn't directly under a draft.

Josh was stirring a cup of tea filled with honey and lemon, thinking that his sore throat and throbbing sinuses were a consequence of running on nervous energy all the time Glass Carat was underway. It was the price he paid to do whatever he could to make sure Marty came back safe and sound. His "home remedy" recipe really called for a shot of Scotch as well, but he was on duty and not in his stateroom. Discreetly bending rules was one thing— openly breaking them was another.

Seventh Fleet was ordered by CINCPAC to organize and manage the search for *Crescent Moon* and *Crescent Star* until they entered Third Fleet's area of responsibility. The staff's command center had the search areas plotted, and when the P-3s reported the finding of one of the ships, Josh would be called.

Shivering, Josh initialed a draft of a message asking CINCPAC to assign surface ships to board and search the freighters once they were found. All he needed were their latitude and longitude to release the message.

Chapter 13—DIFFERENT MISSILE ROE

Tuesday, July 11th, 0934 local time, Broutana Bay

Because of where Simushir sits in its time zone, both sunrises and sunsets are relatively late, all year round. At the height of summer, the sun was visible from about 0600 to 2145. Major Kim preferred these long days to the dark and cold of winter.

His command center was on the west side of the bay in a natural cave. It had a small entrance that a man could easily slip through, and opened into an area approximately 10 meters by 20 meters. They used crushed lava from the settlement to even out the floor. To provide power, they tapped into the electric line that ran from the fishing support facility to the drug lab on the northern end of the bay. They also had a small emergency generator they could use to power the radios and phone system.

Dampness was evident in the shining condensation on the lava walls and drips from the ceiling. To protect their equipment, Major Kim's men sheltered their electronics with plastic sheeting from discarded packing material stretched over a wood frame. It gave the command center a surreal look. The electronics heated the cave, making it 10 degrees Celsius warmer than outside.

With Major Kim's approval, at 0800 every morning, two of the *Osas* were driven to one of eight prepared revetments so crews could practice using the search radar to track aircraft. Today, they were in the revetment closest to the eastern shore of the island. Major Kim half-listened to a called-in report while he finished a discussion with one of his sergeants on possible locations for a live-fire range.

"This is *Wasp One*. We are tracking an aircraft headed toward the island. We are switching to the optical tracker to see if we can identify the airplane."

Major Kim's specific instructions to Captain Jung, who was supervising crew training, were clear. *Osa* crews were to practice tracking airplanes but not switch to engagement mode nor shoot a missile without his approval.

"This is *Wasp One*. The aircraft is a four-engine American electronic reconnaissance aircraft, similar to the ones that fly up and down the coasts of our homeland. Range twenty kilometers and the plane is headed toward the island."

A different voice spoke. "Turn on the target tracker."

Major Kim yelled *"NO!"* and snatched up his handset. "Captain Jung!" No answer.

"Aircraft is almost in missile range at twenty kilometers."

Major Kim tossed the handset to the surprised soldier standing watch. "Keep trying to call Captain Jung! If he answers, tell him I order him not to shoot." He ran to the MULE just inside the cave entrance, fired it up, and floored the gas pedal. The MULE bounced along the rocky shoreline road, barely under control. He was halfway to *Wasp One's* revetment when he saw two missiles leave the launcher less than five seconds apart.

The Simushir Island Incident

0935 local time, on board an Air Force RC-135,
call sign Highlighter Zero Five

Copilot First Lieutenant Jimmy Butler could see the brown shape of Simushir Island. Streaks of snow were visible in the narrow ravines of Mount Milna and Prevo Peak. It looked as if their plane were closer than the planned 15 nautical miles, but the navigator hadn't given them a course correction. He decided to wait and see if the aircraft commander, Major Gus Sanderson, said anything. As a "newbie," he didn't want to ask a dumb question. Instead, he updated his log about a fluctuating oil temperature on the number three engine which was running a hundred degrees hotter than the other three. When he finished, the flight engineer handed him a cup of water.

Just as he took a sip, a horn blared, signaling a missile had targeted them. Jimmy Butler felt every muscle in his body tighten with dread. If the target tracker on the missile locked onto their airplane, the pitch and frequency of the beeping would go higher, or worse yet, become a steady tone.

Major Sanderson rolled into a 60-degree left bank away from the island—which dumped Butler's water into his lap—shoved the throttles to the stops and pushed the yoke forward. Their only hope was to outrun the missile or decoy it. "Pilot to crew, everybody get strapped in. We're targeted and evading. Break, break. Navigator, get off a Mayday with our position and keep sending it until someone answers."

Sanderson, who'd been flying Rivet Joint electronic aircraft since earning his wings 11 years ago, had been shot at before. It wasn't unusual for the Russians or the Chinese or the North Koreans to launch missiles at the intelligence-gathering airplanes, or to intercept them with fighters. Over the years, many U.S. reconnaissance airplanes had been shot down. Sanderson accepted the losses and the danger as part of the job.

"Jimmy, arm the chaff and flares."

Butler looked up at the overhead panel and found the chaff and flare control panel. He pulled the red cover on the arming switch down and forward, so he could lift and move the toggle switch to the armed position. A red light came on, indicating that the circuits were connected to the launchers. "They're armed."

A voice filled with fear filled his headset. "Boss, this is Sergeant Yankovitch. They're SA-8s and they're using the I band radar. Missiles are about five miles from us. They'll lock onto us any second."

"Roger that." Sanderson glanced down at the air speed indicator. The needle was just over the red line. "Jimmy, punch out chaff bundles every five seconds starting now."

Jimmy Butler was a newcomer to the 1st Strategic Reconnaissance Wing, and this was his first deployment. "Pumping out flares and chaff now." He was trying to keep his cool, but the higher-than-normal pitch of his voice gave him away.

Sanderson lowered the nose slightly. The RC-135 was going 50 knots over the red line and accelerating. He'd let the speed increase until the airplane started to buffet, telling him he was approaching transonic speeds. He noticed the muted bangs of flare or chaff bundles had stopped, and yelled, "Jimmy, keep pumping out the chaff and flares!!!"

"I'm trying! Only a few fired! I've recycled the circuit breaker and turned it on and off, but nothing is happening."

The missile warning system shifted into a high-pitched warbling sound. Sanderson shoved the nose down a few more degrees to gain more speed, but once an SA-8 locked on, that was all she wrote. He said aloud, to no one in particular, "Oh shit, we may be fucked."

The Simushir Island Incident

0736 local time, on board U.S.S. Blue Ridge

Josh was studying a chart of traditional shipping routes across the Western Pacific where ships spotted by the P-3s were plotted. None of Crescent Shipping's ships were on the list, which Josh thought was downright strange. Were the freighters deliberately maintaining radio silence and avoiding the most direct routes?

He was walking a pair of dividers across the chart to determine how far a ship sailing at 12 knots would get from Simushir every 24 hours when the overhead speakers crackled. "Mayday, Mayday…this is Highlighter Zero Five broadcasting on all frequencies. Two *Geckos* fired at us from Simushir. Am now eighteen nautical miles directly east of the island and evading."

Everyone in the command center looked up at the speakers and froze.

"Blackbeard, this is Aphrodite One Two. Am closest airborne asset and will try to assist Highlighter Zero Five." The voice was calm.

Josh saw the stricken looks on the faces of the men in the command center and spoke calmly. "No need to talk with either aircraft now. Highlighter Zero Five's crew has its hands full. I know it's hard, but we're going to have to wait. Plot the current positions for Highlighter Zero Five and Aphrodite One Two using the info from Oh Tee Six Us." That was the acronym for the Officer in Tactical Command Information Exchange System (OTCIXS), which collected hourly reports from ships and aircraft on the network.

Josh wondered who would be the poor bastard sent to search for the wreckage if the plane went down.

0937 local time, on board Highlighter Zero Five

Antennas and pods protruded from the RC-135V's airframe. The Boeing 707-based airplane was not designed for high-g maneuvers, and it was already shaking from the airflow around the antennas that were slowing it down. Sanderson was approaching uncharted territory, flying 75 knots faster than the max allowable airspeed. His best hope was to head away from the missile and run it out of fuel. The screeching sound from the radar warning system increased as the missile got closer. Sanderson kept trimming the nose down, trying to get the most speed out of the four-engine jet. He hoped it would not come apart from the stress.

The airplane was descending past 19,000 feet when the SA-8 missile's proximity fuse set off the warhead. Both pilots heard the thump, and fragments from the missile's warhead sounded like rocks thrown on a galvanized metal roof. Cabin pressurization disappeared in a whoosh. Loose paper flew around the cockpit as Sanderson grabbed his oxygen mask and pulled it on. A glance at the flow indicator showed the lifesaving gas was flowing. Soon they would be below 15,000 and wouldn't need it anymore.

Warning and caution lights flashed. Instruments for the number three and four engines on the right wing went crazy. Gently, Sanderson leveled the airplane out at 13,000 feet and pulled off his oxygen mask, glad he could still control the airplane. From years of skiing in the Rockies, he knew he could breathe comfortably at this altitude.

Butler's voice hadn't returned its normal pitch, but it was closer. "Boss, we're losing fuel out of the right wing, number one hydraulic system is out and the number three engine has flamed out."

"Jimmy, you and the flight engineer figure out what we've lost. No emergency checklist will cover what's wrong, but it'll give us some guidelines. Meanwhile, I'll try to keep us wings level and out of the water. Break, break. Navigator—give me a heading to the nearest long runway in Japan. Break, break. Yankovitch—what happened to the second missile?"

The sergeant's voice sounded relieved. "Don't know, sir—but it didn't hit us, and that's all that counts!"

0940 local time, Broutana Bay

Major Kim grabbed Captain Jung by the shoulder and spun him around, banging the captain's head on an electronic equipment rack in the cramped compartment of the *Osa*. "Why did you fire in spite of my direct order?"

"Whenever U.S. spy planes come near or cross our twelve-mile limit, we shoot them down. It is my duty, sir."

"Captain, it is *not* your duty to shoot at any airplane without my permission! Simushir is not in the Democratic People's Republic of Korea, it is sovereign Russian territory. We are guests here."

"Then I am defending a fellow socialist country. The airplane was a threat, sir."

"How do you know that? What threatening action was it taking?"

"Sir, it is an electronic reconnaissance plane recording information about our defenses. It could provide information to fighter bombers who could destroy us."

"So does shooting at it! Now they know exactly what you were trying to keep them from finding out! Get out of the vehicle—you are under arrest."

"Sir, you cannot arrest me. I did my duty. I work for Deputy Minister Thaek, not you."

"Captain Jung, on Simushir I am the senior officer from the Democratic People's Republic of Korea, and therefore you work for me. Get out of the *Osa*, or I will shoot you right now."

Major Kim drew his pistol and pointed it at Jung. Without taking his eyes off Jung, he spoke to the other members of the five-man crew. "What happened to the missiles?"

The vehicle commander answered fearfully. "Sir, one exploded near the American airplane. I think the second missile ran out of fuel. It fell into the ocean."

0752 local time, on board U.S.S. Blue Ridge

As the senior officer present in the command center, Josh made sure tape recorders were set to record all radio communications. Then all the men waited for distant events over which they had no control to unfold. The churning in Josh's gut was an indication of the rising tension.

"Mayday, mayday, mayday, this is Highlighter Zero Five. Anybody copy?"

Josh reached for the handset, grateful that the RC-135 was still in the air. "Highlighter Zero Five, this is Blackbeard. We copy. Aphrodite One Two is en route to your location. What happened?"

"Blackbeard, Highlighter Zero Five. One of the two SA-8s exploded under our right wing, and our number three and four engines shut down. We lost pressurization and our number one hydraulic system, and our right aileron is not working. We are trying to put out electrical fires in the lower equipment bays. The right wing and fuselage tanks were punctured, and we're not sure how much fuel we have left. We are level at one-two thousand and heading two one zero."

In response, a calm voice sounded over the radio. "Highlighter Zero Five, this is Aphrodite One Two. We're seventy, that's seven-zero, miles behind you. Copy?"

"Highlighter Zero Five copies."

A voice spoke from the doorway. "What's happening?"

Josh swiveled to see Vice Admiral Maize. He summarized recent developments and what he hoped would happen next. "When Aphrodite One Two joins up with them, they will be able to assess damage."

"I'll alert CINCPAC. Captain Haman, you've got the watch." Vice Admiral Maize turned to the others. "Attention in the Command Center, Captain Haman now has the command center watch and Commander Cabot is the assistant watch commander. Captain, do you need a full watch team?"

"No, sir, not yet." Josh considered. "Just a couple more ops specialists, someone from intel and our Air Force liaison officer—"

The radio cut him off. "Blackbeard, this is Highlighter Zero Five. The fires are out, and we're treating four crew members for burns. Can you vector a tanker to us?"

Josh walked to the front of the compartment. "Everyone listen up! Highlighter Zero Five doesn't have enough fuel to make it back to Okinawa or even Yakota, so they have two options: ditching or bailing out. Task one: we need to find a seven-thousand-foot runway or longer in Hokkaido, and *pigeons* to that runway and to *Belleau Wood*." *Pigeons* was Naval Aviator speak for bearing and range. "Use OTCIXS and start a plot. Task two: Commander Cabot, call *Belleau Wood* and get them started on a rescue plan they can execute with a few minutes' notice. Tell them to look at picking up men who bailed or ditched. The pilot of Highlighter Zero Five has control problems that may make a successful ditching difficult, if not impossible. That is going to be his call. We need to be ready for either option. Get sea and air temperatures in their area. When the Air Force liaison officer gets in here, have him find out if they will even consider ditching a 135-series aircraft. Task three: call Kadena to get a tanker launched."

"Blackbeard, Aphrodite One Two is at Highlighter Zero Five's four o'clock at about twenty miles and closing."

An operations specialist pointed to a chart on the wall. "Sir, we've got the EP-3E's position plotted on the big board."

"Thanks." Josh picked up the handset and keyed the microphone. "Aphrodite, roger that. Break, break. Highlighter Zero Five, Blackbeard. Can you copy some data?"

"Go ahead, Blackbeard."

"Highlighter Zero Five. Pigeons from your position to nearest runway on Hokkaido is two three zero for four five zero nautical. Nearest American surface asset is the amphibious assault ship *Belleau Wood*, in a joint U.S./Japanese task force with lots of helicopters. They're one seven zero for forty nautical from your current location. Water temperature in their area is a balmy forty-nine degrees. Say souls on board."

"Blackbeard, Highlighter Zero Five copies. We have twenty-seven, that's two-seven souls on board."

1003 local time, on board Highlighter Zero Five

Sanderson trimmed out as much of the rudder and aileron pressure as he could. Keeping the plane level still required pushing left rudder and holding left-aileron-pressure on the yoke.

Jimmy Butler leaned over the center console. "Boss, the engineer and I have been through the numbers at least three times. Short answer is, we don't know how much fuel we have left. Best guess is, we have forty to fifty minutes to flame out."

"So, we're not going to reach Hokkaido?" It really wasn't a question.

Butler shook his head. "Not a chance."

Bailing out from an airplane flying straight and level was safer than trying to ditch an airplane whose handling was unpredictable. *Damn, I wished I had insisted that we all wore exposure suits. Did we use up all our luck surviving the missile hit only to die of hypothermia in the water?*

"Tell the crew to get their parachutes and move to their bailout stations. We're going swimming." At least there would be a rescue team on the lookout for them. Some of them might survive.

0804 local time, on board U.S.S. Blue Ridge

Josh looked around the command center. "Commander Cabot, where's the boss?"

Marty walked over to answer. Part of what he wanted to say was not for general discussion. "In his office, listening on the repeaters. CINCPAC designated Seventh Fleet as the on-scene commander and told the boys in light blue to stop trying to communicate with Highlighter Zero Five. They've got enough problems to solve without being pestered by requests from flag officers, especially after the Air Force didn't have any good options, and—without saying it—indicated the crew was on its own."

"That's good news."

"It gets better. Kadena got its alert tanker airborne in five minutes and is flying at max speed toward Highlighter Zero Five."

"Marty, this will be over long before the tanker gets there. It's two or three hours away, at best, and I don't think Highlighter Zero Five has the fuel to stay airborne that long. Please tell the boss thanks, and I'll do my best not to screw this up."

1028 local time, on board Aphrodite One Two

Lieutenant Commander Harrison eased back on the throttles on the EP-3E to slow the closure rate. They were a half mile behind the crippled RC-135, and he could see a thin white stream of vaporized fuel coming from several places on the wing and under the fuselage. Harrison rolled the yoke slightly to slide the airplane to the right and line up the nose of the EP-3E with the right wingtip of the RC-135. Sitting between the two pilots, Chief Aviation Jet

Engine Mechanic Ron Samson leaned forward on the jump seat. In addition to being the mission's flight engineer, he was one of the detachment's maintenance crew and Harrison wanted him to get a look at the RC-135.

Everyone in the EP-3E was strapped in and had their parachutes on.

Harrison had told his copilot, Lieutenant Junior Grade Al Richter, that flying two large airplanes like the RC-135 and the EP-3E in close formation is akin to a male hippo trying to mate with a female elephant. Richter, who in Navy terms was a nugget —i.e., a first tour Naval Aviator right out of flight school—had his Nikon F with a 100mm lens in his lap. He would have the best view, so his job was to monitor the instruments and take pictures once they got in close. Harrison defined "close" as roughly 50 feet, stepped down, from the RC-135. His plan was to get underneath Highlighter Zero Five, stay long enough to get a good look and back away to give the Air Force crew their assessment. His big fear was that the RC-135 would shed another piece of metal that would hit the EP-3 with possibly catastrophic results.

Harrison turned the knurled knob under the throttles to reduce the friction and make it easier to make slight adjustments in the power settings of the four Allison T-56 turboprops. When the relative motion between the EP-3E and the RC-135 stopped, he nudged them a skosh forward.

The nose of the EP-3E was now 50 feet below the tail of the damaged airplane. Richter unlocked his torso harness and leaned toward the instrument panel to click off pictures.

Harrison keyed the mike. "Highlighter Zero Five, this is Aphrodite One Two. We're in position. We'll slide under the belly and then give you a call."

"Aphrodite One Two, we'll do our best to hold altitude and keep it wings level."

Harrison clicked the mike button twice as he rolled the yoke slightly to the right and nudged the throttles forward, to compensate for the increased drag of the roll so it could move under the RC-135. He stopped the relative motion with a bit of left aileron so the cockpit of the EP-3E under the right wing-root of the RC-135.

"Boeing makes a good airplane," Chief Samson murmured. He appreciated good piloting skills, and good engineering.

Through the holes in the fuselage, they could see where the fire had blackened the lime-green zinc chromate paint on its structure. The number three engine was wobbling on its mount and might come off soon. If it came off while they were there, it would hit the P-3, and they would be dead in seconds. The inboard flaps were gone along with the landing gear doors on the right side, and the tires on the right main-mount were shredded. Black oil and red hydraulic fluid were spreading out along the wing and fuselage, and fuel was streaming from the wing and belly of the RC-135.

"Seen enough?" Harrison wanted to get an accurate picture of the damage, but also wanted to minimize the danger to his own airplane.

Chief Samson had a grim tone as he spoke. "Yeah. They're lucky to be in the air."

Richter finished off the second roll of film and said, "I got good photos."

Harrison gently retarded the throttles a smidgen. Once they were about 100 feet behind the RC-135, he rolled the airplane to the right and added enough throttle to maintain a loose right-echelon, 300 feet away and slightly below the RC-135. Relieved, Harrison took a deep breath before speaking. "Time to give them the bad news. Navigator, give me both SATCOM and the UHF."

0832 local time, on board U.S.S. Blue Ridge

After listening to the description of the damage, Josh pulled the handset for the Satcom radio down from the overhead. "Highlighter Zero Five, say intentions, over?"

"Blackbeard, Highlighter Zero Five. How soon will a tanker arrive?" Gus Sanderson still held out hope take on enough fuel from a tanker to make it to a runway.

"Highlighter Zero Five. One scrambled from Okinawa, but he's at least two point five hours out. Blackbeard suggests you head toward *Belleau Wood*, call sign Victory, who has been alerted. Low-altitude bailout looks like the best option. Our Air Force liaison officer concurs with our assessment and recommendation. *Belleau Wood* is working on a rescue plan. It's your call." Josh grimaced after he spoke the last words.

"Blackbeard, Highlighter Zero Five. We've come to the same conclusion. Best bailout altitude is angels two. It'll give us time to get everyone out and still keep us close together." Josh could hear the dejection, apprehension and fear in the man's voice.

Then a new voice spoke. "Highlighter Zero Five, this is Victory. We copied all prior transmissions. When you arrive, we will have helos airborne and assigned to pick up each crew member as they land in the water. This should minimize problems with hypothermia. Suggest you fly upwind about half mile from the line of ships as you bail out. Over."

"Victory, Highlighter Zero Five. Will do."

"Highlighter Zero Five, this is Victory. Wind is five to ten knots, and sea state is rolling swells, pretty calm for this area. Plan is for the first helicopter in line gets first survivor, and so on. We'll have at least twenty-five helicopters airborne so your crew won't be in the water long. We're putting boats in the water as well. Over."

"Victory, Highlighter Zero Five, roger."

Josh took a deep breath. What he had to say next was hard. "Victory, this is Blackbeard. Once everyone is out of Highlighter Zero Five, destroy Highlighter Zero Five once it is clear of the task force. Shootdown is authorized. Acknowledge, over." Everyone in the command center looked at him.

"Blackbeard, Victory. Understand shootdown of Highlighter Zero Five is, repeat *IS*, authorized *AFTER* bailout is complete."

Josh acknowledged the confirmation. The idea of shooting down an American aircraft turned his stomach. But the damaged airplane had to be destroyed in a place where pieces could not be recovered, like the Kuril Trench where the water depth is between 20,000 and 34,000 feet. The phone on the table buzzed, and he picked up. "Captain Haman."

"Good plan."

Josh recognized Admiral Maize's voice. "Thank you, sir. Any suggestions?"

"Nope. You're doing just fine. All I could do is screw it up. And if you tell anyone I said that, I'll have your ass." The phone went dead.

"What are you smiling about?" Marty was watching Josh during the conversation.

"You don't have clearance for what I just heard."

1043 local time, on board Highlighter Zero Five

Gus Sanderson rolled wings level about a mile to the west of the line of ships. He and Butler had swapped flying so they could strap on their parachutes. Level at 2,000 feet, with the RC-135 trimmed to maintain 220 knots, he gave the order to bail out and radioed Victory that they were leaving the airplane.

"Highlighter Zero Five, Victory. See you on board. Drinks are on us!"

Sanderson heard two bangs in sequence as the forward and aft doors were popped out. He held the left aileron in, and when he released the yoke, the airplane started to gently roll to the right. He corrected and watched Butler get up and head aft.

Seconds later, the intercom buzzed. It was Butler. "Boss, I'm at the aft bailout station. Everyone else is out." And with that, Jimmy Butler dove into the airstream.

Sanderson took a deep breath, released his harness and made sure it wasn't snagged on his parachute harness before he got out of the seat. "Goodbye old lady, you did your job!" The RC-135 stayed straight and level and only started to roll as he dropped out of the crew entry hatch, clutching the ripcord handle. As soon as he was clear of the airplane, he pulled the ripcord, hoping the parachute rigger had done his job well.

0823 local time, on board U.S.S. Blue Ridge

Josh stared at the overhead speakers, feeling like a fish out of water. The search-and-rescue pilot in Josh wanted to be on the scene, and scenarios on how he would make the rescues as quickly as possible ran through his mind.

Josh turned to Marty. "These guys are jumping with no rafts into very cold water, probably without exposure suits. And my guess is, it has been a long time since they performed a bailout drill or trained on parachute water entries. I want to get all twenty-seven back, but will be happy with any number greater than twenty."

"Pessimist," Marty murmured. "I know what the task force is going to do. If they all get out and their chutes open, I'd be surprised if we lost anyone."

It was an agonizing wait. Josh was full of nervous energy and paced back and forth, the distance limited by the phone cord to the radio he clutched in his hand. At long last, a call came through. "Blackbeard, Victory, over."

Josh flexed his fingers to relax them and realized that he'd had the handset in a death grip since the bailout began. He expected bad news, and his fingers hurt. "Victory, Blackbeard, go."

"Blackbeard, Victory. Rescue complete. We have all twenty-seven, that is two-seven, crewmen from Highlighter Zero Five on board Victory. All are in the sick bay, getting checked out. Aphrodite One Two is en route home plate with photos of the damaged airplane and the bailout. Over."

Josh forced himself to maintain radio discipline. "Victory, this is Blackbeard. Outstanding!" He wanted to say "out-fucking standing," but didn't. "Well done! We're all smiles here." Relieved, he slumped clumsily into his chair.

"Blackbeard, Victory. Copy that. We had SEALs or Marine Recon team members jump into the water as soon as Highlighter crew members bailed. They helped get them out of their parachutes and ready to be pulled out of the water. Initial sitrep follows. Three of the four burned crew members will need hospitalization for second- and third-degree burns. When we get close to Misawa, we'll fly them ashore so they can be medevac'd to Pearl. The remainder of Highlighter Zero Five's crew is being dried out and fed. One crewman, Sergeant Yankovitch, saved the data tapes of the SA-8s shot at them. He sealed them along with the mission tapes in Ziploc bags and stuffed them into his flight suit before he jumped. Tapes are being copied now."

"Outstanding. Blackbeard copies."

"Highlighter Zero Five was destroyed by surface-to-air missile and wreckage was seen to fall into water about twenty thousand feet deep. Over.

"Victory, Blackbeard Zero Zero Actual says Bravo Zulu!"

0941 local time, on board U.S.S. Blue Ridge

Now that the emergency was over, Josh was wondering who'd fired the missile. It was an act of war; so was it a North Korean or a Russian—or someone else?

The flag yeoman opened the door and stuck his head in the N6 compartment. "Captain Haman, Commander Cabot, sir, the admiral wants both of you in his conference room post haste. The rope is looking for the N2 and the N3, so if you see either, bring them with you."

"Will do. Tell him we're on our way."

Josh picked up his notebook and a yellow pad. "No rest for the weary. Wonder what's up?"

"Not a clue." Marty led the way.

The admiral's aide was standing by the door. "Gentlemen, go right in. He's just finished talking to CINCPAC."

Josh and Marty looked at each other with raised eyebrows. As they came in the door, the admiral motioned to the empty chairs.

"Gentlemen, CINCPAC wants to pass on his congratulations on an outstanding piece of work this morning."

"Thank you, sir. The *Belleau Wood* and her task group did all the work," Josh pointed out.

Admiral Maize tapped his notes. "This is coming from the White House, and I need to pass it on. First: no one is to take direct action against Simushir. Second: we are to continue surveillance missions, but no aircraft are to close to less than twenty-five nautical miles. Three: the State Department is going to put quiet pressure on the Russians to make the shoot down their problem. The Russians have allowed North Koreans to fire on an American plane from their territory, using Russian-made missiles. State's position is that many international arms trafficking laws were broken; for now at least, it's the Russians' problem to sort that out.

The Simushir Island Incident

"Next subject. We can stop any ships in international waters that left Simushir that we suspect are carrying drugs. Either a DEA or Coast Guard representative has to lead the actual search of the vessel as a law enforcement matter. If we find any drugs, we can seize the vessels.

"Last item. Two *Spruance*-class destroyers—*O'Brien* and *Leftwich*—will leave Pearl within twenty-four hours. They will become Seventh Fleet assets as soon as they clear the harbor. Each ship will have a SEAL platoon, plus DEA and Coast Guard officers on board. We will have the men and resources we need."

Friday, July 14th, 1995, 0745 local time, Honolulu

Jeffers was beyond pissed, he was livid. Vice Admiral Gainesville had just called and informed him that the official results of the flag continuation board were out—and he would be placed on the retired list at the end of the fiscal year. In other words, he would not be "continued"—which meant that, at the end of the fiscal year, he was retiring, whether or not he wanted to. His Navy career was over.

Jeffers immediately put a call through to his close friend and fellow ring-knocker, who was now CINCLANT—only to be told, regretfully, that there was nothing to be done. What CINCLANT didn't say was that he wasn't going to risk his chance to become the Vice Chief of Naval Operations, which was a stepping-stone to becoming CNO and maybe Chairman of the Joint Chiefs, to save his friend's career. Instead, he told Jeffers to be happy he would retire as a rear admiral, and use it to make millions in the civilian world. If he played his cards right, he could become a member of a board of directors or get a high-paying position at a defense contractor.

But becoming a civilian was not something Jeffers wanted. The Navy had been his whole adult life, and he knew nothing else. He was mad at the Navy and angry at himself. In the past, he was always promoted and his peers fell by the wayside. Now, *he* was the one who was done.

The next morning, Jeffers woke up at 0326 and could not go back to sleep. He lay in bed plotting how he could get revenge. Then he dressed as if he were going for a run. He found a pay phone at a gas station in Aiea Heights, put his loose change on the polished steel shelf below the phone, next to the business card of a reporter from the *Washington Post*, and started to dial.

Monday, July 17th, 1995, 0414 local time, M.V. Crescent Galaxy

Major Kim closed the door of his stateroom and dogged it shut. Inside the room, a disheveled and furious Captain Jung was gagged and handcuffed to the bed. There were documents and tapes on the desk detailing recent events on Simushir, along with the keys to the handcuffs. Jung was now the DPRK's problem. Kim had problems of his own. Once the consular official returned to the embassy and reported him missing, Kim would be declared an enemy of the state. He didn't have much time.

In his backpack, he'd carefully packed three sets of clothes, two towels, and a pair of running shoes, wrapped in several layers of plastic and sealed with duct tape. The pack also contained one of the ship's life preservers to keep it buoyant. His identity documents —North Korean passport and national identity card—were double ziploc bagged in a pouch pocket of his camouflage uniform pants.

Crescent Galaxy was approaching Hong Kong Island. Kim went to the side of the freighter, tied one end of a 30-meter climbing rope to the railing, and tossed the rest over the side. Using his legs to bounce away from the ship as he rappelled down, Kim stopped long enough to unsling his pack and loop the straps around his left arm. Three meters above the water, he flexed his legs, pushed out as hard as he could, and let go of the rope. He hoped he landed far enough from the ship's side to avoid being sucked into the ship's screw. He landed with a splash and struck out. Swimming as strongly as he could, he put distance between himself and the freighter.

The *M.V. Crescent Galaxy* slid past and away, and Major Kim aimed himself toward a cluster of bright lights a quarter mile away. The life preserver from his stateroom kept the backpack buoyant as he towed it through the water. He was more worried about being run over by another ship than he was about being attacked by a shark, but sea traffic was light at this time of not-yet-day.

He came ashore among large rocks. Hidden from the road, Major Kim dried himself and changed into civilian clothes, re-pocketing his documents. Kim shoved the wet towels and a large rock into the leg of his uniform pants and tossed it into the water. Somberly, he watched it sink. Then, after removing all identifying markers, he did the same with the shirt. It disappeared under the surface. The life preserver was tossed next, and Kim watched it drift into the harbor. *That is my past life floating away.*

Kim clambered up on to the road and headed toward Hong Kong's central business district. On the way, he flagged down an empty cab whose driver was heading into the city to begin his day's work. The cab dropped Kim off at 1 Queens Road Central, right in front of the headquarters of the Hong Kong Shanghai Bank. By his watch it was 0546; Kim found a place to eat breakfast and waited for the bank to open.

At an open restaurant's news rack, he picked up the *Hong Kong Free Press*. At 0903, Kim walked up to a teller window at the Hong Kong Shanghai Bank branch and slid a withdrawal slip through the slot. She asked for his ID and didn't react when she saw his North Korean passport with its Hong Kong visa. The teller checked the computer to make sure that he had the requested funds before she counted out 9,600 Hong Kong dollars. It left 200 Hong

Kong dollars in the account he'd opened on his first trip to Hong Kong with unspent expense money. In U.S. dollars, Kim had just over $1,100.

Outside the bank, he hailed a cab and gave the cabbie directions to a building two blocks from his final destination. When he disembarked, he looked for signs of surveillance. Seeing and sensing none, he walked down the street and through the gate of 9 Ice House Street.

Kim saluted a startled Marine guard and spoke in accented English. "Good morning, I am Major Chin Hae Kim of the Special Forces of the Democratic People's Republic of North Korea. I wish to defect and seek asylum in the United States." Kim held out Adair's coin. "One of your SEALs left this behind on Simushir."

1115 local time, Beijing

Vice Admiral Pak had traveled to China to meet with his Chinese counterpart, Vice Admiral Chow, at the People's Liberation Army Navy headquarters. So far, the meeting had been very productive. Admiral Chow had just agreed to sell six of China's newer *Whiskey*-class submarines and several trainloads of surplus spare parts for North Korea's aging *Romeo*s at very favorable prices. The deal was good for both countries: the North Korean Navy would get a much-needed upgrade, and the Chinese would offload subs they no longer needed and parts for which they no longer had any use.

"Have you heard about the damaged Russian submarine?" Admiral Chow was fond of talking about potential enemies in informal, one-on-one conversations.

"I heard one had an accident in the Sea of Okhotsk and was towed to Vladivostok." The transcripts Vice Admiral Pak read hadn't revealed anything more than that the sub had needed to shut down its nuclear power plant after an explosion. They were fortunate. Before he left North Korea for this meeting, he'd signed the form letters that told 54 families that their sons died gloriously in the service of their country. So far, his Dear Leader had not summoned him to a meeting, so that was a headache for another day. Meanwhile, Admiral Pak had an opportunity here and now to glean information about submarines, and the *Victor III* was one of the Russian Navy's most modern nuclear attack submarines. "Do you know what happened?"

"No. It is in a covered dry dock, and the Russians aren't saying anything. We heard it was hit by a torpedo." The Chinese admiral said this without any trace of emotion at reporting an act of war that had potential for triggering global conflict.

Pak allowed himself to appear to be surprised. "How so?"

Chow was eager to share what he knew. "The rumor is it was fired upon by another submarine." Chow took a sip of his tea and looked over the edge of the cup. His tone of voice was neutral. "Probably the same unknown submarine that sank the Russian *Udaloy* destroyer."

Admiral Pak took a long drink of the now-tepid green tea, holding the cup before his face. Chow wasn't going to ask, *Did one of your subs fire a torpedo at a Russian submarine?* "I am sorry to say that one of our submarines is overdue."

"I am sorry to hear that," Chow said soberly. As a fellow submariner, he knew this probably meant the submarine was in pieces on the bottom of the ocean. "Do you know why?"

"No. Our sub's last reported position was near the island of Iturup." Iturup was 300 kilometers south of where the torpedo incident had taken place.

"Do you know about the commercial development of Simushir? I understand the fishing boat facility should be operational by the end of the year."

Vice Admiral Pak took another sip of tea. What the Chinese admiral just told him amounted to this: As soon as the announcement is made that the settlement is open for business, the Chinese will send a ship in to take a look around.

"I understand the investors are pleased with the progress." This was as neutral an answer as he could give. Again, he wasn't going to volunteer anything.

"The Americans are not very happy about having their aircraft shot down," Chow said, looking for a place to put his empty teacup.

"It was an unfortunate incident."

"Yes, it was." Vice Admiral Chow looked down as he spoke. "Sometimes the Americans can get very aggressive, and our junior officers cannot contain their desire to protect their country. Our intelligence people are embarrassed because they didn't know our fellow people's republic had acquired *Osas*."

Yes. Broutana Bay was supposed to be a commercial operation, not a military one. Firing the SA-8s had changed all that. General Jang was furious and intended to sacrifice Captain Jung for his stupidity. But this was not information Admiral Pak would share. It would cause his country to lose face.

"When the Americans come close to our country, we shoot at them, and so do you. I do not know why they were shot at, and I know very little about surface-to-air missiles, or my country's plans to acquire them. That is not the Navy's purview."

The Chinese Admiral just looked at him for a few seconds. "I will have my chief of staff contact your Captain Chin, once the contracts are ready for your final review. When they are signed, return them to me via diplomatic pouch." The chubby Chinese admiral rose to his feet and offered his hand, signaling the meeting was over.

"Excellent. I am sure they will reflect the terms of our agreement. Thank you for your support."

Vice Admiral Pak strode outside the building toward the waiting embassy car. Several blocks from his hotel, he asked the driver to stop, saying he wanted to walk the rest of the way. "Take my briefcase and wait for me in the lobby."

Few of the pedestrians gave the blue-uniformed officer striding along the sidewalk a second glance. Only a close inspection of the gold-striped shoulder boards with two silver stars would tell the observer that he was not an admiral from the People's Liberation Army Navy. He was walking casually, his hands clasped behind his back, enjoying the summer sunshine and the wind blowing away the pollution.

He could not stop thinking about Deputy Minister Thaek. *His inquisitiveness tells me that our Dear Leader has started the end game to take over our drug operation. The loss of the submarine and the shoot down of the American airplane will make it easy for him to concoct a story to use to arrest me.*

All this made returning to North Korea… problematic. But escaping North Korea, or even the People's Republic of China, was difficult. He did have a Singaporean passport at the Half Moon office in Beijing, but to go there in uniform would make him conspicuous. Within hours, his country's Ministry of Safety and Security would learn of his visit, which was not on his official agenda. Questions would be asked, leading to an arrest warrant. A wave of panic swept over Admiral Pak.

The sharp crack of a flag whipped by the wind caught Pak's attention and made him stop and look around. Beijing was full of large red flags snapping in the wind.

Vice Admiral Pak felt his uniform made him a marked man on this street unless he continued on to his hotel. Even just stopping for more than a few seconds would raise questions.

As he approached the U.S. embassy, he saw a Chinese policeman managing the line outside the entrance to its visa section, speaking into a hand held radio. The policeman saw Pak and headed toward him. Acid fear laced with paranoia coursed through Pak's body. Rather than freeze, he crossed the street and pushed his way past another Chinese policeman guarding the gate under the sign, *U.S. Citizens Only* in English and Chinese. Once inside the lobby, Pak sprinted toward an open elevator.

Two Marines grabbed Pak, shoved him into an empty room, and closed the door. He stood there silent and unresisting as they patted him down. Gunnery Sergeant Acton recognized the intruder's uniform from an exchange tour with the Korean Marine Corps and said in Korean, "Admiral, what can I do for you?"

"I am Vice Admiral Kim Sun Pak of the Navy of the Democratic People's Republic of Korea." He pulled his identity card and North Korean passport out of his breast pocket and handed it to Acton. "I am the commander of the North Korean submarine fleet, and I wish to defect and seek asylum in the United States."

"Sir, I will have someone check you out. Please wait here. Would you care to sit down?" Acton pointed to a steel chair in front of a gray desk, then stepped out to make a call from a phone in a nearby office. The other Marine remained in one corner of the room, his pistol drawn and ready to use.

Acton re-entered the room. "Admiral Pak, we can speak in either Korean or English. Which is your preference?"

"English. I hope I will speak it more, and my accent is not bad."

Gunnery Sergeant Acton smiled at Pak's attempt at humor. "Your English is just fine, sir. If you find you feel more comfortable in Korean, there are several of us who speak it fluently." He looked intently at the admiral. "We are going to take you to meet several members of the embassy staff. What you say during the first few minutes of the conversation will go a long way toward establishing your identity as well as helping the United States determine whether or not we accept you as a defector."

"I understand." It must, Admrial Pak reflected, be a difficult decision. Persons seeking asylum might be fleeing danger, or they might be attempting to infiltrate a country as spies or agents.

In a small conference room, two Americans, who identified themselves as "Mr. Smith" and "Mr. Jones," grilled Pak for an hour. Jones would leave the room with a handful of notes, only to return and ask another series of questions. Then, Smith would leave, and the process was repeated. Vice Admiral Pak assumed that the session was being recorded and that they were calling CIA headquarters for instructions. It was not, after all, an everyday occurrence for an admiral of a hostile foreign power to request asylum.

The North Korean was careful not to give any details about Simushir. He suspected the Americans would be squeamish about giving asylum to a leader of a drug-manufacturing organization. He didn't want to give them any reason to put him back on the street in Beijing. If they did, he would be dead in a few unspeakably miserable days.

Pak looked at his Rolex. "Excuse me—while I understand the need for you to determine who I am, I must tell you that if I don't appear at my next official function, which is at five today, my government may try to kidnap my daughter, who is here in Beijing, and my wife, who is in Singapore. The North Korean Ministry of State Security knows the address of my daughter because we had to provide it on the visa application.

"Do both women know you planned to defect?"

"Yes, but they did not know when."

"What is the address of your daughter?"

Mr. Smith wrote it down as Pak gave it to him."

"Is she there now?"

"Yes. She is expecting me to call between four and four-thirty. We were planning to have dinner together after I meet with our naval attaché and his staff."

"Do you have a code word to let her know it is time to defect?

"Yes."

"We are going to send some men to her apartment. Please give me the code word and any other information that our men can use to assure her that they came from you."

"Please let me call her to give her the code while your men are on the way. This way, she will be ready."

"Before you call your wife and daughter, I want you to understand that after you identify yourself and are assured they are not under pressure or being held by your countrymen, I will give them specific instructions which they must follow. When you make your calls, there will be men from our embassies a few minutes away. I need to give your wife and daughter a password so they know the men are from our embassy. We will call your daughter first and then your wife. Do you understand?"

"Yes, I do."

Smith nodded his head and, armed with the information and a description, left the room and came back with a phone. He plugged it into a wall outlet. "Call your daughter. Our men will be there in fifteen minutes."

Pak made the call. He was smiling when he hung up. "She will be ready."

"Now let's talk about your wife. Where is she?"

"The Raffles Hotel in Singapore. She is staying there under a different name. When she left for an officially sanctioned conference in Beijing, I told her I was looking for a chance to defect and told her to go to Singapore as soon as she could." Pak rattled off the necessary information, and Mr. Smith made the phone call.

Monday, July 17th, 1995, 1107 local time, Los Angeles

After his first night at Sappho's, Jin-tao Yi waited a week before he returned to Vegas to convert more cash into checks. Every night he was in Las Vegas, he went to the club. For a young man with a healthy appetite for sex, Sappho's was paradise.

Now that he was a "regular" at the club, Jin-tao had come to appreciate the difference between the *manjokcho* women and the women he met at Sappho's. At home, having sex was an act they were required to perform. Here, the women came because they wanted to have as much sex as they could, to receive as well as give pleasure.

The club limo usually brought him back to his hotel between one and two in the morning, which let him "gamble" in the afternoon and go back to Sappho's around nine in the evening. By the end of the second weekend, he had 30 checks for amounts between $8,700 and $9,600. It was time to fly to the Cayman Islands.

Tuesday, July 18th, 1995, 1507 local time,
George Town, Cayman Island

At the Hyatt Regency on 7 Mile Road on Grand Cayman, Yi held a glass of Maker's Mark in both hands and stared at the TV set behind the bar. The woman he'd been talking to had turned down his offer for dinner later, and he was wondering what to do when a man slid onto the bar stool next to him.

"It's bloody rough when a sheila turns you down cold. Feels like a kick in the crotch, don't it, mate."

Jin-tao turned to the stranger and cocked his head. He was missing Sappho's already. It was so much better when everybody wanted the same thing.

"Names Angus Sydney. You look like you're ex military. Did I get that right?"

Yi nodded, afraid to say anything.

"You still in?"

"No."

"You don't sound like a bloody Yank. What country?"

"Korea. Marine Recon."

"I'm bloody impressed. Are you interested in working for a company where you can show your skills every day and get paid a ton of money for it?"

Yi nodded. "Sure. Who wouldn't?"

Sydney fished a business card out of his wallet and put it on the counter. "I saw you come out of the Hong Kong Shanghai Bank office today. My guess is you were doing the same thing I was, and that's depositing checks you don't want the tax man to know about. Call me at the number on the card. I work for a company called Security Resources and we're all ex-Special Forces. We do the bloody shit work no one else wants to take on. We're more interested in what you can do, not your past. Starting pay is ten thousand U.S. a month."

Wednesday, July 19th, 1995, 0543 local time, Hong Kong

Inside the consulate compound, Gunnery Sergeant Herman stood by the open door of the second vehicle in the convoy. Satisfied all was in order, he pointed to the door of the second car. Once Major Kim was inside, Gunny Herman twirled his right hand over his head and the gates to the compound opened.

At this time of the day, there was little traffic on the downhill stretch of Garden Road leading toward Des Voeux Road Central, where the three vehicles made a left turn. They traveled to the corner of Man Yiu Street, where they turned right and headed toward the docks.

If anyone was going to try to intercept them, Herman figured it would be at the section of road where five streets came together and they had to stop at the traffic light. The radio in Herman's car came alive. "The helicopter is orbiting over the harbor and will land when you get here." Even at this hour in the morning, the authorities insisted that every helicopter making a pickup stay in orbit until its passengers were ready and waiting in the small shelter at the top of the stairs, just under the helipad.

The convoy's diplomatic plates did allow the three vehicles to pull up to the front door, instead of parking a distance away. A member of the ferry service's security team waited to lead them to the heliport. Herman, Kim, and four armed Marine escorts were all wearing woodland cammies and Kevlar vests. Just before they got on the elevator to the roof, the ferry employee spoke into his hand-held radio and the H-3 from Helicopter Anti-Submarine Squadron 12 began its approach. Once it landed, Major Kim was escorted out to the H-3. Fifty miles east of Hong Kong, they landed on the forward end of the angled deck of *U.S.S. Independence*. Then Major Kim was escorted to a twin-engine, carrier based, anti-submarine warfare S-3B sitting on the number four catapult. Kim was strapped into an empty sensor operator ejection seat behind the two pilots, and the aircrewman gave him a quick brief on how to use the seat as well as how to get out of his parachute harness.

The H-3 lifted off and entered an orbit on the starboard side of the ship to act as plane guard. The catapult's tow bar pulled the S-3B along the deck to a launching speed of 130 knots, so it could begin the five-hour, 1,800-mile flight to NAF Atsugi.

When it touched down, a smiling Josh Haman and Marty Cabot were waiting on the ramp. Behind them, the Seventh Fleet H-3 was waiting with its engines running and the blades turning. After introducing themselves, Major Kim and Marty strapped into the passenger seats. Josh did a quick walk around before he climbed into the cockpit for the flight to the Seventh Fleet flagship. It was good to be in the air again. And something about Major Kim's manner told Josh that here was a man he wanted to get to know better.

Some words floated up in Josh's mind, an echo of a Rudyard Kipling poem he'd read as a boy. He murmured, "*Oh, East is East, and West is West, and never the twain shall meet, Till Earth and Sky stand presently at God's great Judgment Seat...*"

Marty must have overheard him, for he joined in on the next line. "*But there is neither East nor West, Border, nor Breed, nor Birth...*"

To Josh's utter astonishment, Major Kim's voice came resonantly in on the fourth line. "*... When two strong men stand face to face, though they come from the ends of the earth!*"

1303 local time, Sinuijiu, DPRK

At 1300 the inspection of the special forces brigade was over, as were the office briefings. General Jang told his aide, Captain Meong, to take the rest of the day off. Tomorrow they were scheduled to take the 1730 train to Pyongyang. Captain Meong was delighted. This allowed him to go out with friends he'd served with before.

Alone, Jang pondered what a friend in the Ministry of State Security had recently told him, that Major Kim had committed suicide. Jang didn't believe for a minute that Kim would take his own life. Suicide, however, was often a cover story for political assassination, and since Jang had vouched for Kim's political reliability, his own neck might be in a slowly tightening noose.

He hadn't shared this tidbit of information when he'd suggested to his wife, Ji-ae, that she accompany him to Sinuijiu, but he had used their code word. She had replied with a vigorous nod and a smile that any hidden microphones would never see.

That afternoon, Jang and Ji-ae walked from their hotel to the southern end of the Sino-Korean Friendship Bridge, where they showed their internal passports and authorizations to cross into the People's Republic of China. Only trusted North Korean citizens had the prized endorsements on their internal passports, allowing them to shop in the People's Republic of China between 0900 and 1800. Technically, any purchases were subject to import duty, but the fees were never imposed.

Jang was in uniform and, like many North Koreans going across the Sino-Korean Friendship Bridge into the People's Republic of China to shop, he carried an expandable duffel bag, suitable for carrying large quantities of merchandise. His wife had a similar bag to go with her purse.

When they reached the shops, General Jang bought four silk shirts, two sport coats, and three pairs of dark trousers at two different men's shops. These, along with a new pair of shoes, went into his duffel bag. In another store, Ji-ae bought two fashionable dresses, three skirts and four silk blouses, in varying shades of her favorite colors, maroon and gray.

The couple walked farther into the Yuanbao district to Jinshan Street, pretending to window shop, using store windows as mirrors to see if they were being followed. General Jang looked at Ji-ae, who nodded in agreement.

They went up the stairs at the Hanting Express Passenger Terminal on Shine Road. In the men's room, General Jang changed clothing. His uniform and all his insignia went into one of the shopping bags, which he stuffed into a trash can in the large waiting room. It would soon be on the way to a dumpsite. He flushed his North Korean identity papers down the toilet.

Ji-ae went into a women's bathroom and also changed clothes. Then she pulled up the thick silk-wrapped metal stiffener at bottom of her purse to get to their Singaporean passports, Singaporean National Registration Identity Cards, credit cards and drivers' licenses. According to these documents, they were now Yong and Yan Chao. She also had business cards indicating that Yong Chao was the vice president of operations for the Half Moon Chemical Company.

At the ticket window, she purchased two first-class tickets to Dalian. When her husband walked up, she handed him the tickets and his documents. To even a suspicious policeman, it looked ordinary and commonplace.

Jang saw two North Korean border guards walking down the platform and gently nudged his wife toward the door of the first-class car. Gracefully, she mounted the steps and disappeared from view. Before he could follow, one of the guards tapped Jang firmly on the shoulder; the other gestured to see his papers. Jang handed over his Singaporean passport and forced himself to be calm. The guard scrutinized at him and looked at the photo several times, then fanned through the pages of his passport, which showed several visits to the People's Republic of China and Dalian. As he handed it back, the guard said, "Have a good trip."

Still fearful, Jang boarded the train just before the doors closed and rejoined Ji-ae in the first-class car. Both breathed sighs of relief when the train started rolling.

Jang held his wife's hand and whispered, "So far, so good."

Soon the train was well underway, and out the window they could see the West Sea. Chun Lee Jang leaned back, closed his eyes and tried to relax. Thirty minutes out of Dandong, the conductor, accompanied by two-armed policemen, entered the first-class compartment. The conductor held out his hand. "Tickets!"

Ji-ae, who spoke better Mandarin than Chun Lee did, handed them to the conductor with a big smile. The conductor looked at the pair, punched holes in the tickets, and handed them back.

When the conductor left, Ji-ae rested her head on his shoulder and whispered in her husband's ear. "I'm scared."

"Me too. Try to relax and be positive. Deep, slow breaths help. Think of our future outside Korea. We have a good plan and we will get to Singapore."

The train lurched to a halt and Chun Lee and Ji-ae left the first-class compartment. From the window, he surveyed the platform and the station. Three policemen were making their presence known but were not being intrusive. At a pay phone at the station, Jang dialed the number of the Half Moon plant in Dalian. The suspicious woman who answered the phone needed convincing that he was, in fact, Chun Lee Jang, before the plant manager came on the phone. He apologized and gave them the name of a restaurant by the docks where they would be met.

Three days ago, just before he'd left for Beijing, Admiral Pak had silently given Jang the Crescent ships' schedules. Taking this as a strong hint, Jang had timed the inspection in Sinijiu accordingly.

It had been a difficult decision—take the overnight express from Dalian to Beijing and from there board a flight on a non-Chinese airline, or get on a Crescent-owned ship in Dalian and disappear over the horizon. He'd decided the ship option was less risky and harder to track. But Jang had never been to Dalian before, and maps of any kind in the Democratic People's Republic of Korea were illegal.

Chun Lee hailed one of the few cabs waiting at the station and Ji-ae gave the driver the address. Before they entered the restaurant opposite the docks, Jang scanned the area, looking for signs of surveillance as if he were studying a target he was about to assault.

He saw a tall fence protecting the docks, the customs and immigration office, and a guard shack restricting access to the piers. Guards wearing the uniform of the People's Liberation Army and carrying AK-47s patrolled the fence. Both he and Ji-ae were afraid that, at any second, officers from the Chinese Ministry of State Security would rush out and arrest them.

The couple picked a table in the back and ordered a bottle of mineral water, for they were very thirsty. Glad to be out of the sun and heat, they put their bags against the table behind them.

Two men, one a dark-skinned man wearing a white bridge cover and the other an Asian, entered the restaurant together and looked around. Jang decided to take a chance and waved. The two men approached.

The Asian bowed slightly. He introduced himself as Mr. Guan, Half Moon's factory manager. "And this is Captain Yamani of the *Crescent Star.*"

Guan handed Jang two envelopes. "These papers will allow you to board the *Crescent Star,* which is leaving tonight. Once you are on board, you cannot leave the ship. Captain Yamani will now escort you through customs and immigration to the *Crescent Star* and show you to your stateroom. He apologizes, but it has a bunk bed. It is the only guest room with two beds."

Jang took Guan's hand in both of his. "It is fine. Thank you very much for your help. You will be rewarded."

Thursday, July 20th, 1995, 1212 local time,
on board Windmill One Five, a P-3C maritime patrol aircraft
At 15,000 feet, the expression "the broad expanse of the Pacific" applies. The crew was searching the areas off the so-called shipping lanes for freighters with the word *Crescent* in their name.

The Simushir Island Incident

Each time they spotted a ship, either visually or on radar, they descended to 200 feet and flew up the starboard side of the ship so a sensor operator stationed in the aft observation bubble could snap pictures.

A mile past the ship, the plane would climb to 500 feet, turn steeply to the left, and descend back down to 200 feet to make another photo pass along the port side. If they couldn't read the name, they'd bank away and make a 270-degree turn to the right and come back across the stern of the ship.

Lieutenant Adrian Turnbull, the patrol plane commander, had the right outboard engine shut down to save fuel. At the weight they were flying, the P-3 flew comfortably on three engines. Six hours into the mission, she was totally bored. So far, they'd looked at 11 ships, none of them owned or operated by Crescent Shipping. The only excitement came when they buzzed a ship and the crew or passengers waved—or made rude gestures.

The phrase that "flying is hours and hours of boredom, punctuated by moments of stark-raving terror" applied to most maritime patrol plane flights. Turnbull preferred boring, which was why she'd chosen P-3s. This was her last deployment, nearly the end of the third phase of her life's plan. The first had been to be awarded either an Air Force or Navy ROTC scholarship after high school. A New Jersey native, Adrian had attended Rennselaer Polytechnic Institute paid in full by a Navy ROTC scholarship.

Phase two meant getting into and through flight training. From the outset, she'd wanted to fly P-3s because it facilitated phase four —a job as an airline pilot. Naval Aviators referred to the patrol plane units as "airline pilot training squadrons." Her father's brother had been in the Air Force and flown four-engine C-124s. When his commitment was up, he'd been hired by United Airlines.

Turnbull had turned in her letter of resignation last June to be released from active duty on September 30th. American Airlines had already hired her, and her offer letter said she would start on October 16th, 1995. Her CO had assured her that she would make the class date, unless …. It was the phrase "unless superseded by the needs of the Navy" that bothered her. Now would be a really shitty time for World War III to start.

The only reason she was on the current detachment was that the number of sorties hunting for Crescent Shipping vessels meant the squadron needed experienced plane commanders.

"Pilot, this is radar. We have a break bulk freighter at zero three zero relative at seventy nautical."

"Got it." Turnbull rolled gently to the right and eased back on the three throttles while she trimmed the nose down. "Descending now."

Turnbull kept the four-engine patrol plane at 5,000 feet until they were five miles behind the ship, then dropped to 200 feet. What she saw caused her eyes to widen in surprise. "Tacco, this is the pilot. Ship's name is *Crescent Moon.* I repeat, we have *Crescent Moon* in sight. Start a plot on the ship."

Tacco stood for Tactical Coordinator, the Naval Flight Officer responsible for navigation, employing all the plane's sensors, and long-range communication. "Will do, boss."

1015 local time, on board U.S.S. Blue Ridge

The search for the two ships that had left Broutana Bay continued. As the days went on, the search area expanded, stretching south from Adak, Alaska, and north from Hawaii. Across the most direct route from the Kurils to California or the upper half of the Baja Peninsula, P-3 crews searched each area and photographed hundreds of ships.

"Blackbeard, Windmill One Five, over."

Josh had walked into the command center a few minutes prior for a quick update. After listening to the report, he told Windmill One Five to remain in contact and stand-by for further instructions.

Another P-3C, call sign Trixie Zero Eight, called in with the location of the *Crescent Galaxy.* Operations Specialist Second Class Burleson studied the plot he was maintaining on a chart. "Sir, based on OTCIXS, the destroyer *O'Brien* is about a hundred nautical from the *Crescent Moon,* and can intercept in about four to five hours. The destroyer *Leftwich* is about eighty nautical and four hours from *Crescent Galaxy.* Both destroyers topped off within the past twenty-four hours. I'll let them know, and they should be able to intercept well before either freighter gets to the Mexican or U.S. coast."

Josh smiled. "I love it when a plan comes together. Great work, Petty Officer Burleson! Send out an Op Immediate message. Then call them on the satellite phone to confirm and make sure they know that if they find drugs, they are authorized to seize the freighters, by force if necessary, and escort them to Pearl."

"Thank you, sir, and will do."

1526 local time, Honolulu

David Seul banged the payphone down on the hook and then looked around, embarrassed he'd let his anger show. He didn't like the conversation he'd just had because it got him directly involved in a business in which he no longer wanted to participate. However, he didn't have much choice in the matter. A contact in Macao, from the time when Seul was building a drug distribution network in Hawaii, had leaned on him to help a man tasked with a job in Hawaii. Seul knew damn well that "job" meant "hit."

Seul was in the middle of a transition that he had wanted since he was young man. The recent conversation reinforced his conclusion that he needed to move to a place where he could start fresh and live how he wanted, and the sooner the better. Once the assassin left Hawaii, so would he.

Saturday, July 22nd, 1995, 0632 local time,
on board Crescent Moon, *middle of the Pacific Ocean*

At sea, Konstantin Mallas wore his white bridge cover with the crest of Crescent Shipping the entire time he was on deck, only taking it off when he entered his cabin to sleep. On the bridge, he could enjoy his food, read the latest weather forecast, and study the chart showing their progress toward *Crescent Moon's* destination. He could also check the radar plot and survey the surrounding sea with his binoculars. He'd inherited the 10 x 50 Zeiss binoculars, made in the late 1920s, from his grandfather, who had also been a ship captain. They were heavy and the black paint was worn off in places, but the optics were as good as any binocular made today.

The ship was, by his standards, in good repair. Two years ago, *Crescent Moon* had spent four months in dry dock, having her bottom cleaned, a new screw installed, and long-needed maintenance performed on her engines and loading equipment. Since coming out of the yard, the most noticeable difference was that it took fewer turns of its screw to make 12 knots. This meant the ship now burned less fuel per day. Mallas could feel a slight vibration in the steel deck under his feet as the *Crescent Moon* plowed through the water at 12 knots, at a slight angle to the swells. It caused the ship to settle into a gentle corkscrew motion.

For all of his carefully cultivated situational awareness, Mallas didn't see *U.S.S. Leftwich,* just over the radar horizon, plowing through the water at 25 knots. Nor could binoculars show him the two helicopters following *Crescent Moon's* wake, 100 feet off the water.

The *Leftwich,* a *Spruance* class destroyer, had made radar contact late yesterday afternoon and used its SLQ-32 V2 electronic surveillance system during the night to stay just outside the range of *Crescent Moon's* radar. In the growing dawn, *Leftwich's* commanding officer sent the ship's crew to flight quarters, and as soon as both helicopters were airborne, he ordered the ship to general quarters.

The peacefulness of the scene around him made it easy for Mallas to be complacent. In these waters, there usually wasn't a ship within 50 miles of the freighter. Even so, he made a point of scanning the horizon and periodically glancing at the scope. He was just about to get a mug of coffee when a blip appeared on the radar—and the vector showed the unknown vessel was on a collision course. Suddenly, the blare of a radio transmission broke the peace and quiet of the bridge.

"Crescent Moon, Crescent Moon, this is U.S. Navy warship U.S.S. *Leftwich.* Please heave to and prepare to be boarded."

Mallas stared at the speaker as if he hadn't heard or understood the command. Then, the captain of the *Leftwich* repeated his order. The helmsman gave Mallas a *What do you want me to do?* look.

A matte dark-gray helicopter appeared off the port side at 200 feet, with a machine gun pointed at his bridge. Turning around, he saw a similarly armed light-gray helicopter on the starboard side.

"Crescent Moon, this is the *Leftwich.* If you do not slow down in the next thirty seconds, we will fire a warning shot; if you do not stop, we will fire directly at the *Crescent Moon."*

Mallas snatched up the microphone to reply. "Warship *Leftwich,* we are in international waters, I do not have to stop for any ship. Your demand constitutes an act of piracy." Mallas then flipped the switch and asked the sailor in the radio room to bring him his satellite phone.

"Crescent Moon, heave to, immediately. We have reason to believe you have a large quantity of illegal drugs on board headed for the United States."

"Warship *Leftwich,* this is *Crescent Moon.* We are carrying pottery, dishes and furniture. We do not have drugs on board. Your threats are a violation of international maritime law."

By now, Mallas could see the *Leftwich* through his binoculars. The ship's white bow wave was clearly visible.

"Crescent Moon, heave to *IMMEDIATELY!"*

Both helicopters peeled off to orbits a half a mile aft of the freighter. Mallas saw smoke and a pillar of water 30 meters in front of his ship and 50 meters to starboard, then heard the double booms from the *Leftwich's* forward gun. "Helmsman," Mallas said, "all ahead slow. We will comply."

The matte dark-gray helicopter pulled into a hover over the bow of *Crescent Moon,* and eight heavily armed men came down two ropes and spread out over the freighter. As they did, Mallas called his Crescent's operations center in Hong Kong via the international maritime satellite network. He hurriedly explained that *Crescent Moon* was being boarded by the U.S. Navy and hung up seconds before Lieutenant Boyd Dickinson, U.S. Coast Guard Academy, class of 1989, knocked on the entrance to the bridge.

Lieutenant Dickinson smartly saluted before saying, "Captain Mallas, we are searching your ship. If we find illegal drugs, the United States will take control of the *Crescent Moon.* Do you understand?"

"I do. However, I inform you that we are in international waters and my company will consider this an act of piracy."

Dickinson said politely, "If we don't find any drugs, the United States will apologize. In the meantime, we will do our duty and search *Crescent Moon.* Will you tell me, what was your last port of call?"

"Dalian."

The Simushir Island Incident

We have pictures of the Crescent Moon in Broutana Bay. "Did *Crescent Moon* make any stops along the way after leaving Dalian to either take on or unload cargo?"

Before Mallas could answer, a Coast Guardsman yelled over the short-range radio net. "Lieutenant, we've got the mother lode! Two pallets of what looks like heroin bricks in the forward hold. We're going to test samples to make sure."

Saturday, July 22ⁿᵈ, 1995, 1035 local time, Honolulu

Chin-yi Moon was the third North Korean Special Forces officer hired by Half Moon and smuggled into the U.S. Like the others, he was based in LA and had, over the past year, carried out a series of assassinations. Moon didn't care who the individual was or what he did, only that he did the job and quietly slipped away.

The front desk clerk at the Moana Hotel handed him a note with a number to call. After hanging up, Chin-yi walked to Kapi'olani Park. Sitting on the bench specified in the call was a woman wearing a red Hawaiian dress with a white flower print. Long black hair fell to her waist. She was wearing sunglasses and reading a newspaper. Next to her, there was a box wrapped in brown paper resting on top of a 9" X 12" manila envelope.

The clothing and location matched what he'd been told, so Moon sat down. He looked through the trees to the surf, less than a hundred yards away, and spoke the phrases given to him.

"I guess there's not much surf today."

"You should have been here yesterday, it was really calm."

"That is what I heard."

The woman did not look up from her newspaper. "When you finish your business, you will bring what is in the box back to me and I will dispose of it. Then, you will leave the island immediately."

Moon nodded. "That is what I plan to do."

* * *

The box had his weapon of choice, a Tokarev along with a suppressor, five magazines and a box of 50 rounds of sub-sonic, North Korean made ammunition. The envelope had the address and photographs of his target, and a map of Honolulu: enough for him to scout the location and plan his hit. He made two reconnaissance trips to the neighborhood.

Monday, July 24th, 1995, 0327 local time, Honolulu
The bougainvillea along the driveway went all the way to the back end of the carport and gave him a shadow in which to hide. The side door was locked, and it took a few seconds to pick the lock. Inside, nightlights provided enough illumination.

Chin-yi's crepe-soled shoes let him walk silently on the hardwood floor. At the end of the hall, he found a solitary form in the bed. From two meters away, he fired one round in the back of the head. There was a jerk, then stillness. He walked over and felt for a pulse. There was none.

Tuesday, July 25th, 1995, 0822 local time, U.S.S. Blue Ridge
Marty Cabot was the phone, buying a round-trip ticket to Hawaii for the 26th of August. He made a couple of notes on his pad so he could give Uilani the dates, flight numbers and times. They'd talked last night, planning the vacation that would be just the two of them, surfing off Oahu every day for two weeks, no messages, no meetings, no phone calls. Purchase completed, he grinned, hung up the phone, and started reading the report on what the Coast Guard had found when they searched the freighters *Crescent Moon* and *Crescent Galaxy*.

The STU-III on his desk rang. Seeing it was from JICPAC and that the caller was in a Top Secret facility, he assumed it was

Uilani or someone from her staff. He pressed the answer button and then the encrypt button. Instead of Uilani's cheerful voice, it was Jake Garza. As he listened, Marty's face drained of all color. "Nooooo!!!!!"

Josh heard the howl of pain and dashed into the bullpen. Marty was bent over in pain, arms wrapped around his middle. Tears streaked his agonized face. Josh snatched the handset and punched the speakerphone button.

"This is Captain Haman. What's going on?"

"Josh, Jake Garza here. I'm sorry to say this. Last night, Uilani Ka'anapali was murdered. We need to ask both of you some questions. I know it is hard, but we have to. Time may be of the essence."

Marty, still hunched over from the emotional pain, nodded. Josh spoke. "Go for it, we're both listening."

"Intelligence Specialist First Class Kirkland notified us. He became concerned when Uilani didn't show up for work, and called her house. When she didn't answer after three tries, he drove over, used a key she had given him for emergencies, and found her body." Garza paused. "Do either one of you know who else on her team had access to the info she was gathering on Simushir?"

Marty held up his hand as if to say, *I'll answer*. "Petty Officer Kirkland is her de facto number two. He was doing all the photo work. And then there was a guy by the name of Bill Hamilton, ex-Air Force, NSA, who did the signals analyses. I met both of them last time I was there."

"Did she ever say anything about either one?"

"Yeah. She asked me to help write Kirkland's annual evaluation. She thinks he should be a chief, and Rear Admiral Benjamin wrote an endorsement for the chief selection board and recently awarded him a Navy Commendation Medal. She thought

Hamilton was a C player and wanted to replace him. Look at his personnel jacket."

"We will."

"Anyone told her parents yet?" Marty was wiping his face but he was still crying.

"Yes, Rear Admiral Benjamin is with them now. This has got four-star visibility and CINCPAC wants answers soon."

Marty held up his hand so Josh knew not to speak, but it was a struggle to get the words out. "I'm coming to Hawaii for the funeral. Will you let Uilani's parents know?"

Garza answered quickly. "I'll call them."

Josh put his hand on his Marty's shoulder, wishing he could make his friend's pain go away. "Marty, go pack. I'll tell the boss and get the admin officer to book you a flight to Honolulu. Take as much time as you need." Josh waited until Marty left, then asked Garza the question on his mind. "Any idea who killed Uilani?"

"No. Whoever did it was a pro. The assassin was using a Tokarev, which we know because an empty shell rolled under a dresser, and we think the assassin didn't want to stay in the house to look for it. Here's the thing: there have been a bunch of drug-related hits in LA and San Diego using a Tokarev Type 68."

"But why did they go after Uilani? How'd they get her name?"

"We don't know; that's what we're trying to figure out. Our theory is the bad guys found out she was involved in gathering intelligence on Half Moon, Simushir, and the Kuril Island company. They struck to send a message."

"Jake, go find the bastard who did this."

Josh ended the call just as Marty re-entered the N6 compartment. Josh pointed to his office and closed the door when both were inside. Marty slumped into a seat, and Josh leaned his back against the door. There was a long moment of silence before Josh took a deep breath and said, "Marty, you had to say this to me once. I listened to you then. Listen to me now. Promise me you won't take this into your own hands. Promise. I don't want to have to visit you in Leavenworth."

Marty's answering look was combined anger, hurt and determination.

The bad guys, Josh realized, had no idea of the fury they had just unleashed on themselves. He felt his gut clench. He was deeply afraid his friend was about to go rogue.

And he knew exactly how Marty felt. Josh had never entirely gotten over the murder of his first wife and their family. He'd finally avenged their deaths—discovered revenge wasn't all it was cracked up to be. Even though he'd killed the bastard who'd pulled the trigger, the confrontation had evoked haunting memories of what could have been.

Chapter 14: VENGEANCE

Wednesday, July 26th, 1995, 0656 local time, Tokyo Bay

Crescent Star was approaching the bay of Japan's capital. Captain Yamani ordered the ship to slow to three knots. A small launch flying the Japanese flag was already waiting for the bulk freighter. Two uniformed Japanese customs officials climbed aboard via the Jacob's ladder, followed by a man dressed in a business suit.

The trio were escorted to the wardroom, where Yong Chao, the former General Chun Lee Jang, and Yan Chao, the former Ji-ae Jang, bowed slightly in welcome. The Japanese Immigration Bureau officer and his female associate acknowledged Yong's bow with one of his own, then held out his hand as if to say, *please be seated.*

"I am Senior Inspector Amaya, and this is Inspector Fuse. The purpose of this meeting is to facilitate your transfer to Narita Airport, where you will be able to board your flight to Singapore."

Yong nodded his head, and Yan sat quietly. As Chao's wife, she would not be part of the conversation, yet, in the wonderful way of the Orient, Inspector Fuse was a woman and would participate.

Amaya continued. "We will board my launch to Chiba on the east side of the Tokyo Bay. There, we will take an Immigration Bureau van to Narita International Airport where Inspector Fuse and I will escort you to the first-class lounge in the departure area. We are treating you as passengers in transit, who will not be officially entering Japan. Therefore, you cannot leave the airport's transiting passenger area. Inspector Fuse and I will wait with you until you board and the flight takes off. Is this agreeable?"

Yong said, "Yes, it is perfectly acceptable."

"Excellent, we will now proceed." Amaya gestured to the other man at the table, who had not been introduced.

"Mr. Chao, my name is Hisao Goda, and I am Crescent Shipping's agent in Tokyo. I have your first-class tickets to Singapore on a flight leaving late this afternoon. In addition, a driver will meet you when you exit immigration in Singapore. He will take you to your apartment."

Yong turned toward Senior Inspector Amaya as if to ask, what's next?

"Your passports please. We must make sure they are not suspected of being counterfeits."

Fuse took each passport in turn and compared them to a list containing passport numbers that the Bureau had flagged as possibly counterfeit. She then checked another list for individuals wanted on international warrants. Inspector Fuse smiled as she handed the passports to her superior. A sharp nod of her head told Inspector Amaya that neither passport was on either list.

Inspector Amaya returned the passports to the former General Jang. "Mr. and Mrs. Chao, if you will meet me on the deck with your bags, we will leave the *Crescent Star* and take you to the airport."

Waiting on the pier was a small van. Inspector Fuse climbed into the back seat as Amaya showed the Chao's the middle two seats before getting into the front seat, next to the driver. Once on board, the driver turned on the lights and siren and they left the Immigration Bureau compound. Soon they were speeding down Highway 14.

A car abruptly changed lanes in front of them. The van's driver slammed on the brakes and swerved to avoid an accident. There was a crunching of metal as the van's nose went up the concrete divider, and the van rolled. Bags, briefcases, and loose items bounced off the humans and tumbled about.

The van's roof partially collapsed on impact and Jang heard the scraping sound of metal on concrete. What he didn't see was the trail of gasoline from the ruptured fuel line. Sparks from the metal-on-cement friction ignited the fuel, and before the van slid to a stop it exploded in a ball of flames. Everything and everyone inside were incinerated.

1849 local time, Honolulu

David Seul opened the latest envelope from Bill Hamilton and shook out the contents onto the open space of his highly polished teak desk, accented by an antique letter opener, a clock, and a small Wedgwood vase containing three silver Parker pens and several mechanical pencils.

He smoothed his dress beneath his knees as he sat down, then pulled on a pair of latex gloves, making sure his manicured fingernails didn't rip the thin material. Next he took a loupe from a desk drawer and studied the photos. Satisfied, he inserted the prints back into a fresh 9-by-12-inch envelope, sealed it, and slid it into a larger envelope for a courier company. He frowned faintly.

The package was a link to a past he'd hoped he'd put behind him, and a reminder of the nine-month nightmare that had been his trial.

The Simushir Island Incident

Born Gil-su Jang, David Seul had always been the black sheep of the Jang family, but despite his father's disapproval of his sexual preferences, he'd always done what was asked of him to the best of his ability. Eventually he'd won grudging acknowledgement, even a degree of respect, from his father Ju-won Jang couldn't argue with the results.

In 1979, at the age of 22, he'd been sent to Thailand to build a network of opium suppliers. The work was difficult, dangerous and, at times, bloody. There had been occasions, deep in the jungle that straddled the Thai and Laotian border, when he'd had to do his own dirty work to send a message to other suppliers. While he was honorable and met all his commitments, he expected others to do the same. One did not cross Gil-su Jang.

The organization in Southeast Asia prospered during the Vietnam War. Afterwards, Gil-su Jang was sent to California. His mission: build a distribution network for heroin and methamphetamines in the United States. It took eight years. As a cover, he worked out of Half Moon's office in Long Beach.

In 1980, Gil-su Jang finally became a U.S. citizen named David Seul. He told his father that he was turning over his drug business to his subordinates, and bought six struggling hotels—three on Oahu, two on Maui, and one on the big island of Hawaii. In less than a year, he turned all six into profitable, five-star properties, before branching out to operate popular nightclubs and highly rated restaurants. *Finally, he was out of the drug business!!!*

Then in 1990, the State of Hawaii—along with the FBI, DEA, BATF and the IRS—spent untold millions trying to convince a jury to convict him on racketeering and drug-trafficking charges. The state's case fell apart in the courtroom when both star witnesses admitted on the stand that what they'd witnessed had taken place over a dozen years before. The jury took less than an hour to deliver a "not guilty" verdict based on the statute of limitations.

During the trial, Seul never once communicated with his family. It was something he had to fight and win on his own. Every day he remembered his father's admonition to him as a teenager: do not bring disgrace to the family. In other words, you may do what you choose, but you must not cause the Jangs to lose face.

After he'd had time to reflect on the trial, David decided that the millions he'd paid his attorney's law firm to defend him was well worth it. He now had iron clad, legal proof that his businesses were squeaky clean.

After the verdict, Seul put the hotels and clubs in a real estate investment trust that specialized in the hospitality industry. It paid him a percentage of the profits, and he no longer was involved in the day-to-day management.

Still, in the back of his mind, he suspected one of the alphabet soup of federal agencies still kept him under surveillance. Seul also worried that the attorney who'd prosecuted the case was still smarting from his loss. The man had political ambitions and didn't care whose lives he destroyed in the process of making a name for himself. Fear of having to go through that again made David very, very careful.

However, he had an interest in the Simushir operation. Two years before it began, Cho Rhee had asked him to help develop the plan. Reluctantly, and only because it was family, he'd agreed on the condition that he had no part of its execution.

And then one day a bookie had approached him through one of his legitimate clients, and said he had a problem and maybe David Seul could suggest a solution. When David found out where Hamilton worked, he realized that here was a golden opportunity to learn what information American intelligence had about Simushir and Half Moon. And it cost Seul nothing, because Half Moon made the payments.

The Simushir Island Incident

Still, Seul knew Hamilton would eventually be caught, because Hamilton was a *shlemiel*, and any investigation would lead back to him. When he'd discussed the risk with his relatives at Half Moon Trading on a recent trip to Hong Kong, he'd been told to maintain the relationship. Simushir, they said, was far too valuable, and Half Moon needed to know what the Americans knew. But David had an end date in mind, and it was fast approaching. If his departure caused him to become estranged from his family, he was okay with that. He'd been there before. And if he were arrested, Seul had a plan for that eventuality as well.

He rose gracefully and went into the bedroom to apply his make-up, admiring the results in the mirror. Then he put the package into his briefcase went to his club, rated as one of best nightspots in Honolulu. There he gave the envelope to the club manager, who—as usual—ordered an employee to deliver it to Cathay Pacific's airfreight office, where it would be secured as carefully as if it contained diamonds and flown to Macao.

With the last business task of the day completed, Seul went into the bar to meet his date.

Thursday, July 27th, 1995, 1538 local time, Pyongyang
Thaek sighed, and patted the pocket where his cigarettes were stashed. The conference rooms all looked the same: gray walls adorned with large portraits of the Dear Leader and his father, smaller ones of Lenin and Stalin. On the wall opposite the door of this room, there was an original painting of men in Korean People's Army uniforms surrounded by dead American and South Korean soldiers.

For a change, Kim Jong-Il was on time—a signal that he was very interested in the conversation about to happen. Thaek waited until his Dear Leader sat in the largest chair in the room at the end of the table before he sat down. On the mirror like surface, he could see the lights hanging from the ceiling.

"Deputy Minister Thaek, how certain are you of the information you sent me?" Kim Jong-Il leaned back in the chair, which was much nicer than the other twelve in the room.

Thaek spoke formally. "Very certain, sir. Our Chinese friends photographed Vice Admiral Pak entering the American embassy in Beijing. He left the next day on an American Air Force airplane."

This was a very serious matter, and if presented the wrong way, could be Thaek's ticket to a re-education camp. He had assured the Dear Leader that Pak was reliable. He desperately wanted a cigarette, but right now his number one priority was to keep the Dear Leader from thinking Pak's defection was his fault. He told himself that nicotine withdrawal would help keep him focused.

"What else?" There was a harshness in Kim Jong-Il's voice that Thaek had never heard before.

"Major General Jang and his wife have also disappeared. They crossed the bridge and walked to the stores in Yuanbao but never returned. The Chinese surveillance tapes of the Yuanbao train station do not show any recognizable images of him. We conclude he avoided the cameras or changed clothes."

Kim Jong-Il banged the palm of his hand on the table. "Incompetent bastards! I thought you had both men watched, with orders to arrest them if they attempted to leave the country!"

"Yes, Dear Leader, I did. I called the head of security in our embassy in Beijing to remind him of the importance of watching Admiral Pak. We have agents all over Dandong and the Yuanbao District, and they were alerted when Jang and his wife crossed the river. They were followed into a crowded market, where the agents lost sight of them."

Kim Il-Sung pursed his lips. It was obvious to Thaek that his Dear Leader was trying to contain his anger. Under the table, his hands were shaking.

"Could the Jangs have used another name?"

"It is possible, Dear Leader. The Chinese tell us the passports and visas for the passengers on the Beijing and Dalian trains were all in order."

Kim Jong-Il slammed his hand down on the table again. "So, Major General Jang disappeared into thin air?"

Thaek tried to keep from wincing. "We will find them." The individuals at their embassies who hunt for traitors have already been ordered to find the Paks and the Jangs—and eliminate them.

"And what about this Major Kim?"

"Sir, we know only that sometime in the early morning hours he slipped over the side of a ship named the *Crescent Galaxy*."

"You told me that Major Kim was one of our best special forces soldiers."

"Yes, sir. All our reports said he was very reliable. Major General Jang vouched for him."

"Is Kim married? Are his parents still alive?"

"No, sir."

"Any chance he disappeared into the fleshpots of Hong Kong?"

"That is always possible. If it is so, we will find him."

"Do you think Major Kim is dead?"

Thaek felt his stomach twist. This wasn't going well, but it wasn't his fault. "No."

Kim Jong-Il leaned forward. "Then where is Major Kim?" The Dear Leader didn't wait for Thaek to answer. "Tell me why three good men desert? They had money and privilege. Why would they betray me?"

Thaek had no answer for that one. He couldn't very well tell the Dear Leader, *They probably suspected we were planning to eliminate them.* It was definitely time to change the subject. "There is one more thing."

"More bad news?"

"No, Dear Leader, an interesting piece of information."

"What is it?"

"Major General Jang has been using three of our soldiers to eliminate competitors to our drug business. I sent all three of them messages telling them I am now their control."

"That is a good move. We can use them to kill Jang, Kim and Pak." The Dear Leader's index finger tapped the table. "They and their families are to be considered enemies of the state. If you can't bring them back to the People's Republic for trial as traitors, eliminate them."

"Yes, Dear Leader."

"One more thing. I am going to decorate, not punish, Captain Jung."

1950 local time, Oahu

Uilani's will specified she was to be cremated and her ashes spread on the waters of Kaneohe Bay. Rather than ride in the mourner's outrigger canoe with her parents and brothers, Marty rented a surfboard and paddled out into the bay to watch Uilani's parents, brothers and sisters take turns spreading her ashes on the calm water.

It was closure, but it didn't alleviate the pain. Marty wanted revenge.

During a lonely dinner at a Mexican restaurant in Oahu, it was all he could do to focus on Dick Couch's novel *SEAL Team One* and not think of Uilani. On his way back to the Hale Koa Hotel, Marty saw Bill Hamilton enter a McDonalds. He was carrying a large manila envelope. Marty's curiosity went to general quarters when he saw, through the large window, Hamilton sit at a table and hand the envelope to an Asian man.

Marty watched the Asian man leave and walk toward a Crown Victoria, trailed by a bodyguard. Another man was already in the driver's seat. Marty flagged down a cab and pointed at the Ford. "Follow that car."

The cabbie looked at Marty as if he were crazy, so Marty slapped a $20 bill on the front seat. "I said follow that car, or do I call my friends in the police?" The acceleration slammed him back into the seat.

The maroon Crown Victoria was easy to follow. It made straight for the airport, and when it finally stopped, the Asian man got out, accompanied by the two bodyguards. The cabbie turned to Marty. "Do you know who that is?"

"Haven't a clue." Marty leaned forward. "Humor me."

"*That* is Mr. David Seul. The cops went after him big time for being a major drug dealer, but they couldn't pin anything on him. Believe me, they tried. It was in all the papers for months. He's Korean, I think."

"Thanks for the warning." Marty dropped two more twenties on the front seat and followed Seul's retinue to the Hawaiian Air ticket counter. He stood in line behind one of Seul's bodyguards and heard him buy three tickets to Hilo on the big island of Hawaii. Marty glanced at Mr. Seul, who was sitting in a chair reading a paper.

In the gate area, Marty dropped a quarter into a pay phone and dialed Jake Garza's home number. "Jake, I just saw Bill Hamilton pass a thick envelope to a man my cabbie identified as David Seul, who is headed to the big island."

"Wow!!!! I'll have someone meet you."

"No, don't. My guess is Seul knows all your people. I'll find someone else."

Marty hung up and dialed another number. "Master Chief Jenkins—Commander Cabot. Sorry to bother you. I need a favor."

Friday, July 28th, 1995, 0026 local time, Pyongyang
The day his mother left for Singapore was the day Seong Pak realized he would never see her again. The tears in her eyes were the giveaway. Then, when his father said he was going to Beijing for a week, the youngest Pak realized the end game had begun.

Neither of his parents had included him in their discussions about leaving their homeland. He didn't want to know so he didn't have to worry about putting them at risk when, not if, he was interrogated by a Ministry of Safety and Security officer.

Today Seong had gone to the doctor. He was weak from pneumonia and believed he was dying. The doctors gave him antibiotics and told him to go home and rest. Better, Seong decided, to die in his bed than in the hands of the Ministry of State Security.

When the knock came, Seong didn't bother to get up to answer the door. He was carried to a car that brought him to the ministry's headquarters. In a windowless, concrete-walled room, he laughed as he was slammed into the chair and chained down. This was his victory. Those he touched and those who breathed the air he expelled from his ravaged lungs would share his pneumonia.

Captain Dokgo punched Seong in the solar plexus, slapped him hard, and demanded to know what was so funny. Seong's diseased lungs struggled to process oxygen and send it to his brain. He gasped, "I don't know where my parents are, and if you beat me, I will die before the interrogation is over. You will get sick, and the joke will be on you."

"Seong Pak," Captain Dokgo snarled, "you will answer all my questions or you will *wish* you were dead."

"I don't know where my parents are. You can beat me all you want, but I can't tell you something I don't know."

Dokgo nodded to one of the soldiers in the room, who hammered Seong in the chest with the butt of his AK-47. Seong's eyes bulged out in pain. His heart, starved for oxygen and shocked by the blow, stopped working. Seong Pak fulfilled his karma.

1020 local time, JICPAC, Naval Base Pearl Harbor

Marty walked to the opening of Hamilton's cubicle, two doors down the hall from Uilani's empty office. As he entered, Jake Garza and Chief Warrant Officer Davies, from the Navy's Criminal Investigative Service peeled off into a nearby conference room. Without introducing himself, Marty grabbed the chair next to Hamilton's desk, spun it around and sat down with his chest facing the backrest.

"Who are you?" Hamilton asked in quizzical, unconcerned voice.

Marty wasn't interested in pleasantries. "Do you recognize this man?" He plopped a mug shot of Seul on the desk.

Hamilton swallowed very hard and flushed. His cheeks and forehead turned bright red.

"I repeat, do you know this man?"

Sweat started to bead on Hamilton's forehead as he stared at Marty.

Marty's palm slammed down on the table. Hamilton jumped in his chair, and his Adam's apple bobbed as he swallowed several times.

"Answer the fucking question."

Hamilton stared at him silently.

"Let me tell you why I am here. Last night, I saw you enter the McDonalds on Keeaumoku Street and hand this man a manila envelope. What was in it?"

Hamilton licked his lips and swallowed hard. Despite the cool room temperature, perspiration continued to form on his forehead.

Marty stared at the intelligence analyst. "Hamilton, I am not here to fuck around. His name is David Seul and either you answer me or I get word to him that you ratted him out, right after the Navy Criminal Investigative Service takes you out of here in handcuffs. You've got ten seconds to make up your mind."

"I'm a dead man either way."

"Ah, the man speaks."

"Who are you?"

"I am Commander Marty Cabot, United States Navy." Marty thought he saw a flicker of recognition in the man's eyes. "I am here for two reasons. One, I think you are a traitor. Two, the woman I loved was assassinated, and I believe she was targeted using information you gave Seul."

"I didn't have anything to do with her... Uilani's..." Hamilton stammered, "her death."

"What did you give David Seul?"

"What kind of deal can I get?"

"That's not my department." Disgusted, Marty turned to the sailor standing in the doorway. "Petty Officer Kirkland, will you please ask Chief Warrant Officer Davies and Special Agent Garza to join us?"

1730 local time, Honolulu

Marty and Jake put on their sunglasses as they exited the DEA's headquarters. Marty turned to the DEA agent. "After listening to Hamilton, I don't know whether I need a bath or a drink more. What's next?"

"A plane ride to the Big Island, followed by more fun and games. You interested?"

"Are we taking down David Seul?"

"Yeah. We've been looking for a reason to raid his house for years. Now we have it, with the search warrant based on Hamilton's statement."

"Expecting trouble?"

"Always do. I'd rather go in with overwhelming force and not find anything than get ambushed."

"I want in."

"Figured you would."

Marty jerked his head in a hard nod. "How are you going to get to him?"

"We've had a sniper team in position above the house for the past four or five hours. They'll radio us if Seul leaves. Any sign of resistance and we'll shoot."

"How come the FBI is not leading this? It's espionage."

"It started with drugs, and that's my turf. And they don't have the talent in Hawaii for a takedown like this. We do."

2020 local time, the Island of Hawaii

Seul's house was at the north end of a cul-de-sac, several hundred feet above the coastal road. All the front window had unobstructed views of the ocean.

Jake and Marty joined some of Garza's men at an overlook on the coastal road, where people could park and watch the surf pound the volcanic rock. Garza explained the plan and made sure everyone had equipment, then the team set out, loaded into four armored Suburbans.

As they approached the dwelling, one of the two guards by the gate raised an AK-47 to fire, but a fusillade of M-16 rounds took him down before he pulled the trigger. The other opted for survival by raising his hands.

In a hallway, the DEA agents found Seul, wearing a pink blouse and gray skirt, carrying documents to a shredder. At the point of a gun, he dropped the documents and raised his hands above his head. He was told to back away from the papers strewn on the floor.

Just before Marty entered the house, he saw movement in the shadows of the garden and dodged. A bullet smacked into the marble next to his head. Marty shouted, "There's another, and he's running!"

Jake keyed the mike on his handheld radio. "This is Garza. Runner on the west side of the house. Send backup."

Marty was already in pursuit, and he'd drawn the Glock 17 that Garza had just issued to him. He was wishing he'd spent some time on the range with it. The man Marty was chasing turned slightly as he ran, and fired. A round hissed past his head. No sound and no flash meant that the shooter was using a suppressor.

SMACK!!! A bullet struck Marty's Kevlar vest, and it felt as if someone had hit him in the chest with a hammer. Adrenalin kept him going forward. Another round punched him in the chest—a sharp, stabbing sensation followed by a dull ache. He wasn't dead, but he might have broken ribs.

He fired two rounds at a dark silhouette next to a bush. The shots flushed a man carrying a pistol, who ran among the trees to make himself hard to hit.

A bullet kicked up dirt by Marty's foot and another smacked into the eucalyptus tree he was using for cover. He responded with two rounds of his own.

He looked around slowly, using peripheral vision to search the grove of thick banyan, eucalyptus and cedar trees. Behind him, Jake was pressed up against a large cedar tree. Marty yelled "Cover me!" and held up three, then two, and when he showed one finger, Jake pivoted around the tree and fired three double taps.

As soon as Jake began firing, Marty dashed toward another tree, then to a second and third to get between the runner and the road. There was no return fire in his direction, but peering around the three-foot diameter of a cedar tree, he could see a young Asian male about 15 yards away. The man had his back pressed against a tree, and he'd just ejected a magazine from his pistol.

Now! Marty pointed in the direction of the shooter, held up two fingers once and again before he pointed at the target. He hoped Jake understood his gesture to mean two more double-taps. Then he held up three fingers, and as soon as he got down to one, he started to move.

Double taps from Garza's gun kept Marty from hearing a first shot go by, but a second bullet sent bark flying from a tree just before he reached it. On the run, Marty fired two rounds before he got behind another tree, nine yards from where he thought the assassin was hiding. There was no return fire.

Cautiously, he poked his head around the tree and saw the man running toward him, aiming the pistol and carrying what looked like a small sword. Marty fired twice; and the man staggered and went down with two spreading bloody blotches on his chest. By the time Marty kicked the *wakizashi* away, the man's eyes had a vacant stare.

"You okay?" Garza loped over, still scanning the area. He stared at the two center mass hits visible on Marty's chest, imbedded in the rip-stop nylon cover of the vest.

"Shit. I didn't know he hit you."

"I felt them, but I see the kevlar did its job. The bastard almost got on top of me with his *wakizashi*. That would have been a problem." Kevlar was designed to stop high-speed bullets; it was not as effective against blades.

"He should have given up."

"I don't think it was in his nature."

Jake smiled. "You know what they say, never bring a knife to a gunfight."

Back in the house, two members of Jake's team were cataloging the documents they found.

"Let's go talk to Mr. Seul."

Seul was handcuffed and sitting on his couch. Seul's hands, Jake noticed, were neatly manicured. The nails even seemed to have a clear polish on them. Jake stood in front of him and demanded, "Who's the guy in the yard?"

"That would be Chin Yi Moon. I gather you caught him." Seul knew perfectly well that an ordinary arrested suspect should never, ever volunteer any information to the police beyond his own name and address—the only disclosure required by law. But he was about to play a bigger game.

"I can read what's on his driver's license. Who is he really?"

"First Lieutenant Chin Yi Moon of the Korean People's Army. The North Koreans are very good at getting their citizens into this country as sleeper agents. He's one of many loaned out as professional assassins. After two years or so, they go back."

"Why was he at your house?"

"He came to bring a pistol back for me to destroy." This was not the time to tell Garza that Chin Yi's flight was scheduled to leave for LA in the morning.

"Did you send him to kill Uilani Ka'anapali?"

Mr. Seul smiled at Garza. "I gather you are the special agent-in-charge?"

"I am. Answer my question."

"No. I just provided a gun and ammo."

"Who tasked him?" Marty interjected.

"And you are, let me guess, Commander Cabot or Captain Haman." Mr. Seul gazed at Marty speculatively. Marty didn't say a word.

"I'll take that as a yes." Mr. Seul turned to Jake Garza and spoke almost primly. "We need to talk about what I can do for you.

It is far more than what you see here. For example, I can give you names, contact details, information on who tasked Lieutenant Moon, and how the North Koreans get their assassins into the United States. I can also help you bring down a drug operation bringing in a ton or more of Asian Pure heroin into LA every month. And I can lead you to several of the largest drug distributors in Hawaii and the Southwest."

"In return for what?"

"Disappearing. I would not survive very long in jail. I know way, way too much. Even if you kept me in solitary and away from the general prison population, you wouldn't be able to protect me. It would just be a matter of time before someone killed me, even at Club Fed. So I will give up my U.S. citizenship and never come back."

"We need to see proof of what you are saying."

"I understand. You just have to keep me alive until I meet my end of the bargain. Then, I disappear."

"How do we know you won't go back into the drug business?"

"Ahhhhh, that is simple. I am tired of wondering whether the next person I talk to is either a policeman or an assassin. It is time to completely retire."

"Don't you think you are signing your own death warrant?"

"No, Agent Garza, I don't think so. I have several identities I have never used that are known only to me. My part of the bargain is I give you information I have gathered over the years. It is…" Mr. Seul tapped the side of his head, "up here and nowhere else, except a few innocent looking address books."

"Where are the books?"

"In a bank vault on Oahu."

"Let me get this straight. You're going to give us a brain dump to fill in the blanks to solve a murder, help us shut down a heroin pipeline, and give us enough evidence to shut down several large drug operations in Hawaii and California. And then, for that, we let you board a plane and disappear?"

"Correct. And no offense, Mr. Garza, but this is not your decision to make. You are an errand boy. Please call someone who can contact someone who has real authority. You have nothing to lose, and I will wait." Calmly, he smiled in the agent's face.

Chapter 15: RETRIBUTION

Sunday, July 30th, 1995, 1321 local time, Honolulu

Marty and Master Chief Jenkins were in a secure conference room so Marty could use a STU-III to contact Seventh Fleet.

"Josh, Master Chief Jenkins says 'Hi.' He is attempting to stay retired and out of the operational world but can't. He blames you for his problem because you seem to find ways to keep getting him involved."

"Tell him that's my job!!!"

Marty recounted the raid, and how preliminary ballistic results confirmed that the Tokarev Lieutenant Moon had fired at him was the same weapon used to kill Uilani.

"In a grim way, that's good news," Josh pointed out. "You wanted revenge, and you got it—completely and directly—without making trouble for yourself."

"Garza is waiting for his folks in D.C. to approve the deal with Mr. Seul. Then the formal debriefing can begin. I'll be part of it, because there are links to Half Moon Trading. It may help us separate fact from fiction and figure out what to do next."

"Good." Josh paused. "When are you coming back?"

"Not sure. I'm waiting to get a crack at Seul, and I need to sort out a few things."

Thursday, August 3rd, 1995, 0735 local time, U.S.S. Blue Ridge

With the daily intelligence briefing over, Admiral Maize walked slowly to the podium. Usually when he wanted to offer guidance or make suggestions, he did so from his chair. Going to the podium added an air of formality and seriousness.

The three-star admiral looked around the room and held up a copy of the *Washington Post* as if it were contaminated. "Gentlemen, someone with classified knowledge of the shoot down near Simushir Island blabbed to a reporter. Needless to say, CINCPAC is hard pissed because there is very sensitive information in the piece. The shit has hit the fan and is being flung all over the place. The chairman of the Joint Chiefs wants a very public hanging of the leaker. So, let me get to the punch line."

Admiral Maize looked around the room, meeting the gaze of every man in it. "The legal officer will interview each of you. Your sworn statement will be recorded and transcribed. You will be asked to sign copies of the transcript and a letter certifying you did not talk to the *Washington Post* reporter. The interviews will happen today, starting with me. I am confident no one on this staff was the leaker, but I ask you all to fully cooperate. Please do not make this any harder than it has to be. That is all."

1117 local time, on board U.S.S. Blue Ridge

Admiral Maize sent for Josh. As soon as he entered the office, the admiral waved him to a chair. "I don't have much time, so I am going to get to the point—you need a break."

"Sir?" Josh gave the admiral a puzzled look.

"Sign this. Trust me—it's a good deal."

Josh looked at the Navy form, in which he acknowledged that he was to be given access to another code-word-compartmented program called *Red Siren*. He scribbled his name and handed the form back without asking the obvious question.

"Just four people on this staff—the N2, the chief of staff, me, and now you—have access. Commander Cabot will be read in when he gets back. *Red Siren* is the debriefing of the head of North Korea's submarine force—Vice Admiral Kim Sun Pak—in Hawaii. He may have some information on the Kuril Island Development Corporation and Half Moon Trading, and since you are already in the know, you are going to get what he knows out of him."

"Yes, sir. When do I leave?"

"As soon as we can get you off this tub."

"Yes, sir."

"And one more thing. I am extending the temporary-duty orders for thirty days after you finish the debrief. Go spend it with Rebekah and your kids. By the time you get back, I'll have figured out how I am going to get along without you."

"Sir? My tour is not up until the end of the year. Am I being relieved?"

"Yes, but for the right reasons, Josh. You are not being fired." It was the first time the admiral had ever addressed him by his first name. "You're one helluva naval officer. Several flag officer friends recommended I add you to my staff, and they were right. It has been my absolute pleasure and privilege to serve with you. The Navy rotates officers early all the time. I am writing a special meritorious fitness report, which will be favorably endorsed by CINCPAC, saying you walk above the water because you don't need the rocks. Admiral Gainesville will help make sure you are at the head of the list when ship CO billets are handed out. The Navy needs officers like you out at the sharp end of operations, not tucked away in a back room sorting messages. The younger officers and sailors need to see that the Navy has warriors—and mentors—like you."

Admiral Maize smiled. "We're trying to get you one of the big amphibious ships that has an embarked Marine Air Group, based in San Diego. When you get back from leave, you can begin the official turnover to Commander Cabot, who will be your replacement. He'll be filling a captain's slot while still a commander, which will help get him promoted. He's also getting a meritorious fitness report."

"Thank you, sir."

The two men shook hands firmly.

2358 local time, Hong Kong harbor

Three men, clad in black pants, black cotton turtlenecks and black ski masks, remained in the shadows while a fourth, moving with the focused stealth of a SEAL, slid up to a door next to a loading dock to pick the lock. He wasn't worried about being spotted; the lights on the dock, shot out the night before with a pellet gun, still hadn't been replaced.

He opened the door, and all four entered the building. Each carried a backpack and a shoulder holster with a Browning Hi-Power pistol and three spare 15-round magazines. None of them were expecting a firefight; the pistols were "just in case."

To avoid alerting the security guard in the lobby that someone was using the freight elevator, the four men climbed the stairwell. The only noise was the barely audible soft squishing sound made by crepe-soled shoes. On each landing, the men paused to listen. Hearing no activity, they kept climbing until they reached the seventh floor.

Gently, the front man pulled down on the lever until he heard a soft click, indicating the latch had released, and cracked open the stairwell door. The hallway was dark and empty.

The Simushir Island Incident

Two large wooden double doors were the only ones on this floor. A large brass plaque announced that these were the offices of Half Moon Enterprises, Ltd. On the other side, a series of smaller plaques indicated a slew of subsidiary companies. These doors were locked. The man who had unlocked the outer door stepped forward, lock-picking equipment once more in hand. It took thirty seconds of fiddling before the door could be opened.

Inside, the four split up and searched the empty offices. Nightlights left on by the tenant made it easy to navigate through the halls. Flashlights provided additional light when needed. In a back room of what looked like an accounting department, they found what they were looking for: a large safe. A few doors down, they found a storeroom containing boxes of financial records, neatly arranged on shelves, and another safe.

Out of the lock-picker's backpack came a stethoscope. He pressed the small paddle against the safe's steel door and started to slowly turn the dial. The other three took up guard positions. This was a much better lock. It took two minutes of patient work before the heavy door of the safe swung open. "There we go," the man murmured. He spoke with a faint Australian accent.

The safecracker then went to the storeroom safe, while the front man used a flashlight to examine the contents of the accounting department's safe. On the bottom shelf were five rows of U.S. bills stacked ten bundles high, each bundle wrapped with the mustard-colored band denoting they were hundreds. But Marty Cabot wasn't in Half Moon's offices looking for money. He wanted intelligence the Navy could use. Still, he gestured to the two other SEALS to pack up the bills. This had to look like a robbery motivated by greed. With any luck, the men who ran Half Moon Enterprises, Ltd. would be too busy suspecting each other to guess the truth, that it was an unsanctioned raid by rogue agents of a foreign power.

On the top shelf was a green ledger book. Marty flipped through the pages. It had notes and numbers he didn't understand; but on one page he found a list of ships, dates, ports of call, and a column headed by a single letter, "K," as in kilos. The ports were all in Southeast Asia. Underneath the ledger was a pile of papers in English and Chinese, with numbers and dates that looked familiar. The book and the papers went into Marty's backpack.

In the second safe they found more files, mostly corporate records of board meetings. They were about to leave when one of the members tapped Marty's shoulder. He pointed to a wall safe they had previously missed, hidden by a photo of Hong Kong's skyline.

With one man stationed in the reception area, the other two gathered around the wall safe and its electronic lock. Their safecracker said he didn't have anything that could unlock it.

Marty responded, "Yes, we do. Det cord."

"It will make a hell of a mess and let people know we were here."

Marty responded quickly. "I'll live with that. It'll look even more like a robbery." He set to work, winding thin strips of the cord around the hinges and another around the handle.

The cord went off with a loud bang, and Marty wrestled the door off the safe. Inside, there was another green ledger, titled *KIDC*. Another book consisted of columns of numbers along with dates. The contents of a separate blue folder also looked important, so all three were added to the backpack.

It felt like hours, but in reality, the team was only in the office for eight minutes. They retreated the same way they'd come.

Friday, August 4th, 1038 local time, Pyongyang
Thaek was in panic mode. With shaking, nicotine-stained fingers, he stubbed out the last of his first pack of cigarillos and

tore open a second. The lighter in his hand wavered as he brought its flame up to ignite the next one. A cloud of smoke obscured the ceiling.

With Jang and Pak gone, the drug business was his to run, and at first the changeover had gone smoothly. He'd already found a shipping company to replace Crescent, whose owners frequently carried clandestine cargoes for his country. The owners were pleased; they said a pallet or two of one kilo bricks of Asian Pure would be a lot easier to smuggle than several tons of ammunition. And Thaek was arranging to replace Half Moon's workers on Simushir with men from his country who were experts in drug production. They were scheduled to leave next week.

His problem was that neither Jang nor Pak had given him their contacts for raw opium. The precursors for the methamphetamines were easy enough; they were bought from the People's Republic of China and shipped to Simushir from a Chinese port.

Thaek picked up his phone and called a certain very select number from memory. The man who picked up was the head of the Ministry of State Security's clandestine operations branch. The two had known each other since they'd started at the ministry.

"Sagong." Byong-ho Sagong never bothered to state his department name or title when answering the phone. Those few who had his direct line already knew who he was.

"Byong-ho, it is Kwang-sik." Thank inhaled deeply. Right now, his friend was probably lighting a cigarette of his own and leaning back in his chair.

"And how may I help the Deputy Minister do the people's work and carry out the wishes of our Dear Leader?" These words were spoken to appease any political officer who might review the transcript of the call.

"I have two questions. First, do we have any contacts with the Sinaloa cartel?"

There was a pause. "We do. Why?"

"The People's Republic has a relationship with the Sinaloas but a link has been broken. We need to re-establish contact and our Dear Leader would like it to run through your Room 39 operation." The purpose of The Central Committee Bureau 39 of the Korean Workers' Party was to generate cash—through counterfeiting foreign currencies, manufacturing and selling illegal drugs, and arms sales.

"How high in their organization?"

"All I have is a name, Luis Padilla, who I believe runs their distribution in Los Angeles. We provide them with processed heroin."

"And the second question?"

"Do we have contacts in Southeast Asia or elsewhere that can provide large quantities of raw opium?"

Sagong took a deep breath, hungrily sucking smoke into his lungs as he contemplated what he was going to say.

"I was wondering when you would call me about this. We supply both the Gulf Cartel and the Sinaloas with weapons and ammunition. Our contacts are very high in the organization. We have contacts in Myanmar and Laos to whom we provide advisors and weapons. They pay us with money from their sale of raw opium. What is your objective?"

Thaek rubbed his forehead. "We have a drug factory that has lost its supplier of raw opium. The Sinaloas have committed to buy at least a ton a month of its product, called Asian Pure." He didn't want to sound desperate when he added, "This is priority of our Dear Leader."

"Give me a few minutes and I will call you back."

The Simushir Island Incident

Saturday, August 5th, 1995, 0836 local time, Honolulu
Jake Garza gazed thoughtfully at a box sitting on his desk. It had been delivered via an overnight courier service. *Someone paid a pretty penny to send this to me.* As a matter of policy, the box and its contents, two large padded envelopes, had been X-rayed, bomb-sniffed, and checked for fingerprints. Nada for the envelopes; whoever had prepared them must have worn gloves. None of the prints on the box were in the DEA's, ATF's or FBI's criminal databases. They most likely belonged to mail handlers.

The DEA had determined the address in Hong Kong was not real. Based on that, Garza assumed that the name—H. Hopkins—would not check out either.

Garza had come in on his day off, rather than wait until Monday to find out what was so screamingly important to some anonymous sender. He cleared off a small conference table, unfolded the blade on his pocketknife, and slit open both packages. One at a time, he dumped out the contents, being careful to keep the two piles separate. Before he touched up any of the documents, he pulled on a pair of latex gloves.

Garza flipped through the pages of the two ledgers. It didn't take him long to figure out he was looking at a list of heroin shipments for the past five years. It had dates, quantities, and ships, along with a code he guessed represented the buyer. The notes column was in Chinese; when it was translated, he would learn more.

He guessed the letters *KIDC* on the second ledger stood for the Kuril Island Development Corporation. The ledger listed bribes paid to Russian officials by name, including bank transfer information, along with the dates. It also listed the money being spent on each supplier, including equipment and invoice numbers, and suppliers for the heroin factory on the north side of Broutana

Bay. Other items included the bonus paid to Managing Director Lee to take on the project.

The loose papers were a mix of contracts and agreements, as well as hand-written lists. One of the contracts seemed to be an agreement between the Kuril Island Development Corporation and the Russian Maritime Administration.

Translating the Chinese and deciphering the codes could potentially deliver a mother lode of information to the DEA, but the material presented two problems. One: how would he keep it secret? Two—and much more difficult—how could he use it?

It hadn't come from a confidential informant or any listed source, so a sharp defense attorney could claim the documents were elaborate forgeries. He had no proof, no chain-of-custody regarding their origin—and he suspected they had all been stolen.

However, he could use them to gather officially obtainable evidence.

Garza wanted them in a safe place, out of the DEA offices. He called the *Blue Ridge* to talk to Josh, only to learn that Haman was off the ship on temporary duty. He then called Master Chief Jenkins, who immediately offered to temporarily store the documents as intelligence on Simushir.

Monday, August 7th, 0945 local time, Oahu

From Honolulu International Airport, the drive to Schofield Barracks up Hawaii's Interstate Highway H2 was spectacular. It went right up the center of the island between its two mountain ranges. On the right were the ridges and peaks of the Oahu Mountains and national wildlife refuge. On the left was the Waianane Mountain ridge with its heavily forested slopes. Josh guessed the surf must be up on the north side of the island, because many cars had surfboards on their racks and the drivers seemed to be in a hurry. And then there were tourists, who didn't seem to know where they were going, or who were looking at the scenery and failed to stay in their lane. *But then*, Josh mused, *I am also a tourist. It's just that the scenery I am here to visit is different.* He didn't know what to expect. Debriefing a defector, much less a North Korean vice admiral, wasn't something he'd done before.

At Schofield, Josh drove to a specified address, an empty house reserved as quarters for visiting colonels. An armed guard with a clipboard checked his orders and ID, then ushered Josh inside. A balding man sat at a card table, in front of which was a single folding gray chair. On the desk was a STU-III, connected to an outlet in the wall.

"Captain Hamam, I'm Ike Henderson, the lead interrogator and a DIA analyst. The North Korean Navy is my area of expertise. It is my job to brief you on your upcoming interview. I remind you that any notes you take will be left with the briefing team, who will review them. The DIA will determine what can be sent via courier to Seventh Fleet."

Josh nodded. He'd more-or-less expected the DIA would try to make this difficult.

Henderson looked like a scholarly mouse, with big ears and glasses taking up much of his face. "Debriefings are the purview of trained interrogators. However, CINCPAC insisted that you be given time with Vice Admiral Pak. The purpose of this conversation is to make sure you understand the format of the debriefing. Each session is limited to a maximum of two hours and is taped. Other intelligence officers will be in the room. They will also take notes and listen to Admiral Pak's answers. They have the authority to end the session if you ask questions that are not appropriate." Henderson spoke in an emotionless monotone. "When you come back for your session, please be in civilian clothes. We're trying to keep this low key."

Josh wondered if the monotone diction was natural or acquired. "No problem."

"Captain, we've allocated one session to you. Will that be enough?"

"The honest answer is, I don't know. Until I pick his brains, I can't tell you."

Henderson nodded. "Then we will be flexible. We have you scheduled for today's last session, which starts at 1600. Will you be ready? If not, we can pick another time."

Josh looked down at his uniform. "I'll change and be ready."

Henderson nodded. "One last item, please confine your questions to only those relating to his involvement or North Korean involvement with the Kuril Island Development Corporation's facility on Simushir."

Josh nodded. "I understand. However, I would like to ask him about recent North Korean submarine operations that Seventh Fleet believes are related."

"It is my understanding submarine operations are not your area of expertise."

Josh corrected this misapprehension. "As Seventh Fleet's chief of staff for operations and plans, everything that goes on in our AOR is in my area of interest if it affects our operational planning."

Henderson frowned. "I was not told you were interested in submarine operations. Therefore, I cannot allow any questions from you on that topic."

"Even if they were in and around the central Kurils and may be related to the Kuril Island Development Corporation facility on Simushir?"

Henderson shifted in his chair. Compartments concerning the intelligence from Pak were well defined. Now this Navy captain was challenging those divisions with a strong argument.

"Mr. Henderson, I suggest you call Captain Billingham on the CINCPAC staff. I am sure he will approve any questions I have about North Korean submarine ops in support of the Kuril Island Development Corporation."

"I will do that before you come back."

"Thank you, sir."

1046 local time, Honolulu

In his BOQ room, Josh called the *Blue Ridge* and got the message that Jake Garza wanted him to call immediately. When he called the agent, Garza asked if they could meet at Master Chief Jenkins' offices, so Josh headed for Pearl immediately after hanging up. *So much for a swim in the pool or some beach time.*

He parked the rental car in a spot that was reserved for "O-6 and Above," which made showing up on time a lot easier, and headed inside.

"Glad you could meet me here." Jake Garza held out his hand, which Josh shook firmly. Then Josh faced Master Chief Jenkins.

"Good morning Captain, it's great to see you." The burly and very fit retired master chief gave Josh a playful bear hug.

"Good to see you again, Master Chief."

Jenkins escorted his two guests into a secure conference room. Josh looked at the DEA agent. "Okay, guys. What is so urgent?"

Garza pointed to two ledgers and a stack of papers on the table. "I got a mysterious package. What you see had to come from a Half Moon office safe. I have no idea who sent it to me. Josh, do you know how these were acquired?"

Josh shook his head. "No."

"I can certainly use the intel." Jake picked up a green ledger. "This book shows all their drug shipments for the past five years. This book," Jake pointed at the other green ledger, "shows what they bought and spent on Simushir Island. We'll know a lot more when they are all translated. Master Chief Jenkins' friends have the necessary language skills."

"Jake, why are you working out here rather than the DEA offices?"

"This place is secure and out of the way."

Josh's mind made the leap. *This way you don't have to worry about leaks, or answer questions about how you got them. That tells me you weren't born yesterday.*

"My two guys who just left the room are experienced at looking at this kind of stuff and figuring out what it means. I told them that if there is a leak of any kind, Master Chief Jenkins' friends will do unmentionable things to them with dull serrated knives." Josh looked at Master Chief Jenkins, who gave him a look of feigned innocence.

Jake looked through the sheets and pulled out one from the middle. "This is a list of major drug dealers in Mexico and in the U.S., with addresses and phone numbers. Some of these guys we'd identified—some we hadn't. There are dates next to some names that looked familiar, so I compared them to murders in LA and San Diego. And guess what? They matched."

Josh held out his hand for the papers. "I need copies of all this. This is what I am looking for."

Garza waved his hands over the ledgers. "I'll give you as much as I can."

Josh put the sheets he was still holding down on the table one at a time, giving him time to think. "Jake, can you give the master chief and me a few minutes alone?"

Jake glanced from one to the other. "Sure. I need to take a piss." He sauntered out.

Master Chief Jenkins closed and latched the door, then sat down.

"Master Chief, I don't know but I can guess where this came from. There are too many coincidences. Marty was in Hong Kong on his way back to the *Blue Ridge*. So, first question, if Marty is hauled in front of the long green table, will you get hit with any of the mud?"

"No, sir."

"Did you know he was going to Hong Kong?"

"Yes, sir."

"Did you know if he was going to see anyone?"

"Yes, sir. We both know the names."

Josh didn't want to ask the question that would force the master chief to either lie to him or betray a confidence. At this point, the less he knew the better, and he could never ask Marty. "I just hope this doesn't ruin a fine career."

"He knew the risks, sir. They all did. Some things matter more than careers. In this case, Truth."

1540 local time, Oahu

The drive back to Schofield Barrack gave Josh time to script questions. He suspected he already knew most of the answers, but they needed Pak's confirmation.

Josh was in a hurry to get back and was driving 75, well over the 60 mile an hour speed limit. Briefly, he imagined the conversation he would have with any police officer who pulled him over.

Police officer—"Sir, is there some emergency?"

Me—"Yes, sir, there is."

Police officer—"Would you care to tell me what it is?"

Me—"I can't, other than it is a matter of national security."

Police officer—"With all the military bases on this island, all of Oahu can say that. Please explain."

Me—"I have to question a North Korean defector who is part of a major drug ring bringing tons of illegal drugs into the U.S. every year. Officers like you have to deal with the effects of Asian Pure on the street. "

Musing about this mythical conversation almost caused Josh to miss his exit. Self-chastised, he drove at the speed limit and parked in the driveway of the house. On the horizon, dark cumulous clouds suggested that it would rain soon. He went inside, wondering if the information storms would be as violent as the brewing thunderstorms.

Overhead, a fan stirred the air. The foyer windows were closed, the drapes drawn. The room was furnished with a worn couch, a coffee table, and two armchairs that had seen better days. Josh recognized the furniture as "contemporary BOQ."

Ike Henderson introduced Grant Willow, who would be the other intelligence officer in the room. Willow was wearing a golf shirt embroidered with the silhouette of a submarine and its name *U.S.S. Parche.*

When Josh entered what appeared to be a living room, Vice Admiral Pak stood up. He was dressed in a pair of khaki slacks and a golf shirt with the Naval Air Station Barbers Point golf course logo. Josh thought it was ironic that they were, apart from the color of their golf shirts, wearing the same style clothes. It was, he thought, a uniform of sorts.

"Captain Haman, it is good to meet you. I have read your biography."

"My bio?" Josh was taken off guard.

"Oh, yes. When you were assigned to Seventh Fleet, our Russian friends sent a summary from the file they keep on you. Most impressive."

"Uh, thank you." *I guess.* "But we're not here to talk about my career."

The Simushir Island Incident

"I understand. I just thought you might like to know your enemies still take an active interest in your professional and private life."

Shit! Does that mean what I think it means? But whether or not there is an assassin assigned to take me out—or worse, my family—is a question for later in the session, or maybe a follow-up one.

"Admiral, the subject of this session is to talk about what you know about the Kuril Island Development Corporation facility on Simushir."

"I know very little, other than Kim Jong-Il directed me to provide submarines to support it."

"So, you know nothing about the facilities on the island?"

"As I said, very little."

"Vice Admiral, before I continue, I want to remind you the willingness of my country to offer you asylum is dependent on the truthfulness of your answers. If we find you are providing misleading information or lying, the United States may put you on a flight back to Beijing with a connection to Pyongyang."

"Captain, we," the Vice Admiral waved to the others in the room, "have gone over this several times. There is no need to threaten me."

Out of the corner of his eye, Josh could see Henderson start to react. "My apologies, Vice Admiral, it was not my intent to threaten, only to remind you of the conditions of this debriefing."

Josh reached into his briefcase and pulled out a file marked Top Secret/SCI/Glass Carat. "I'd like to show you some recent photos of Simushir."

Josh placed a series of eight-by-ten-inch black and white prints on the table between them. The first one showed a group of soldiers on the rim of Zavaritzk Caldera. Each successive blowup Josh put down showed a closer view until the very grainy last one. Despite the loss of resolution, Major Kim's face was recognizable.

Then he laid out photographs showing the *Osas* with their surface-to-air missiles taken on Simushir and soldiers in their Korean People's Army uniforms. Pak picked up the photo of Major Kim.

"Vice Admiral, the officer in the picture you are holding is Major Chin Hae Kim of the Korean People's Army's Special Forces. The man standing next to Major Kim is a man by the name of Ryu who has a doctorate in geology."

Josh watched Pak's face, looking for a hint of what was going on in his mind. They may have been playing poker, only Josh wasn't bluffing. He had a royal flush in spades.

"Here are several more. I apologize for the bad light, but these pallets have about 200 bricks of heroin, known as Asian Pure. The photos were taken inside the building on the north side of Broutana Bay. This picture shows one of the pallets being loaded onto a freighter by the name of *Crescent Moon*, owned by Crescent Shipping and chartered by Half Moon Trading. The ship was seized on the way to the United States, and the crew arrested."

Josh opened his briefcase and handed over a color photograph, a close-up of Major Kim. "This picture was taken a few weeks ago in my office on the *Blue Ridge* during Major Kim's debriefing after he defected."

The photo fluttered to the tabletop as the air went out of Vice Admiral Pak's lungs. Josh had the goods on Pak, and he'd just dropped the hammer. "We know you met Major Kim several times. We know you were involved in the Simushir operation up to your eyeballs; and from documents now in our possession, we know you were involved with Half Moon Trading." Josh paused. "In light of this, would you like to start telling the truth?"

Vice Admiral Pak took a deep breath and leaned back. *If they send me back to Beijing, the Chinese will turn me over to the Dear Leader. I will be tortured to death.* "If I tell you information U.S.

officials might consider criminal, will the United States' offer stay the same?"

Henderson chimed in. "Yes, assuming what you tell us checks out." Translation—the value of Pak's intelligence to national security outweighed his criminal activity.

"Then, Captain Haman, what do you want to know?"

"Let's start with how the operation was conceived?"

Pak began with Kim Il-Sung approaching Pak's father with the idea of manufacturing and selling illegal drugs as a way to generate cash for the regime. The Jangs owned opium dens throughout Korea and southern China and ran other illegal businesses, and the Paks owned and operated pharmaceutical factories, so they were ideal partners to start an illegal drug business. In Kim Il-Sung's mind, this was a way to make money for the regime and compensate two friends after his government had shut down their family businesses in the mid-1950s.

What evolved was a state-owned enterprise with two product lines. One was reverse-engineered and manufactured prescription drugs sold in third world countries at a tenth of the price of the legitimate drug. The second line was illegal drugs—uppers and downers, and heroin. Using processes developed in the fully equipped pharmaceutical factories, they had created a much purer, higher grade and much more addictive drug they named Asian Pure.

In search of more cash, first Kim Il-Sung and then his son, Kim Jong-Il, had wanted to sell the illegal drugs in the United States. Half Moon had the cover and Crescent owned the ships to bring the drugs to the U.S. David Seul set up the initial operation, but to increase their sales, they needed a partner with an existing network. Their agreement with the Sinaloa cartel required Half Moon to decimate Sinaloa's competitors. Jang offered the use of special forces soldiers trained as assassins to carry out the missions. Until Kim Il-Sung died in '94, he approved the assignments. Now, Pak said, they were approved by Kim Jong-il.

Josh asked. "How many assassins were sent to the U.S?"

"I know of three: Jintao Yi, Chin Yi Moon and Dae Ho Muk. I don't know if there are any others."

Josh handed Pak the list of names given to him by Jake Garza. "Is this the list of competitors who were eliminated? Are any of your relatives involved with Half Moon in the U.S?"

Pak took a deep breath while he decided how much he should reveal. He wanted to protect Cho. "My niece Cho Rhee handled the negotiations with Luis Padilla, the head of the Sinaloa cartel in Los Angles. She works for Half Moon and Crescent Shipping, managing all the information on payments and shipments through a law firm in Macao. I do not think she is involved in any of the killings." Pak hoped Cho was out of the U.S. by now.

"Why did they use Tokarevs? It's a very distinctive weapon, and the only real clue we had."

"That's easy. The assassins wanted our competitors to know who did the work. For these men, it is a matter of professional pride."

"Admiral, how do they get the weapons and ammunition into the U.S?"

"I believe the weapons and ammunition come in on Crescent ships. After the ship clears customs, someone from the crew delivers the pre-addressed package to one of those mailbox stores. The assassin picks it up from there. It is pretty simple."

"How did the assassins get into the U.S?"

Pak shook his head. "I don't know."

"What other relatives are involved in Half Moon and Crescent that you haven't told me about?"

"Jang has a brother who was born Gil-su Jang. He now goes by the name of David Seul."

There's another family connection! "Why did you set up the factory in Simushir?"

"It was an out-of-the-way location, where we could convert opium into heroin in large quantities without interference and ship it all over the world. We figured you Americans wouldn't pay attention to ships going and coming to Simushir. The fishing boat support facility is a cover for the factory."

"Why all the North Korean soldiers on the island?"

"Ahhhhh." Admiral Pak shook his head over tented fingers. "Originally, we sent Major Kim and a small team to explore the island and provide security. When I left, the Dear Leader was planning to deploy missiles that could attack Japan and the U.S. with chemical and nuclear warheads. That was never part of the original plan—our plan."

A silence fell over the room. Willow's face went pale. Henderson looked as though he refused to believe it. He blurted out, "Are you serious?"

The former admiral glanced at Henderson and then looked Josh straight in the eye. "Yes. It is the plan of a madman."

"Where did the *Geckos* come from?"

"The what?"

"I'm sorry. The *Osas* that were used to shoot down an American reconnaissance aircraft."

"I don't know. More than likely, Half Moon had an agent set up a dummy company to make the purchase and then dissolved it."

"So who maintains the relationship with Half Moon and the Kuril Island Development Corporation in North Korea, now that you are gone?"

Pak leaned back against the couch, hoping his answer would lead to that bastard Thaek's death. "Kim Jong-Il ordered General Jang and me to pass on everything we know about the illegal drug business to a man by the name of Kwang-sik Thaek, who is a

Deputy Minister of Safety and Security. We knew that assigning Thaek to work with us was Kim Jong-Il's first move to taking over the drug business, which meant it was time to leave. Both General Jang and I warned Half Moon. We arranged that if we were eliminated, or disappeared, Half Moon would cut off contact with the North Korean government."

"Does Thaek task the assassins now?"

"We're back to that?"

"Oh, yes, we are. My best friend's fiancée was murdered by one of these men. She was also a senior employee of our federal government. So I am interested both professionally and personally. So answer my question."

Vice Admiral Pak cocked his head and looked at Josh through half-lidded eyes. From reading the Russian dossiers, he knew he was dealing with a dangerous man. It would be better to have this man as an ally, or at least as a neutral, than as an enemy. And Pak very much wanted Thaek neutered and sent to a re-education camp where he could experience the horrors inflicted on those he'd sent there. "Yes. Thaek likes to order people killed."

"Where is General Jang now?"

"I don't know."

"Did he get out of North Korea?"

"I don't know. I hope so. I tried to warn him and provide a way."

"Will the…" Josh stumbled for the word, "the *president* of Half Moon or any of its executives talk to us, or to the British?" *We need to corroborate our evidence.*

"I doubt it. Why should they? There is no way you can compel them to speak to you. Half Moon will claim they are a legitimate business, and even if you were able to work through the maze of corporations and agents, you will never find proof they were involved in illegal drugs. Besides, they are only one of many companies providing what your countrymen are so desperate to buy. If you think heroin use is a problem, handle it at your end."

Josh put his pen down, surprised by how tired he was.

Saturday, August 5th, 1995, 0945 local time, Honolulu

Two cars were winding their way through Admiral's Row in base housing, where the high ranking officers lived. The first car was black and had two blue flags with four white stars flying from either side of its front bumper. The second vehicle, painted a dull Navy gray, followed at a discrete distance. Inside the admiral's car were two passengers: CINCPAC and a Navy captain. The captain's shoulder boards bore the silver mill rinde between two gold oak leaves insignia of the Judge Advocate General. The Navy JAG Corps adopted the mill rinde because it is the French symbol for justice, based on the old saying, "The wheels of justice grind slowly but exceedingly fine."

The black car parked in a space overlooking the harbor. Before getting out, CINCPAC turned to the other man in the back seat and said, "Stay here unless I send for you. I am hoping we can do this the easy way, not the hard way." Then the Commander in Chief, Pacific Command walked up the steps to the door and knocked.

"Admiral, this is a pleasant surprise. Please come in." Jeremiah Jeffers stepped back and opened the door.

"Thank you." CINCPAC headed toward the living room.

"What can I do for you, Admiral?"

"Is there someplace private we can talk?"

"Yes, sir, right here. Sandy is out shopping. Please have a seat. May I get you some coffee?" CINCPAC could see boxes and packing material in the dining room. The hutch where the china once was displayed was empty.

"No thanks." CINCPAC sat down and got right to the point. "Jeremiah, did you talk to a reporter at the *Washington Post?*"

Jeffers flushed. "Why are you asking?"

"Out in my car is a JAG officer from CNO's staff. There is second car with agents from the Naval Investigative Service and the FBI. Do I need to rephrase the question as an order? Until September thirtieth, you are still a rear admiral on active duty in the United States Navy."

Jeffers clasped his hands and hung his head before he looked up. "I did."

"How many conversations did you have?"

"Several."

"Several is a vague number. How many did you have?"

"Three long ones."

Wrong answer. "Investigators have proof there were more." CINCPAC let his words sink in before he asked the question he most wanted answered. "Why? Why did you do it, Jeffers?"

"Why do you think? I was angry at being forced to retire. The Navy is a military organization and the public has a right to know when we step out beyond our traditional missions. Shutting down commercial entities legally chartered in another country is not our job! We could have started a war, and the American public needed to know the truth."

"That was not your call. I'm the one the President holds accountable for operations in the Pacific theater. That's why there is a State Department representative on my staff. That's why I talk to the Chairman of the Joint Chiefs frequently. That's why I brief the President and advisors and answer their questions. My decisions and my actions were all approved by the President. And for the record, the Navy has been performing diplomatic missions since the day it was born. Simushir is just another example."

There was a long silence before Jeffers spoke. "Let us say we have a professional disagreement."

"It is more than that. You violated your oath of office by giving a reporter classified information. So let me get to the point as to why I am here. Your retirement orders have been amended. Instead of retiring as a rear admiral, upper half, you will now retire with the pay and rank of a captain. Before you object, CNO has already spoken with the Chairman of the Joint Chiefs, the Secretary of the Navy, the Secretary of Defense and the President. All have signed off on the paperwork."

"Are you telling me I am being busted two ranks?" Jeffers looked like he couldn't believe what he was hearing.

"Yes." CINCPAC paused. "You do have a choice."

"Which is?" Jeffers was struggling to contain his simmering anger.

"I tell the JAG officer out in the car you have refused to accept retirement as a captain, and you will be arrested and charged. You will remain a rear admiral up through the time the court martial makes its decision. If you win, you retire as a rear admiral. Who knows, they may agree with you once they hear the evidence. If you lose, you get whatever punishment the court imposes. The court has the power to reduce you in rank to any grade they wish, take your retirement benefits and pension away, or toss you in jail —or all three."

"How long do I have to decide?"

"When I walk out the door, I have to tell them. The CNO is hard pissed you were the source and wanted to haul you in front of a court-martial, so it took a lot of convincing on my part to give you the option."

"This is what I get after twenty-seven years of loyal service to this country and to the Navy?"

"I didn't make the calls to the *Washington Post*—you did. The higher you are in the Navy, the greater the penalty. If you'd called the reporter after you retired, the rules are different. But you made the call while you were still on active duty, and you have to live with the result. And frankly, Jeffers, your actions were not those of a patriotic, dedicated Naval Officer but of a vindictive, selfish man who believes his friends will protect him, no matter what." He wanted to ask, *What were you thinking, and how arrogant can you be?*—but didn't.

Jeffers' eyes started to water.

CINCPAC held out a blue folder. "The new orders are in here. I'll allow the retirement ceremony to go on as planned so you can preserve the fiction you are leaving the Navy as a rear admiral. The only people who will know the truth are you, whoever you tell, and the Defense Finance and Accounting Service."

Sunday, August 6th, 1995, 2203 local time, Oceanside

From where they were sitting on their deck, Josh and Rebekah had a clear view of the Pacific. The sun had already disappeared below the horizon. Rebekah snuggled into Josh's shoulder, enjoying the moment. Her long hair, now stylishly streaked with gray, cascaded over Josh's shoulders. "It is great to have you around, with no cruise scheduled."

"Amen. It's also great to be back in the States. Answering inane questions from staff weenies in the Pentagon and Hawaii was getting very, very old."

"Do you know when your new orders are going to arrive?"

"Seventh Fleet should get a call any day, and then the paperwork stream starts. There's always a chance it could be a ship based in Norfolk.

"I hope not. With Stan sick, I don't want to leave my mother alone."

While he'd been away, Rebekah's stepfather had been diagnosed with an inoperable brain tumor and given less than six months to live.

Josh spoke softly. "Admiral Maize and Admiral Greenville are trying to get me a ship based in San Diego, but there are no guarantees. We may not have a choice."

Rebekah picked up her head and looked directly in his eyes. "Yes, we do. You can retire and do something else. You have twenty-plus years of service. As you keep telling me, making captain means you've had a very good career."

"I'm not ready to hang it up yet." Josh bristled a bit. It wasn't the first time Rebekah brought up retiring from the Navy. But he understood that Rebekah wanted to stay near her mother. He was dreading the thought of helping his wife grieve for her stepfather with whom she had a strained and often contentious relationship.

"I don't mean to demand that you retire, but if the orders are not what you want, you can call it quits."

"True. I'll call the *Blue Ridge* tomorrow and see if they've heard anything. Once I know my rotation date, I'll go back and do the turnover with Marty. It shouldn't take long."

"Make it no more than two weeks on the ground." Rebekah leaned her head on his shoulders. "I miss you when you're gone."

2319 local time, Los Angeles

Through Byong-ho Sagong's organizational contacts, a source of raw heroin was found. Confident he could now supply the Sinaloas, Thaek made a call. Sagong listened in without contributing. The Sinaloas said they were unhappy with the $110,000 per kilo price Padilla had negotiated with Cho Rhee, and Thaek readily agreed to reduce it to $95,000 a kilo.

Then Thaek asked who was going tell Padilla. The Sinaloas' man said, "I'll let you deal with Padilla as part of our agreement to take out competitors. He cost us $15,000 per kilo."

By the end of the day, a package was on its way to Dae Ho Muk. As soon as he received it, Muk began watching Padilla's compound. By the end of the third day, he knew the guards' schedules and the patterns of their perimeter patrol.

He parked his battered Chevy Silverado on the dirt well off the side of the road and headed up the steep mountain toward the house. Behind him shone the lights of Los Angeles. Dressed totally in black, he was invisible as he worked his way up the hill, through scrub trees and brush. He covered the last hundred yards patiently and worked himself into a dark area near the retaining wall. Slowly, he raised his head and spotted the guard a few feet away, walking toward the far end of the house. As soon as the guard disappeared around the corner, Dae climbed over the wall and dashed to where a screened-in porch jutted out from the house.

Muk drew his *wakizashi* and pressed his back against the wall. Hearing the soft footfalls of the returning guard, he raised the short sword above his head and waited, then stepped forward and brought the blade down in a slashing motion when the guard came around the corner. The blow cut through the guard's neck, slicing through a carotid artery and a jugular vein, and nearly severed his head. He had no time to cry out.

The assassin caught the dying man and lowered him to the ground. One down. From his reconnaissance he knew there were three more. He took the fallen guard's AK-47 and ammunition, then stealthily approached the building. Slowly, he raised the latch on the door to the screened-in porch. It released with a soft click. Muk's crepe-soled boots crossed the concrete and tile floor silently. A set of French doors led to the rest of the house. Muk twisted the knob and found it not locked.

In his bedroom, Luis Padilla pushed a button to change the TV screen from the local news to his video security system. He went from one camera to the other, just in time to see a black-clad man open the French doors.

Padilla grabbed his Glock 17 9mm pistol from the drawer in his nightstand and yelled, "Salvador, there's a burglar coming into the house!"

Before Muk opened the unlocked door, he peered through the curtains and saw the back of a man's head on the couch, watching TV. His orders were to make the kill bloody to send a message, but for this man, his suppressed Tokarev was the best weapon, so as not to alert the others. Pistol in right hand, he slowly turned the knob. When the latch gave way, he pushed open the door.

Salvador Alzado had barely heard Padilla's voice over the sound from the TV, but it was enough warning for him to grab his AK-47 and stand up and scan the area—just as the French door opened and a dark figure slid through. He brought the weapon up to fire, his voice belligerent and annoyed. He spoke in Spanish. "Who the fuck are you?"

Those were the last words he would ever utter. Two bullets slammed into his chest. Alzado staggered back, jerking the trigger on the AK and sending a short burst into the couch before a third bullet entered his brain.

Muk ran toward the hallway, where the third guard, Dominque Ramos, was charging out of a room with his AK-47 pulled into his shoulder, ready to aim and fire.

Muk shoved the *wakizashi* into the guard's gut. As the man screamed in pain, Muk used his boot to shove him back to withdraw his sword. Then Muk shot him in the head.

The delay allowed the fourth guard, Jorge Castillo, to fire a hurried five-round burst from his AK-47. Muzzle rise caused all but one bullet to miss his attacker.

Muk felt a burning sensation in his abdomen as the 122-grain round, traveling at over 2,300 feet per second, shoved him backward into the wall. He forced himself forward, ignoring the pain from what he suspected could be a fatal wound, if he did not get to a hospital. His life didn't matter. He had a mission to finish; then, and only then, would he tend to his injury. Reflexes and training took over. Muk fired once, twice, and a third time. In the dim light, he saw his target stagger from the impact.

Castillo put a hand on his chest, trying to stem the blood flowing from three holes in his body while his brain told him his heart was destroyed. He looked up at Muk and, as his eyes glazed over, fell forward.

Padilla had turned off the lights, closed the door, and retreated to the corner of his bedroom that was out of line-of-sight from the doorway, yet gave him a clear view of anyone who entered. He cursed when he realized that he'd left a light on in the bathroom. With gunshots echoing in the hallway, he didn't dare run across the room to turn it off and give up his hiding place. He made sure there was a round in the chamber of his pistol and wedged himself further into the corner. He would shoot anyone who came through that door without knocking first and shouting, "Boss, are you ok?"

Muk leaned against the wall and looked down. He was losing blood, and the pain was intense. *I will not die until I kill my target.* He dumped out the partially emptied magazine; better to have a fully loaded one in case he needed more than two or three shots. The fresh one almost slipped out of his bloody hand, but he jammed it home and released the slide to chamber a bullet. He took a deep breath and walked slowly toward the closed door at the end of the hall, stumbling a little. The *wakizashi* slipped out of his bloody hand. Instead of picking it up, he pressed his left hand to his stomach, trying to stem the flow of blood.

The Simushir Island Incident

There was no time for subtlety. Muk banged the door open and lurched forward. Two bullets went hissing past his shoulder. Muk fired in the direction of the muzzle flashes and tried to move to make himself a harder target. Moving hurt. Another bullet zinged by his head. Seeing the form of a man, he fired a fast double tap at the shape—then another. Muk saw his target recoil from the impact of the four bullets, one after another.

Luis Padilla spat blood as he breathed. Blood was oozing out of holes in his chest and stomach. He put one hand on the end table to help keep himself upright as he aimed for one last shot. He managed to stand long enough to see the back of his assailant's head fly off as his last bullet entered the man's eye. As he fell dying to the floor, Luis Padilla had the satisfaction of knowing he'd killed the man who killed him.

Monday, August 7th, 1995, 1115 local time, Honolulu
Jake Garza gazed out his window, watching the activity in the bay and trying to decide where he would go for lunch. His direct line rang. Very few outside DEA headquarters had this number.

"Special Agent Garza?"

"You've got him. Who's this?"

"This is Lieutenant Doug Proudfoot from the Los Angeles Police Department's Special Investigations Unit."

"What can I do for you?"

"Our local DEA liaison officer says you have a special interest in North Koreans who kill people with a Tokarev. Is that correct?"

"Yes, it is." Garza pulled his feet off his desk and flipped the sheets on the yellow pad to a blank page. "What do you have?"

"Last night, Luis Padilla, the local head of the Sinaloas, was killed here in LA." Proudfoot described the scene he'd visited earlier this morning.

"What do you have on the shooter?"

"His driver's license says his name is Dae Ho Muk. Heard of him?"

"He's on a list we have." Garza shared some of what he'd learned from David Seul and Admiral Pak. "Muk's death means that two of the three are dead. But we have no idea where the third, Jintao Yi, is."

1722 local time, Long Beach

Cho Rhee had selected a local channel for some background noise as she changed into something suitable for a workout out at her favorite dojo, a few blocks from her house. The words "shootout at the home of one of the leaders of the Sinaloa cartel" got her attention, and she strode, half-dressed, into the living room. An excited reporter was standing by the front gate of Luis Padilla's home, telling the world how the maid found six bodies when she came to work that morning. The station cut to photos of the faces of the dead men, one of whom was identified as Dae Ho Muk, a Korean.

Cho Rhee decided not to go to the dojo.

No one seeing her calm face and relaxed posture would guess how fast and furiously she was thinking. Why had Padilla been targeted? She came to the conclusion that someone new was controlling Muk, and had different plans for the distribution of Asian Pure. *Where does this leave me?*

Alarmed, Cho set in motion a plan she'd created months ago. Her first act was to confirm a first-class seat to Singapore, using a ticket with open dates. There was a seat available on the flight leaving just after midnight. Swiftly, she packed three bags. Then she left a message on her landlord's answering machine, saying she was moving out, the keys were on the kitchen counter, and he could keep the deposit and anything in the apartment.

The Simushir Island Incident

Friday, August 11th, 1995, 1336 local time, U.S.S. Blue Ridge

Marty Cabot studied the fax he'd just been handed, from the U.S. Consulate in Hong Kong. It was a recent article from the *International Herald Tribune.*

KURIL ISLAND PROJECT SHUT DOWN

HONG KONG—The Kuril Island Development Corporation announced it was stopping development of the Simushir Island facility. Earlier this year, the company started an ambitious project to create a fishing boat support facility on Broutana Bay at the northern end of the uninhabited island. Construction work started immediately in order to have the former Soviet sub base ready for operations this fall. These plans have been cancelled due to much higher than anticipated costs of readying the facility and economic difficulties facing its principal investor.

The press release from the Kuril Island Development Corporation also stated that the company was going to evacuate the island and minimize any impact to the island's fragile environment. The heavy equipment delivered to the facility at Broutana Bay will be left on the island until a decision can be made about its disposition.

Deputy Minister Valerie Dimitriov from the Russian Federation's Maritime Administration said, "The Russian Federation is disappointed the project will not be completed. Russia will take possession of the new buildings and any remaining equipment left on the island as per the terms of the lease."

When asked, the Deputy Minister said he believed all the Kuril Island Development Corporation personnel will be off the island by the end of August. However, he would not comment on why he thought the Kuril Island Development Corporation abandoned the project, or whether there were armed forces from another country on the island. Nor would he comment on whether he thought the shooting down of a U.S. electronic surveillance airplane on July 9th had led to the decision by the Kuril Island Development Corporation to shut the project down.

Marty scratched his head. Once Seventh Fleet verified the place was shut down, it would end its surveillance. The best way to find out what the company had left behind was to go to Broutana Bay.

He badly wanted to find out if the SA-8s were still there, as well as the drug lab. He wondered if Admiral Maize would sponsor another reconnaissance mission.

1344 local time, Broutana Bay

Managing Director Lee made sure he was the last person on the island. He double-checked the placement of the plastic explosive, then shot holes in the bottles of chemicals so they would leak on the floor and feed the flames. Then he set the timer. The two-hour fuse gave him plenty of time to drive from the settlement to the pier and board the last ship.

1548 local time, on board Aphrodite Five Three

Marty was busy sketching out the operations and reconnaissance plan for a return visit to Simushir when the phone on his desk jangled. A radio call had come in from a four engined EP-3E, Aphrodite Five Three, assigned to take pictures of Broutana Bay. Marty said he'd be right over.

"Aphrodite Five Three, this is Blackbeard November Six Actual, go ahead."

"Blackbeard, Aphrodite Five Three is passing twenty-five miles east of Simushir Island. There's a ship leaving the harbor, and we just saw an explosion on the northwest corner of Broutana Bay. Now there's a fire burning up one of the buildings. We're pretty sure the freighter is one of Crescent Shipping's boats. Copy?"

"Aphrodite Five Three, Blackbeard copies. Did you get a good view of everything around the harbor?"

"Blackbeard, Aphrodite Five Three, that's affirmative. The SA-8s are parked in a row in the sheds. The earth-moving and construction equipment are parked in rows on the helipad."

"Please expedite getting us the imagery." Marty hung up the handset. He still thought that a trip back to Simushir was warranted.

Saturday, August 12th, 1995, 2317 local time, Escondido

It was a terrible analogy, but the thought passed through Josh's head that with Sasha out on a date, and Sara and Sean spending the night at the houses of their friends, the Haman's four-bedroom house was as quiet as a morgue.

"How about a refill before we go to bed?" Rebekah leaned away from their cuddle so Josh could get up during a commercial break. They were watching a broadcast of the movie *In Harm's Way*. Both could recite many lines, but they still loved watching the old John Wayne movie about World War II.

"Sure."

Josh was in the kitchen, emptying a wine bottle into their glasses, when Rebekah heard a click. Figuring that someone had forgotten to lock it properly, she headed toward the door. That's when she saw the handle turn and the door crack open, just enough for stainless step forceps to reach for the safety chain.

"Josh!" Rebekah screamed, "A burglar!"

A man clothed in black, face covered with a ski mask, flung open the door and stormed in. Rebekah grabbed the floor lamp next to her and swung it like a baseball bat. It slammed into the intruder's mid-section and sent his pistol flying across the room. She aimed the bottom of her foot to buckle his knee, but missed and struck his thigh. Nonetheless, the dual blows staggered the man.

Rebekah stepped back and swung the lamp again, this time in an upper cut motion to catch the intruder in the neck and jaw. Before he could recover, Josh tackled him. Both men were momentarily stunned when they slammed against the wall, caving in the sheetrock.

Jintao Yi recovered first and hit both sides of Josh's head with the base of his palms at the same time. Horribly disoriented, Josh involuntarily relaxed his bear hug. Yi shoved the taller, heavier man off and stepped back, his hands raised and his feet positioned as if he was about to engage in a karate match. Josh's stomach churned and fear spread through his body. He was sure he would lose in hand-to-hand combat against a North Korean Special Forces soldier.

Yi looked around for his pistol. It was lying a few feet away, halfway between Josh and Rebekah—whose angry, defiant body language warned him this was not going to be an easy battle. Jintao reached behind his back, confident the *wakizashi* would end this fight in his favor. The man was his first target. He would kill the woman later. Slowly, very slowly as payback for the blow from the lamp.

"Here!!!" Rebekah tossed Josh the remains of the lamp, now nothing more than a five-foot metal pole with a baseplate. Josh moved forward. The assassin was waving his sword in small circles. With blinding speed, he engaged. But Josh had practiced kendo and still had the reflexes of a former Olympic-class skier. Each of Jintao's strikes were marked by a clanging sound as the short sword banged off the steel. Josh's jabs forced Yi back and kept the *wakizashi* from slicing him open.

Yi's focus on Josh gave Rebekah an opening. She snatched up a table lamp, pulling the plug from the wall socket in the process and plunging the room into darkness, and threw it at the North Korean's head. He dodged instinctively and it hit his shoulder. The lamp shattered, scattering broken glass on the floor, and Jintao Yi retreated again. Strobes from the black-and-white movie on the TV gave a fluctuating illumination to three grim faces.

"You must be Jintao Yi," Josh said it in a quiet but firm voice, keeping the pole pointed at the North Korean and trying not to sound afraid. He wanted to buy time.

The North Korean soldier cocked his head. "How do you know my name?"

"I know all about you... how you got here... who controls you... why you are here." He shifted his position to bring himself closer to a long, thin black object leaning against the wall in the corner behind a large overstuffed chair. He was supposed to have hung it on their living room wall, along with the framed inscription, but hadn't gotten around to it despite Rebekah's nagging. She thought it would be a great conversation piece. "Did Deputy Minister Thaek send you to kill me?"

"Yes. And your family."

Josh slid his hands to one end of the metal rod and threw it at Jintao Yi. The assassin knocked it aside, but his movement gave Josh time to reach the honey-do. As he drew the *katana* out of its wooden sheath, he felt again how well balanced the sword was.

It had been made in the traditional manner of heating the steel, hammering it, re-heating the metal and folding it over in layers before they are beaten flat again. Captain Nagumo had presented the traditional weapon of the Japanese warrior in an elaborate, somber ceremony attended by senior officers from the Japanese Maritime Self-Defense Forces and the Seventh Fleet staff. He remembered Nagumo's words as he presented him with the sword. "This is Japan's gift to a true samurai."

The gift had been in recognition of his progress at Kendo, which he had taken up early in his tour of duty in Japan at Nagumo's suggestion. Nagumo had said Kendo—the modern version of *kenjutsu,* the Japanese art of sword fighting—was how he maintained his warrior spirit. After watching Josh use a test sword, the old sword maker said according to Hitoshi's translation, "His technique is crude, but effective." Later, when Josh tested the blade that was to become his *katana* against three straw dummies, the sword maker noted, "He is beginning to polish in his skills."

The North Korean froze at the sight of the long, gleaming *katana* held in a ready position. *Can this American really use it, or is he just mimicking stances he's seen in movies? I think it is the latter.* "You will lose this battle, and I will kill your whole family." Jintao lunged at Josh, thinking Haman's *katana* would make a wonderful trophy. Thaek had told him to make an example of the Navy captain, and killing his family would earn him a large bonus.

Josh's hands were positioned on the handle to maximize the striking power of the weapon. He parried the lunge and following strike. "We'll see." Josh side-stepped around the chair into an open area in the living room, reminding himself this was not a kendo dojo drill, but a real sword fight. He hoped his crude technique was indeed, as the sword maker had said, effective. "Rebekah," he called out, "get my .45 and call the police!"

Jintao Yi's first *shitake-waza,* or attack move, had been designed to wound and maybe unnerve the American. He dismissed Josh's first parry as luck. Yi moved in for a quick kill. Short sword versus long sword was something they'd practiced in North Korea with bamboo swords called *shinai,* and he'd always won.

Josh parried Jintao Yi's attacks by stepping back and to the side in *nuki-waza* defensive moves. After each strike, he made sure his sword was positioned to threaten the North Korean. Rather than carry out his favorite move—in which, after he stopped an attack, he reversed his grip and struck from the opposite side—Josh held his ground. *I am not going to remain defensive if I see an opening. Nor am I going to let him slice me open.*

The clashing blades met and crossed in a series of thrusts, counter thrusts and slashes, and Josh reacted without thinking. Instinct and hours of training in the dojo was, at least for now, keeping him alive.

As they slashed and moved, the two men swapped sides of the room. In a sudden flash of light from the TV screen, Josh could see the North Korean's left sleeve wetting with blood.

Maybe all those beatings and lessons in the dojo were worth it. I got the first cut; but be careful, asshole! Remember Marty's favorite saying about knife fights—"Everyone gets cut. The winner is the one with the fewest deep ones!!!"

Jintao, feeling the pressure of time, attacked. Josh stepped back at an angle and, with a diagonal upward movement of the *katana,* knocked the *wakizashi* off to the side and followed with a downward right-to-left slash. He felt the sword slow down before it came free, and he brought it back into a near vertical position in front on his right side, ready to defend against an attack.

The stunned look on Jintao's blood-spattered face made Josh pause. Blood was pumping from the severed aorta and from the deep slash down through his breastbone. The point of the Korean's *wakizashi* stuck in the floor momentarily, then the short sword tumbled over as Jintao Yi's dying body fell into a growing pool of blood. Josh looked at his *katana.* It was dripping blood on the carpet.

* * *

After the police arrived, Josh wrapped his arms around Rebekah and they huddled in their bedroom while the medical examiner removed Yi's body. The detective recorded their statements and watched how they, once the area was cleared, recreated the fight. The carpet squished with undried blood as Josh went through the steps and moves he had made. When the police were finished, the Hamans were told they couldn't stay in their house because it was now a crime scene. His *katana* was taken as evidence, and Josh wondered if he would ever see it again.

Fortunately, Sara and Sean were with friends. Rebekah called the families and explained the situation. Sasha returned, and the three of them packed clothes and toiletries for the whole family. It was well after three in the morning when they walked into a two-room suite at the Hilton Hotel, near San Diego's airport. They would stay there until the police finished their investigation, the house repaired and cleaned, and the carpet replaced.

Josh couldn't sleep. Around five a.m., he eased himself out of bed and went into the bathroom. The image he saw in the mirror was of a haggard, tired man.

On missions I put myself in danger, and I know the risks. When I recited the oath, I wrote a blank check to the Navy, saying that I will defend the Constitution and the United States. The implication was that I would do so to my last breath.

An attack on my family is another matter. They never took that oath. I can accept that I may die in service to my country, but if they were killed as a result of my Navy career and I survived, I don't think I could ever forgive myself.

Josh leaned on the bathroom counter and continued staring at the image in the mirror.

This attack was along the lines of what the old KGB would do. Luckily, none of us were physically hurt. Hopefully, it will not cause my children any long-term emotional harm. They are old enough to know what I do for a living and, despite the kidding, they are proud of me. But the risk of being the child of a naval officer was an abstract idea until last night.

Rebekah understands the significance of the oath I took. She was born in Israel, her father was killed in one of its many wars. Death of members of the armed forces is the price one pays for freedom. If she hadn't been so alert and so fierce, Yi might have accomplished his mission. Still, she was shaken, and so was I.

An old feeling, one Josh had felt when his first wife Natalie was murdered, returned. It had simmered in him and never gone away until he'd pulled the trigger that ended the life of Nikolai Volkov, the KGB officer who'd ordered the hit that killed her, their unborn child, and her parents.

Josh could feel the rage and anger boiling up. He wondered how would he deal with it. Would it destroy his life, or could he move on?

It took me 17 years, luck and opportunity to reach Volkov. How long would it take me to get Thaek? Am I going to try?

"A penny for your thoughts?"

Josh turned to see his wife standing in the doorway of the bathroom, wearing nothing but an open robe. Josh opened his arms so they could hold each other. Later, they would talk. It would be painful—but necessary.

Sunday, August 13th, 1995, 1248 local time, San Diego

The Cohen's house in La Jolla was set back from the street. Typical of many three-bedroom homes in La Jolla, it had a large covered patio in the back, where—weather permitting—the family congregated. Tonight, the adults were eating dinner on the patio. A smoldering coldness forestalled any conversation other than what was needed to pass food around the table.

Stan Cohen sat at the head of the table. He was drawn and pale, showing the effects of the cancer that was sapping the life out of him. He looked over his shoulder to make sure his grandchildren were inside, then he turned on Josh, eyes filled with hatred. "You almost got my daughter and grandchildren killed. How dare you let that happen?"

Josh didn't answer, knowing anything he said would infuriate his father-in-law, who lashed out at everyone and everything. Stan was going through the natural phases, and now he was at anger, knowing the end of his life was near and not wanting to die. He had not yet come to acceptance. Josh wondered if Stan ever would, in the brief time remaining to him.

"Answer me. Do you want to share your death-wish with your family?"

"That's not true and you know it."

"Well, if this government didn't provoke countries, we wouldn't have people out there trying to kill you, now would we?"

"This had nothing to do with U.S.-North Korean relations or the lack of them. This is about putting a major heroin producer out of business."

"Oh, so now you are in the narcotics law enforcement business? Is there nothing you war-mongers don't want to take over?" Stan was a graduate of the University of California at Berkeley and, in 1953, had protested the war in Korea. Fifteen years later, he'd protested the one in Vietnam. Several times he'd been jailed for civil disobedience, and he believed his record was one reason none of the big accounting firms had wanted to hire him. He and several of his anti-war friends had opened a CPA practice, and had included in the partner agreement a provision that none of them could be fired for protesting a war. His opposition to all things military was core to his opposition of Josh dating, and then marrying, his stepdaughter.

"Stan, one of the missions of the United States Navy is to support law enforcement agencies."

The Simushir Island Incident

His stepfather-in-law snarled. "Everywhere you go, death and destruction follow. Your first wife was assassinated, and now you've endangered my daughter and grandchildren, and that is *totally unacceptable*. This will never end. They will always be in danger. I will go to my grave knowing they may soon follow me long before their time."

Josh didn't say anything. The truth was, he was afraid the North Koreans would try again.

Stan Cohen took a long swallow from his glass of iced tea. "I want you and Rebekah to get a divorce. If you don't, I will spend whatever it takes to get a court to force you two apart. I've changed my will so any property Rebekah gets from my estate is on the condition the two of you are no longer married or living together. The lawyers will file the lawsuit on Monday. The sad part is, I won't be around to see you two split. If I were still alive when it happens, it would be the happiest day of my life. My lawyers and I think we can get a judge to agree you have put my daughter and her children in mortal danger too many times and end the marriage to ensure their safety."

"I don't think that is a good idea. I don't think you can get a court to force us to separate." Josh responded. He didn't want to ask if Stan's wife Leah would carry out the threat.

"I think I can. There's enough evidence. Your first wife and her mother were collateral damage when the KGB killed her father. This could happen to my Rebekah and my grandchildren. I think a court will agree this is not a healthy home environment for kids."

Rebekah faced her stepfather. "Stan, I won't divorce Josh, and I don't think Mom will continue pursuing this obsession of yours. You've tried to break us up ever since we started dating. Every year it's a new scheme. Stop it. Enjoy knowing Josh and I are happily married and have given you three wonderful grandchildren. Why ruin that?" She squeezed Josh's hand as she spoke. "If you make any effort to try to force us apart and don't change your will back to what it was, you will never see me or your grandchildren again before you die."

"What do you mean by that?"

"To you, it will be the same as if we were dead."

From the doorway to the kitchen, Leah screamed. "Stop it! All of you!"

Leah came over and stood in front of her husband. "Stan, I will not allow you to break up this family because you hate Josh. For years, you have been searching and praying for a way to get him out of your life. You've wasted thousands of dollars in legal fees. Now you're dying, and do you want them to remember your hate? Instead, you should want to spend as much time as you can with them. You should want to be remembered as someone who enjoyed their happiness—not someone who tried to ruin it."

Stan looked at Josh, not at Leah. "The best way to protect my daughter and my grandchildren is to get this bastard out of our life."

"Stan, let me remind you that Rebekah is *my* daughter. You never adopted her after we were married. Josh is *my* son-in-law, and his children are *my* grandchildren. I will *NOT* let you destroy this family. Period."

"We need to rid this family of this, this militaristic cancer! There is no other way we can ensure the safety of my—*our*—grandchildren and our daughter."

Leah tossed the dishtowel on the table. "Stan, I've had enough of your bullshit. If you don't change your will back to what it was and cancel this lawsuit, you will find yourself very alone for the last few months you have in this world. I will take you to a hospice and not visit you, so you can face death by yourself. Remember that if you sign those papers."

Chapter 16: DÉJÀ VU ALL OVER AGAIN

Monday, August 28th, 1995, 0730 local time, Washington D.C.

Mr. Ki-Jung Ka, formerly Kim Sun Pak, resplendent in a new charcoal gray Brooks Brothers suit, light blue shirt and red-striped tie, entered the lobby of a modern office building on the corner of North Highland Street and 11th Street North in Arlington, Virginia. The building was the headquarters of the Center for Naval Analyses, which had agreed to hire him. Before taking Pak on as an analyst on the North Korean Navy and politics, the center had reached a complicated internal government funding agreement so his stipend and benefits were paid by three parties—the CIA, DIA and the Navy—and all three would sponsor the Paks' applications for U.S. citizenship.

As part of the agreement, the former North Korean admiral filed a complete financial statement with the CIA, detailing all his assets and their location, and terminating his financial relationship with Half Moon. He would also have to file taxes with the IRS and provide the returns to his employer.

The last conditions of the Paks' asylum agreement were that they could not leave the D.C. area without the permission of the

CNA, and all contacts with foreign nationals must be reported. As long as the Dear Leader was alive, Pak would spend the rest of his life looking over his shoulder, waiting for an assassin from North Korea to kill him. His former Dear Leader was relentless in hunting down and killing high level defectors, no matter what the public relations cost. *Would I become one of them?* Over time, he hoped, that fear and threat would go away.

Assuming they met all the terms and conditions of their agreement, three years from the day he began work at the Center for Naval Analyses, the Paks would become American citizens. Because neither Kim Sun's wife, So-yi Pak, nor his daughter, Eun-mi, had attended medical schools whose accreditation was recognized in the U.S., they could not practice medicine. To earn new medical degrees, both women enrolled in courses so they could apply for internships and then residencies in their medical specialties.

Thursday, September 7th, 1995, 1000 local time, San Diego

A little over four weeks after the sword fight, the cancer in Stanley Cohen's brain won. A simple, varnished wood coffin containing his remains rested at the bottom of the grave. Its only decoration was a wooden Star of David, in a darker stain, glued to the top.

During the last days of his life, Stan had kept his feelings about Josh to himself. He hadn't wanted to lie in the ground forgotten.

Josh stood at the head of the grave between his wife and mother-in-law, with his arms around their waists. As they listened to each of Stan's three partners say a few words, he pulled them close. The eulogies over, the rabbi led Leah, Rebekah and those standing around the grave in the Kaddish, the traditional Jewish prayer for the dead.

The Simushir Island Incident

In Hebrew, the words have a simple, unforgettable rhythm to them…*Yitgaddal veyitqaddash shmeh rabba be'alma di vra khir'uteh*…Josh could recite the 36 verses of the prayer by heart. He had said it every day for a year after his first wife was murdered, and it was seared into his memory. Both Josh and Rebekah believed everyone has someone to mourn. Today, it was someone very close.

Rebekah leaned on Josh as they got to the last verses. *Oseh shalom bimromav, hu berakhamav ya'ase shalom alenu, v''al kol yisra'el, v''imru amen.* The hardest part was coming next.

Josh steadied Leah while she pushed the shovel into the loose mound of dirt and then dumped it onto the casket. The dull, hollow thuds from the clods of dirt resonated as they rose from the grave. He could feel his mother-in-law cringe in emotional pain as she heard the thumps echo through the coffin. Leah started with a load in each corner before tossing several onto the center of the coffin. When the coffin was almost covered by dirt, her tears had stopped. Satisfied with her share of the work, Leah handed the shovel to her daughter.

Rebekah did what she had to do. She plunged shovel into dirt and dumped the first load onto the barest spot. A second followed, then several more, each one covering a bare area. Rebekah looked down at the coffin, now covered with an uneven layer of dirt, then up to the sky. "Stan, I thought I would never say this, but I love you and will miss arguing with you."

* * *

As a psychiatrist, Leah specialized in grief counseling, and now she was trying to come to grips with losing her second husband and deciding what to do next with her own life. She was wondering if she should retire or continue practicing. Leah took the advice she gave patients—see a grief counselor and wait at least six months to a year before making major decisions. Waiting took the pressure off. Even without the insurance payoff and the settlement from Stan's partners, money was not an issue. Self-worth, while adjusting to being single again and keeping busy, was.

In the midst of helping his wife and her mother deal with their loss, Josh's career in the Navy marched on. One afternoon he got a call from the Bureau of Naval Personnel in Washington, D.C. Josh was being ordered to report to the 13-week Prospective Commanding Officer's School at the Naval War College in Newport, Rhode Island. The class started on September 18th and ended on December 15th.

His ship would be the amphibious assault ship *Tarawa* that would begin workups for a Pacific deployment in the middle of next year. Its homeport was San Diego. The change of command would take place in mid-January after he completed the PCO school.

The commanding officer tour was a mixed blessing. It was good for his career; and, to some extent, it restored the rhythm of their life as a Navy family. But Rebekah knew, from experience, that Josh would be consumed by the challenges of taking a ship to sea as its commanding officer. She dreaded being once again mom and dad to their three kids while he was gone for six months, but this time, she had an ace in the hole.

After Stan's death, they made Leah a bigger part of their family's everyday life. It was a way for both women to deal with their grief. Now Leah didn't have to ask about her grandkids' activities, she participated in them on a regular basis, and it gave new purpose to her life.

Saturday, December 16th, 1995, San Diego

The Simushir Island Incident

Rebekah picked up Josh at the airport in San Diego, hugging him tight and kissing him with three months of stored up passion. Instead of heading straight home, they made some stops along the way to do some shopping for Hanukah. When they opened the door to their restored home, the message light was flashing on the phone. Josh pushed the "play" button. The rear admiral in DC had left his home phone number, asking Josh to call him as soon as possible. Josh made the call, while Rebekah put groceries and gifts away. When she returned to the living room, Josh faced her, a stunned expression on his face. Rebekah waited for him to tell her what the call was about.

"The admiral asked if I could take over command of the *U.S.S. Peleliu* immediately, here in San Diego. Its CO just died of a heart attack. *Peleliu* is scheduled to leave on deployment on February 7th."

"Oh. What did you tell him?"

"I said I'd need a few days to get my clothes cleaned and celebrate with my family."

Rebekah didn't know whether to congratulate her husband or burst into tears. A February deployment meant Josh would miss Sean's graduation from high school. But this was exactly what he'd worked for. Ship command. She couldn't not be happy for him. And she knew Sean would be too.

Tuesday, December 26th, 1996, 0700 local time, San Diego

Commissioned in 1980, *Peleliu* was the last amphibious assault ship of the *Tarawa* class to be built. With a loaded displacement of 39,400 tons, the ship—named after the bloody battle for the island of Peleliu—was about the size of a World War II *Essex*-class aircraft carrier.

Josh stopped at the pier end of the gangway that led up to *Peleliu's* quarterdeck. He put his briefcase onto the concrete pier and looked at the 820-foot long, Navy gray ship that towered over him. From where he stood, he could see men and women moving boxes from where they were stacked on the aircraft elevator into the ship through the open doors into the hangar deck. On the flight deck, he caught glimpses of men and women jogging.

His emotions went from the gamut of excitement to fear and self-doubt to remorse, because in a few weeks *Peleliu* was deploying. Once again, he would be leaving Rebekah who, while he was gone, would play the role of mother and father; and he would miss six months of his children's young lives.

Taking the 50+ officers and 900 enlisted men that made up the crew and 1,800 Marines in the 11th Marine Expeditionary Unit to sea on *Peleliu* for six months was going to challenge his skills as a leader and as a naval officer. Just running through the scenarios of what he might face was sobering.

Yet Josh was excited, because he realized that once he stepped onto *Peleliu's* quarterdeck, he was about to realize a life- and career-long dream of commanding a ship. Getting to this point was the culmination of hard work, courage, luck and admittedly, help. Not just from officers with whom he served, but also from Rebekah, who'd steadfastly supported him throughout his Navy career.

Peleliu was considered a major command, one of the best equipped amphibious assault ships on the planet. Being selected as its commanding officer was a giant step forward in his navy career. If he screwed up by running *Peleliu* aground, or by banging the amphibious assault ship into a pier, or worse, colliding with another ship, or, or, or… his career in the Navy was effectively over. The possibilities for a major mishap were endless. On the other hand, if the ship did well, he would, in all probability, be selected for admiral.

The Simushir Island Incident

His job was to lead and do his best to accomplish whatever tasking *Peleliu* was given.   That was the goal; and with that thought, Josh took a deep breath, did a cursory self-inspection of his khakis, and started up the brow.

At the top of the *Peleliu's* gangway, Josh saluted the officer of the deck and handed her his green ID card. Lieutenant Junior Grade Kathy Heller suddenly realized she was the first person on the ship to meet their new skipper. "Welcome aboard, sir. We've been expecting you. I'll ring the executive officer."

She nodded to the petty officer standing the watch, who keyed the ship's first main communication system and blew into his whistle, known as a bosun's pipe. When the distinctive, high pitched warbling of "All Hands" died down, the bosun's mate rang the bell on the side the quarterdeck. The petty officer spoke into the microphone. *"Peleliu* arriving."

The week's *Navy Times* had run an obituary about Josh's predecessor, a Vietnam War veteran who'd flown H-3s and had picked up a Gemini space capsule after it splashed down in the Atlantic. In the list of changes of command, the publication noted Captain Joshua Haman had assumed command of *Peleliu.*

Thursday, February 29th 1996, 0916 local time, Mayang-do, DPRK
When Lieutenant Commander Sang-mi Seomun arrived at fleet headquarters for a pre-sail meeting with the flotilla commander, the commanders of S-207 and S-211 were already present. All three commanders had taken their submarines on exercises in the area off the Russian coast in the East Sea.

Their flotilla commander entered the room, accompanied by a civilian smoking a cigarillo. The commanders exchanged surprised glances as they stood. Submarine missions were supposed to be top secret. The flotilla commander had a grim look on his face as he introduced Deputy Minister Thaek from the Ministry of State

Security. Seomun hated the secret police and everything they stood for. Thaek's presence in the room made him uncomfortable.

Thaek stubbed out what remained of his cigarillo and unrolled a map on the conference table, then outlined a detailed plan that Seomun had to admit was a well-thought-out ambush. There was no explanation of why this particular target was a target of interest. Seomun wondered if any further details would be included in his sealed sailing orders, which he had to open in the presence of the political officer once they were at sea.

Tuesday, March 4th, 1996, U.S.S. Peleliu, *at sea off Okinawa*

At first Austin Rankin, a Navy commander and *Peleliu's* Executive Officer, was wary of his new skipper. He'd heard that *some* highly decorated aviators were assholes. He'd never been in combat himself, and often wondered how he would perform.

But this new commander seemed almost embarrassed by the ribbons he'd earned. Most of the time, rather than wear his seven rows of ribbons, his skipper just wore the minimum allowed by regulations—the first three rows. At the top were the blue and gold ribbon of a Navy Cross with a single silver star, signaling a second award; a recently awarded Legion of Merit for his leadership and performance as a member of the Seventh Fleet staff; and the blue, white and red ribbon for the Silver Star medal with two little silver stars, indicating three awards. Many of the Marine Aviators on board were Vietnam vets who'd earned Distinguished Flying Crosses and Air Medals. In Haman's "rack," they were on the second row.

As soon as he took command, Josh went all over the ship, talking to the sailors in his command and hearing, firsthand, what they did. During the first week, he had a chiefs-only meeting and one with just the first-class petty officers, no officers or chiefs. Later, he met with the E-5s and below in three separate meetings.

In each one, he explained what he planned and took questions. Notes he took during the meetings led to action items for the ship's department heads. Even at sea, he'd leave the bridge to talk with members of his crew, as well as with those Josh often called, "my honored guests"— the Marines aboard *Peleliu.*

Josh began holding drills while the ship was still in port. On his third day aboard, he started with a counter-terrorism drill. It caught the rapid response team by surprise and earned their leader an unpleasant one-on-one meeting with the ship's captain. Three or four times a day, there was some type of drill. Early on, Josh Haman led the debrief on what went right and what went wrong during the drill.

Once they were underway, the drills got more intense and complicated. Two days out of San Diego, en route to Hawaii for the Operational Readiness Inspection, several officers complained through their department heads that they didn't like the way Josh was pushing their departments. Their comments led to one-on-one meetings with *Peleliu's* new skipper where their concerns were addressed, or they were told to get their shit together and do their jobs or they would be replaced.

By the end of the second day of drills, Rankin realized his captain was using the scenarios to teach his subordinates how to think and operate under pressure and not to follow procedures like robots. The skipper gave several officers who didn't meet his standards a second chance, and if they failed again, they were reassigned. As Captain Haman reminded his officers and chiefs in meetings, combat is a very unforgiving environment. Nothing goes exactly as planned, and a damaged ship's systems don't fail the way they do in the manuals. In critical roles, he wanted only those he could count on.

Officers who initially doubted Josh's approach came to admire his style. The most junior sailors pushed their peers and superiors to be better. Pride, built on confidence, filled the *Peleliu's* passageways, and the crew worked as an efficient team. All of this made it easy to be the ship's executive officer. Along the way, Commander Austin Rankin was learning lessons in leadership he'd never learned at the Naval Academy. They were, he realized, lessons he would be able to put to good use, not only if and when he got his own command, but more immediately.

Peleliu's first stop was Pearl Harbor, where they were to participate in the battle group operational readiness inspection (ORI) before heading west to participate in exercises. A ship or task force that failed would not be allowed to continue westward until they made a satisfactory grade. For COs, failure could be career ending.

Josh used the 2,600-mile transit from San Diego to Hawaii to test his crew and watch how his officers and men performed. At the end of each drill, he picked a department, gave them a scenario and asked what they were going to do and why. He wanted to see what kind of crew he'd inherited, and the "But-I-just-took-command!" excuse would be no excuse for failing an ORI.

The ORI lasted three long days, over which duration Josh managed to snag about 6 hours of sleep total. *Peleliu* didn't pass the ORI—it aced it. In an announcement, Josh congratulated the crew and gave credit to his predecessor for preparing them well. Three days of liberty at Pearl Harbor for the crew followed, before *Peleliu*, along with its escorts, departed Hawaii. Next stop was Okinawa for detailed briefings on an exercise with the South Koreans called Foal Eagle.

Beginning in 1976, the South Koreans and the Americans had held a large annual joint exercise known as Team Spirit. One of its major events was an amphibious landing on the east coast of South Korea which was both a practice assault and a reminder to the North Koreans that the U.S. Navy could land a sizable force on the

The Simushir Island Incident

Korean peninsula. In 1992, Team Spirit had been cancelled. The exercise was carried out in 1993, but then cancelled again the next year by President Clinton as a carrot to the North Koreans while he negotiated a nuclear arms deal. In 1994, Team Spirit was replaced with a series of command-post exercises called Reception, Staging, Onward Movement, and Integration of Forces, RSOMI for short, along with a smaller scale series of exercises involving men, ships, and airplanes. RSOMI was replaced by an exercise called Foal Eagle in 1995. *Peleliu,* along with a battalion landing team and 30 Marine Air Group 33 helicopters, was going to be one of the exercise's main participants for Foal Eagle '96.

And then, just as they left Okinawa, word came down that Foal Eagle '96 was cancelled. *Peleliu* and the supporting carrier task force were assigned to conduct training off the east coast of Korea that would include inserting and extracting Marine reconnaissance teams. The ship was instructed to be prepared to conduct an amphibious assault on short notice. Seventh Fleet designated Josh as Commander, Task Group 76.1.5; his ship, *Peleliu*, as Task Unit 76.1.5.1; and its escort, the *Perry* class frigate *Sides*, as Task Unit 76.1.5.2.

Wednesday, March 13th, 1996, 0943 local time,
on board U.S.S. Peleliu *in the East Sea (Sea of Japan)*

Josh loved being at sea, and he loved the pressures of being a ship's commanding officer. The captain's chair on the inboard wing of *Peleliu's* bridge was 150 feet above the sea, giving the captain a panoramic view forward and of the entire flight deck. If the commanding officer wanted to look out the starboard side, there was a similar chair on the other side of the bridge. It was a good observation post when *Peleliu* was connected to an oiler via hoses to take on fuel, or getting supplies from a replenishment ship. It was also a good place to sit and think.

Josh was taking a break from reading the stack of messages that came in a never-ending flow. He let his mind wander and admire the beauty of his surroundings. Despite its 820-foot length, *Peleliu's* bow pitched up and down in the long, six-foot swells. Peering through the window, he studied the puffy, white cumulus clouds suspended above the tranquil ocean. On the flight deck, helicopters were being repositioned for the flight operations scheduled to start after dark.

Seven decks below, Marines were pre-flighting two H-46 helicopters for a night insertion of a Marine reconnaissance team in a mountainous area 20 miles south of the demilitarized zone. Last night they'd put one team ashore, and tonight they were going to put in a second. Four nights from tonight, both teams would be extracted as part of the reduced exercise schedule.

To give the *Peleliu* and *Sides* more sea room, Josh took his task group to the deep water between the island of Uleung-do and the city of Uljin on the east side of the Korean peninsula. Josh planned to close to within eight to 10 miles of the South Korean coast before launching the H-46s. *Sides* was stationed 10 miles to the north-northwest, at the edge of the visual horizon, positioned between *Peleliu* and North Korea. A half hour before flight operations began, *Sides* would move to a plane guard position, astern and off the starboard side of *Peleliu*.

"Captain, CIC."

Josh pushed the lighted button and picked up the handset that connected him to the ship's combat information center. "Captain, aye."

"Sir, the tactical action officer on *Sides* sent us a message. They've been tracking a sonar contact for hours, and classified it as a probable North Korean *Romeo*. Sub's position is approximately twenty-five miles away and three three zero at fifteen from *Sides*. It is not a threat to either ship."

"We'll head to the southern end of our assigned box. Tell *Sides* to maintain that track. Also, check with the exercise controllers to make sure there isn't a U.S., Japanese or South Korean sub in the area."

Josh hung up the handset. "Officer of the deck, change course to two two five."

"Aye, aye, Captain" Kathy Heller replied. "Helmsman, left standard rudder to course two two five."

For a few seconds Josh contemplated the sea through the thick glass separating him from the cold, forty-degree air, then he headed toward the chart table. He felt his ship heel slightly as it turned. The petty officer maintaining the manual plot on the nautical chart stepped aside. Josh picked up the dividers, calibrated them on the longitude line on the chart, and used them to walk off distances between *Peleliu, Sides,* and the reported position of the North Korean *Romeo*.

Back in the captain's chair, he picked up the handset and selected the secure satellite-radio circuit that Seventh Fleet monitored. *A little bit of paranoia may be a good thing.* Once he saw the green light indicating a link to *Blue Ridge* had been established, he pressed the push-to-talk key. "Blackbeard, Blackbeard, this is Big League Zero Zero Actual, over."

"Big League, this is Blackbeard, go ahead."

"Blackbeard, this is Big League Zero Zero Actual. Is Blackbeard November Six Actual available?" November Six Actual was Marty.

There was silence, then a different voice. "Big League Zero Zero Actual, this is Blackbeard November Six Actual. What's on your mind?"

"Blackbeard, our playmate is tracking a North Korean *Romeo* near *Peleliu.* Two questions. One—any info on recent deployments or changes in tactics based on the discussions in Hawaii? Two—

have you seen any recent intel on Thaek and his activities?" The assassin's attempt on his life was still fresh in his mind.

"Big League, this is Blackbeard. Let me get back to you. Enjoying the cruise?"

"Blackbeard, Big League. Thanks, and affirmative." Josh didn't want to get into bantering with his good friend; Lord only knew who was monitoring the circuit.

A lighted button on the red phone indicated a new incoming call. "Go."

"Captain, Combat. Sir, based on the sound profile, the *Romeo* is hull number S-211. It took a while to identify him because he's been running on batteries. This confirms it is a North Korean submarine."

"Thank you. Tell *Sides* to maintain a position and have its SH-60 armed so it can drop a torpedo if needed. I don't trust the North Koreans." *My paranoia is showing.*

"Aye, aye, sir."

"I want the plot on the tactical distribution system repeater up here on the bridge."

"Already done, sir. The *Romeo* is designated Sierra One."

"Excellent." The Navy's Joint Tactical Information Data System showed an up-to-the-minute plot of all the ships, aircraft and submarines around the *Peleliu*. Just before they'd left San Diego, the latest version of the secure ship-to ship and ship-to-air data link equipment—called *Link 16*—had been installed.

Josh adjusted the distance rings on the display so the scope showed everything within a 50-mile radius marked by distance rings at five-mile intervals. Just beyond the 25-mile ring, a red "V" with a dot in the center and a line showing direction of travel gave the sub's course and speed, labled Sierra One. The arrow pointed in the direction of *Peleliu.* A green circle with a dot in the center represented *Sides,* now 15 miles to the south and east of the "V."

CO of sub 211, what are you trying to do? Get close so you can brag to your buddies you did it? You might get a medal. Or is Thaek still trying to kill me?

A moment later, Marty called back.

"Big League, this is Blackbeard November Six Actual. Intel says they are expecting the North Koreans to be very aggressive this year to show they are not a pushover while they negotiate some kind of nuclear arms treaty."

"Blackbeard, can you define aggressive? They like to make threats when we're exercising with the South Koreans, but it is usually bluster. Or does N2 think they may want to create a major incident with plausible deniability? Over."

"Big League, I asked, and he doesn't know. Boss says you need to be prepared for anything. Over."

"Blackbeard, Big League, roger. Anything else?" *Marty, you were on the same goddamn list I was. They have a folder on you as well.*

"Big League, Blackbeard, negative. Good luck, and go get 'em, tiger!!!"

"Thanks. Big League Actual out." Josh ended the call and pushed another button. "Combat, ask the executive officer, the Marine Air Group commanding officer, both our operations officers, and our intelligence and senior tactical action officer to meet me in my at-sea cabin in ten minutes."

The captain's at-sea cabin wasn't very large. It had a bed, a chest with a fold down desk, a chair and a small table with two more chairs. One bulkhead had a door leading to a private head with a shower. When Josh arrived, two of the officers were standing by the doorway and one against the wall; the first three to arrive had already claimed the chairs. Josh sat on the bed to address them all.

"Here's what's going on. We have a North Korean sub tracking us. Seventh Fleet expects the North Koreans to be aggressive during what is left of these exercises. Right now, *Peleliu* is the biggest major asset closest to North Korea. We're going to sprint south for about two hours at twenty knots and then slow to about five knots and deploy the noisemaker. I already tasked *Sides* to track the sub and arm its SH-60 with a torpedo. Any questions or comments?"

Commander Rankin, executive officer and surface warfare officer, made notes in the little green spiral book he kept in the breast pocket of his uniform shirt. He found Josh's leadership style to be a breath of fresh air. Haman was blunt, tough, fair, and cared about everyone who served under him. And there was the intensity in his eyes that focused on you like two laser beams.

"One, Skipper. We need to let our boss know what we're doing."

"We will. Ops, call them and confirm our intentions with a message."

"Yes, sir. How does the move affect the exercise, if at all?" The operations officer was responsible for helping Josh make sure *Peleliu* "made" each of its scheduled events. The North Koreans may or not be up to something, but the exercise scores would most assuredly affect careers.

"We're going to be thirty miles farther south from our originally planned launch point."

"The helos should be okay on gas, but it'll limit the time they can spend finding the landing zones. I'll have them fly to the beach and then up the coast. We may have to launch a bit earlier, so we'll change the air plan."

"What we do will depend on what the *Romeo* does." Josh turned to Lieutenant Commander Avery Newsome, *Peleliu's* senior tactical action officer. A good TAO was expected to be a walking encyclopedia of facts, figures and information about potential threats, as well as the ship's own defensive systems. *Peleliu* was dependent on escorts for protection against almost any threat, and they only had the one escort. Its own self-defense weapon systems were minimal. "TAO, keep me in the loop with what *Sides* learns."

Next, Josh turned to his operations officer. "If we change the launch time, do we have to notify anyone?"

"No, sir. All we have are times on target for the landing zones. As long as our helos stay below a thousand feet and get there at the right time, we're okay. If we have a new, significantly different launch time, or if they want to fly higher, we'll notify the Air Force. You know how touchy they are about everyone complying with their air tasking order."

"XO, we're going to burn a lot of fuel during our sprint. Can we make it to our next underway replenishment date, or do we need to bump it up? Also, make sure the engineer can give us twenty-five knots when I want it. We may need it in a hurry."

The XO ran numbers through his head. "Skipper, no problem. We just topped off yesterday, and we haven't burned much. But I'll check with the engineer when I give him the news that you're going to want to go 'warp factor nine' on a moment's notice."

"Did we leave anything out?"

Before anyone could answer, the speaker next to the desk blared. "Captain, this is Combat. *Sides* just reported that the *Romeo* is snorkeling and headed toward us. The sub fired off a short message in the high frequency band. *Sides* recorded and sent it to JICPAC for analysis."

"Very well."

Josh continued. "In a few hours, the *Romeo's* batteries will be charged and the fun may really begin. By then, we'll be well south. If the sub's commander really is taking an interest in us, our shift in position will force him to move, and we'll continue to track him. Gents, the chess game has begun."

U.S.S. *Peleliu's* Korean Area of Operations

1642 local time, on board U.S.S. Peleliu *in the East Sea*

After plowing through the water at 20 knots for 120 minutes, Josh ordered the *Peleliu* to slow to five knots and turn seaward and east, away from the Korean peninsula. Once on the new course, Josh ordered the Nixie acoustic decoy deployed.

The vector for the *Romeo* still pointed in *Peleliu's* direction. The display showed the sub's speed to be five knots, which was as fast as it could go on its diesels while submerged and charging its batteries.

The phone jangled.

"Sir, this is Newsome. *Sides* has another contact out to our east, south of the island of Ulleung-do. Their TAO thinks the island masked the second sub from its towed array, which is why they didn't pick it up earlier. It is classified as a probable North Korean *Romeo* and is on your scope as Sierra Two, about twenty miles to our east and moving in our direction."

"How many sonobuoys does a LAMPS helo carry, and how many can it process?" Josh thought it was 16, but some had been upgraded. LAMPS was the acronym for Light Airborne Multi-Processor System, which is how the SH-60B helicopter was designated in the fleet.

"Twenty-five, sir."

"Find out how many sonobuoys *Sides* has on board. My guess is she is going to need a bunch. Also, see what other assets we can request. I don't want to cry wolf yet, but we may need some help."

"Yes, sir."

Josh resisted the urge to go down to the Combat Information Center and take charge. He'd tested Newsome and his assistant TAOs with complex tactical problems during workups and in drills on the cruise west. Now they were doing it for real. *It is so hard. I need to stay calm, cool and collected, even though my gut tells me that something bad is about to happen.*

He snatched the handset just as it started to ring. "Captain."

"Sir, an SH-60 can process sixteen sonobuoys using the LAMPS on board and send sixteen back to the frigate, so a total of thirty-two can be processed by the ship and the helo. *Sides* has a hundred and twenty buoys on board—that is just shy of five full reloads. *Midway* and TF-76 have a P-3 supporting them, but it is going home in about an hour. *Midway* also has an H-3 squadron, but we're more than a hundred-fifty nautical north of them. To give them on-station time, we'd have to hot-fuel them. *Nimitz* is even further to the south in the Tsushima Straight. She's got a squadron of S-3s, but their air plan doesn't start until ten tonight. We can, if you want, ask for one of the P-3s based in Misawa and on Okinawa, or the S-3s."

"Good info. Ask for a P-3 and get me a circuit to *Belleau Wood*. After I get off the radio, ask the XO and ops officer to join me."

Am I over-reacting? Paranoid? Am I losing it?

Rear Admiral Jay Abbott, the amphibious group commander aboard *Belleau Wood*, said plainly that he didn't think the two *Romeos* were a serious threat, but he reluctantly agreed to assign another *Perry*-class frigate, the *Crommelin*. It would refuel and rendezvous with the *Peleliu* early in the morning. He denied Josh's request for the P-3.

Abbott had spent six years running procurement programs in the Pentagon. Before that, he'd commanded a frigate assigned to a NATO task force, which spent most of its time in port or steaming in formation for photographs. Not a warrior, Abbott had been given command because he was well connected and needed a task group command to make him more competitive for his second star. Admiral Jeffers had lobbied hard to get his friend the billet.

At a pre-deployment briefing in San Diego, Abbott had expressed surprise that his task force was expected to plan and practice opposed landings on a regular basis. The Marine colonel on Seventh Fleet staff had politely reminded Abbott that Task Force 76's primary mission was to land the Third Marine Expeditionary Force whenever and wherever tasked.

The Simushir Island Incident

Abbott's intel and ASW officers should have the latest information gleaned from Vice Admiral Pak, so they should be familiar with the DPRK Navy's tactics. I can't go over his head to Vice Admiral Maize and ask for assets. I have to figure out a way to get Seventh Fleet to provide direction to Abbott.

"XO, level with me. Am I nuts?"

"No, sir," Rankin replied. "I think you are being very prudent. Amphibs like us are big juicy targets. Look, the *Romeos* could just be out here trying to get into a firing position as an exercise. But they might be planning an attack launch they can later explain away as an 'accident', but by then it will be too late for *Peleliu*. In either case, we have to make it difficult—if not impossible—for them to target us. This is great real-world training, and if their subs *do* try something, we'll be ready. Like you, sir, I don't want to take the first hit."

"Our advantages are speed and sensors." Josh was thinking aloud. "We can run from them, and as long as we don't stumble onto a third sub and find ourselves boxed in, we're okay. But the launch and recoveries later tonight make us predictable."

The ops officer spoke up. "Not if *Peleliu* keeps moving in a random pattern. We can always vector the Marine helicopters to us. The subs can't go far or fast on batteries. Just remember, we only have two sensor platforms, and if you're not careful you'll wear out the SH-60 crews."

"Using our radar will make it easy for the North Korean subs to home in on us—"

"Captain, Combat," the blaring speaker interrupted.

"Captain, aye."

"Sir, *Crommelin,* which is now Task Unit 76.1.5.3, is on its way at twelve knots, heading north-northwest to stay shore-side of the second *Romeo*. She can't go any faster with her array deployed. When she is within fifty miles, she'll slow down and contact us for tasking her SH-60. She has a hundred and two sonobuoys on board. And based on our request sent to CTF 76, Seventh Fleet is sending us a P-3 from Okinawa, call sign Watchdog Zero Nine. It gets here in about an hour. Skipper, I have more."

"Excellent. Go."

"*Sides* has a firing solution on both subs and is staying outside of their torpedo range. The CO wants to know if the rules of engagement have changed."

The rules of engagement said they were not to take the first hit, and to attack only if threatened. Interpreting "threatened" opened oneself to the second-guessers on the other side of the long green table. *To me, a North Korean submarine moving into a firing position IS a threat.*

"Thanks for the update. Tell the captains of *Sides* and *Crommelin* that the ROE have not changed. They are to consider a sub opening the outer doors to its torpedo tubes within torpedo range of his ship or *Peleliu* as a hostile act. Anything else?"

"Yes, sir. Sierra One is now fifteen miles to the north and closing. The other sub is seventeen miles to the east. On present courses, they will be within fourteen thousand yards in about two hours."

In other words, *Peleliu* would soon be in range of the *Romeo's* Yu-3 anti-ship torpedoes. The Chinese-made, 553-millimeter diameter "fish" swam at 30 knots and had a range of about seven nautical miles.

"Mr. Newsome, I want to talk to both captains as soon as *Crommelin* is in radio range. Let *Sides* know we are going to sprint southeast for about an hour to open the range and to make it easier for *Crommelin* to close on us. Then get me a course, speed and time to get back to our original launching point for the Marines."

Josh returned his attention to the meeting. "XO, where were we?"

The Simushir Island Incident

"We were talking about *Sides'* helo crew. Sir, I've had combat pass the word to land their helo, do whatever maintenance they need, and get ready to be a pouncer. I'll have Newsome pass the same guidance to the *Crommelin.*"

"Outstanding. Now I want to brief the crew."

1821 local time, on board North Korean submarine S-204

Lieutenant Commander Sang-mi Seomun was not happy with his sub's political officer. Chul Bac was a weasel. Seomun, who'd been in the People's Navy for almost 14 years, noticed that when Bac was around, his men were sullen and were much more careful in what they said or did. Seomun suspected that one or two more members from the General Political Department were planted among his crew. He had his guesses, but kept them to himself.

S-204 was at periscope depth, waiting for an answer to Seomun's latest transmission, sent just before the submarine finished charging its batteries and submerged.

The atmosphere in the submarine's control room was tense. In his brief message, Seomun had reported contact with a large surface ship that matched the indicators of his target. Seomun had bluntly asked headquarters to confirm his written orders to sink the ship and kill any surviving officers.

In the orders packet was a picture of the captain of the *Peleliu.* But Seomun believed that surfacing to kill survivors was wrong and made him a war criminal. It would also make it easy for others to find and sink his submarine. *I have a horrible feeling that we are viewed as expendable. My crew feels it, too.*

The decoded response was short and blunt. "Orders confirmed. Failure to execute them will result in court martial. Thaek.*"

Seomun went to his cabin, unlocked his safe, and took out the pistol he had been issued, along with the three spare magazines. He pulled back the slide and made sure a round was in the chamber of the Tokarev, ready to fire. The pistol went into his right pants pocket, the spare magazines into the left.

1946 local time, on board U.S.S. Peleliu *in the East Sea*

In his at-sea cabin, Josh picked at his cooling dinner of chicken teriyaki and studied the chart spread on the table. Current positions, courses and speeds of his task group's ships and the North Korean submarines were all marked. After the Marine helos completed tonight's missions, he would no longer be constrained by an exercise event schedule and could move as he chose.

Is this the beginning of Thaek's end game? His gut told him Thaek was involved, but he had no proof.

The phone rang.

"Skipper, Assistant TAO here." Josh recognized the Georgian drawl of one of the junior tactical action officers. "Sir, you've got an urgent call on the INMARSAT satellite phone from Seventh Fleet."

"Patch it through." Josh waited.

"Josh, it's Marty. We can be informal, I'm using a STU-III."

"What's up?"

"We've been monitoring the HF radio transmissions between the *Romeos* and their headquarters. From partial decrypts, JICPAC is pretty sure *Peleliu* is the target of some type of action."

"Marty, why am I not surprised?"

"Because, my friend, you are a paranoid cynic."

So, I am not crazy after all. "Only because they sent an assassin to kill me and my family. Who else have you told?"

"You're the first because you're the target. Admiral Maize is on the phone with CTF 76 on the *Belleau Wood* as we speak. He's politely introducing him to the real world. Rear Admiral Abbott will get firm direction to give you all the support you need and stay out of your hair. My guess is, Maize will tell Abbott that if he doesn't, his ass is grass and he can kiss a second star good-bye. Vice Admiral Maize is also calling the head-shed in Korea and letting him figure out how much to tell the ROKs. Saying too much will give away our code-breaking capabilities."

"Great. What else?"

"Expect a change in the rules of engagement. The lawyers back at CINCPAC are working on a mod just for this exercise. Our JAG officer is trying to light a fire under the collective asses of CINCPAC's legal beagles. You know as well as I do, by the time they figure it out and run it up and down the chain of command twenty times, the shooting will have either stopped or they'll have it so convoluted you and I will never figure it out."

"I won't hold my breath."

"Josh, one last thing."

"And that is?"

"Admiral Maize said—and I quote—protect your ships and men, and if you need to, make the other guy go home in a body bag. In other words, don't take the first hit—unquote. He doesn't want a U.S. ship to be torpedoed on his watch, so he'll back you to the hilt if you think you need to take out a North Korean sub or two."

"Tell Admiral Maize thanks for the support and I'll try not to fuck it up. I know he's hanging his fourth star on my decisions. I'm glad men matter more to him than a promotion."

"It is not the first time he's done that. And he said there is no one he'd rather have in this pickle than you. Don't make him look bad, and don't let it go to your head. Oh, Jack's here for a couple of weeks as the staff's exercise action officer, along with a bunch of reservists because they have more Foal Eagle and Team Spirit experience than any current member of the staff. Gotta go."

2016 local time, on board U.S.S. Peleliu *in the East Sea*

As Josh entered the CIC, a sailor announced, "Captain is in combat." A large "W" shaped console on an elevated pedestal was surrounded by control boxes for radios so they could communicate with the outside world as well as anywhere within the ship. Cords for handsets dangled from the overhead.

The senior tactical action officer, a brand-new lieutenant commander, was at his station where he'd been for most of the day, along with his number two. "Did either of you listen in to the call I just had?" Josh demanded.

The TAO gave an affirmative nod. "Good, then I don't need to repeat it. I presume you don't make a habit of listening. Do not discuss it with others; that's an order."

Both men nodded emphatically.

"Good, I want to ambush the ambusher, so to speak. We need to force the North Koreans' hand, so we need options. Let's start with the assumption *Peleliu* is the bull's-eye."

"Skipper, do you want to be in on the brainstorming?"

"I'd like to be, but no. Come up with three scenarios and we'll go through the pros and cons. Think like you are a North Korean, and assume Thaek believes his life is on the line so it is either him or me. We'll pick the option we think is best, and the other two become the basis for Plans B and C. You have sixty minutes, so be practical. Come up with the options first, and then we can flesh out the details. Call the bridge when you are ready."

"Sir, who is this Thaek guy?"

To come up with the best scenarios, they need to know. Josh took a deep breath and told both men what he thought he could, given neither were cleared. They now understood why their lives, along with the lives of their shipmates, were on the line.

Josh had been up since 0530 after just three hours of sleep the previous night and a quick hour's nap after lunch, and now he was running on adrenaline. Ensconced in his chair on the bridge, he selected the button for the 1MC so his words would be broadcast on speakers located throughout the ship.

"Sailors and Marines on *Peleliu*, this is the captain speaking. In just a few minutes, we are going to both flight and general quarters. Earlier this evening, I told you two North Korean submarines were stalking *Peleliu*. They still are. While this is not unusual, our intelligence suggests they are planning some kind of action against our ship. The North Koreans are very unpredictable, so we are going to be flexible and prepared for whatever they throw at us. In other words, when we go to general quarters, it is not a drill. This is not part of the exercises."

Josh paused to let that sink in. "Two of our frigates, *Sides* and *Crommelin,* are tracking the North Korean subs. *Peleliu* will remain at general quarters until we are assured the danger to our ship has passed. As events evolve, I will keep you informed. I have faith in every one of you, and we will, if need be, write another chapter in the proud history of *Peleliu* the ship, the Marine Corps, and the Navy. That is all."

Once the gong sounding General Quarters began, Josh climbed down the ladders from the bridge to CIC, which was just below the hangar deck. As he'd learned at the PCO School, in the "new" Navy, warship captains "fought" their ships from the combat information center, not the bridge.

2315 local time, on board U.S.S. Peleliu *in the East Sea*

Josh had asked one of the assistant TAOs to bring a chart to the command center with *Peleliu's* movements plotted, along with those of the *Sides, Crommelin* and the two North Korean subs.

Surrounded by large screen displays and radarscopes, he felt old fashioned using the chart, but it gave him a better feel for the tactical picture than the clinical-looking, abstract symbols on a large screen display. He was an old dog who had both old and new tricks.

The handset overhead jangled. Newsome reached up and grabbed it. After listening for a few seconds, the lieutenant commander turned to his captain. "Skipper, P-3 call sign Watchdog Zero Niner has laid the sonobuoy patterns we requested and is orbiting thirty miles to the west of us at angels 10. Unfortunately, he has no weapons on board."

"Got it. Thanks." Josh sat down in his chair, trying not to betray his nervousness. He hated what he called "pre-combat waiting." His mind never stopped working and playing out potential scenarios, most of them bad. This time it was worse, because he held the lives of almost 3,000 sailors and Marines aboard *Peleliu* in his hands, along with the 350 men on the two frigates. If the shit hit the fan, all were trusting in his judgment. What made it worse was that he didn't know if this was going to be an exercise or a firefight.

In front of him, three 80-inch screen displays were set up so the one on the left was the air picture, with the symbology showing the ships' helicopters and the P-3. On the right, the ships and submarines were portrayed, along with the sonobuoy lines. The center display showed the combined air, surface, and sub-surface picture.

One North Korean sub was to the north and east, the other coming from the west. Vectors showed them headed straight toward *Peleliu*. Both subs had snorkeled again.

Okay, Thaek. What do you have planned?

Nearly an hour later, the phone rang. "Skipper, this is the air controller. The Marine helos just went feet wet. They should be back here in twenty-two minutes, at 0014. We'll launch another H-46 to act as a plane guard when the helos are ten minutes out. We also have a boat ready to launch if needed."

Josh looked at the air picture display where two semi-circles with dots in the center and vectors pointing to the ship had passed the line representing the Korean coast. Each had the altitude, heading, course, speed, transponder code and call sign under the symbol. To Josh, it looked surreal, like something out of a *Star Wars* movie.

If a helicopter had to ditch and Marines died, the second-guessers would question his not having kept a frigate nearby and assigned to the plane guard mission. The book said you needed one helicopter and one ship. He had one helo and a boat. It wasn't like he hadn't requested more backup.

Tuesday, March 14th, 1995 0019 local time,
on board DPRK sub S-204 in the East Sea

Heat from the electric equipment inside of the sub counteracted the cold sea temperature, making the inside of the sub a comfortable 18 degrees Celsius (64° Fahrenheit). But with the fans and the ventilation system turned off to reduce the battery drain, it was starting to get stuffy.

"Comrade Commander Seomun, why are we still at periscope depth?" Seomun turned from the chart table to face his political officer. Lieutenant Bac was rocking on the balls of his feet, his hands clasped behind his back.

Seomun hated him. The man delighted in questioning every order he gave. He often demanded aloud in his shrill, questioning tone, "What would our Dear Leader think of...?" He tried to contain his irritation. "Because there is no need to go deeper. It would only waste precious battery power."

Bac was not to be dissuaded. "Going below the layer will make it harder for the Imperialist Americans to detect us."

Seomun wanted to say, "You moron, with their sensors they have to know we are out here already because we ran our diesels. As soon as we try to attack, they will sink us. Staying this close to the surface gives us a chance to survive." Instead, he said, as politely as he could, "I am staying at this depth because occasionally I raise our radar receiver so I can get a bearing on the American ship."

Bac nodded. "I see." He then disappeared down the passageway, heading aft, and everyone in the control room breathed a sigh of relief. Seomun assumed he was headed toward his cabin to write something in his journal that would be turned over to his superiors at the end of the cruise.

0249 local time, on board U.S.S. Peleliu *in the East Sea*

The CIC area was kept cooled to about 60 degrees Fahrenheit to protect the computers from overheating. Everyone in the space wore a long-sleeve shirt and a jacket or sweater. Josh pulled his leather flight jacket on and zipped it up. He liked the feel of the fur against the back of his neck when he leaned back in the chair.

Three message boards were piled on the table next to his chair. He'd put them down when he realized he couldn't focus on them anymore. *If Peleliu is hit by a torpedo, I'll have more important things to worry about, and they'll still be there in the morning. Or maybe they'll be floating in the Sea of Japan. If we haven't been sunk, the one thing that is certain is that the pile will be a lot bigger. Messages! Arrrrgggggghhhh!*

"Skipper?"

Josh sat up and looked over at the lanky Newsome. The man didn't sit in a chair, he folded himself into one. "Watchdog Zero Niner reports low frequency machinery noise associated with a possible third submarine. *Sides* is reporting a contact in the same area. We're correlating the data and the new contact, designated Sierra Three, will pop up on the screen as soon as the computers update. Both *Sides'* and *Crommelin's* helo crews are now on two-minute alert. Their SH-60s are fully mission-capable and armed with two Mark Forty-Six torpedoes each."

From experience sitting alerts, Josh guessed the crews were in their seats in the helo waiting for the order to launch. "Who told them to load the weapons?" *Shit, I don't remember doing that.*

"I did, sir. They won't have time to go back and load if the subs open their torpedo-tube doors. If nothing else, it is good practice. Based on your guidance, we're prepared."

"Very well. Good move." The knot in his stomach just got even tighter, and fresh adrenalin began to flow. *The third sub is the anvil; the other two were the hammers flushing the prey called the* Peleliu. *And the North Koreans just lost all grounds for plausible deniability. Game on, Thaek! Now I am fully awake.*

Hurry up and wait. For over an hour, Josh watched the computer-generated pictures update. Occasionally, a sailor wearing a headset would make a grease-pencil mark on a display and then key his mike.

The TAO approached. "Skipper, both Watchdog Zero Niner and *Sides* confirm Sierra Three is a North Korean *Romeo*, hull number two zero four. The sub's course is one zero zero, speed two knots. I'm guessing it has been lurking out here for a day or so— we would have heard him if he'd lit off his diesels. He can't have much charge left in his batteries. For planning purposes, we're going to assume he has about four hours left."

"TAO, I concur. It is a perfect setup to try to sink us. When will *Peleliu* be in torpedo range of Sierra Three?"

"Sir, based on the current tracks of Sierra Three and *Peleliu,* we enter the sixteen-thousand-yard ring in about two hours. North Koreans tend to shoot at twelve-to-thirteen thousand yards on a closing target. They want you at ten thousand yards, max, if you are a crossing target. Sierra One is outside twenty-five miles from us and closing but not near any of our escorts. Sierra Two is fifteen thousand yards from *Sides.*"

"TAO, fifteen minutes prior to our reaching the sixteen-thousand-yard ring, launch Lamplighter Three Six."

Nearly two hours later, Josh watched as the half circle representing the SH-60 helicopter, call sign Lamplighter Three Six, moved toward the red V on the large-screen display indicating the location of Sierra Three.

He turned to the tactical action officer. "Are you sure the sensor operators can hear Sierra Three open its outer doors on a sonobuoy?"

"Yes, sir." The man's Southern drawl made the first word sound like three syllables. "They tell me it is a very distinctive mechanical noise, followed by the sound of rushing water when the tubes are flooded. If they open, we'll hear it."

"Okay, here's the plan. Opening their torpedo-tube outer doors at this range is a hostile act; make sure it is logged as such. Once we get inside fourteen thousand yards, if either the frigates or the helicopters hear that noise, have Lamplighter Three Six drop the warning charges. Tell Lamplighter not to waste time asking for permission, just drop charges and report. If Sierra Three shoots, Lamplighter is cleared to drop his torpedoes without asking permission. Also, make sure I have an open circuit to both our boss and Seventh Fleet."

"Already done, sir. We have clearance to use Seventh Fleet's dedicated net. I suspect CINCPAC and the Commander, United Nations Command, in Seoul may be listening as well."

"So we have a star-studded audience to the morning's festivities. Just do your job, and don't worry about the book or second guessing. That's my job."

Newsome chuckled. "Sir, may I ask you a question?"

"Go for it." Josh needed to talk to someone. The knot in his stomach was getting tighter and tighter. Despite all the activity around him, he'd never felt the loneliness of command as he did now. There was no Marty Cabot or Jack D'Onofrio around with whom he could share his fears.

"Sir, we're basing our whole plan on the assumption that the info we got on North Korean subs is good because it is very detailed. Is it too detailed to be true?"

"Fair question. Call over the ASW officer and I'll tell both you of you." The time it took the submariner to walk over gave Josh time to let his brain come up with an answer that wouldn't violate the security of *Red Siren*.

"My source is Roger Billingham, the ops officer on the CINCPAC staff and one of CINCPAC's resident experts. He's a fast-attack guy, who has experience chasing these guys all over the Sea of Japan. He told me that he wouldn't have given the info to us unless he was sure the dope was good."

The submariner nodded. "Thank you, sir. That's good to know."

Josh could hear the radio calls from the recovery in the background and resisted the urge to go back to the bridge to watch the helos land. If something went wrong, he'd find out soon enough.

It would be daylight in about an hour. Josh sent a message up the chain of command, asking if they could be released from exercise participation until the danger from the three North Korean subs had passed. The reply was, Exercise Foal Eagle was politically important; the Commander, U.N. Forces Korea was reluctant to change the schedule. He still wanted the practice amphibious landing.

Josh activated the com for "'All Hands."

"Good morning, this is the captain speaking. There are now three North Korean submarines stalking *Peleliu*. Our escorts, the frigates *Sides* and *Crommelin,* are also at general quarters and have helicopters ready to pounce. If *Peleliu* begins to maneuver at high speed, you'll know we are under attack without me having to tell you. I will do my best to make sure we do not take the first hit and our task force finishes what the North Koreans start. I am confident *Peleliu* can handle anything the North Koreans throw at us. *Peleliu* is ready because *you* are ready. This is what all the drills and training were about. Remember, luck is the intersection of smart, hard work and having a good plan. We've done the former and have the latter. That is all."

After he hung up, Josh couldn't help but think about the World War II battle for the island of Peleliu. It was one of the bloodiest, nastiest battles of the island-hopping war in the Pacific. It had been projected to last less than a week. Instead, the two-month battle cost more than 2,000 Marines their lives and wounded another 8,000. The National Museum of the Marine Corps summed up the fight for the island as "the bitterest battle of the war for the Marines."

0618 local time, on board submarine S-204 in the East Sea

One had to be a realist when one went to sea in an old submarine. Mechanical problems, some more serious than others, were routine. Lieutenant Commander Sang-mi Seomun often told his crew that their primary job at sea was to keep water out of the people compartment.

It was, he thought, suicidal to attack ships with excellent antisubmarine warfare capabilities. Seomun wondered how long he and his men were going to live once they launched the torpedoes.

He felt the whole mood in the control room change when he announced to the crew that S-204 was about to commit an act of war. The only person in the control room who was smiling was Bac. The arrogant political officer didn't grasp the dire consequences of firing a torpedo at an American Navy ship.

Seomun took a deep breath, looked around him, and quietly commanded, "Fire one."

The young sailor standing by the firing tube panel turned to his captain. "Captain, are you sure?"

Before Seomun could answer, Bac pulled a pistol from his belt and shot the sailor in the head. He pointed the gun at the assistant. "Fire the torpedoes as you were ordered—*NOW!*"

The sailor hesitated, looking at his captain for confirmation. Bac shot him in the chest and spun around, his pistol sweeping the control room. He picked up the handset and ordered petty officer Chul Haeng to come to the control room. Haeng, who was one of the men Seomun already suspected worked for Bac, came from his battle station in the forward engine room. Bac handed him a Tokarev, along with a spare magazine.

"Shoot three torpedoes at the American amphibious ship," Bac commanded. Haeng pushed the firing button for torpedo tube number one. The sub recoiled slightly as compressed air shoved the torpedo out of the tube. When the torpedo room confirmed it was launched, Haeng did the same for tubes two and three.

Again Bac swept the control room with his pistol. "We have done our duty. Now we wait to see if we need to finish our duty.

Seomun, you are relieved. I am now in command. Steer toward the American ship and take us down to seventy-five meters."

0620 local time, on board U.S.S. Peleliu *in the East Sea*

Even in the combat information center, Josh could feel the rise and fall of the forward end of the flight deck as *Peleliu* plowed through the eight-foot swells. As soon as the helicopters touched down, Josh ordered *Peleliu* to increase its speed to 20 knots. For the plane handlers on the deck, the increased wind and the ship's up and down movement made life more difficult as they repositioned helicopters with small tractors. Even so, minutes after the second helicopter touched down, both were chocked and chained down.

"Skipper, *Sides* and P-3 Watchdog Zero Niner confirm Sierra Three has fired three torpedoes." Newsome tried to sound calm, but couldn't keep the pitch in his voice from rising.

"Start the music. Turn acoustic torpedo countermeasures on." Josh was issuing the first of a sequence of commands he'd briefed to his executive officer, who was sitting in his seat on the bridge.

Josh reached for the handset connecting him to the bridge. "XO, all ahead flank, starboard to zero four zero. We're about to fuck up the sub's firing solution."

Right after he hung up, the TAO reported. "Sir, Nixie decoy is deployed. Coming up on twelve thousand yards from Sierra Three. Lamplighter One Two is airborne and mission capable. On my mark, twelve thousand yards... three, two, one. Mark! Twelve thousand yards."

Peleliu started to heel and surge forward as the steam turbines fed their 70,000 horsepower to the ship's twin screws. Inside CIC, everyone could feel the increased vibration.

Josh punched a button on the console and spoke into the handset. "Engineer, give me all those extra ponies you've been talking about. We need 'warp nine' now."

"Sir, we've got full pressure on the steam turbines. Passing twenty knots right now, and should have twenty-five in a minute or two."

"Great." Josh turned to the lieutenant commander. "TAO, in our turn, how close are we going to get to Sierra Three?"

"Sir, at the apex of our turn, we will be approximately nine thousand, five hundred yards from Sierra Three. But I don't think his fish have the speed or range to reach us once we are we're running away at twenty-five knots."

"Okay—let's pray our plan works. If not, we'll be practicing damage control for real!"

The pitch in the voice of the petty officer manning the scope went up an octave as he called out, "Range just passing below ten thousand yards. *Sides* reports four enemy torpedoes in the water— one aimed at *Sides* and three at us. *Sides* is evading and has countermeasures in the water."

"Let me know when we start opening the range. Has either of the Lamplighters dropped its torpedoes yet?"

"Lamplighter Three Six's torpedo is in the water and pinging. The helo reports it appears to have locked onto Sierra Three."

"Who shot at *Sides*?"

"Sierra Two. *Sides* reports it fired an anti-submarine rocket down the bearing line of the torpedo."

"Sir, first torpedo is inside two thousand yards. Second one is at three and the third is at five. All are closing."

"Skipper, this is Lieutenant Junior Grade Heller on the bridge. XO said to tell you that *Peleliu* is making twenty-seven knots and that's all she's got."

Josh could hear confidence warring with fear in Heller's voice as she spoke. "TAO, sound the alarm." When the ten seconds of blaring, warbling noise subsided, Josh activated the button for all hands. "This is the captain. All hands, brace for possible torpedo hit."

Josh wished he could look outside in the direction of the approaching torpedoes to see if he could see their wakes. He'd probably seen too many World War II movies about submarines; modern torpedoes probably didn't run shallow enough to generate wakes. Instead, he was stuck in a blackened room in the belly of the ship lit only by red and pale-blue lights, surrounded by repeater scopes and large screen displays. Suddenly, Josh felt trapped.

A muffled explosion rocked the *Peleliu*. Josh held on to the arm rests as *Peleliu* nosed down into the water. He breathed out slowly, waiting for his world to explode, or for another torpedo to hit. Nothing bad happened. The ship didn't stagger, fire alarms didn't go off, and more importantly, the ship wasn't slowing. He breathed in again.

"Captain, Combat, the Nixie decoy took a direct hit."

"What about the second and third torpedoes?"

"*Sides* said they stopped running. Probably ran out of propellant and sank to the bottom. There are no more torpedoes in the water from any of the North Korean subs."

"What's the status of the Mark Forty-Six torpedo from Lamplighter Three Six?" Josh had a mental list of questions.

0623 local time, on board submarine S-204

Both political officers kept sweeping the compartment with their pistols to intimidate Seomun's crew—his former crew. The red light made the blood from the two dead sailors look black as it pooled on the steel floor. The smell in the chamber was noticeably worse from gunpowder and dead men.

The Simushir Island Incident

The pinging of a Mark 46's sonar and the singing of its screws got louder as the torpedo headed toward the submarine. In a quiet, authoritative voice, Seomun addressed Bac. "We have not yet sunk our target. If you want to accomplish your mission, you need to evade the torpedo. I suggest you let the crew deploy our decoys and go back to periscope death."

Bac considered, then nodded. At periscope depth, they would be able to watch the American ship sink.

If I resume command, I will probably get shot. But we are all going to die unless I act. The depth gauge showed S-204 at 40 meters. "Make turns for eight knots and take us up to periscope depth as fast as you can," Seomun ordered. "Launch two decoys now. Reload the decoys, and—on my command—launch two more."

He felt the nose pitch up sharply and the depth gauge start to decrease. He waited until the launchers were loaded and launched the second set of decoys. It was probably too late. The Mark 46 torpedo had probably achieved a fix and would maneuver to follow.

He was right; the decoys didn't work. The torpedo slammed into S-204's hull and exploded. The sub shuddered, and Seomun yelled, "Emergency surface! Blow all ballast tanks!"and lunged for Bac, who was thrown off balance by the sudden change in the sub's pitch. Seomun slammed the political officer into the hull, and Bac's pistol went flying. Chul Haeng fired wildly, trying to hit Seomun, before two sailors wrestled his gun away from him. The first bullet ricocheted around the control room. The second struck the sailor manning the stern planes. As he fell backward, he pulled the wheel controlling the aft planes, and the sub pitched up even more as it took on water in the aft torpedo compartment.

Seomun stepped back from the stunned Bac, pulled out his pistol and shot the political officer in the face. By now, Chul was subdued, and Seomun walked over to the second political officer and executed him.

The ringing bells and alarms in the background didn't give him time to gloat. He had a sub and crew to save. If there was another political officer on board, Seomun hoped the man had enough sense of self-preservation to leave the rebellious commander alive long enough to do his job.

0628 local time, on board U.S.S. Peleliu

"Captain! Lamplighter Thirty-Six reports a Mark Forty-Six exploded, and hears sounds consistent with a sub trying to surface. There's more. A second explosion in the vicinity of Sierra Two, and *Sides* reports sounds consistent with a submarine sinking. *Crommelin* reports Sierra One is retiring to the north at about three knots."

Josh looked at the TAO as a plan formed in his mind. "Newsome, direct *Sides* to close on the surfacing submarine. Tell it to fire a warning shot, and if the sub does not go dead in the water, sink it. If the sub goes down, I want to pick up any survivors. Give the helmsman a course and speed to Sierra Three's position. If it is still on the surface when we get there, we'll stand off by about five hundred yards. Let's go to flight quarters and launch the *Cobras* on two-minute alert. If that son of a bitch tries to shoot another torpedo, I want *Sides* and the *Cobras* to fill it full of holes with their rockets and cannon."

"Aye, aye, sir."

"I need to talk to our boss. If anyone else other than Seventh Fleet calls, tell them to stand by." Josh suspected CIC might be getting a stream of radio transmissions from the chain of command, wanting to know what was happening. He wanted them to focus on their jobs, not answer calls from second guessers sitting in some command center thousands of miles away. Those people had access to the same Joint Tactical Information Distribution System that he did.

"Aye, aye, sir, I got it. That was in the brief—"

"Sorry. I forgot. Different subject. I want a couple of boats made ready to pick up survivors. Make sure there are armed Marines in the boats, ready to shoot if the North Koreans try anything. These are my orders: pick the North Koreans up if they are willing. If not, leave them in the water. Don't force the issue."

"Skipper, Lamplighter Three Six has a visual on the surfacing sub and reports the sub is down at the stern. The crew has four rafts out and are abandoning the sub."

Josh ordered the quartermaster to reduce speed to 15 knots and called the air boss to announce flight quarters. He pushed the "All Hands" button on the 1MC. "This is the captain speaking. We just had three torpedoes fired at *Peleliu* and one at *Sides*. One hit our Nixie decoy. That was the explosion we all heard and felt. The good news is that there is no damage to the *Peleliu*. *Sides* was not hit and sank the sub that attacked her. A helicopter from *Sides* dropped a torpedo on the sub that shot at us and damaged it. We are now closing on that North Korean sub to pick up survivors. Any sailors or Marines who speak Korean fluently may leave their battle stations and muster immediately on the hangar deck, by the aft elevator. We need volunteers to go in the boats so we can communicate with the survivors. That is all."

Josh looked at Newsome. "Tell *Sides* and *Crommelin,* well done. Have both *Sides* and *Crommelin* keep one of their SH-60s airborne and armed until I give them the all clear."

The TAO nodded, and Josh poked the button for the ship's communications center. "This is the captain. Give me the SATCOM circuit to our boss, CTF 76 and Seventh Fleet, so I can tell the world what just happened and what we are about to do."

0753 local time, on board U.S.S. Peleliu *in the East Sea*

Josh walked up to the bridge. He wanted a break and to stretch his legs, and to see sun and sky. The 15-knot wind was enough to create whitecaps, and along with the 40-degree Fahrenheit air temperature was enough to give one the chills. He wanted to change his clothes, take a shower and shave. That pleasure would have to wait until he ordered the ship to secure from general quarters and resume normal operations.

A smiling Kathy Heller handed Josh a set of powerful binoculars, and he walked out on the starboard wing of the bridge. The seas had calmed and *Peleliu* was rolling gently, 700 yards from the damaged North Korean sub. The sub's stern was below the surface, and only the bow and conning tower were visible. It looked like a World War II picture of a dying U-boat.

"Sir, the TAO wants to talk to you." Josh nodded acknowledgement to Rankin and returned to the captain's chair. He let the glasses hang down on their strap as he settled in. Weary, but alert, he keyed the mike. "TAO, this is the captain."

"Sir, we have three boats in the water to bring survivors to *Peleliu*. Injured sailors get priority. We have a medical team standing by on the well deck."

"Search them all thoroughly for weapons and anything else that can go bang. Make sure that our guys do not board the sub. The crypto gear is not worth the risk of losing sailors."

"Yes, sir, understood. Our plan is, once the North Koreans are on board, we'll separate them and have the docs check them out before we let them off the well deck. We have about a dozen volunteers who speak Korean."

"TAO, after the North Koreans are looked over, let them shower. We'll issue new clothes. Find the political officer and hold him by himself."

"Yes, sir, that's in the plan."

The Simushir Island Incident

"Once the prisoners are all on board and the sub sinks, and assuming Sierra One doesn't do anything stupid, we'll secure from general quarters."

* * *

With its well deck flooded, the lowered stern of *Peleliu* was just under the surface of the water, allowing members of Marine Recon to launch four Zodiacs, which sped toward the sub crew's rafts. Each had three armed Marines on board, plus a Korean speaker. The first boat also had two corpsmen.

With Sierra One well out of torpedo range, Josh felt the risk was acceptable. He believed *Peleliu* was the ship best equipped to handle 40-plus North Korean prisoners.

From the bridge, Josh watched a Marine bring the raft alongside the sub's bow. A second Marine helped North Korean sailors onto the Zodiac while the third kept his rifle ready. Each Zodiac filled up with ten prisoners and returned to the well deck.

Each prisoner was searched for weapons and checked by the hospital corpsmen. Then, at a distance from the arriving men of at least 12 feet, a Korean-speaking sailor quietly asked each man two questions. "Who is your political officer?" and "If allowed, do you want to go back to North Korea or seek asylum in South Korea?" Those who elected to go back home were put in a group at the aft end of the well deck. The larger group, those who sought asylum, were put in another group farther forward, close to the ladder leading up into the ship.

The last boat brought the sub's captain, who told the Marines that there were four dead men still on the submarine. The sub's captain wanted to leave them on board and had opened the S-204's seacocks to sink it.

As soon as the last North Korean was on board, Josh ordered the *Peleliu* back up to 12 knots on a southerly heading, away from the scene. Satisfied that the ship was no longer in danger, he ordered the crew to secure from general quarters.

The phone on the bridge rang. Wearily, Josh pulled it down. "Captain."

"Sir, the sub's captain has asked to speak to you. He has his logbook, codebooks and written orders."

"Very well. Ask the XO to relieve me on the bridge. Bring the North Korean captain to my in-port cabin, along with an interpreter and an armed Marine."

Josh made his way down to his in-port cabin, which was just below the hangar deck. There was a large metal desk in the office portion of the cabin, a separate bedroom and bathroom, and a small dining room. The office wall was adorned with reprints of photos taken during the bloody battle for Peleliu.

When he heard two raps on the door, Josh put his Colt .45 Model 1911A1 on the top of the desk, by his right hand, and said, "Enter." The Marine guard stuck his head in the door. "Sir, the captain of the North Korean sub, the TAO and an interpreter are here, along with two Marines."

"Send them in."

The first man reeked of sweat, diesel fuel, and kimchi. He carried a dirty white bridge cover under his left arm. Standing at attention, he was at most five-foot-two and weighed maybe 120 pounds. He was followed by Newsome carrying a large gray oilskin pouch, which he put on the table. A petty officer third class, in dungarees, and two armed Marines, wearing woodland camouflage uniforms, followed the officers.

One Marine took a position off to one side, and the other stationed himself behind the North Korean officer. Both held their . 45's muzzles down, in a ready position. The TAO directed the man in dungarees to stand beside the desk next to Josh. "Captain, sir," he said, "I am Operations Specialist Third Class Choi, and I will be the interpreter."

"Excellent. Petty Officer Choi, where are you from?"

"LA, sir."

"Please stand at ease." Josh was trying to reduce the intimidation factor. "How old are you?"

"Twenty, sir."

"Where are you assigned?"

"Combat, sir. Most of the time I'm on one of the radar scopes."

"Excellent. So, you were in CIC when all this happened?"

Choi's answer was an excited, "Yes, sir."

"Have you been speaking to the prisoners?"

"Yes, sir. They've been very talkative."

"What have they been saying?"

"Several were surprised how fast we fired back at them. The Mark Forty-Six hit their sub in the aft torpedo room and flooded it. One of their engine compartments also flooded."

"They're lucky most of the crew got out."

"Yes, sir, and they know it. Several said there was a fight between the captain and the political officer and his assistant. I was sent up here before I got more details."

"Very well." Josh considered. "I understand our prisoner has something important to say to us. I want you to concentrate on getting the translation right. If you don't understand the sub's captain, ask for a clarification. We're going to record both his words and yours for intelligence purposes."

"Yes, sir."

Josh smiled. "One more thing, Petty Officer Choi. What is said in this room stays in this room."

"Yes, sir—I understand."

"Excellent. Please ask our guest to stand at ease and tell him who we are. And explain that we are not trying to be rude when we ask him to repeat information."

The TAO pushed the record button on the two cassette recorders. Petty Officer Choi nodded and turned to the North Korean. He bowed at the waist as a gesture of respect and then spoke. The North Korean captain nodded in return, then turned to Josh and bowed before he spoke, pausing every few words to allow Choi to translate.

"Captain Haman, I am Lieutenant Commander Sang-mi Seomun of the North Korean People's Navy and captain of submarine S-204. I do not speak English. I do not want to return to North Korea and would like to live in South Korea or come to America." He nodded emphatically to confirm this statement.

"Captain, are you alone in wanting to defect?"

The North Korean looked at Petty Officer Choi, who translated.

"No, most of my men do not want to go back to our homeland." Again, a nod for emphasis.

Josh bowed slightly and nodded in acknowledgement. "Please ask him if he will help identify those who want to defect from those who will do so just to become spies. Tell him that any defectors will be fully debriefed as part of being granted asylum. It is a nonnegotiable requirement."

Petty officer Choi and Lieutenant Commander Seomun spoke at length before the American turned to his commanding officer. "Captain, Seomun believes if the U.S. or South Korea offers them asylum, they will accept these terms.

The captain spoke some more, and Choi translated Seomun's description of the fight in the control room. "Sir, he and his men will help us find the third political officer, if there is one."

"Excellent. Petty Officer Choi, have the contents of that pouch been searched?

"Yes, sir, it was cleared before he left the deck. The captain says these are the sub's logs for the past year, the submarine's code books, and his personal copy of his orders."

"What do the orders say?"

Choi translated, and then there was a dialogue between the two men that went on for several minutes before the American turned to his captain. Petty Officer Choi's face was pale and his voice subdued.

"Captain Haman, he says his submarine was assigned to wait in ambush and sink *Peleliu.* If you were among the survivors, you were to be killed as soon as you were identified."

Josh wasn't surprised. "Ask him if he knows the name of the person who issued those orders." Petty Officer Choi nodded, spoke and listened to the answer. It was followed by a second exchange in Korean. Josh assumed Choi was getting a clarification.

"Sir, Lieutenant Commander Seomun says all three submarine commanders were given their orders in person by Deputy Minister Thaek from the Ministry of Safety and Security in Mayang-do before they sailed. Thaek said you are an enemy of the People's Republic, that you kidnapped Vice Admiral Pak, who—at one time —commanded all North Korea's submarines. Seomun did not want to start a war with a surprise attack. He radioed headquarters to clarify his orders. The response confirmed his orders and said if he failed to do his duty, he would be court-martialed. He brought a copy of that message with him."

"Petty Officer Choi, do you read Hangul?"

"Yes, sir."

"Ask him if his copies are decoded and, if so, could he show them to you."

Petty Officer Choi translated, and the North Korean pointed to an envelope. Choi opened it, making sure not to damage the fragile pieces of rice paper. He almost dropped the envelope when a copy of Haman's official Navy photo fell out. "Sir, these are his actual orders and a copy of the message confirming them. The documents use several words I am not familiar with, but the gist—excuse me, the content—directs him to find and sink *Peleliu* and any escorts trying to stop him. It does say to kill any officers who survive."

Josh slammed his fist on his desk as he struggled to contain his anger, causing Choi's head to snap back. "Thaek was willing to risk starting a fucking war just to kill me. Un-*fucking* believable!"

Josh turned to the North Korean. "Petty Officer Choi, translate what I just said—make it clear that I am not angry at *him*. Then ask him if there is anything else he would like to tell us?"

After translating his question, Petty Officer Choi focused on the long answer. "First, Lieutenant Commander Seomun apologizes for having any part in the attack. A political officer actually fired the torpedoes before Seomun killed him. Second, Seomun believes his country would be destroyed in a war with the United States and many innocent people killed. He does have one question."

"And that is?"

"Do we know what happened to the other two submarines?"

"Tell him that we sank one in addition to his, after it fired on *Sides*. The other is still out there, and we're watching its movements. Right now, it is not a threat to us or any other American ship."

Before Choi finished his translation, Josh saw tears welling up in Seomun's eyes. He spoke, and Choi translated. "I had many friends on both submarines, and many are now dead because of a..." Petty Officer Choi said a few words, and the North Korean nodded. "... because of a madman."

The Simushir Island Incident

"Petty Officer Choi, please escort Lieutenant Commander Seomun down below. Make sure he knows his men must not attempt to do any harm to anyone or anything on this ship. We will do our best to get them asylum, but there is no guarantee."

Chapter 17: JUST DESERTS

Monday, April 1st, 1996, 1348 local time, Broutana Bay

In an inflatable boat, Marty, Lieutenant Adair, and the three other SEALs of the previous mission left *La Jolla* and motored to the settlement. Reconnaissance phots showed that the facility had been abandoned, and Vice Admiral Maize had gotten approval for a second visit. Past the rolling swells of the caldera's entrance, the harbor was calm. There was no one other than birds to greet them.

For Marty, it was a chance to visit a place that had occupied so much of his attention over the past few months. He also wanted to find out why Major Kim had a love-hate relationship with the island. He broke away from the team, which had specific reconnaissance objectives, and climbed Mount Uratman.

Marty was stunned by the spectacular view from the top of Mount Uratman. He had an unobstructed view of the harbor, the Diany Strait to the north, the island to the south, and the Pacific Ocean to the east. The view was well worth the long hike. He now understood why Major Kim said the island had a unique, captivating beauty. The only sounds Marty heard were from the local bird population and the Pacific Ocean pounding on the volcanic rocks. He felt as though he could feel the island awakening from its long winter slumber.

As soon as the SEALS were headed ashore, *La Jolla* had submerged in the deep waters of the Diana Strait so only its radio antenna was above the surface. Other than to check in every hour, Marty didn't expect to use his radio during the daylong visit.

Adair reported there was nothing to see where the drug lab was once located. All that was left was a seared cement foundation, burnt steel frame, broken and charred glass, and a scorched pier.

None of the doors on the buildings were locked. Inside the office building, the SEALs found emptied file cabinets. The other buildings were clean as well, down to the empty toilet paper holders in the bathrooms. No attempt had been made to seal or preserve the buildings, other than to make sure all the doors and windows closed. The keys to the locks were in clear plastic bags taped to the walls. Unused construction material and supplies were neatly stacked, ready for someone to pick up where the Kuril Island Development Corporation's efforts had stopped.

Marty unscrewed the brass plaque outside Managing Director Lee's office door. It read "Kuril Island Development Corporation, a Hong Kong company." He felt it was an appropriate souvenir.

All the SA-8 missiles and reload packs were gone, but the *Osas* launchers were parked in a neat row in a shed a short walk from the main office. Inside the one with soot and scorch marks from missile exhaust, a SEAL connected the battery cables. In the driver's seat, he turned on the ignition and waited for the glow plugs to heat up before he pushed the starter button. The diesel engine turned over and rumbled to life. With the engine idling, he turned on the vehicle's systems and let the *Osa's* fire-control system warm up. Then he shut down the engine and removed the vehicle's fire-control computer.

Tuesday, April 2nd, 1996, 1430 local time, Hong Kong

After the break-in to their secure office, Half Moon installed armored doors at the entrance to its suite and stronger doors and locks to other rooms requiring additional security. After-hours access now required entering a six-digit code, unique to each authorized user, and insertion of a company identification card before an electronic cipher lock released the latch. Later in the year, they planned to add a fingerprint scanner to the front door for after-hours entry.

The insulated walls and the closed heavy, teak doors assured the board members of Half Moon Trading and Crescent Shipping of total privacy. As an added precaution, a white noise generator, which randomly changed frequencies, made electronic snooping impossible.

The first item on the agenda was electing Managing Director Chan Ho Lee as President of their new Vietnamese subsidiary. His responsibilities would be to expand two plants, one that made small animal-shaped vases from clay, and another that made fertilizer, some of which was sold to local government agents who, in turn, sold it at a profit to farmers. The rest was bagged and shipped overseas, along with the vases. The two factories were side-by-side and a few kilometers down the Mekong River from Ho Chi Minh City. Each had its own pier, once used by the U.S. Navy.

In a separate area, walled off from the main factory, a different group of workers turned opium from Laos and Cambodia into Asian Pure. The opium was loaded onto ships owned and operated by another shipping company called Global Transport. Through a maze of corporations, Half Moon and Crescent Shipping owned Global.

The second item was to return General Jang's shares to the company's treasury. The Japanese had been kind enough to inform

Crescent's agent in Japan of the death of General Jang and his wife.

The third item led to a spirited debate. Some board members argued that Cho Rhee had stolen money from Half Moon. However, examination of the records indicated the full amounts had been deposited, and only anything over $95,000 for each kilo had been withdrawn—as per her agreement with Half Moon. The Half Moon board decided no action of any kind would be taken against Cho Rhee; she had simply been collecting her commission.

Friday, April 5th, 1996, 1000 local time, Panmunjon,
on the 38th parallel between North and South Korea

Vice Admiral Maize stood behind the long table opposite six senior Korean People's Army officers. The one-piece wooden table had a white line running down the middle. The north side of the table was the territory of the Democratic People's Republic of North Korea. On the south side, the table and the land under it belonged to the Republic of Korea.

To the left and right of Admiral Maize were the U.S. Army and Navy members of the United Nations Command, along with a Korean general and an admiral who was the Commander, U.S. Naval Forces, Korea. Maize had asked to attend for two reasons. One, *his* ships were attacked; and two, he wanted to lead the discussion with the North Koreans.

In the complicated organizational chart of the United Nations Command, the Naval Component Commander, or NCC, was the Commander, Seventh Fleet. It was through his NCC "hat" that Vice Admiral Maize asked to lead this meeting.

Behind him, a mix of armed U.S. and South Korean soldiers stood at parade rest, eying the members of the Korean People's Army opposite them. At any of these meetings, there was a very real possibility the North Koreans might do something provocative. Each meeting with the North Koreans was tense because only a cease fire, not a peace treaty, had been signed in 1953, which meant South Korea, along with the 16 countries whose troops fought in the conflict, were still at war with North Korea.

Six three-inch-thick notebooks rested on the table in front of Admiral Maize. Each light-blue front cover was embossed with the seal of the United Nations. Admiral Maize had an additional dark-blue padded folder with the Seventh Fleet crest sitting on top of his notebook.

He looked to the east end of the room and nodded. No introductions were made, nor were there any handshakes with the North Koreans. The only information about who the North Koreans were was the name and rank in Hangul on each tented paper sign. In Maize's briefing, he had been told the North Koreans rarely used their real names.

With great ceremony, two guards, one a member of the People's Army and the other of the South Korean Army tapped a small triangle at the same time. The pleasant tone was followed by the sound of chairs legs scraping across the wooden floor as everyone with a seat at the table sat down.

Admiral Maize put his headset on and waited until the interpreter told him each member acknowledged he was "on line." Maize opened his blue folder, with the gold number seven and three gold stars, and began to read. The 18-point, bold-face type was marked to tell him when to stop to allow the translation to catch up. At the pauses, he looked at the six North Korean officers across the table one at a time—all of whom, he had been told, didn't really need the translation.

The North Korean generals stared at him with blank, expressionless faces. Maize felt like he was speaking to a wall. His words became part of the official record of the ongoing attempts to negotiate a peace treaty between the Democratic People's Republic of Korea, the United Nations, and the Republic of Korea. Maize described the chronology of the shoot down of the RC-135 and the attempted sinking of the *Peleliu* as part of his narrative about the recent attempts to create a military base on Simushir.

He referred to Lieutenant Commander Seomun's orders and photographs, which had required presidential approval to be included in the notebooks. There was no outrage or anger in his words as he spoke in measured tones. When he finished, Admiral Maize closed the folder and nodded to an aide standing behind him, who slid the six notebooks across the white line so that one was positioned in front of each North Korean. Translations into Hangul of his speech, as well as copies of each document to which he'd referred, were inside each binder.

None of the North Koreans moved to look inside the books. After what felt like hours but was less than a minute, the senior North Korean sucked a noisy breath through his teeth and said—in English—in an annoyed tone, "Admiral, everything that you said is a fabrication of the CIA and their South Korean lackeys. It is, therefore, not worth discussing."

As soon as he finished speaking, chair legs scraped loudly as each North Korean officer pushed back his chair, stood up, and walked out of the room. They left the notebooks untouched on the table. Their movement was so coordinated, it appeared to VADM Maize to have been rehearsed.

Wednesday April 10th, 1996, 1006 local time,
Naval Base, Pearl Harbor

Bill Hamilton stood when the judge, who wore the uniform of an Army colonel, entered the wood-paneled military courtroom, and sat when instructed to do so. The blinds were drawn so one could not see in or out of the courtroom. At his table, next to him, was his civilian lawyer, as well as a Navy lieutenant commander from Pacific Fleet's Judge Advocate General office. The only others present were the court recorder and the three Naval Investigative Service officers sitting behind the prosecutors, along with the two armed Marines wearing military-police armbands.

He pled no contest to the charges of espionage leveled against him, in return for a lighter sentence and details on the information he had passed to Mr. Seul.

Rather than risk a trial and the possibility of being incarcerated for life, he and his lawyers agreed to 10 years in prison and a fine. He could apply for parole after six years if he "minded his Ps and Qs" in prison.

The judge looked up as a signal he wanted everyone to pay attention to what he was about to say. "William Archibald Hamilton, please stand. This court has reviewed the plea agreement and will now officially pronounce its sentence. It took into account your willing cooperation, as well as your years of service to this country and information provided to the Honolulu Police Department, which allowed them to arrest and bring your bookie to trial, as well as your testimony, which helped gain his conviction."

The judge put down a piece of paper. "Paying off a gambling debt is not an acceptable reason to betray your country. Your treasonous actions helped a criminal enterprise import illegal drugs into this country and led to the murder of a senior Naval Intelligence analyst, Uilani Ka'anapali."

The judge clasped his hands on the desk. "My conclusion is that your gambling debts made you a target for blackmail. Other than murder and rape, espionage is, in the opinion of this court, the most heinous crime a member of the military or intelligence establishment can commit. While I cannot overturn the plea agreement, it is in my power to change some parts. Rather than being eligible for parole in six years, I am changing it to eight. In addition, you will forfeit any and all benefits you accrued working for the government. Your sentence begins today, and I have instructed the Navy to arrange transport to Leavenworth." He hammered the desk with his gavel. "This court is adjourned."

Bill Hamilton bowed his head so the judge could not see his smile. It could have been worse. Mr. Seul hadn't spilled the beans on all the money he'd been paid. He had 400,000 dollars sitting in a Swiss bank account, accruing interest. When he walked out of prison, he would have a nice nest egg to start over.

Tuesday, April 16th, 1996, 0756 local time, Pyongyang

Deputy Minister Thaek bounded up the long stairs to the building, then shifted his weight impatiently as he waited in line to go through security. There was the usual pat-down search and examination of his identity documents and the contents of his briefcase. When the guards finished, a lieutenant guided him to a small, windowless conference room in a wing unfamiliar to him.

The single steel door led to a room with two slate-gray steel chairs on either side of a small metal table, which was bolted to the floor. If he had bothered to look around the room, he would have noticed that the floor sloped slightly toward a drain under the table and, behind one picture, there was a cabinet containing a reeled hose.

His appointment with the Minister of Safety and State Security was for 0830. Almost 60 minutes later, Thaek was still waiting, and seething with impatience. He had other meetings to attend later in the morning.

At the sound of the door latch he looked up to see Captain Young Jae Jung enter with his hands clasped behind his back. Unlike most of the officers in the building, Jung was wearing his camouflaged utilities. If he'd been wearing his working uniform, one would have seen the ribbon for the Order of the National Flag, the second highest award for service to the Democratic People's Republic of Korea. It had been pinned on his chest by Kim Jong-Il for directing the shoot down of the American electronic surveillance jet. "Kwang-sik Thaek." Jung spoke his name tersely.

Thaek was annoyed by not being addressed by his title nor saluted by a man who worked for him. "It is *Deputy Minister* Kwang-sik Thaek to *you*, Captain Jung."

"Kwang-sik Thaek." Jung spat out the words as if they were dirty. "And it's *Major* Jung to *you,* blind man!"

Thaek looked again and was astonished—Jung, indeed, wore the insignia of a People's Army Special Forces major. *When did that happen?*

Jung continued. "Our Dear Leader has decided that you carried out operations without his approval, which led to the loss of two valuable submarines."

"Bullshit! Our Dear Leader approved everything I—" Thaek stopped abruptly when he saw the business end of a Tokarev Type 68's silencer. A moment later he fell in a heap to the floor, blood spilling from the hole in his forehead.

Major Jung touched Thaek's throat to make sure the inert form was dead. He admired his handiwork, although the entry wound was a half-centimeter to the left of where he'd aimed. As he stood up, he smiled. He realized how much he liked this kind of work.

Jung opened the door to let in two soldiers. They stuffed Thaek's body into a large black zippered vinyl bag and pulled it to the side. Then they pulled out the hose and rinsed the floor before swabbing it with soap and disinfectant and washing it thoroughly. When Jung was satisfied, the soldiers rewound the hose and closed the door, making sure the picture was square with the walls. They left carrying the black body bag. It had been bought from a firm in Hong Kong, which makes them in the People's Republic of China for police departments in the United States.

The Simushir Island Incident

Friday, April 19th, 1996, 0726 local time, Broutana Bay

Managing Director and now President of Half Moon Trading, Vietnam, Chan Ho Lee stood on the deck of well-worn "landing ship, tank," a.k.a. an LST, built in 1944, as it approached Simushir. The ship was perfect for what Half Moon Trading needed, and the People's Republic of Vietnam had been more than willing to charter the ship for needed cash.

The captain nosed the ship against the black beach of crushed lava. The ship's ramp groaned as hydraulic actuators lowered the 52-year-old steel to the ground. The crew set two anchors on the rocks, and dropped a third over the stern.

Managing Director Lee drove a Honda TRXTM 200, with 10-liter gas cans strapped to its luggage rack, over to where the MULEs were parked in a neat row in front of what the North Koreans had briefly used as an armory. He checked to see if there was any gasoline left in the tank of the first MULE in the row, and there was. He twisted the key and it coughed a few times, started, and belched smoke before settling into its normal lumpy idle. The 12-man maintenance crew accompanying Mr. Lee fanned out to each piece of heavy equipment brought to Simushir, made sure batteries were connected and charged, added diesel as needed, started the engines, and, after allowing them to warm up for 30 seconds, drove them onto the LST.

Managing Director Lee gunned his all-terrain vehicle and sped toward the shed where the *Osas* were parked. He attached two kilos of Czech-made Semtex plastic explosive under the fuel tanks. The timers were set for a three-hour delay. Yes, they were valuable; but Half Moon's management had decided it wasn't worth the risk of selling them, as that would bring more unwanted attention to the company.

One last thing to do. Managing Director Lee wanted the plaque from his office as a souvenir. When he saw it was gone, his eyes narrowed. He wondered who'd taken it.

The LST was in the Diana Strait when Managing Director Lee, standing on the wing of the bridge, heard a faint thump. Through his binoculars, he saw a large pillar of smoke. If the explosions didn't destroy the *Osas*, the fire would.

Saturday, April 27th, 1996, 2212 local time, Bangkok, Thailand

The U.S. government held Seul in a secluded safe house on Oahu until the information he provided checked out. He was then driven to the Honolulu airport. where he boarded a non-stop flight to Hong Kong, and then, after several phone calls to confirm an appointment and money transfers, and a three-hour wait, he boarded a Royal Thai Airlines flight to Pattaya. He arrived in Thailand 30 hours after he finished his exit debrief.

The next morning, David Seul became the trans-woman Yeong Gim. The sex change surgery was something he'd wanted to do for years. Except for his meetings with Bill Hamilton, Seul had been living as a woman most of the time. Many of the managers of his businesses knew him as Cynthia Seul.

Ten days later, when she walked out of the clinic, she felt the best she had in years.

Friday, May 3rd, 1996, 2236 local time, Washington, D.C.

After the shit storm over his discharge subsided, Steven Higgins still couldn't find a job. No one would hire him. Even law firms that specialized in left-wing causes turned him down. Those who were candid in their answers said his background would be used by their opponents and could detract from their ability to win in court for their client.

The Simushir Island Incident

Higgins took contract work as a legal analyst; but the work, while lucrative, was spotty. What he wanted was a steady salary. What he really wanted was the look of respect, or fear, on every face that turned towards him.

He'd sublet his townhouse in D.C. and wanted to move back home, but his father refused. The World War II veteran had learned more about his son's Navy career from the newspaper articles than from his boy's own mouth. Robert Higgins could no longer look his son in the face and contain his anger. Time and love might heal the wound; but for now, Robert Higgins didn't want his son around. His mother hesitantly suggested that he use some of his savings to travel a bit, see the world, relax and enjoy himself.

Higgins called Greenpeace USA, headquartered in D.C. Initially, they turned him down; but in early January they needed legal help, and he was offered a job. He changed his hair style, bought dark glasses, and moved back to D.C. A condition of his employment was that his name would not appear on any legal filings, press releases, or on the staff's public roster. He was, as it was explained and often repeated, expected to remain in the background as an independent contractor. The situation gnawed at him that others would get credit for his work; but it was, he decided, better than doing nothing.

After drinking several beers with his solitary dinner at a Chinese restaurant, Higgins pulled into the garage of his townhouse. He slipped the six-speed transmission of his special-order 1990 Pontiac Firehawk—a gift from the Chevrolet dealer in Madison, Wisconsin while he was a Congressman—into neutral before pulling the parking brake.

He pressed the button to activate the garage door and leaned back against the headrest, enjoying the sensation of leather, tired from a 12-hour day of fluorescent lights and hard chairs and way too much to drink. Higgins decided he would rest for a few minutes before he got out of the car. Behind him, the garage door closed.

Early Saturday morning, a neighbor noticed smoke coming out from under the bottom of a garage door and called the fire department. When the door was opened, they found Steven Higgins, still in the driver's seat, dead from carbon monoxide poisoning. Since there was no suicide note to go with the high blood alcohol level, the coroner ruled it an accident.

Robert Higgins had his son's body flown back to Madison, where it was buried on the family plot. The gravestone read, "Steven Higgins, beloved son" over his dates of birth and death.

Thursday, May 16th, 1996, 2010 local time, Sydney, Australia

Cho Rhee ordered an expensive bottle of champagne to go with her dinner at an Asian fusion restaurant in Sydney known as The Rocks. She was celebrating. Earlier in the day, she had sworn allegiance to Australia and become an Australian citizen under the name of Mi-ja Byeon, the name on the Hong Kong passport she'd used to travel from LA to Singapore. Cho Rhee no longer existed.

Cho had applied for Australian citizenship at its Singaporean embassy, knowing the Australian government gave preferential treatment to applicants willing to invest at least 500,000 Australian dollars in local businesses or the Australian stock market. Her supporting documents included statements from her London-based broker, who had obligingly changed the names on her accounts to show Mi-ja Byeon was a wealthy young woman. She was not asked how or where she got the money. In the interview, the immigration officer asked her if she was wanted for any crime or was a fugitive. To both questions, her "No" was emphatic.

The Simushir Island Incident

Six weeks after arriving in Sydney, Cho's loan for a beach house in Manly was approved. Putting 50 percent down had helped her establish credit.

Once the house was tastefully furnished, Cho bought several small employment agencies and began to merge them into a chain. She lived on the income produced by the agencies, only drawing money from the Asian Pure commission account to buy the house and to make the initial purchase of the employment agencies. Now an eligible and attractive woman in her late 30s, she learned to surf as a way to meet men.

Monday, July 22nd, 1996, 0721 local time, Tucson, AZ
Charles Kim, formerly Major Chin Hae Kim, now a naturalized citizen by the order of the President of the United States, looked at himself in the mirror. After completing a 26-week course, he now was a U.S. Border Patrol Officer and in a uniform he was proud to wear. Ahead, Kim had the required four months of field training.

He asked for and was granted his wish to be assigned to teams that track and arrest drug smugglers coming from Mexico. Kim wanted this mission because he would be helping protect American citizens from the poisons made by companies such as Half Moon. And, unlike the special assignments from that bastard Thaek, he wouldn't have to worry about being either shot or sent to a re-education camp because he knew too much.

During two weeks of debriefing, he'd explained everything he knew about the Democratic Republic of Korea's People's Army and its Special Forces. As part of the agreement the Border Patrol made with the CIA and DIA, Charles Kim would be granted leave if either agency needed his services.

He had one other commitment that he gladly made to his adopted country. Two nights a week, he was taking the citizenship course required of all naturalized citizens. And, he was teaching himself Spanish to go along with his English, Korean, and Russian.

Another benefit of the course was that he was meeting other future U.S. citizens. In the class, there was a female refugee from Venezuela whom he liked. She lived with relatives who had been in the U.S. for a decade. Last Saturday, they had invited him over for dinner. He'd had to limit what he told his hosts when, after a delicious meal of Venezuelan dishes, everyone took turns describing how they came to the United States of America.

Kim liked the Heckler & Koch P2000 pistol he just slid into his holster. The German made 9mm pistol was a much better weapon than the Tokarev he'd carried in the North Korean Special Forces. As he'd proved on the range, the P2000 was more accurate, more reliable and easier to shoot.

He put the forest green campaign hat worn by agents on his head and adjusted the position so that sweat band was just below his hairline. Satisfied, he looked around the one bedroom apartment. Bookshelves lined an entire wall. He had spent many hours in the local bookstores, new and used. Once he finished field training, he would buy a small home in Tucson with a loan guaranteed by the federal government. The former North Korean Special Forces officer was glad he would never be cold again.

Friday, July 26th, 1996, 0900 local time, San Diego
Josh leaned back in the captain's chair, completely relaxed as a harbor pilot guided the helmsman steering *Peleliu* into San Diego harbor. Its six-and-a-half-month deployment was almost complete.

After the incident in the Sea of Japan, *Peleliu* met its commitments and participated in an exercise with Filipino marines. The ship made port calls in Singapore and Hong Kong before venturing down to Perth, Australia, and then across to Melbourne and Sydney before heading to Hawaii and home.

When *Peleliu* stopped at Pearl Harbor for four days, CINCPAC asked to come on board. He was accompanied by the Commander of the Pacific Fleet. After honors were rendered, Josh led them to his in-port cabin. He considered offering them each a drink of scotch, then decided it would be a bad idea.

Once the door was closed, a smiling CINCPAC took the lead. "I thought I would deliver the news to you in person. Vice Admiral Gainesville asked me to tell you that you are on the flag list that will be published while *Peleliu* is en route to San Diego. Let me be the first to offer you congratulations."

The four-star held out his hand. Josh took it, not knowing what to say. Being promoted to admiral was something that happened to other people, not him. He managed, "Thank you, sir."

The three men talked for almost an hour, mostly about Simushir and the incident in the Sea of Japan.

The Navy's Tiger Cruise program permits family to sail on board the ship of their service members from Hawaii to San Diego, so there were many dependents on board. Josh had decided to put on a show. On his command, selected members of the crew "manned the rail" dressed in their summer whites as the ship entered San Diego harbor. By custom, those who volunteered to man the rail were guaranteed to be the first ones off the ship. The dependents, massed on the hangar deck with their luggage, would be the next to leave.

While *Peleliu* was nudged to the pier by four tugs, Josh stepped onto the wing of the bridge and listened as newly promoted Lieutenant Heller and the harbor pilot gave commands. Once the tugs were alongside, there was little he had to do. Yet, if something ugly happened, as the captain of the ship, it would be his fault.

The slow movement gave Josh time to scan the pier with binoculars. He smiled when he saw Rebekah and their three children standing in a cluster of other wives.

Josh heard Heller say, "Captain, we're tied up."

He ordered "Engines, all stop." The loss of vibration and the sudden calm felt to Josh as if he had teleported to shore ahead of his crew.

Finally, I am home and back in the United States to stay. I can enjoy being with my family and have some peace.

The END

Epilogue

At his change of command ceremony, a month after *Peleliu* returned to San Diego, Rear Admiral (select) Josh Haman awarded medals to deserving members of his crew. Before the end of the ceremony, CINCPAC, who was a surprise attendee, gave a short speech and then ordered Rear Admiral (select) Joshua Haman to come front and center. He awarded him a Distinguished Service Medal for his actions both on the Seventh Fleet staff and as commanding officer of *Peleliu.*

Later in the year, Commander Austin Rankin made captain and was given command of the amphibious ship *U.S.S. Denver. Peleliu's* operations officer was screened for command and was sent to *U.S.S. Tarawa* as its new executive officer.

Josh Haman's next assignment was on the Commander, Naval Air Forces, Pacific Fleet, staff—based in San Diego. After a year and half, he was given command of an Amphibious Group based in San Diego and led it on an uneventful six-month cruise to the Western Pacific. On the way home, he was promoted to Rear Admiral, Upper Half, with two stars on his collar.

When he learned his next assignment was a procurement billet in the Pentagon, Josh decided he'd had enough and retired. Rebekah and he bought a house and 500 acres of land north of Durango, Colorado, where they are often seen skiing. Josh helps coach young ski racers.

Marty Cabot was selected for captain in the spring of 1996. He finished his tour as the Seventh Fleet N6 and was send to Tampa as the number two SEAL at Special Operations Command.

The scar created by Uilani's murder was slow to heal. After two years in Tampa, he requested that he be assigned to the Naval Base, Coronado. Instead, he received orders to the Seal Development Group in Dam Neck, VA. For a SEAL captain, the billet was a ticket to becoming an admiral, but Marty declined. The lure of a star was not enough for him to stay in the organization that had brought him so much joy, as well as unspeakable pain. It was time to retire.

Back in San Diego, Jack D'Onofrio brought Marty into his organization with the caveat that he buy rental properties. With Jack's guidance, Marty's portfolio of profitable rental properties grew quickly, and he enjoyed being the number two person in a real estate property management business.

Despite the best efforts of the wives of Jack D'Onofrio and Gary Nash, as well as Rebekah Haman, to match him with another woman, Marty was reluctant to open up, fearing that it would end badly. It took the three women three years, but finally, they introduced Marty to a woman with two boys, whose husband had died suddenly. Within months, the boys captured his heart, and six months later, Marty Cabot was married.

Late in the spring of 1996, Gary Nash was officially notified that he'd been selected for Rear Admiral. The selection was contingent on his agreement that he accept a two-year assignment in the Pentagon as the number two JAG officer in the Navy. He asked for time to consider the requirement.

Accepting the promotion meant that he would have to leave the law firm that he'd founded for at least two years. He agonized over it for several weeks before deciding to accept. After the two years, he could either retire or rejoin his old firm—or do something else. The future, in his mind was bright. It was just a new set of challenges.

The History of the Soviet Base on Simushir

In 1987, those running the Soviet Navy decided that it needed a support base for its diesel submarines on Simushir in the Kuril Islands. While the reasons were not made public, the limitations of the diesel electric submarines that made up the majority of Soviet sub fleet were probably behind the decision.

The primary limit on deployment length for a nuclear-powered sub is food. Crew endurance is also a factor, but the natural limit on how much food can be stored on board is what brings a nuclear submarine back to port.

Diesel submarines (even those with the new air-independent propulsion systems) are much cheaper and easier to build and support than nuclear subs, and they are quieter and smaller. However, they have significant limitations—far lower sustained speed, a much smaller load of torpedoes, mines or cruise missiles, and, just like nukes, limited food storage. These restrictions encouraged the Soviets to look for a base to give them ready access to the Pacific Ocean without having to pass through narrow straits that could be mined or controlled by potentially hostile nations.

Simushir was ideal. It gave the Soviet Navy a base in a strategic location, halfway up the Kuril Islands and close to the Diany Strait, the deepest, widest strait from the Pacific Ocean to the Sea of Okhotsk. Basing subs in the Kurils eliminated the need to transit from Vladivostok (~1,100 nautical miles), Komsomolsk (~1,000 nautical miles) or Magadan (~980 nautical miles) and increased the diesel electrics on-station time.

It also provided a place they could come for repairs. Soviet diesel (as well as nuclear) submarines had, and continue to have, far more mechanical problems than their Western counterparts.

At its peak, approximately 3,000 Soviet citizens were stationed on Simushir. The base contained magazines for torpedoes and other weapons, food, fuel, and a small hospital. Anti-aircraft guns and surface-to-air missiles defended the garrison.

Cost, along with the difficulty of keeping the base supplied, is probably what led to the Russians' decision to abandon the facility. In addition, the Russian Navy had acquired a growing number of longer-range nuclear submarines comparable to the U.S. *Los Angeles*-class. By 1994, all the Russians were gone, and they left behind pretty much everything they brought except the weapons.

If you are interested, there are companies that offer tours of what they advertise as the "Secret Soviet Sub Base." There was, however, nothing secret about it. U.S. satellites routinely photographed it and monitored what ships and subs came and went.

About The Author

Marc Liebman

Naval Officer, Business Executive, Entrepreneur and Author

Marc retired as a Captain after twenty-four years in the Navy and is a combat veteran of Vietnam, the Tanker Wars of the 1980s and Desert Shield/Storm. He is a Naval Aviator with just under 5,000 hours of flight time in helicopters and fixed wing aircraft. Captain Liebman has worked with the armed forces of Australia, Canada, Japan, Thailand, Republic of Korea, the Philippines and the U.K.

He has been a partner in two different consulting firms advising clients on business and operational strategy, business process re-engineering, sales and marketing; the CEO of an aerospace and defense manufacturing company; an associate editor of a national magazine and a copywriter for an advertising agency.

The Liebmans live near Aubrey, Texas. Marc is married to Betty, his lovely wife of 50+ years. They spend as much time as they can visiting their seven grandchildren.

If You Enjoyed This Book
Visit

PENMORE PRESS

www.penmorepress.com

All Penmore Press books are available
directly through our website

BIG MOTHER

BY

MARC LIEBMAN

Big Mother 40 is a story well told and one in which aviation and special warfare veterans of the Vietnam conflict will identify, and about which they will tell their friends. Younger readers will enjoy the book simply as a great adventure.
— Michael Field, Captain USN (retired) Wings of Gold, Winter 2012 issue

Liebman skips macho combat images to plunk us into the deeper connections of war, from fear and courage to the truer realms of human relationships. His detail is authentic, and he lends even greater validity to the operations he describes with valuable author notes at the back of the book including a historic analysis of the time, military glossary and roster of characters. Despite the book's intensity and detail, the story is fast-paced. For a book you won't forget, you have to read BIG MOTHER 40.
Bonnie Toews, Military Writers Society of America, January 2013

PENMORE PRESS
www.penmorepress.com

CHERUBS 2
BY
MARC LIEBMAN

In combat, there is a fine line between being overly cautious and cowardice. It's Josh Haman's first tour in Vietnam and he's fresh out of the training command - a "nugget" in Naval Aviator parlance. Josh Haman has to figure out on which side of the line the combat search and rescue detachment's officer-in-charge stands. Untested and without a lot of experience, he has to make a career and life and death decision and live with the consequences.

Josh gets his first taste of the unpredictability of Naval operations when he is picked to be a pioneer in flying helicopters in Navy special operations. He, and Marty Cabot, a Navy SEAL, become pawns in inter-service politics. The two of them are ordered to fly missions that could, if not carried out successfully, have international consequences

PENMORE PRESS
www.penmorepress.com

Forgotten

By

Marc Liebman

The Forgotten are six Americans who did not come home at the end of the Vietnam War. Kept hidden in a remote camp in the jungle near the Laotian/Vietnamese border, their captor – a People's Army of Vietnam lieutenant colonel – has them converting raw opium into morphine base. His goal: ransom them back to the Americans for millions years after the war ended.

Before she married Randy, Janet Pulaski was an anti-war activist and a member of the Students for A Democratic Society's Action Wing. After he's shot down, she's sent to Cuba to learn how to be an assassin and makes an interesting lifestyle choice.

When the U.S. learns of their existence in 1982, two men, one a former POW and the other a CIA operative want the POWs dead. Their existence could send one to jail and the other to a firing squad.

"Forgotten by Marc Liebman is a great read. It's one of those stories that grabs hold on page 1 and takes you on a rollercoaster ride. The plot is amazing, something quite unique, and is full of twists and turns." – Anne-Marie Reynolds for Readers Favorite

This is a giant whopper of a sex thriller with violence and bloodshed on most pages, along with that nymphomanical ex-antiwar activist turned assassin. If you love books like this, it's the one is for you. ... Forgotten is well written and held this reader's attention throughout.

Daniel Wilson, The Vietnam Veteran

Forgotten wasn't predictable or cliché, and sometimes it was cutthroat and harsh, and other times I was nearly breathless from the intensity and violent passion. Other times I was chuckling aloud at the witty banter.

Leo Gregory, Indie Book Reviewers

penmorepress.com

RAIDER OF THE SCOTTISH COAST
BY
MARC LIEBMAN

Which serves a Navy better? Tradition and hierarchy, or innovation and merit?

Two teenagers – Jaco Jacinto from Charleston, SC and Darren Smythe from Gosport, England – become midshipmen in their respective navies. Jacinto wants to help his countrymen win their freedom. Smythe has wanted to be a naval officer since he was a boy. From blockaded harbours and the cold northern waters off Nova Scotia and Scotland, to the islands of the Bahamas and Nassau, they serve with great leaders and bad ones through battles, politics and the school of naval hard knocks. Jacinto and Smythe are mortal enemies, but when they meet they become friends, even though they know they will be called again to battle one another.

"This is Marc Liebman's first foray into the age of sail, and what a densely packed, rattling yarn he has produced... The twists and turns of the breathless plot see the two main protagonists cross again and again in a story that never lets up its pace." ~ Philip Allan, author of the award-winning Alexander Clay series about the Royal Navy during the Age of Sail.

PENMORE PRESS
www.penmorepress.com

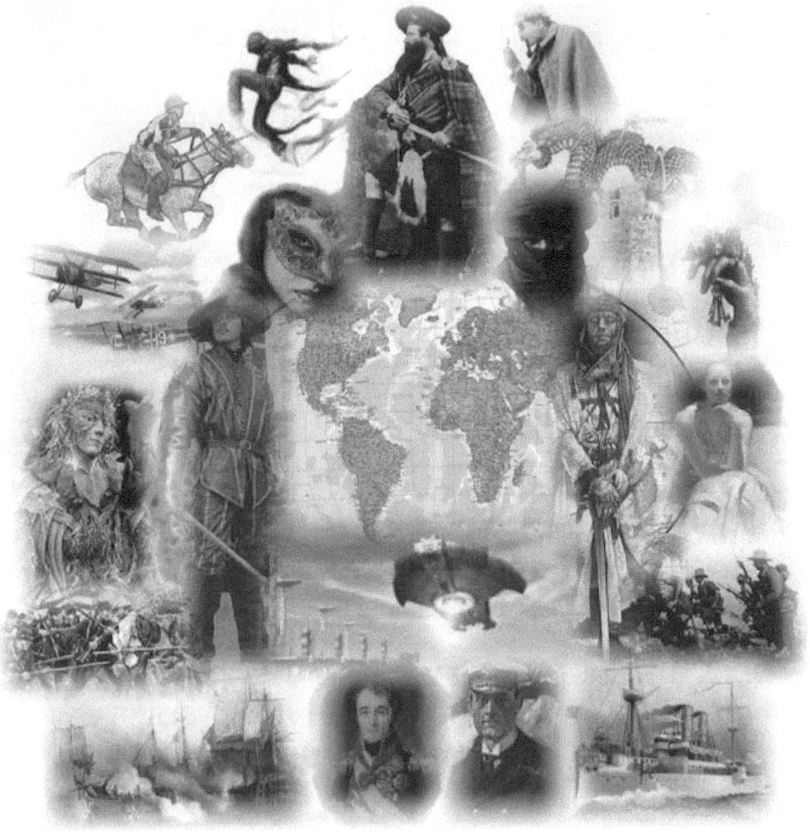

Penmore Press

Challenging, Intriguing, Adventurous, Historical and Imaginative

www.penmorepress.com